Praise for *After the Fall*

"Peter David mixes wry humor . . . with tense drama. . . .
[His] narrative is populated by a vast array of previously
minor characters from the screen incarnations of *Star
Trek*, all vividly fleshed out into well-rounded personalities. . . . This is a whole new *New Frontier*, but no less
welcome."

—Sci-Fi Online

"Peter David takes the series in a daring new direction. . . . [Plenty of] audacious surprises. . . . A whole lot
of fun."

—Treknation.com

Praise for Peter David and
Star Trek: New Frontier®

"Peter David is the best *Star Trek* novelist around."

—*Starburst*

"A new *Star Trek* novel by Peter David is always a good
bet. . . . David has made good use of minor characters
from the *Star Trek* universe."

—SF Site

"He effortlessly makes the most of his own characters
while developing some from small-screen *Trek*."

—*Dreamwatch*

Star Trek: New Frontier novels by Peter David

In chronological order

STAR TREK
NEW FRONTIER®

MISSING IN ACTION

Peter David

Based upon
STAR TREK: THE NEXT GENERATION®
created by Gene Roddenberry

POCKET BOOKS
New York London Toronto Sydney

POCKET BOOKS, a division of Simon & Schuster, Inc.
1230 Avenue of the Americas, New York, NY 10020

This book is a work of fiction. Names, characters, places, and incidents are products of the author's imagination or are used fictitiously. Any resemblance to actual events or locales or persons, living or dead, is entirely coincidental.

Copyright © 2006 by CBS Studios Inc. All Rights Reserved.
STAR TREK and related marks are trademarks of CBS Studios Inc.

 CBS and the CBS EYE logo are trademarks of CBS Broadcasting Inc. All Rights Reserved.

This book is published by Pocket Books, a division of Simon & Schuster, Inc., under exclusive license from CBS Studios Inc.

Originally published in hardcover in 2006 by Pocket Books

All rights reserved, including the right to reproduce this book or portions thereof in any form whatsoever. For information address Pocket Books, 1230 Avenue of the Americas, New York, NY 10020

ISBN-13: 978-0-7434-2959-7
ISBN-10:   0-7434-2959-1

This Pocket Books paperback edition January 2007

10 9 8 7 6 5 4 3 2 1

POCKET and colophon are registered trademarks of Simon & Schuster, Inc.

Manufactured in the United States of America

For information regarding special discounts for bulk purchases, please contact Simon & Schuster Special Sales at 1-800-456-6798 or business@simonandschuster.com.

THE PAST

We are Borg.

Our current location is unknown.

Theory: Enemy action attempting to disorient us.
We cannot be disoriented.

We are Borg.

We are as one. One who are many, and many who
are one. We can be neither disintegrated nor pulled
apart. That which attempts to resist us invariably
tries to sever our unity. Such attempts will always
fail, for we cannot be resisted. Resistance is futile.

Futile. Summarizing the hopelessness of the situation for any who endeavor to oppose us.

We are currently faced with a situation.

We have assimilated . . .

The Queen will command a full report, and we
must accommodate, for we are Borg.

Assimilated . . .

New technology.

Tunnel.

Summary as follows: We have assimilated new
technology from a race we have designated as
Species B221. Technology determined to be a conduit. A means of moving through space with an
efficiency and speed that far surpasses that of simple light speed. It is technology we do not currently
possess. It has now been assimilated.

The technology, designated "a transwarp conduit," was not completed. Simply under development.

Had we known, assimilation might not have been undertaken. We could have permitted them to continue their development of the transwarp conduit so that we could then assimilate completed technology. Instead, that which we have absorbed is unfinished. Lacking in full functionality.

But we are Borg.

We are complete unto ourselves. Therefore, if we have assimilated the technology for the transwarp conduit, then we must be able to complete it ourselves. That is the way of the Borg. We complete what we find, and improve it beyond anything that its creators might have been able to conceive.

This Borg vessel—the ship that is making this report—was assigned by the Collective to test the transwarp conduit, as it has been developed, retooled, redesigned, and completed by our Collective mind and will. Whatever the outcome of this initial test, and whatever the fate of this segment of the Collective, all information and results will remain part of the Borg core. If we are destroyed, the development will continue. The transwarp conduit will become a weapon in the arsenal of the Borg. The technology will yield its secrets to us. That outcome is inevitable, and nothing can change that.

Resistance is futile.

We are . . . Borg.

We activated the transwarp conduit at precisely two-twenty-one-set-one-set-two. The mechanisms within our vessel functioned perfectly, or so we believed. The conduit appeared in space at heading of one-eight-one-mark-five. We approached the opening and took readings on the energy output from within the conduit. That was all we had intended for the initial experiment. The conduit, however, functioned beyond expected parameters.

We were pulled in. As we passed through, this vessel was strafed by energies of uncertain origins. We believe they had a variety of effects upon us, but we do not know precisely what those might have been. We are still processing information and plan to have specifics soon.

Although we did not expect to be drawn into the transwarp conduit, we did anticipate the possibility. We had projected potential scenarios in which our vessel would emerge at some other point in our galaxy, or perhaps another galaxy altogether. These anticipatory scenarios evolved from the fact that the conduit's original developers had not yet found ways of limiting and channeling the technology's potential. Since we had not been completely certain that we had accomplished our aim in tailoring the technology to our needs, we did not know what would happen once the conduit was activated.

Our current situation is outside even the most liberal parameters that we had developed.

We do not believe we are in our galaxy.

We do not believe we are in another galaxy.

We are not even certain we are in our known universe.

Our surroundings are alien to anything that we have experienced before. We are not in space. We are in an environment that is entirely viscous. At first we thought it the fluidic space that serves as the point of origin for the troublesome Species 8472. But that seems not to be the case, since it contains fundamental trace elements that are not present in any biochemical analysis performed upon that species. If anything, the viscosity seems far greater than the environment of Species 8472. We are able to move within it, although not without effort. It resists our attempts to scan it. Although it is difficult to be certain, we believe there are traces of biogenetics all about us. Nevertheless, with the current status of our scans, it is nearly impossible to determine where it is, or how readily we can assimilate it for our own needs. There are also trace elements of oxygen and hydrogen permeating the thickening layers surrounding us.

We are attempting to reactivate the transwarp conduit so that we can return immediately to our own space, although we do not know for certain whether such attempts can or will be successful. At the moment, we . . .

Wait.

Something is coming toward us.

Our scanners remain unable to determine specifics. It appears to be another vessel. It is not Borg. We do not know the nature or background of the oncoming vessel. It is far larger than this vessel. It has noticed us and is approaching us in a manner that suggests an aggressive posture.

We are not concerned. We are not deterred.

We are Borg.

We will conquer. We will assimilate all that endeavors to stand in our way.

The vessel is almost upon us.

It is contacting us.

It seeks to communicate with us.

Perhaps it is intending to surrender so that . . .

No.

It intends to attack us.

We are informing it that it is proceeding from a false assumption. It cannot conquer us. It is we who will assimilate it, and not the reverse.

It does not know what it has encountered.

It does not realize that its time of dominance in this sphere is over.

It looms before us now, five times our size. Its inordinate size has lulled it into a false sense of security. It does not understand that it is at our mercy.

And we have no mercy.

We are Borg.

We will inform it.

"We are Borg. You will be assimilated. Resistance is futile."

We wait.

It responds.

Processing assessment of tone and intent.

Assessment completed.

It is expressing amusement.

Obviously it does not appreciate the gravity of its situation. It appears to be preparing to fire upon us.

We will destroy it and assimilate its remains.

"You will be assimilated. Resistance is fu

THE FUTURE

The Spectre

i.

Commander Soleta, late of the Federation, dedicated agent in the service of the Romulan Praetor, sat in her quarters aboard her stealth vessel and thoughtfully studied the data chip that she held delicately between her fingers.

"I wonder who died for it?" she said aloud.

She knew that someone had. Xyon, the cheery spacegoing pirate who had obtained it for them, had as much as said he'd had to kill someone to obtain it. She wondered who it might have been. She wasn't concerned about the morality of it. She had been given a specific assignment: to get information on the new weapon the Orions were developing. She, in turn, had made use of Xyon's unique talents, and he had gotten the job done. So here it was in her hand, and Xyon had needed to get it over someone's dead body.

Had it been an innocent? Had it been someone of no real consequence? Was it, perhaps, an Orion spy who had tried to get in Xyon's way? And what of that spy? Knowing Xyon, he had probably left no traces of the body, or bodies, so it would remain a permanent mystery.

Weapons systems. Sometimes she felt as if the universe was a massive chess game being played, where one side would come up with a weapon that another would put into check, and the other side would simply develop a new weapon to overcome the previous one. And so on and so on, greater and greater weapons, more and more impressive means of annihilating races, planets, star systems. She had to wonder if someday, someone would develop a weapon so powerful that there would be no such thing as a "check" for it. Instead it would be check, mate, and game over.

"Who died," she said again, staring at the chip, continuing to turn it over in her hand, "to try and keep this information from us? So that we can use it, build the weaponry ourselves, or figure out how to thwart whatever it is the Orions make . . . until, of course, they overcome us in turn. Perhaps . . ." She set it down carefully upon her desk. "Perhaps we should try and cease the endless cycle for once."

A small model of a Borg cube sat upon her desk, a gift once given her by Elizabeth Shelby—something of a Borg expert—and her only possession from her previous "life." She picked it up, hefted it. It had satisfactory weight to it. She brought it up and held it over the chip. It would take such little effort to bring it smashing down upon the chip, crunching it into uselessness. Then the nameless Orion, who perished in an attempt to keep a secret, would not have done so in vain.

Her hand did not tremble in the slightest, not betraying in the least the indecision within her. Then, very slowly and carefully, so as not to risk damaging the chip, she lowered the Borg-ship model and placed it gently next to it.

A useless impulse left over from a time when I had a conscience.

There was a buzz at her door. She called out, "Come."

Her tribune—the Romulan equivalent of a first officer in Starfleet—stood in the doorway. His name was Lucius and for as long as he had served under her, Soleta hadn't the faintest idea where he stood in terms of his loyalty to her. He maintained a resolute poker face in all dealings with her, remaining always stiff and formal. He never appeared to relax or let down his guard with her. Then again, as near as she could determine, he never let down his guard with anyone. It was possible she was overanalyzing, or perhaps even underestimating the wisdom of keeping one's guard up at all times.

Lucius had uncommonly pale skin for a Romulan, which provided a sharp contrast to the darkness of his hair. His face was almost triangular, and his eyebrow was so perfectly arched that Soleta suspected he trimmed it to make it come out that way. His pointed ears were long, tapering, and elegant. He was only a year or two older than Soleta, but he had an almost regal bearing that made him seem even older. As someone who was half Vulcan and half Romulan, Soleta envied him somewhat. After all, Lucius knew exactly what he wanted and who he was, and so set out to get it. Soleta . . . well, there were days when Soleta didn't have the slightest idea what she wanted or who she was.

This was shaping up into one of those days.

"Hail, Tribune," she said evenly.

"Hail, Legate," he replied. He preferred that alternative Romulan term for captain to the "Commander" favored by others of her crew. When she had asked him point-blank why he would use the more archaic term, he had been utterly forthright in replying: "Because you have served in the Romulan military for a fraction of the time that I have. 'Commander,' to my mind, is a title earned through years of service. Not accorded by imperial whim to a latecomer with a history that is . . . dubious. However," and he had squared his shoulders, "if you wish to register a complaint with the Praetor, and he instructs me to address you in that manner, then naturally I will comply. Or you can naturally request another second-in-command, who might prove more . . . flexible."

It was certainly tempting to do so, except that Lucius had a stainless record, was an experienced hand, and also commanded tremendous respect from subordinates. He could be of tremendous use to her, if only he'd cooperate. "And how will the rest of the crew view me, if my second-in-command is not referring to me by the proper title?"

He had pondered that a moment, and then nodded. "I can see how it might possibly sow disrespect among them. Very well. I shall refer to you as 'Commander' in the presence of others, and 'Legate' privately. Would that be acceptable to you?"

She had considered that, and then nodded. "I hope, Tribune, that eventually I will live up to your standards of excellence."

"As do I, Legate," he had replied.

Since then she and Lucius had maintained a calm, cordial relationship. But he still referred to her by the more antiquated rank. It had been annoying at first; however, she had come to be amused by it, even asking him what she would have to do in order to be addressed by him as "Commander."

"Convince me you could kill me," he had replied. "Then you would have my full respect."

"I see," she had deadpanned. "Well . . . I'll keep that in mind."

Having put the Borg cube aside, she sat back in her chair, her fingers intertwined and resting upon her lap. "Do you bring me news, Tribune?" she asked. "I'm growing a bit bored sitting here, waiting for the next instruction from the Praetor."

"As am I, Legate," he said. "Unfortunately, the situation has not improved. I am here to inform you that another communication cycle has passed and we still have not received instructions from either the Praetor or his recognized emissaries as to how we are to deal with the information chip."

She gestured for him to sit in the chair opposite her. Naturally he did not. He did, however, acknowledge her invitation to informality by drifting over toward the chair and resting one hand lightly upon it.

"Our orders were most clear," he said. "Once having met up with Xyon and recovering the data chip from him, we were to withdraw from the immediate area and wait for rendezvous information."

"The Praetor does like his secrets," Soleta said regretfully. The individual they were supposed to turn the chip over to was then supposed to proceed with the ship to a hidden scientific research location. Praetor Hiren preferred to keep weapons knowledge secluded from those under him whenever possible, on the assumption that they might use it without authorization against enemies of the Empire or—even worse—against the Praetor himself. It was certainly a paranoid way to live. Then again, as the old saying went, just because one is paranoid doesn't automatically mean that people *aren't* plotting against you. She shook her head. "Even so . . . I've grown accustomed to his caution, but this is beginning to exceed reason. I feel as if we're wasting time out here . . . ours and his. What's the point of commanding a stealth vessel if we can't utilize it?"

"There seems to be very little," her tribune agreed. He paused and then said, "Might I suggest an 'activity' to engage us while waiting to hear?"

"Are you suggesting sex, Tribune?"

He looked startled for a moment, but then actually smiled. "I have . . . vague memories of such activities. But merely vague ones."

"I can sympathize." Soleta gestured for him to continue.

"You have a permanent order to keep abreast of the movements of the *Excalibur* and Captain Calhoun, especially if they come within our sphere of interest."

"Yes," she said cautiously. "Has that occurred?"

"If coming within ten thousand klicks of us constitutes 'within our sphere,' I would have to say yes."

Her eyes widened. As far as distances in space were concerned, ten thousand klicks wasn't much at all. It wasn't enough to provide a threat of collision, but relatively speaking, it was spitting distance. "Why so close?" she asked. "Were they looking for us?"

"I do not believe so," said the Tribune. "They were heading into Thallonian space. Our trajectory projection indicates that—if they do not deviate from their present heading—they are on a direct course with the planet Priatia."

"Priatia?" Soleta frowned, trying to call to mind what she remembered of the world. During her time on the *Excalibur*, she had certainly spent enough time in Thallonian space. She had used what little downtime she had in a productive manner, researching every planet that she was able to find out about.

She knew the Priatians. Knew they had their legends and beliefs about a race referred to as "the Wanderers" who supposedly once dominated the Thallonian region. That new and emerging civilizations in Thallonian space—including, naturally, the Thallonians—had taken over worlds previously inhabited by the ancestors of modern Priatians. In so doing, they had effectively marginalized the Priatians, leaving the descendants of the once planet-spawning race to lick their wounds. The Priatians were left to complain that, eventually, the Wanderers would show up and restore Thallonian space to its proper balance. In some ways, they reminded her a bit of the Redeemers . . . except they weren't especially dangerous. Just . . . eccentric.

Still, if they had done something to attract the *Excalibur*'s attention, then there was every possibility that they were more dangerous than Soleta had previously credited them with being. After all, it had been some time since she'd been assigned to Thallonian space, and it wasn't as if she'd been making huge endeavors to remain up-to-date.

"I wonder if it has anything to do with the war," she said thoughtfully. Although they had been fairly isolated, they'd intercepted random unguarded broadcasts that had enabled her to keep abreast of current conditions. She knew that the new Thallonian Protectorate had fallen into disarray, people choosing up sides in an all-consuming battle between the House of Cwan and the House of Fhermus and their respective allies.

"I suppose it is possible," the tribune said. He regarded her askance. "Do you still blame yourself for it? For the war?"

"I never 'blamed' myself, Tribune," she corrected him. "What I said at one point was that I wondered if I wasn't partly responsible. From what we understand, the entire mess is somehow related to Kalinda, sister of Si Cwan, and her lover, Tiraud, son of Fhermus. And I was the one who informed Xyon, Kalinda's former paramour, that she and Tiraud were to be wed. Xyon acted as if that news meant nothing to him, but now I'm wondering what chain of events he may have triggered."

"From what we're hearing, Legate, Tiraud is dead. Killed on his wedding night by Kalinda herself."

"Yes, I know, but I don't believe that," said Soleta, shaking her head firmly. "It makes no sense at all. What does make sense to me . . ."

"Is that Xyon killed him?"

Now Soleta nodded. "Yes. Exactly. I think Xyon killed him, Kalinda is covering for him, and Xyon's father, Mackenzie Calhoun, is rushing in with the *Excalibur* to try and salvage the situation."

"But what does any of that have to do with Priatia?"

Soleta opened her mouth to respond, then closed it again. She scratched her chin thoughtfully, and then said, "I have absolutely no idea." She paused and then looked puckishly at Lucius. "Perhaps we should try to find out?"

"Are you suggesting, Legate, that we head out after the *Excalibur* and see precisely what they are up to?"

"I see little point to sitting here and accomplishing nothing. Perhaps the *Excalibur* is involved in something that could affect Romulan interests."

The tribune did not reply immediately. She waited for him to respond, and when he did not, she prompted him with "Is there something on your mind, Tribune?"

"The *Excalibur* was your former assignment, before you joined the Romulan Empire," said Lucius. "So it is natural to wonder—"

"Whether I'm motivated less by my loyalty to the Romulan Empire, and more by some leftover sense of being beholden to Captain Calhoun?"

"It had crossed my mind," he admitted. "I should point out, Legate, that my personal musings are merely that and no more, and will not impact in the slightest upon my obedience."

"Ah, but will it impact on your ever-valuable opinion of me?"

He shrugged, feigning indifference. Or perhaps it was no feint, and he simply didn't give a damn.

"The ultimate purpose of this vessel, Tribune, is as a spy vessel. It is not a 'sit around and await orders' vessel. So . . . we might as well find something to spy on. And Captain Calhoun is as good a something as any."

"Shall we set course for Priatia, then?"

"I think we shall."

He bowed and saluted. "As you command, Legate, so shall it be done."

She watched as he walked toward the door. "And Tribune . . . you *are* aware I was just joking about having sex. Right?"

"As with matters of respect, Legate . . . I could never be lovers with someone if I did not think they could kill me."

She stared at him. "You're a very twisted individual, Tribune."

"I simply have my standards, Legate," he replied, and headed off to the bridge to carry out his commanding officer's orders.

ii.

("Captain!" Kebron shouted. "Sensor readings indicate massive tachyon surge directly to starboard!"

"On screen!"

They had a clear view of something gargantuan swirling in space, like a massive whirlpool of energy. Energy crackled as if the very ether itself had come to life, and then it spit out a huge vessel the likes of which Calhoun had never seen.

"That's it!" Xyon shouted, pointing at the screen. "That's the ship that came after me! The one that took Kalinda!"

"Doesn't look like any mirage to me," said Calhoun. "Red alert! Morgan, shields up! Kebron, full phaser batteries online!"

The new arrival swatted them.

That was what it felt like, at least. Something, some sort of energy barrage, slammed into them just as their shields came up. The shields withstood the impact, preventing the Excalibur *from being shredded, but they weren't sufficient to stop the ship from spiraling out of control, as if the far larger vessel had simply reached through space and knocked them aside.*

Throughout the ship, crew members were hurled this way and that, slammed into walls, ceilings. No one knew which way was up or down.

The whirlpool of energy coruscated on the screen directly in front of them, and Tania Tobias was shrieking, and Morgan was calling out, "We're out of control!" as if that needed to be said, and Xyon was shouting Kalinda's name, and that was when a tumbling Calhoun struck his head on a railing.

The world began to spiral into blackness from the impact, and the last thing he heard before blackness claimed him was the apologetic voice of Keesala saying over the still active com link, "Please understand that we have nothing but the highest regard for you. Unfortunately, it appears you've gotten in the way." And then came another voice, at the last possible moment, also filtered, shouting his name, and it sounded like Soleta of all people, but she was gone, long gone, another failure of which this new incident was only his latest and possibly his last . . .

And then the world went dark and he was gone.

Seconds later, so was the Excalibur . . .)

Soleta was on the bridge of the *Spectre* when they drew within range of the *Excalibur.* The starship had fallen into orbit around Priatia. Her gaze riveted to the viewscreen, she felt a curious tugging at her heart that was not remotely in keeping with the sort of attitude she felt she should have toward her former vessel. The bridge of the *Spectre* was remarkably cramped in comparison with a Federation starship bridge. Instead of the commander's chair being in the center of it, Soleta's chair was on a raised structure in the back, enabling her to look down upon the entire bridge in one sweeping view.

"Keep your distance, Centurion," she told her helmsman, an extremely capable young pilot named Aquila who possessed a brashness Soleta found surprisingly refreshing.

"I hope you're not concerned about detection, Commander," said Praefect Vitus from the tactical station. Gruff and aggressive, he was all for throwing the *Spectre* into any manner of challenges, confident in the ability of his ship to prevail. "The stealth capability of this ship is second to none in the galaxy."

"That's as may be, Vitus," replied Soleta. "But I can tell you from personal experience that Mackenzie Calhoun has almost a sixth sense for danger that borders on the supernatural. I have absolutely no interest in doing anything that could possibly trigger it." She turned to the com officer. "Maurus . . . are they talking to the planet's surface?"

"Yes, Commander," said Centurion Maurus. "But it's scrambled. It'll take me a few minutes to punch through and tap into the frequency."

"Keep at it," she said. "I want to know what they're saying."

"You used to be the science officer on that vessel, Commander," pointed out Lucius. "Perhaps you have some insight that can expedite the process . . ."

Soleta shook her head. "The frequencies are stacked on a random-oscillation variable," she told him. "Makes it harder to listen in. And since it's random, your guess is, quite frankly, as good as mine. It'll be as much luck as anything else if Maurus is able to listen in."

"I don't need luck, Commander," Maurus said confidently. "My skill will suffice."

"Your confidence is appreciated, Centurion," she replied. "Make certain to—"

"Commander!" It was Vitus who had called out to her. He was far too veteran an officer to show fear or even be disconcerted. But the concern in his voice was obvious. "I'm detecting a tachyon spike . . ."

Soleta was immediately out of her seat and at Vitus's side. She had too much of the old science officer instincts in her to just sit about while someone else did the analysis. If it irritated Vitus, he gave no indication. She studied the readings, feeling—not for the first time—that Starfleet equipment was superior to what the Romulans had to offer. Still, this was sufficient.

"Something's forming out there," she said after a few moments. She looked up at the screen. "Something big. Helm, bring us back another five thousand klicks. Maurus, forget about trying to eavesdrop. Open up a direct channel to the *Excalibur*."

It was a frozen moment on the bridge as all eyes turned to Soleta. "Commander," said Lucius slowly, "are you suggesting we drop stealth . . . ?"

"I am suggesting nothing, Tribune. I am *ordering* a direct channel to the *Excalibur*. Centurion Maurus, why don't I have it yet?"

"Hailing the *Excalibur*, Commander," Maurus said stiffly.

Soleta turned and was surprised to see that Lucius was standing right there, barely half a foot away from her. In a low tone that suggested burning anger and suspicion, he said, "With all respect, Commander, this is a breach of proto—"

She cut him off. "If something happens to the *Excalibur*, I want to find out who the hell they were talking to. I want to know what's going on, and if that means—"

That was when the sounds of chaos came over the com unit. Maurus made no attempt to hide his surprised reaction as a cacophony of barely controlled pandemonium filtered through the *Spectre*.

She heard a woman screaming, and shouted reports coming from all over the bridge. Voices that she knew, although it was as if she were recognizing them from a lifetime ago. Before she could focus on it, try to discern what everyone was saying, Praefect Vitus was calling out with a measure of alarm that matched what was happening on the *Excalibur* bridge. "Commander, tachyon readings off the scale! Something's forming in front of us . . . something huge. It's . . . a vessel, Commander!"

"On screen!" called out Soleta, but it was already appearing on the monitor even as she ordered it. Her eyes widened as she said, "It's too big. Reduce image size so I can see it more clearly!"

"That *is* with image size reduced," Vitus said. At helm, Aquila audibly gulped.

"Back us up another ten thousand klicks, Aquila," Soleta said evenly.

The *Spectre* promptly moved even farther away from the debacle that was unfolding before it, and Soleta was finally able to get a clearer view of what they were dealing with.

The design was completely asymmetrical, which made it look like no other vessel Soleta had ever seen. It was almost as if the various parts of it had been stuck together haphazardly, a series of tubes affixed to pulsing globes. It resembled the model of a gigantic molecule.

It loomed before the *Excalibur*, looking ten times as

big. Energy was crackling around it, and suddenly something huge, swirling rippled into existence in front of the embattled starship. They were clearly trying to hold their position, but some sort of monstrous forces were exerting themselves upon the ship, dragging it forward despite its best efforts.

"*Calhoun!*" Soleta shouted, the name bursting from her almost against her volition. The outburst prompted glances from her bridge crew, and she could see the suspicion in Vitus's eyes, but she ignored them.

It was hard for her to discern whether what she was seeing was genuine, or some bizarre trick of light, a distortion unrelated to reality. But it seemed to her that the *Excalibur* was actually twisting back upon itself, bending around as if it were made from rubber. Unimaginable energies had taken hold of it, swirling around the ship like some sort of cosmic sinkhole. It bore a resemblance to transwarp conduits such as she had seen the Borg use, but it was different, and the energy readings she saw on Vitus's board didn't match up precisely either. This was something different, with molecular-contortion capabilities that were unlike anything she'd seen.

It was no doubt a trick of perspective, but the *Excalibur* appeared to get smaller, smaller. It seemed to take an excruciatingly long time instead of the seconds it truly required, and then the energy wheel—for such did it look like to Soleta—spun in and upon itself and vanished. She thought she saw a brief little burst of energy that might have been the *Excalibur* right before it disappeared, but she couldn't say for sure.

And then it was gone.

"What in the name of the Praetor is that thing?" whispered Aquila.

"I don't know," said Soleta. "But I'd very much appreciate, Vitus, some hard information so we can answer Aquila's very reasonable question."

"It's not there," said Vitus.

"What?" She turned to him, her face a question. "Are you saying it's a mirage?"

"I'm saying that whatever's there, our sensors aren't picking it up," Vitus told her. "All I've got is the residue of the tachyon emissions, but that was likely generated by whatever that rip in space was. I'm telling you, Commander, that thing . . . it's almost as if it's fake. An illusion."

"Care to bet our lives on it?" asked Soleta.

He met her gaze without wavering. "Absolutely."

"All right. Arm weapons. Drop cloak. Prepare to fire."

"Aye, Commander."

Lucius approached her and stepped in close. "With all respect, Commander, what's the point of this exercise? We're designed for observation, not for battle . . ."

"If that thing is truly what it appears to be, then it poses a threat to the Romulan Empire . . . to say nothing of everyone else I can think of," Soleta said. "Determining the nature of potential threats falls well within our purview. Wouldn't you agree, Tribune?"

Lucius nodded. "A valid point, Commander."

"Thank you. Vitus . . . ?"

"We've decloaked and are awaiting your order to fire, Commander. But without sensor lock, I don't have a confirmed target."

"Praefect, it's only slightly smaller than a planet. Do you need me to come over and aim for you?"

"No, Commander," he said stiffly.

"Excellent. Best guess, then. And . . . fire!"

The *Spectre*'s weaponry cut loose, torpedoes lancing through space and hurtling directly at the ship. Soleta watched intently, waiting to see if they would pass through the ship harmlessly, as would be expected if it was truly just a gigantic illusion.

The torpedoes struck hard against the vessel and then dissipated.

"All right. We have a problem," said Soleta.

"Commander," Aquila said, clearly working hard to control the concern in his voice. "I . . . think we've gotten their attention."

"Now we have an even bigger problem."

Aquila was right. The gargantuan vessel had simply been stationary in space, but now it was turning on some vast, unseen axis and was starting slowly but determinedly toward the *Spectre*.

"Helm, plot us a course toward the Neutral Zone. Go to cloak, Vitus," said Soleta, feeling that that moment wasn't the best time to throw Vitus's misplaced confidence back in his face. "Run us silent."

Vitus nodded, cloaking the ship and engaging the ion glide so that the *Spectre*—like the ghostly images its name suggested—would be undetectable by any measure known to modern science.

Seconds later the *Spectre* angled away, cloaked in invisibility and silence. The vast ship started to dwindle in their sights, and then . . .

"Commander! They've opened fire on us—!" Vitus shouted.

He barely had enough time to get the warning out before the ship was struck by twin energy blasts that had ripped out from the underside of the much larger ship. Soleta could not remember a time when she'd been in a ship that had been hit that hard, and that counted attacks from the Borg. The *Spectre* spun around, completely out of control, tumbling through space. Soleta's feet left the floor as she was sent sailing through the air, crashing hard against her command chair. Those who had been seated managed to remain where they were, but just barely. Something slammed into Soleta, and it took her a moment to realize it was Lucius. He muttered an apology and pulled himself off her.

Alarm klaxons went off all over the ship, and damage reports flooded in from all sections. "Vitus! Shields?" Soleta called.

"Holding, but just barely!"

"Engines?"

"Still online!"

"Full warp speed—!"

"Commander, if we drop ion glide and go to full warp, they'll be able to detect us—"

"Use your eyes, Praefect! They found us just fine even with the silent drive! Now do as I say!"

"Yes, Commander!"

Still cloaked, the *Spectre*'s warp engines came online.

Time and space bent around it as the *Spectre* threw it-self into warp in a desperate attempt to put some distance between itself and its menacing attacker.

"Here it comes," Aquila said grimly.

He was right. The ship was moving in pursuit of the *Spectre*. Not only was it keeping pace with no discernible effort, but it was beginning to close in. "We need more speed," Lucius snapped at Aquila.

"We're already at maximum!"

"Concentrate all remaining deflector power to rear shields," Soleta ordered, "and all remaining available energy, reroute in the engine."

"It won't be enough," Vitus called out. "We could stand and fight . . ."

"And get slaughtered," Soleta said with conviction. "Maintain speed."

For a good long time after that, nothing was said. The bridge crew of the *Spectre* watched with intense fascination as the larger ship continued to pursue them. It drew closer and closer with a sort of steady implacability.

"I wonder why it hasn't fired at us?" said Lucius.

"I don't know," Soleta said. "But we're not exactly in a position to question our good fortune."

Closer it came, and nearer still, and Soleta fancied she could practically feel them breathing down her neck. She toyed with the idea of trying to open a hailing frequency, to perhaps talk terms of surrender. But she discarded the notion before it even had time to solidify in her thoughts. There would be no discussion of the *Spectre* being captured. She would be letting down the Praetor, her crew, and herself. Mackenzie Calhoun would *never* have entertained surrender options, and she would do no less.

The pursuing ship filled the entirety of their screen. Soleta felt as if their whole universe had been reduced to that ship. That there was nothing in all of existence except that vessel and them. "Aquila," she said very softly, as the ship loomed behind them and she braced herself for the inevitable discharge of their weapons. "How far until the Neutral Zone?"

"Three hours, twenty-seven minutes," he replied with a sense of inevitability, knowing—as she did—that it was hopeless. They would never get within sufficient range of home to expect to encounter other Romulan ships that might be able to aid them. That was probably a good thing. Considering how formidable their pursuer was, the chances were that anyone who did attempt to help them would suffer the same fate.

"Very well. Prepare to jettison my log at the first sign of—"

"They're breaking off."

It had been Vitus who had spoken, and he sounded appropriately disbelieving. Soleta couldn't quite accept it either. She approached him, resting her hands on his tactical board. "Are you sure?"

"They're slowing," he said. "That much is definite. And I believe they're beginning to change course."

"Are you detecting any weapons activity?"

"No."

They watched in stunned disbelief, afraid to accept their own good fortune. Vitus was right. It was becoming more evident on the screen that the pursuing ship was slowing down and veering off, allowing the Romulan vessel to depart without so much as another shot being fired.

"But . . . I don't understand," said Maurus. "They had us. Why would they not finish us?"

"Isn't it obvious?" declared Vitus, his voice swelling with pride.

"Enlighten us, Vitus," said Soleta.

"Why . . . they're afraid of us, of course," he said. "They do not know for certain our capabilities, and have decided that pursuing us could possibly lead to their destruction."

"An interesting thought," she said, "and I might be inclined to accept it if no other explanation presented itself. Unfortunately, one does."

"And what would that be?"

She watched the screen grimly as the bizarre vessel swerved away from them, executed a large, leisurely U-turn, and headed back the way it came. "They let us go . . . because they're completely unafraid of us. We pose no threat to them whatsoever. That this pursuit was a warning to stay away, and they didn't obliterate us . . . because we simply weren't worth the bother."

There was quiet in the bridge for a long moment as the significance of her words sank in. She knew that Romulans were a proud race. Her crew would probably rather be blown to bits by a superior enemy than face the knowledge that they weren't considered enough of a threat to be dispensed with.

"Commander," said Lucius, "if what you suggest is

true . . . then this new race, this ship . . . presents a vast danger to the Romulan Empire, should it eventually decide to spread its interests in our direction."

"I don't disagree, Tribune."

"We have to find a way to fight them."

"Not necessarily," said Soleta. She sat down in her command chair, drumming the armrest with her fingers thoughtfully.

"We cannot shrink away from responsibility for the security of the Empire!"

"I wasn't suggesting we do, Tribune. However, in war it can often be useful to let a cat's-paw do your fighting for you, at least in the beginning. Then you can measure their success against your opponent, charting their successes and failures and learning without having to shed a drop of your own blood."

"You're saying," said Lucius, "that we should arrange for someone else to fight them?"

"Yes."

"Who?"

"I was thinking . . . Starfleet."

"And how would you go about arranging that?" he asked.

"It would not be all that much of a chore," she said. "Maurus . . . I assume you have a recording of the apparent demise of the *Excalibur*?"

"Of course, Commander."

"Good," she said. "Prepare to attach it to a blind communiqué. If the recipient knows it's from us, that will cause greater distrust in its authenticity. But sent anonymously through subspace channels, it will be judged solely on the information itself. Can you do that for me, Maurus?"

"Of course, Commander. And the recipient would be . . . ?"

"Admiral Elizabeth Paula Shelby," she said. "Commanding officer of Bravo Station . . . and, for all we know, the newly minted widow of Captain Mackenzie Calhoun."

Space Station Bravo

i.

The night sweats had been fearsome lately.

Elizabeth Shelby was dreaming that she was falling. She had no sense of what she had fallen off, or where she was probably going to land. It didn't even feel as if air was rushing past her, but instead that she was plummeting through a void of pure, black nothingness. Not even stars shone toward her to provide guidance. She reached out desperately to try and find something to grab on to, and the gesture from her dream translated into an identical one in the waking world. The abrupt thrust of her arm snapped her back into wakefulness. She had swung out so forcefully with it that had anyone been sleeping next to her they would have received a solid punch in the head or upper body. As it was, she sat up abruptly, grasping at air. The bedcovers were soaked with perspiration, and her hair—normally curly—was hanging in her face. She brushed it back, squinting in the darkness, then closed her eyes in a vain attempt to shake off the terrifying images that her imagination had conjured.

It had been a disconcerting dream, to be sure. There was no coherent "storyline" to it, or if there had been, then she certainly couldn't recall it. All she was able to retain in her awakening was flashes of images, a sense of jeopardy. Strangely enough, even though she knew she had been the one who was falling, she nevertheless had the oddest feeling that it was, in fact, her husband who was in danger. Perhaps (she reasoned) the sensation of falling she'd experienced represented how utterly adrift she would feel if Calhoun were gone from her world.

She had lost him once. When the previous model of the *Excalibur* had been blown to bits, Mackenzie Calhoun had been missing and presumed dead. She had mourned him, she had dealt with it, and she had moved on . . . only to have him return from the dead, the beneficiary of a miraculous escape. The realization of the Calhoun-sized hole he had left in her life had been part of what prompted her to marry him in the first place.

So even though she knew that she was capable of surviving his loss since she had already managed it once, it did not make her especially anxious to essay the endeavor a second time. Especially since she wasn't entirely confident she would be able to manage it again. Once a lifetime was sufficient; who should have to mourn the same man twice?

She remembered all the times that she had read stories in which brothers or sisters or spouses claimed that they had some sort of paranormal sense of it when something awful had happened to one of their loved ones. Shelby's inclination had always been to dismiss such unscientific, unprovable intuition as pure nonsense.

Despite that, she sat there in her bedroom and braced herself, waiting to receive some kind of unexpected word that something terrible had happened to the *Excalibur*. That would, after all, be the most dramatic, wouldn't it? Dreaming of danger and loss, and an instant later her aide walked in with some sort of horrible news?

It didn't turn out that way. No one knocked at her door or rang the chime or interrupted over an emergency frequency to tell her grim tidings. Shelby slumped back on her bed and, even though she wasn't able to fall into a deep sleep once more, she still managed to drift in an uneasy slumber that prevented her from dragging around the space station the next morning.

The transmission arrived at Space Station Bravo two days later. Shelby's frightful dream had already faded into the farthest reaches of her brain, where useless information generally went to die a lonely death. She was working in her office when her aide, Lieutenant Kassir, entered. Round jawed and curly haired, he now looked unusually grim faced, and the moment she saw him, the dream came roaring back to her.

His description of the transmission's contents was perfunctory, almost noncommittal. It had come into the com office, and he had immediately recorded it onto a data chip and brought it to her personally, rather than simply forwarding it to her. She downloaded the contents and watched it, and then rewatched it, without visibly registering any reaction.

"It's some sort of trick," she said finally, and even Kassir had to admit that it was a logical assumption. The source of the transmission was scrambled and anonymous. The very fact of its anonymity made it subject to suspicion and skepticism.

Furthermore, what it appeared to display was just . . . ridiculous. It purported to show the *Excalibur* overwhelmed by a huge vessel, and then being hurled into some sort of whirling energy portal that swallowed it up. By any reasonable interpretation of what she was being shown, it appeared that the *Excalibur* had been lost with all hands aboard . . . including her husband, Captain Mackenzie Calhoun.

"What planet is that?" she asked, tapping the small world upon the computer screen.

"We've identified it as a world in Sector 221-G called Priatia. It's a—"

"Pri . . . Priatia . . . ?"

"Yes, Admiral," Kassir said.

Shelby didn't move. Indeed, she stayed so frozen in place that Kassir looked concerned. "Admiral," he asked tentatively, "is there some . . . significance . . . to that planet?"

She was surprised how steady her voice sounded. She supposed she shouldn't be all *that* surprised. She was, after all, a professional. "The *Trident*," she said, "was assigned to enter Sector 221-G . . . also known as Thallonian space . . . to investigate the possibility that some sort of technology, similar to the Borg transwarp conduit . . . was being developed or even in use. Although they did not discover any such device in active use, they did find traces of what could be termed a 'sinkhole' in proximity to the planet Priatia."

"And you think that sinkhole could be the transwarp conduit they were looking for . . . and that ship is . . ."

"The only thing I'm thinking right now, Lieutenant," she told him, "is that I want this forwarded immediately to Starfleet Command. No knock on our own people, but they have the experts who can break this thing down to its root command and tell us if we're seeing something real or an invention of a sick practical joker with a holocreation program and way too much time on his hands. Beyond that, I'm not going to think a damned thing until I have to."

"Yes, Admiral."

She handed him the chip, and he turned and headed for the door. There he paused and turned back to her. "Admiral . . ." he said, but then became stuck for what to say next.

Shelby couldn't blame him. What was there to say, after all? He hoped that her husband wasn't dead? She put up a hand and said, "Save it, Lieutenant. This is all very . . . dubious. So it's probably best if we save well-wishing or condolences until we know what's what. All right?"

"Yes, Admiral," said Kassir, who looked relieved that she'd said so, and headed out to do as he was ordered.

Despite her best resolve to the contrary, Shelby then proceeded to accomplish absolutely nothing for the rest of the day. No matter what she tried to concentrate on, her thoughts kept returning to the images she'd seen on the screen. What she wanted to do, more than anything else, was contact the *Trident* and send it to Priatia to examine the area and find out what the hell was going on. But she lacked the authority; she couldn't issue starship assignments. And if there was one thing that Elizabeth Paula Shelby had respect for, it was the chain of command. God knew she'd had enough arguments with Calhoun over that very subject.

So she would wait. She would wait to hear from Starfleet, she would make her recommendations on the best way to proceed, and everything would progress according to the proper way of things.

When she slept, she kept waiting for dreams of falling or of Mackenzie Calhoun in distress to dog her slumber. That would also be dramatic, would it not? Recurring visions of her husband calling to her from some nameless void, either begging for her help . . . or assuring her that he was in a better place somewhere, across a great divide.

Instead she had only dreamless sleep . . . and that bothered her more than nightmares would have.

ii.

Admiral Edward Jellico looked at the image of Elizabeth Shelby on his viewscreen and wished that he could just reach through it somehow and pat the poor woman on the shoulder.

He had lost count of the number of times he'd had to inform wives, husbands, children, of the loss of their loved ones. It never got any easier, which was why nowadays he was grateful that he had subordinates who did that sort of thing for him. In this case, though, he felt it his duty to tell Shelby himself the bad news.

It wasn't that he was insensitive to the losses of the countless other families. There were, after all, a thousand people on the *Excalibur*, and the odds were that every single one of them had families who would have to be contacted and given the awful news:

MIA. Missing in Action.

As far as Jellico was concerned, it was worse than being told flat-out that someone you loved had perished. At least you knew what was what in that instance. When it came to MIA, it condemned those left behind to a sort of twilight existence. They were asked to maintain infinite stores of hope for an eventual return, and in the meantime could not possibly go on with their own lives in any sort of direction. Couldn't mourn, couldn't remarry. A huge gaping part of their existence simply ground to a halt.

It wasn't fair. True, anyone who signed on for Starfleet knew the risks. That didn't make it any fairer.

Still, at least with Shelby, Jellico could be more brutally honest in assessing the situation than he was likely to be with a civilian. "I'm truly sorry, Elizabeth," he said, his fingers interlaced and rested on his desk, "but as I told you, we've scrutinized the transmission extremely thoroughly—"

"He's not dead," Shelby said. She sounded surprisingly dispassionate about it. Jellico didn't know whether to chalk it up to shock or superb restraint.

"Again, as I told you," he reminded her, "we're not officially listing Mac, or any of them, as dead. However, I'm telling you that the odds of them having survived that—phenomenon—are rather small."

"We don't know for certain what that phenomenon is. You said your own studies of the visual record were inconclusive."

"Inconclusive, yes, but the fact is that the *Excalibur* was being subjected to forces that . . . we don't even have a name for them. The type of energies that were unleashed were beyond our abilities to measure . . ."

"You didn't have sensor equipment on site, Admiral," she reminded him. "It's all conjecture you're trying to make based upon what you saw on the screen, sent to us by an unnamed source. Do you at least have some idea who recorded the visuals we saw?"

He shook his head wearily. "Believe me, I wish we did. It might give us . . . something. More than we have now, certainly. The point is, the *Excalibur* was pummeled by unknown forces and hauled away who-knows-where, with no means back, to the best of our knowledge."

"Oh, they have a means back," Shelby said confidently. "They have Mackenzie Calhoun as captain. That's their means back, right there."

"Presuming they survived the trip."

"I don't presume it. I know it. There's no way that . . . he wouldn't . . ."

She stopped talking then and made a visible effort to control herself. Once more he felt sorry for her, but he wasn't about to let that show. Elizabeth Shelby didn't want anyone's pity or sympathy, of that he was sure.

"He's alive," she finally said, nodding slightly as if to convince herself of it. "He survived a ship's exploding to hell and gone. He can survive this. They all can. And there's only one way to determine it. We need to send out another ship. The *Trident*. Mueller knows the area, she can—" She stopped as she saw that Jellico was shaking his head. "Why are you—?"

"We can't."

"We sure as hell can."

"Shelby," he said sharply, "I know this is a difficult time, but I have to ask you to remember whom you're addressing."

"I'm sorry. What do you mean 'we can't'?"

"I don't know if you've been paying attention, Elizabeth, but Thallonian space has turned into a free-fire zone. A civil war's broken out." He leaned forward, making no effort to disguise how disturbed he was by what he was telling her. "Si Cwan and his former allies are at each other's throats. The New Thallonian Protectorate is currently in flames."

"Yes, I know," said Shelby. "The things I've read and heard . . . Kalinda supposedly killing her new husband in cold blood. I know the girl, Admiral. I don't believe she could have done such a thing. At the very least, if she did commit an act of violence against him, then it was self-defense."

"Some agree with you, Elizabeth, and some dis-

agree. The problem is, not only is there this unre-
solved killing, but it's stirred up resentments and dis-
putes going back centuries. It's more than political,
more than a single death. It's tribal. Generational. And
there's nothing we can do at this point except stay out
of the way. In fact, we've been given explicit instructions by the combatants to stay out of their territory.
Under the dictates of the Prime Directive, we have no
choice but to honor that . . ."

"How can we honor it?!" she practically exploded,
standing up behind her desk with such violence that she
banged her knee on the underside. It hurt like hell, but
she didn't allow her face to reflect her pain. "We have
video record of one of our ships—"

"—disappearing," Jellico finished for her. "Show
me a ship in distress, Shelby. Show me a ship that we
can see and react to and respond to, and I'll find some
way of getting around the constraints we're currently
under. But this isn't a crippled ship hanging dead in
space, calling for aid. This is a ship that is no longer
there. Any starship that gets sent in there is simply
going to circle the area and find nothing while presenting a target for the angry forces of the House of
Whatever who are looking for a target and suffer from
itchy trigger fingers."

"With respect, Admiral, you don't know what
they're going to find until we send someone out there.
I fully understand that there's an element of danger
involved in going in there, considering the incendiary
political situation. But Kat Mueller is more than capable of handling herself."

"Would I be wrong in assuming that you would have said exactly the same in regards to your husband before this transpired?"

She opened her mouth to respond immediately, but then hesitated. Finally she nodded and admitted, "You . . . would not be wrong about that, sir."

He forced a thin smile. "Admiral . . . I'm not unsympathetic. You know that. You know that the differences I had with Mac are in the past. That I owe him too much to remain a hard-ass in how I regard him. But this comes from the highest levels. Sector 221-G is off-limits until the local situation has settled down and we are welcomed back into Thallonian space . . . or whatever the hell they're calling it when all of this is over. I can't order the *Trident*, or any ship, in there unless there's a case of dire distress . . ."

"A starship being swallowed by a sinkhole doesn't qualify as dire distress . . . ?"

"This will sound harsh, Elizabeth—"

"It's all sounding harsh, Admiral."

He ignored her as if she hadn't spoken. ". . . but with the ship vanishing, and no sign of any of them surviving it . . . it doesn't fill any definition of 'dire distress' that is currently accepted."

"Need I point out, Admiral . . . that there's the additional concern over a gigantic ship such as we've never seen before?"

"A ship which has yet to cross into open Federation territory."

"So as long as it's wreaking havoc in someone else's territory . . ."

"Someone else who has specifically told us to stay out."

"Dammit, Edward!" Shelby practically exploded. "So what are you telling me? That I'm supposed to just sit here and stew?"

"Not in those exact words, but in so many words, yes."

The muscles in her face worked against each other, giving her the appearance of twitching fiercely. She looked as if she were struggling to form the next words. "I had a dream, Edward," she said finally.

"A dream?" He didn't comprehend.

"I had a dream that this was going to happen. Not this exactly, but that Mac was going to be in trouble and that he was going to need me."

"A premonition," he said, understanding now.

"I never really believed in such things," she continued, "but I do now. And telling me that I'm supposed to do nothing when he needs me . . ."

"Elizabeth," he said patiently, "I can't tell you the number of times I've heard such comments. I know that they—and that you—say them with sincerity. But let's face it. You and anyone who has a family member working in Starfleet have doubtless had any number of bad dreams in which they've believed their loved one is in danger. And then nothing comes of it and they forget all about it. However, when something untoward does then happen, they seize upon the most recent late-night nightmare and hold it up as a premonition. So let's not hold it up to be anything other than what it was, all right? And certainly don't start trying to convince yourself that you were receiving mental summonses for help from Mac that you're now ignoring."

"I wasn't thinking anything like that, Admiral."

"Good."

"What I was thinking was that, if I were in your position, I'd say to hell with whatever the highest authorities in Starfleet and the Federation had to say and I'd be doing whatever I felt was necessary in order to try and retrieve Calhoun."

He fixed a level gaze upon her. "No," he said confidently. "You wouldn't. You would not do that, Elizabeth, and you know it."

She looked about to protest, but then her shoulders sagged. "Probably not. And here's the depressing thing: If the situations were reversed, Mac would."

"Yes, well . . . that's one of the many reasons why you're an admiral and he's remained a captain . . . and very likely will until the end of his career."

"Which," she said distantly, "may have already happened."

Jellico didn't respond immediately. Finally he said, "Let's hope that's not the case."

"Absolutely," said Shelby, making no effort to hide the sarcasm. "Because that's what we're all about, isn't it. It's right in the Starfleet credo: To boldly hope as no one has hoped before."

Shaking his head, Jellico said, "We'll keep you apprised of any changes in the situation. Jellico out."

Her image disappeared from the screen and Jellico sat back in his chair, staring at the emptiness.

He wondered what he was going to do when Shelby—as she inevitably would—ignored orders and spoke to Mueller, who would also ignore orders, and went in to try and find some way of getting to the *Excalibur*, presuming there was any *Excalibur* to get to . . .

Well . . . maybe he'd be wrong. Somehow it seemed that everyone who came into contact with Mackenzie Calhoun sooner or later became infected with an infuriating tendency to act as if they knew better than Starfleet how to proceed in any given circumstance. It was one of the reasons that Jellico had so despised Calhoun, and it had taken extraordinary circumstances to reorient his thinking on that score. Still, the effect Calhoun had on people continued to resonate, and Jellico had to hope that good old Starfleet training would carry the day in terms of respecting the wisdom of the chain of command . . .

The chime at Jellico's office door sounded. "Come," called the admiral.

Jellico's aide entered, looking very concerned. "Admiral," he said. "Captain Picard is on the line. He heard a report that the *Excalibur* had disappeared, that Sector 221-G is off-limits, and wants to know why everyone is just sitting around doing nothing about it."

Jellico rubbed the bridge of his nose with his thumb and forefinger, feeling the beginnings of a sizable headache coming on. This had the makings of an exceedingly long and exceedingly bad day.

U.S.S. Excalibur

i.

Mackenzie Calhoun had no idea how long he remained in darkness, nor did he have any sense of his arms or legs or any other part of his body. This alone was extremely disconcerting, since Calhoun usually had an extremely acute sense of his physicality. When he was quiet and concentrating, he could hear his own heartbeat. Now since he didn't even hear that, he began to wonder if he was, in fact, dead. He didn't think he was because he had every reason to believe that an extremely active afterlife was awaiting him, and here there was simply nothingness. It was too quiet to be true death, he thought.

Then, while he wasn't even dwelling upon it, he detected his heartbeat once more. It was surprisingly calm and steady, all things considered.

One by one, the familiar noises of the *Excalibur* bridge started to crop up. The general ambience he took for granted until it wasn't there anymore.

Slowly he opened his eyes, morbidly curious as to what he would see. As it turned out, the answer was: Not much. The bridge was mostly dark. Only emergency lighting was available. Thanks to that, he was able to see general outlines of his people. One or two weren't moving, and he prayed that it was simply a matter of their being unconscious. The rest were stirring slowly, pulling themselves together as he had been.

"Status report," he called out. He wasn't expecting anything terribly useful to start out, but he felt it necessary to make sure everyone knew he was in one piece and in control . . . or, at least, as much as one could be of a situation that was completely out of control. "Where are we?"

"On the floor, sir," came the unmistakable voice of Zak Kebron, the ship's massive head of security. His huge Brikar body was lurching to its feet.

"Thank you, Mr. Kebron. That's very helpful. Morgan, can you get us full power back online . . . ?"

There was no response, and at first Calhoun thought she was unconscious. Then he remembered belatedly that Morgan Primus, the ship's ops officer, was no longer a human being at all. She was instead part of the computer system, and projected her presence via a hologram. He'd become so accustomed to having her around that her true nature had slipped his mind for a moment. With only emergency systems online, there wasn't enough power available for her to create her holographic self.

This was verified a few seconds later when Morgan's voice, devoid of body, floated through the bridge. "Full power is going to take some time, Captain. Still assessing damage results from all over the ship."

"What have we got so far?"

"Life-support systems minimal, but functioning. Shields down. Weapons systems at bare minimum. Warp engines out, impulse available. Turbolift system out. Sickbay fully functional." That last was no surprise to Calhoun. It was standard operating procedure, in times of emergency, to give priority to sickbay needs on the assumption that medical services would be in demand.

"Give me intraship," he said.

"Not sure if it's function . . . ah! Okay, up and running, at least for now. Go, sir."

"This is Captain Calhoun," his voice echoed throughout the ship. "All department heads, report in"—he glanced over at Kebron, the only one who was on his feet and seemed to have completely shaken off the pounding they'd just sustained—"to Security Chief Kebron. We're working to get all systems back online, so bear with us a bit longer. You're all professionals, and I fully expect that you will continue to act like it. Calhoun out." He paused, regrouping his thoughts as his eyes more fully adjusted to the dimness. He had exceptionally sharp night vision, but this was a challenge even for him. "Sound off, people."

"Here, sir," said Kebron.

"Yes, I knew that, Zak. Anyone else?"

"I'm okay, sir . . . I think," came the unsteady voice of Xy, the science officer.

"Me too," said Xyon, Xy's namesake and Calhoun's space pirate of a son.

No one else spoke up immediately. Morgan he

knew about, but the conn officer, Tania Tobias, was eerily silent, as was second-in-command Burgoyne 172.

"Someone check on Tobias," he said as he spotted Burgoyne lying a few feet away. He crouched next to the Hermat and checked hir over for some sign of broken bones. Calhoun was no doctor, but he had more down-and-dirty surface-war experience than he cared to think about. An inevitable result of surviving as many battles as he had was developing the ability to make quick and accurate diagnoses of injuries that fellow warriors had sustained. So it was with some authority and experience that he was able to determine that Burgoyne was—from the evidence on hand—relatively unharmed . . .

Unless s/he's bleeding internally, in which case s/he could be dead in no time . . .

Oh yes, that was exactly the kind of useful thinking that would benefit his ship and crew.

"Burgy," he said softly, shaking hir shoulder. "You okay?"

Calhoun felt as if an age passed before Burgoyne replied. "I've had better days, Captain," Burgoyne managed to get out.

Calhoun slid his arms under Burgoyne's. "Need help?"

"Yes, actually."

He carefully lifted Burgoyne to hir feet, amazed at hir lightness. Perhaps Burgoyne had hollow bones. He glanced over at Tobias and saw that Xyon was checking her over. Xyon looked up worriedly. "Father," he said, "she's not coming out of it. There's a swelling on her head. Maybe she's concussed."

"Do you think you can get her down to sickbay?"

"Not a problem."

"Remember, the lift is out. You'll have to—"

"Take her down the emergency exit, I know." He slung her over her shoulders as if she weighed less than Burgoyne. "I can manage."

"Thank you. Oh . . . and check on Moke on your way back. Let him know I'm okay and tell him to stay in his quarters until he hears from me."

"No problem."

Stepping carefully in the darkness, Xyon made his way to the emergency exit. He gripped the edges of the ladder with either hand, keeping Tania deftly balanced on his shoulders, and then he clambered expertly down the ladder. Calhoun thought, not for the first time, that his son would have made a hell of a Starfleet officer.

And then his voice floated back up from the exit chute: "I told you that Kalinda was in trouble."

He had to admit that Xyon had done just that. If Calhoun had listened to his son's misgivings earlier, it was possible that a good deal of the trouble they'd encountered since then could have been avoided. But he hadn't, and they hadn't been. There was no use dwelling on it now, though. Calhoun turned in his chair and addressed Xy. "Science officer, report. What hit us?"

From the darkness, Xy replied, "Something big."

"I think we need a bit more than that to go on."

"Something really, really big."

"Upon review, I'd have to concur with the lieutenant," Burgoyne said.

"Gentlemen, I appreciate a dazzling display of repartee as much as the next captain who's thinking of court-martialing his bridge crew. However, I think it important that we focus."

"As do I, Captain," Xy said readily. "But all my instrumentation is down, the monitor is blank," and he indicated the viewscreen, which was, indeed, nothing more than a large black rectangle at that moment, "and I have no data at my fingertips that would allow me to—"

The lights suddenly came up. They looked around in surprise and there were a few ragged cheers.

"All right," Xy continued without missing a beat. "I have a monitor, I have fingertips, and ideally I should shortly have data. Just give me a few . . ." Then his eyes widened as he stared at the now active viewscreen. "What the hell . . . ?"

Xy was normally an unflappable individual, a natural result of the partial Vulcan heritage he'd gotten from his mother, Dr. Selar. But now he was gaping at the screen and making no pretense of anything other than shock.

Calhoun automatically turned to see what Xy was reacting to, as did everyone else.

There were no stars. Nothing. There was just . . .

"What . . . *is* that?" Calhoun said slowly.

The customary darkness of space had been replaced by an environment unlike anything that Calhoun had ever seen. It was thick and pulsing, mostly clear but with a faintly pinkish hue. And it was that way for as far as the eye could see. "Kebron," he said, "can you give me a slow three-hundred-and-sixty-degree scan?"

"I believe so, sir."

The view on the screen angled and shifted around. It was the same in all directions. There were some variations in color and shading, but overall it was consistent.

"What are we, in someone's heart?" asked Calhoun.

"At the moment, Captain, I wouldn't rule anything out," said Xy.

"I can appreciate that, Lieutenant, but speaking for myself, I'd appreciate it if you did, in fact, start ruling some things out . . . beginning with whether or not we're still in our own galaxy."

"Frankly, Captain," Xy told him after a few moments, "I don't even think we're in our own universe anymore."

Before Calhoun could respond, there was a sudden fluttering at the ops seat, a beam of light dancing around Burgoyne. S/he immediately vacated the seat and everyone watched as the light beam turned horizontal and started to expand. Calhoun tensed for an instant, but then he relaxed as the familiar form of Morgan Primus appeared in her place at ops. "Sorry about the delay, Captain," she said.

"Glad to have you back, Morgan," Calhoun said.

"Xy," Burgoyne said, smoothing down the front of hir uniform after having scrambled to get out of

Morgan's way, "is it possible we're in the fluidic universe? The one that species that harassed the Borg came from?"

"I don't believe so," said Xy. "Unfortunately, I'm guessing."

"Guessing? Why are you guessing?" asked Calhoun.

"Because," Xy said, sounding both reasonable and yet frustrated, "I'm not getting any readings on it."

"None? No sensor readings at all?"

Xy shook his head. "It's as if . . . as if they simply can't process the information. As if they're not calibrated for it."

"What could cause something like that?"

"A change in physical laws," Morgan spoke up. Calhoun realized she was the most logical individual to speak on the subject, since she was effectively the entirety of the vessel. "Caused either by our destination, or by the means with which we got there."

"I managed to pick up a few trace elements before the sensors simply cut out on me entirely," said Xy. "Based on it, I certainly wouldn't recommend an EVA. I'm reading cardiotoxins, neurotoxins, dermatoneurotoxins, myotoxins, nephrotoxins . . ."

"The repeated use of the word 'toxins' would seem to be the tip-off, wouldn't it," said Calhoun grimly.

"Yes, sir, it would. I don't even want to think what it would do to an EVA suit."

"But what's it doing to our hull? Morgan, can you . . ." He paused. "I don't quite know how to say this. Can you *feel* anything? On the outside of the ship,

I mean. I know you're in the central computer, but—"

"I can't feel anything out there in the tactile sense, Captain," Morgan said slowly, as if trying to figure out the best way to explain the inexplicable. "But I can send electrical impulses through parts of the ship's hull in a manner not entirely dissimilar from a nervous system. It gives me sensations of pressure, basic environmental data and such. I'm doing it right now, since I thought it a safe assumption that—if you asked—you'd want it done."

"All right then," said Calhoun. "How long will it take you to—"

"It's instantaneous," she said. Her brow wrinkled thoughtfully and she brushed a lock of her hair from her face. Calhoun thought both of those gestures to be a bit amusing. After all, she was a computer entity and didn't really need to "think" at all. Her thought processes were indeed, as she said, instantaneous. Nor did she need to make any sort of physical gesture to adjust her appearance. She simply needed to think and the change would happen immediately. But she retained enough of her humanity that she still felt compelled to at least look like she was giving something some thought and display those little human gestures such as primping.

"It's definitely not the fluidic space that the *U.S.S. Voyager* encountered. I just compared the readings from their own science surveys," she reported. "Its mass is much thicker than that. It's . . . well, it's gelatinous."

"Gelatinous? Okay . . . look, I know you don't have

much to work with. But can we at least get a feel for what's out there? I mean, isn't it possible that we haven't gone anywhere at all? That we're actually inside some sort of . . . I don't know. Enclosure? Some sort of force bubble created by whatever the hell that was?"

"An enclosure within our own galaxy? It's possible, yes," admitted Xy. "Then again, it is possible, as I suggested earlier, that we're in another universe entirely. Or perhaps some sort of pocket universe, an anomaly situated between different planes of existence. But as long as our sensors aren't functioning, I can't determine precisely. Still . . . perhaps I can get us a rough idea of the size of what we're dealing with."

"How?"

"I can use the sonar array dish to generate small-amplitude adiabatic oscillations. If they encounter boundaries, obstructions and such, they will rebound from whatever they strike and be detectable to us if we listen for their reflection. If they don't return, we know that we've got some serious distance around us. Perhaps enough to indicate that we truly are in another galaxy or even universe of some sort. If they do return, we can determine the distance they traveled by measuring the time of the emission of the pulse to our reception of it. We might even be able to construct wave images of whatever it was they ran into. Naturally if we were dealing with deep space, such an alternative to sensors would be fruitless, because there's no air for sound waves to travel upon. But in this gelatinous mess, it should be feasible."

"That's very ingenious," said Calhoun. "Do you really think it will work?"

"It worked several hundred years ago," Morgan pointed out, "back when they called it 'sound navigation and ranging' . . . or, for short—"

"Sonar. Oh. Right." Xy looked slightly crestfallen. "That *would* be sonar, wouldn't it."

"Don't feel bad, Xy," Burgoyne said consolingly. "Nothing wrong with reinventing the wheel every now and then."

"Very well, then. Do it," Calhoun ordered.

"Kebron," said Xy, moving toward the Brikar, "I'll need to do this through tactical . . ."

"Got it." Kebron didn't nod, since he effectively had no neck. He stepped back and allowed Xy to step in and start programming the sensor dish for its newly created purpose.

"Morgan," said Calhoun, as Xy continued his preparations, "do you think you can handle both ops and conn until Tania's back at her post?"

"Of course, Captain." Morgan was speaking matter-of-factly, without any trace of boasting. "In point of fact, since I'm effectively the computer system, I could run this entire vessel all by myself."

"That's a great idea, Morgan, because having a single computer mind running an entire space vessel . . . nothing bad has *ever* happened as a result of that situation."

She frowned. "That was sarcasm, wasn't it."

"Just a touch."

"Oscillation activated, Captain," said Xy. "Generating full-radius scan."

"Excellent. Engine status?"

"We have both warp drive and ion drive available, Captain," said Morgan.

"Can we move through this . . . whatever it is?" asked Calhoun.

"We can, yes," said Burgoyne. "But we shouldn't move at anything more than sublight speed."

"Why not?"

"It would be inadvisable."

"I'm not following, Burgy," said Calhoun.

"Captain . . . light speed functions because we essentially slip into warp space while simultaneously bending a bubble of subspace around us. That's why we don't become bogged down in Einsteinian paradox. It's also why warp speed has been having environmental consequences: because it causes wear and tear on the very fabric of space and time itself."

"So?"

"Oh dear," Morgan spoke up, and now Xy was nodding as well. "I see the problem."

"Yes, so do I," said Xy.

"Excellent, then," Calhoun said, slapping his palms on the armrests of his chair as if the matter was settled. "As long as everyone else understands, I don't see why it's remotely necessary that the captain be right there along with everyone else . . ."

"The problem, Captain, is that we don't know where we are," said Burgoyne. "Subspace, warp space, or any damned space in between. Plus Xy has given us reason to believe that some aspects of the laws of physics might not function in the way that we're accustomed. If that's the case and we activate the warp engines . . ."

"We're taking the chance that we could shred everything around us," said Morgan. "Not only could we destroy our surroundings, but we could theoretically initiate a chain reaction that would work its way through every plane of existence and destroy time and space—the very universe—itself."

Calhoun took this tidbit in. "Okay, yes," he admitted, "I would tend to classify that as 'inadvisable.' Good judgment call. So we proceed on impulse, if we're to proceed at all, is that it? Going to take us a long time to get anywhere. Then again, since we haven't the faintest idea where we're going, I suppose we're not in all that much of a rush. I mean, Kalinda is still a prisoner on Priatia, and the incendiary political situation in the New Thallonian Protectorate threatens to plunge the entire territory into civil war. But what's a massive body count between friends?"

There was silence from the rest of the bridge.

"People," he continued, "I have no desire to bring the entirety of the multiverse crashing down upon our heads. But neither do I want to pretend that we don't have some serious time pressure at work. We need to figure out what happened, and how to reverse it, and we need to do it soon . . . before there's no longer a Thallonian space of any sort to get back to."

There were echoes of "Aye, sir" throughout the bridge.

That was when Xy suddenly spoke up. "Captain, we're receiving rebound information from the oscillation waves."

"I believe the old-fashioned term was 'pings,' " Morgan said.

"We have some pings, Captain," Xy promptly amended.

"You mean we're getting a determination of the perimeters of this place?"

"Not so far," said Xy, crouched over the readings. "But I'm getting a reading on something else."

"What sort of something else?"

"Something big, Captain," and he looked up at Calhoun with clear worry on his face. "Something extremely big."

"Is it the same ship that sent us into this . . . place?"

"It could be," said Xy slowly, nodding. "It could very well be."

"Well then," Calhoun said with disturbing cheerfulness. "Since our priority is getting back home . . . let's head over and introduce ourselves to the neighbors."

ii.

Dr. Selar was accomplished at maintaining her Vulcan sense of reserve and detachment in just about all situations. The qualifier of "just about" invariably related to interacting with her erstwhile mate, Burgoyne 172, and particularly so when matters were stressful.

"I have six injured crewmen down here," she told hir over the intercom, glancing around the sickbay to make certain that everyone was being attended to properly. She knew that all her people were top medical personnel. Nevertheless she double- and even triple-checked their work out of force of habit and training. Deep down, she was convinced that no human could be as capable a doctor as a Vulcan. She would never have said that aloud, since it would doubtless have had a negative impact on her people's morale, but she couldn't do anything about her opinion. "I would very much like to know," she continued, "if any more can be expected in the immediate future."

"*I'm afraid I don't know that at the present time, Doctor,*" said Burgoyne. "*We're still gathering damage reports.*"

"Are we in a hostile environment?"

"*I don't know.*"

"Are we likely to be in a combat situation in the near future?"

"*I don't know.*"

"Where are we?"

"*I don't know.*"

This was precisely the sort of situation in which, were it anyone else, Selar's inflection would not have changed. But because it was Burgoyne, and because of their history together, she was unable to keep annoyance out of her voice. "Thank you, Commander," she said, her tone laden with irony. "This has been an extremely enlightening conversation. Selar out." She heard Burgoyne start to say something in reply, but the connection was obediently severed.

The doors to sickbay hissed open, and Xyon entered,

hauling what appeared to be Tania Tobias along with him. She was barely conscious, her head slumped forward, her eyes looking glazed. "Customer, Doc," he called out. "Possible mild concussion."

"Thank you for your diagnosis, Dr. Xyon." She didn't bother to wait for any of the technicians to come over and lend a hand. Instead Dr. Selar went straight over to them, positioned her arms under Tania, and lifted her clear off the floor.

Xyon made no effort to hide that he was impressed. "That Vulcan strength certainly comes in handy, doesn't it."

"It can," Selar said noncommittally.

"I don't know why you bother with the nerve pinch when you can just break someone's neck so they can't bother you anymore. Why do you?"

She fixed him with a glance. "At the moment, I could not say." She carried Tobias over to an empty diagnostic bed and laid her down. "Did you see what happened? What she struck her head on?"

"Not really," Xyon admitted. "Everything was dark at the time. She was found like this."

"Worlds."

It had been neither Selar nor Xyon who had spoken. Instead it was Tania, who had come around but appeared to be oblivious of where she was or who was with her. She was staring up at the ceiling with great interest, although Selar couldn't say whether she actually saw it or was, perhaps, looking right through it.

"What did she say?" asked Xyon.

"Worlds." It was Tania again, but Selar had the

oddest feeling she hadn't repeated herself in order to accommodate Xyon. Instead she was randomly saying whatever was passing through her mind. "Worlds . . . in worlds . . ."

"What's that supposed to mean?"

It was not an unreasonable question for him to ask, and yet Selar felt unduly irritated by having to take the time to answer it. Instead she was studying the diagnostic readouts, trying to get a fix on Tania's brain activity. "There appears to be no subdural trauma. No substantive damage. However, Doctor, I am always open to a second opinion," she added dryly.

"You didn't answer my question," Xyon pointed out.

She sighed with the infinitely annoyed air of one who does not suffer fools gladly. "If I answer it, will you leave?"

"Deal."

"It was the name of the project she was working on before her . . . breakdown. Worlds Within Worlds. There had been a growing faction within the Federation arguing that terraforming was a violation of the Prime Directive."

"Violation? How?" asked Xyon. "I thought terraforming was only done on planets that had no existing life on them."

"Yes, but the argument went that there was the potential for life and a subsequent civilization on any planet, and the mere act of terraforming amounted to de facto interference."

"That's ridiculous."

She hadn't been looking directly at Xyon, concentrating her efforts on tending to Tobias. Now, however, she glanced at him and said, "I have lived longer than you, Mr. Xyon, and I can tell you with authority that there are very few discussions in the universe that will be quashed simply by dint of the fact that they are ridiculous. In any event, Worlds Within Worlds was conceived as an alternative to terraforming. It involved the creation of artificial spheres in which entire populations would be able to exist. It is a concept that has existed for some time, originally proposed by a physicist named Freeman Dyson and called a Dyson Sphere. Dyson, however, proposed the construction of a megastructure around a star. Worlds Within Worlds entailed the creation of essentially a smaller, far more compact artificial star which would serve as the source of light and energy for the colonists."

"And something happened to her while she was there?"

"Yes. She suffered a mental collapse of some sort. No one knows why. And even if I did know why, I would not tell you, for we would be moving beyond the realm of that which is public record and into the area of that which is—how best to put it—none of your damned business."

"Fair enough," said Xyon. "But if she had, as you say, some kind of breakdown . . . what's she doing here?"

"Captain Calhoun decided to take a chance on her."

"Why?"

"You would have to speak to him about that. Now, if we are quite through . . . ?"

"Okay. Sure, well . . . thanks for the information."

Xyon turned and exited the sickbay, much to Selar's relief. She turned her attention back to Tania Tobias, who was continuing to stare fixedly at the ceiling. Tania's lips were moving, but nothing seemed to be coming out. Selar leaned forward slightly, her extraordinarily sharp hearing serving her well as she realized that Tania was indeed whispering very, very softly. What she was saying, though, provided little guidance for Selar in terms of how to proceed.

"You know nothing," Tania whispered. "Nothing. You know nothing at all . . ."

iii.

Calhoun was absolutely determined not to say "What *is* that?" yet again. He felt as if he'd been asking that entirely too often, and it made him feel as if he was coming across as perpetually clueless. If one was to lead, one should—at the very least—give the impression that one knew as much as, if not more than, those one was leading.

So it was with a feeling of relief that he was able to see the object ahead of them and know, for a fact, what it was.

It had taken them what felt like an excruciatingly long time to get there. Calhoun was accustomed to warp speed, even if it was only warp one. Between traveling at sublight and moving through the fierce viscosity of the gelatinous mass of a universe in which they'd been enveloped, Calhoun felt less like the captain of a sleek starship and more like a flea perched atop the head of a hog slogging through mud.

All the time they had been traveling, Calhoun's mind kept returning to the situation they had left behind. He couldn't believe that matters had improved in their absence. Frustration was welling up within him. He was positive that Kalinda was a prisoner on Priatia, and that the Priatians were behind the civil war threatening to destroy the entirety of the New Thallonian Protectorate. Here was the *Excalibur* with this knowledge, tromping around, unable to do anything about it except pray that something turned up that would enable them to get the hell out of there.

He hoped that whatever it was they were about to encounter, it might provide them with that escape they so desperately needed.

Now, as it came into view on the screen, he realized that he might get his wish . . . but it might not do him any good, either.

"It's not the same ship," Burgoyne said, staring as fixedly at the screen as anyone else there.

Calhoun knew s/he was right. The vessel that they were seeing, although it bore a resemblance to the ship that had attacked them and sent them spiraling into this bizarre realm, was not exactly the same. It had that same cross-tube construction that made it look like a giant molecule, but there were far more tunnels cross-connecting. Also, although it was hard for Calhoun to believe, the damned thing was even bigger than the one they'd encountered. It almost offended his sense of propriety.

Apparently Morgan's thoughts were going in the same direction. "Is it just me," she asked, "or does anyone else think that there comes a time when something is so big it's just ridiculous? I mean, at some point it just becomes showing off."

"Perhaps they have issues," said Kebron. "Captain, permission to speak freely?"

Calhoun rolled his eyes. "Of course."

"That thing is about a hundred times bigger than we are. We'd be insane to approach it."

"I agree."

"And yet we're approaching it."

"And yet we are," agreed Calhoun. "As fast as our stubby little sublight legs will carry us."

"May I ask why?"

"Yes."

Now it was Kebron's turn to roll his eyes. "Why?"

"Because the ship is devoid of life."

That prompted a surprised reaction from the others. Xy glanced at his still-useless sensor devices. "I'm still getting no response from my sensor array, Captain," said Xy. "May I ask—" He stopped himself and started again. "On what do you base that assessment?"

"A gut feeling, Lieutenant."

"A gut feeling, sir?" Xy looked bemusedly at Kebron, as if to make sure that they were both hearing the same thing.

"That is correct, Lieutenant. A gut feeling. A feeling that comes from deep within my gut." He had stepped out of his chair and was staring at the monitor, his hands draped behind his back. "It has guided me through many a hazardous situation. Situations that, I should add, were far more hazardous than this."

"Really?"

Calhoun paused, giving it some thought. "Okay, actually . . . no. This is probably the most hazardous. But let's face it, people: When our instrumentation lets us down, what else do we have to see us through except for good old human instinct."

"Technically speaking, sir, you're not human," Xy reminded him.

"Somehow I knew you weren't going to let that slip by, Lieutenant."

"Captain," Morgan asked, "shall I continue approach?"

"Did I give you an order to the contrary?"

"No, sir."

"Then that's your answer, isn't it."

"Aye, sir," Morgan agreed.

In short order, they had drawn sufficiently close that the ship occupied and then exceeded the dimensions of the monitor. Calhoun knew that they were still a considerable distance from it, and yet it was mammoth almost beyond his ability to comprehend.

But even so . . . he was still not getting any sense of jeopardy from it.

Calhoun couldn't even begin to count the number of scrapes he had managed to avoid or be one step ahead of based purely on his unerring ability to "read" a situation and perceive the inherent hazards. He'd actually once, at the behest of his wife, gone in for testing to see if he had some sort of genuine psionic power. He had always cherished the terse written report that had been issued after he'd received a thorough going-over: "Detailed analysis of Calhoun's brain reveals nothing." He remembered conveying the message word-for-word to Shelby, and she had laughed for a solid five minutes.

He missed her laugh. He missed her.

He wondered if she knew what had happened to him (not that he himself had any clear idea). If she did, she was probably going out of her mind with worry. Calhoun wondered, not for the first time, if he hadn't done her more harm than good by marrying her.

In any event, despite the fact that there was no scientific proof as to the reliability of his "nose for danger"—usually characterized by the hair on the back of his neck rising—he had learned to depend upon it and had never been disappointed. Still, nothing was perfect and nothing was infallible.

As he watched the ship loom larger still, he said, "Just think, Mr. Kebron . . . if I turn out to be wrong and that ship fires a massive weapon of some kind that obliterates us . . . you'll be in a position to laugh at me and say, 'See? So much for your gut instinct.' "

"Why yes, Captain," replied Kebron. "I would consider it personally gratifying if I, along with my crewmates, could lay down our lives for the privilege of being right while you were wrong."

"That's good to know."

"I wasn't serious, Captain."

"I knew that, too."

The space between the bars, which had appeared narrow from far away, had initially appeared far too tight a fit for the *Excalibur* to slide through. Now though, within range of the huge vehicle, it was clear there was plenty of room for the *Excalibur* to pass through the exterior of the ship and into . . . what? He wasn't at all sure what to expect.

But it wasn't a trap. There was no danger.

His instincts were assuring him of that.

Let him be in a universe where the sensors didn't operate. Let him be in a universe where the laws of physics themselves were dubious at best, lethal at worst. Let all of that be true and still, he assured himself, nothing could tamper with his inborn ability to perceive danger to himself and those who depended upon him.

Except . . . what if he was wrong? What if he was indeed putting the life of his crew on the line over a hunch that was no more reliable than a hunch anyone else might have?

As much as the doubts raged within him, his exterior betrayed none of it. He looked relaxed in his command chair, legs crossed at the ankles, giving not the slightest hint that he was anything except completely confident in his course. Sometimes what a crew needed more than a captain who was sure of what he was doing was a captain who gave the appearance of being sure of what he was doing.

"Captain," Morgan suddenly spoke up. "They were in a fight. And I think they lost. Look."

He saw that Morgan was right. He was beginning to see signs of what looked like carbon scoring. Then there was more: Gaping holes that had been torn in various sections. Twisted struts that had been ripped away from their connecting sockets. The design of the ship had hidden such structural defects initially, but the closer they drew, the more evident it became. Morgan was right. They had indeed been in a battle, and judging from the amount of damage they'd sustained, they hadn't come out on the winning side.

"What are those?" Calhoun suddenly said. There appeared to be pieces of something floating through the gelatinous exterior. "Can you zoom in on them?"

Morgan did so. Calhoun studied them. They were thick and tubular, a pale gray. "Xy," he said slowly, "do those look biological to you?"

"They certainly do, Captain. Actually . . . they look like pieces of tentacles."

"That's what I thought," said Calhoun. "As if someone blew up a squid." He looked at the growing array of fleshy pieces hanging there. "A lot of squids," he amended. "Either the ship was a floating aquarium . . . or it was piloted by beings who looked a lot like squids."

"Extremely large squids," added Xy, "judging by the size of the fragments we're see . . . Captain! We're getting ripples!"

"Ripples?" said Calhoun, not understanding.

"The sensors may not be functioning properly, but

I can at least detect movement of the substance around us . . ."

"He's right," Morgan said. It seemed as if she wasn't looking at Calhoun, even though she had turned to face him. Instead she appeared to be looking inward. "There's an undulation against the surface of the ship. Something's moving out here besides us."

"I'm getting a ping back on the sonar," Xy said, adopting the ages-old terms for the technique he was using. "It's behind us. Still a good distance from us, but it's big and it's heading our way."

"Is there a chance it hasn't seen us yet?"

"We're the size of a flyspeck in comparison to this thing," Xy said, indicating the ship that was right in front of them. "There's every chance."

"Morgan. Best possible speed into the ship."

Instantly the *Excalibur* waddled forward on impulse power, penetrating into the heart of the strangely molecular ship. It loomed around them, dwarfing the smaller vessel, and Calhoun was starting to have uncomfortable mental images of an insect wandering all unsuspecting into a web.

Soon there were struts and supports all around them. Judging it to be far enough for their purposes, Calhoun said quietly, "All stop. Put me on intraship."

"You're on, Captain."

"All hands, this is the captain," he said. "We are now running silent. No unnecessary talking or movement from here on in until I give the all-clear . . . or until I sound battle stations. Captain out." He leaned forward and murmured, "Give me a view of what's coming our way."

The monitor image changed. It was hard to make anything out. There was the merest outline of whatever it was that was behind them.

The tension on the bridge was palpable as, hiding within the remains of a derelict ship, Calhoun couldn't help but think that whatever was out there . . . might well be the thing that had attacked the ship they were using as camouflage. If it was capable of laying waste to a vessel as large and powerful as the one they were using as camouflage, the *Excalibur*—for all its resources and resourcefulness—wouldn't last a minute.

The Spectre

With the Romulan Neutral Zone looming less than twenty minutes away, Soleta wasn't able to remain within her command chair. Instead she paced the bridge constantly, so much so that Lucius could not help but comment upon it. "Is there a problem, Commander?"

She swiveled to face him, looking distracted. "Problem, Tribune? What sort of problem?"

Lucius glanced at the other members of the bridge crew, who were watching with open curiosity. Aquila shrugged slightly, which was about all the encouragement any of them were prepared to offer. "To the casual observer," Lucius said gamely, "it would appear that you seem . . . preoccupied."

"I am," she replied. "Lest you forget, Tribune, I was once a science officer in Starfleet."

"I have never forgotten that, Commander," he said politely . . . so politely that it was difficult for Soleta to determine whether or not he was insulting her.

She decided it would be wisest to let the subtext pass without comment. Instead she said, "I am simply trying to figure out what it was we saw swallow the *Excalibur*, and what the nature of that vessel was that came in pursuit of us."

"Whatever it was," growled Praefect Vitus from tactical, "we should be grateful to it. The *Excalibur* was a troublesome vessel, and its captain an arrogant maverick. Anyone who presents a threat to the Romulan Empire is better disposed of."

"A not-unreasonable attitude, Praefect," Soleta said, her Vulcan-trained demeanor of dispassion masking her desire to reach over and tear Vitus's face off. She half-suspected that he was saying it specifically to get a reaction out of her, and she'd be damned if she'd accommodate him. "However, might I point out that we are talking about a phenomenon the true nature of which we do not understand. Which effectively means that, if we are faced with the same threat, we will experience the same fate as the much-despised *Excalibur*. Would you be comfortable with that?"

"If we did so while defending the Empire," Vitus said stiffly, "I would honor such a fate."

"I have no doubt. But are you anxious for it?"

"Well . . . no . . ."

"No. Nor am I," she said. "The readings we managed to take of it while it was happening are woefully inadequate to determine its true nature. Maurus, bring it up on screen again. Let me see it once more."

"Again?" asked Maurus. Then, seeing the look she gave him, he immediately said, "On screen, Commander."

She watched the entire thing unfold yet again, and felt frustration roiling within her as she continued to have no idea what it was she was talking about. "The sensors array behaved as if there was nothing at all strange transpiring," she said aloud to herself. "But subsequent diagnostics indicated that they were functioning perfectly. Why would that be?"

"Again, perhaps it was an illusion?" suggested Lucius. "Perhaps that which we thought we witnessed was not actually transpiring."

"A possibility, but I think not," said Soleta. "We were still able to detect the residue of the occurrence, free-floating tachyons in high amounts that hadn't been there before. It's as if . . ." She stopped her movement and drummed thoughtfully on the helm console. Aquila looked up at her but said nothing. Then she snapped her fingers. "Yes. That makes sense."

"What does?"

"We were seeing something that was not there."

"An illusion, as I said . . ."

"No, Lucius. See . . . a wormhole, which is the closest analogue to what we're witnessing, opens a hole into subspace, where different rules apply in terms of such things as traversing physical distance. But this . . . this sinkhole we're witnessing . . . it's possible that it's opening a gateway to an alternate universe where our physical laws don't apply. If that was the case, the sensors would not be able to detect anything because they literally wouldn't know what they were looking at. So it would either come across as inconclusive or as not even there at all."

"That makes a certain degree of sense," said Lucius cautiously.

"I appreciate the ringing endorsement, Tribune. Still, I'll look forward to meeting with the Praetor's top scientists and learning their opinion of this matter."

As if on cue, Aquila said, "Approaching Neutral Zone border now, Commander."

"Home," sighed Maurus.

Soleta knew he was anxious to return to the homeworld of Romulus. His mate was expecting their first child and, although there was nothing lacking in Maurus's conduct, she knew he was feeling a little distracted. She couldn't blame him.

Every so often she toyed with the notion of what it would be like to have a child of her own. And just as often, she dismissed it.

Moments later, they were through the Neutral Zone, which served as the border to Romulan space. Soleta had tensed slightly, both in the approach and in their passage through the Zone. She knew it was a holdover from the old days when being in a Federation ship that was entering Romulan territory was tantamount to an act of war. A Romulan ship doing so, obviously, was not in any danger. Which reminded her . . . .

"Drop cloak," she said. "Switch from ion glide to standard warp. Run normal space."

"Normal space, aye."

The *Spectre* shimmered into existence. It was virtually undetectable when running invisible and utilizing the ion glide. Soleta saw no reason to be sneaking around or expending ship's energy needlessly now that they were in their own backyard.

"Commander," Maurus said. He appeared a bit

puzzled. "I'm doing a routine scan for subspace chatter . . ."

"Yes?"

"There isn't any."

"None?" Soleta frowned, her arched eyebrows knitting. "That would indicate some sort of communications blackout from the homeworld . . . area ships, everything. Why would that be?"

"I have no answer for you at this time, Commander."

"Keep listening, then."

"Shall I send out a general call for response?"

She considered it. Something about the oddity of what they were experiencing made her even more cautious than usual. "No. Listen for whatever you can detect, but say nothing. Vitus, full sensor scans. If anything's coming our way, I want to know about them before they know about us."

The *Spectre* maintained its course, heading for Romulus. Soleta retreated to her command chair, trying to determine what the reason could be for the odd state of affairs. She had received no recent communiqués from the Praetor, but that in itself was nothing to be especially concerned about. Hers was, after all, a stealth vessel, carrying out missions of extreme delicacy and espionage on Praetor Hiren's behalf. So it wasn't as if she expected any sort of routine communication from him.

Still . . . something seemed . . . off.

She promptly dismissed the notion. What, was she turning into Mackenzie Calhoun, working his way through space by taking guesses and operating on instinct and hunches? She admired the man, yes . . . not that she would have admitted it aloud to her crew . . . but his tendency toward flying on instinct never struck her as any sort of logical way to conduct oneself. There was too much luck involved, and sooner or later, luck tends to run out.

"Commander," Vitus suddenly said, "two contacts, approaching at 227 mark 8."

"Ours? Or do we have troublemakers in Romulan space?"

"Ours," said Vitus. "From their energy signatures, I make them to be the *Dhael* and the *S'harien*."

"The *S'harien* is under the command of Commander Aurelius," said Lucius. "Trustworthy and honorable. He'd be honored to provide us escort straight to the Praetor if we asked him to."

"Excellent," Soleta said, relaxing a bit. Lucius was never wrong about this sort of thing. He commanded the respect of other Romulans that she often secretly wished she could acquire for herself. "Maurus . . . send a hail. Get their attention."

The centurion did as he was ordered, and minutes later, the two Romulan warbirds had come into view. They were approaching slowly, with not the slightest hint of aggression.

"Commander," said Maurus, "the *S'harien* is responding."

"Put them on, Centurion."

The image of an older, stately Romulan appeared. He said nothing, but simply inclined his head slightly at the sight of Soleta.

Soleta decided to make the first move. "Commander Aurelius," said Soleta, with a slight bow.

"Commander Soleta," replied Aurelius. "Welcome back. May I take it that Tribune Lucius is with you as well?"

"I am here, Commander," said Lucius, stepping into view. It was a slight breach of protocol, an inferior officer addressing another ship's captain without so much as a by-your-leave from his own commanding officer. However, Soleta saw no reason to make an issue out of it.

"Yes," said Aurelius, and that struck Soleta as an odd response. Just . . . yes? Why didn't he act as if he was pleased to see his old friend? She glanced over at Lucius and even he seemed mildly surprised by how tepid the reply was.

"Did you accomplish your recent mission for the Praetor?"

Lucius glanced at Soleta, clearly unsure whether he should continue the conversation. Soleta nodded to him and Lucius replied, "Yes. We have achieved our goals for the glory of the Praetor."

"Good. The Praetor has new orders for you. You are to turn over whatever you have acquired and then be dispatched on a new mission."

Lucius made no effort to hide his confusion. "With all respect, Commander, this is . . . a bit unusual. May I see the Praetor's orders?"

"You doubt my word? *My* word?"

"Not . . . at all, Commander, but—"

"I do," Soleta suddenly said, stepping forward. "I answer to the Praetor, Commander Aurelius, not to you. I deal in espionage and sabotage, and it is not in my nature nor in my command prerogative simply to take anyone's word for anything. This is highly irregular . . ."

"These are highly irregular times, Soleta, and I do not suggest you defy me in this manner."

"Saying no is the only manner in which I know how to defy someone, Commander."

Aurelius's face started to flush green with anger, but then he visibly reined himself in and even managed to force a thin smile. "All right, Commander Soleta," he said coolly. "You make some valid points. How about this . . ."

Suddenly Soleta clutched at her stomach and moaned. The gesture clearly surprised everyone watching. "Commander Soleta . . . ?" Aurelius called.

Soleta stumbled toward the tactical station and grabbed it for support. Immediately a concerned Vitus leaned forward, and the moment he did so, Soleta spoke quickly, urgently and barely above a whisper: "Scan for motion detectors and plasma trails." She waited just barely long enough to satisfy herself that her words had registered on Vitus. Then she made a show of turning back to the screen, wincing in pain. "My . . . deepest apologies, Commander," she managed to get out before taking a deep breath and acting as if she had just fought off a wave of pain. "I have been having . . . severe abdominal cramps. Mild case of food poisoning, I fear. It is a trial, but I endure."

"My condolences, Commander," said Aurelius. "Now . . . I was about to say—"

"Yes. Speak, Commander," she said, rubbing her stomach delicately. "You have my full attention. You were saying . . . ?"

"I think the simplest solution to this issue would be for me to beam over there so we can discuss the matter face-to-face. That doesn't present a problem for you, does it?"

"Of course not," she said. She turned to Lucius. "Tribune . . . do you see that as presenting any sort of problem?"

"I . . . no, Commander, I . . . do not," said Lucius, but he was looking at her oddly, as if trying to peer directly into her mind and figure out what she was thinking.

"Good. How about you, Centurion?"

Aquila looked around and up at her, bewilderment on his face. "Me, Commander?"

"Yes. You. I am wondering if you have a problem with Commander Aurelius's plan." She cocked an eyebrow and looked at him expectantly. "Do you feel that your opinion has no worth?"

"No, I . . . I do not feel that way, Commander. I'm just . . ." He cleared his throat and straightened his back. "No, Commander. I do not have any problem with it."

"Commander Soleta," said Aurelius, his suspicions obviously on the rise. "Is it your habit to poll your bridge crew on all your command decisions?"

"It's an experiment, Commander. I'm still a scientist at heart. Indulge me, won't you?"

"Commander, this is—"

She didn't give him the chance to finish the sentence. Instead she turned to Vitus and said, "Praefect? Your thoughts?"

Very slowly, ever so slightly, Vitus nodded and held up two fingers.

It told Soleta exactly what she had suspected.

Vitus had checked the immediate area, at Soleta's instructions, to determine whether there were any other Romulan vessels around that were cloaked.

He had found two. Two more ships, in addition to the ones they were facing, were hiding nearby.

There was only one possible reason that Romulan ships would be cloaked.

Options raced through her mind in seconds. Four against one: the odds didn't favor them for a shoot-out, and the *Spectre* was built more for stealth than battle anyway. They could cloak and try to sneak away, but the cloak drained power from the engine, and they wouldn't be able to use anything approximating maximum speed, or be able to use shields. The moment the ship vanished, all the ships in the area would start firing in as wide a dispersal as possible. All that was needed was for one stray shot to make contact before they could get clear, and that would provide sufficient target for all four ships—or, at least, the four ships that they knew of—to open fire.

Allow Aurelius to beam over? Take him as hostage, try to bargain their way out that way? No. That was Federation thinking. If Aurelius was a hostage, he would just die with the rest of them.

She considered other possibilities as well, discarded

them, and then turned and strode over to the com station. "Well, that settles it, Commander," she said calmly. "Just give me a moment to contact the transporter room. How many to beam over?"

With one quick movement, she reached down and shut off the transmission. Aurelius's face disappeared even as he started to make his response. His image hadn't even faded as she called out, "Shields up! Helm, set course for the Neutral Zone! Best possible speed, now! *Now!*"

Some small part of her had been concerned that there would be confusion, vacillation. That they would ask her what was going on. Any hesitation on the part of anyone to whom she had just barked orders could be fatal, because the clock was ticking down for them the microsecond she severed communications.

Fortunately enough, the urgency in her voice and long years of training were all that was required to spur her men to action. The shields went up instantly, which she had expected since Vitus already had some clue as to their situation. But Aquila was no slower in laying in their path back, and an instant later, the engines came online at full power. The *Spectre* whipped around and started heading with all possible speed back the way they'd come.

They made exactly ten thousand and thirty kilometers before they collided with a cloaked Romulan vessel.

It wasn't a total surprise. Soleta had factored in that possibility when calculating her next move. But space is vast, there were any number of directions they could go, and the odds of them actually coming into contact with a cloaked ship were small enough that Soleta felt it was worth the risk. This was one of those rare instances where Soleta "beat" the odds in an adverse way.

They slammed into the cloaked vessel, sending everyone and everything on the *Spectre* crashing to the floor or into one another. Alerts began screaming all over the ship. Their shields had afforded Soleta's ship a measure of protection, but Romulan energy shields were designed to withstand blasts from pulse weapons or phaser fire. They were intended for deflecting and blocking weaponry that was of the same fundamental nature as the shields themselves. They were not prepared to ward off the full impact of another ship's hull.

Although they were in space where sound didn't travel, Soleta fancied she could almost hear the sounds of tearing, shredding metal mixed in with voices crying out in terror.

"Dammit, Centurion, get us out of here!" Soleta shouted over the din.

"Trying, Commander!" Aquila called back. He eased the ship back, endeavoring to disentangle it from the other vessel. The cloak on the other vessel fizzled and lost power, and a Romulan warbird blinked into existence all around them. Soleta watched in mute horror as the *Spectre*'s efforts to disengage from the warbird caused the warbird to shred from the stress. The *Spectre*'s own shields practically groaned under the strain.

Suddenly the *Spectre* shuddered from several violent impacts. "Commander, the other vessels have opened fire on us," called Lucius.

Right there on the viewscreen, the two already-visible ships were angling toward them, firing as they came. Stray shots would hit the ship they were still tangled with, but obviously they didn't care about that. Now a third Romulan ship was decloaking as well, which could only mean that it was preparing to fire upon them.

The *Spectre* shook once again, but this time it felt different. "We're clear, Commander!" shouted Aquila.

Soleta saw the shattered remains of the other ship floating away from them, along with a number of Romulan bodies. "Vitus, arm rear plasma torpedoes! Aquila—"

"Full speed, aye!" he said, anticipating her next words.

The *Spectre* angled away from the other ships and, seconds later, unleashed a volley of torpedoes behind itself to try and slow down their pursuers.

"Damage report!"

"We've lost forward shields; aft shields at half power," Vitus told her. "Warp engines beginning to run hot; engineering thinks we sustained damage to the coils and recommends shutdown until they can lock it down . . ."

"We shut down the warp engines, they'll overtake us and blow us into scrap."

"Understood."

"What about the ion glide? Can we still go silent?"

"Yes, but the energy drain by the cloak could leave

all other systems, including life-support, dangerously low . . ."

That was when the ship was struck yet again. Soleta staggered and would have fallen except for Lucius reaching out and snagging her, practically shoving her back into her command chair. "Sorry, Commander," he muttered.

"Don't worry about it."

"Commander, aft shields cannot survive another hit!" said Vitus.

"That, on the other hand, we can worry about. Helm, evasive maneuvers!"

"There's too many of them, Commander," replied Aquila, who was doing his best to comply with her orders. The *Spectre* was deft and maneuverable, and plasma cannon blasts exploded around them, just barely missing. But their luck was going to hold for only so long.

Soleta took a deep breath and let it out slowly. "Vitus," she ordered, "divert all power into the cloak and ion glide. Take us silent."

"Taking us silent," said Vitus without hesitation.

"Commander, I won't be able to maintain us at full warp speed," said Aquila. Soleta was fully aware of that, and naturally Aquila knew that she knew. But standard operating procedure required that he inform her of that fact.

"Best possible speed, Aquila," she told him, praying that it would be enough.

She watched the pursuing ships on the monitor screen and waited to see what reaction they would have when the *Spectre* vanished. The problem was, she had absolutely no clue what in the world had happened that would cause this sort of action on their part. Anything seemed possible at this point. And if that was the case, then for all she knew, they'd managed to develop some new technology that would enable them to pursue the *Spectre* even when fully cloaked and running silent on the ion glide.

Certainly the exact same thoughts occurred to the rest of her crew, for they were watching as anxiously as she.

"Shield engaged. Ion glide engaged. We are now running silent," said Vitus grimly, knowing as well as she that the next few moments would determine their fate.

Space, which had been hurtling by them, seemed to slow, and their surroundings shimmered and distorted slightly, as they always did when the shields first came on. The pursuing ships, however, did not appear to be slowing down, and were instead gaining on them steadily.

"Helm, change course," Soleta said quietly. "Bring us to a new heading of 227 mark 3." That would keep them heading in the direction of the Neutral Zone and out of Romulan space, but at a different angle.

Aquila immediately obeyed. Soleta only belatedly realized that she had stopped breathing altogether as she watched them move away from the other vessels. She was waiting for them to realize, to adjust their own courses so that they could continue their pursuit.

No such course adjustment came. Instead the pursuing ships continued in the same direction, moving in a V formation.

"Thank the gods," muttered Maurus.

"Considering what we just went through, the gods have a lot to answer for," replied Soleta, who nevertheless let out a heavy sigh of relief. "Helm, keep us moving hard and steady for the Neutral Zone."

"Commander, that's going to drain our energy reserves to the breaking point," said Vitus. "By the time we make it there, we may be virtually dead in space."

"I'm aware of that, Praefect," she said. "But we have no idea how many other ships are out here, and on what sort of search-and-destroy mission they're on. We have to get clear and into Federation space as quickly as we can, and if we do it uncloaked or with normal engines, we might well not make it and be literally dead in space rather than virtually."

"But Commander," said Maurus, "I . . . I still don't understand. Why did they fire on us in the first place?"

"I don't know."

"Why did they attack us . . . ?"

"I *still* don't know!" said Soleta, wiping sweat from her eyes. She felt a hundred years older and as if she hadn't slept in days. "I can, however, take a guess."

"The Praetor," Lucius spoke up grimly, "is no longer in power?"

Slowly Soleta nodded. "That is my guess as well. And until we know for sure . . . we don't dare go home again."

It was certainly not the first time that Soleta felt no sense of belonging. She had just hoped that the previous time would be the last. Obviously that was not going to be the case . . . and she wondered how often it was going to happen to her before she went completely insane from it.

New Thallon

Excerpted from Lefler's logs:

It's been ages since I maintained a first-person log of what's been going on in my life. It was a practice of mine when I was much younger, and I continued it naturally during my service on shipboard when such logs are standard procedure. But having taken a planetside assignment here on New Thallon, and since marrying Si Cwan, I've fallen out of the habit. Matters, however, have taken a violently downward spiral, and I find myself more isolated and frustrated with each passing day. I crave someone to talk to. But Si Cwan is barely there for me. No one is there for me. And so I must console myself with the sound of my own voice.

Si Cwan has put the planetary defenses on full alert. They are well prepared for any potential attack from the forces of the House of Fhermus. Of the fifty-seven member worlds of the Thallonian Protectorate, they have split almost evenly between supporting Fhermus and Cwan, with a slight edge toward Cwan due to ancient treaties. Thirty of them have sided with Cwan, twenty-seven with Fhermus.

It's madness. All of it, madness.

It's not even as if the alliances necessarily mean any-thing. Many of them are simply economic agreements over boycotts. Various worlds agreeing not to conduct business with the Nelkarites or anyone associating with them. That sort of thing. In terms of actual military might, only a few on either side bring much to the table.

Again, madness I say.

Once upon a time, they were called "member planets" and they sent "representatives." Now they're referred to as "allies" and the representatives have been designated "war-lords." In that way, they are unilaterally granted the right to make decisions and plans in accordance with what Si Cwan wants.

What does Si Cwan want? I can't even begin to know.

He wants Kalinda's name and reputation cleared, that much I can say. He believes Fhermus savaged both by claim-ing that Kalinda had brutally murdered Tiraud in cold blood. And I think Cwan still burns with fury every time he contemplates Tiraud bruising and battering Kalinda. Tiraud, dead, has escaped his wrath. But Fhermus is of course alive and can still be punished. The father being made to suffer for the sins of the son. There's a twist.

I've tried to talk to him. I've tried to talk to Kalinda. It's as if I'm addressing strangers. Si Cwan is consumed by anger and frustration, and Kalinda . . . I swear, it's as if she looks at me through the eyes of a stranger. Could Tiraud's actions have been that traumatic that she regards the entire world with suspicion? Or is there something else, something more sinister?

I'm probably just imagining it. These days, with every-one so tense and a general sense of paranoia in the air, it's understandable that I see plots and schemes everywhere I look.

Si Cwan is meeting today with the warlords to go over the final plans for a major strike against Fhermus. He is one of the most powerful and influential members of the Nelkarite race, and has managed to align most of his world against the House of Cwan. That means that, for Cwan to attack, his plans must encompass the entirety of Nelkar. I've tried to talk him out of this. To remind him of all the Nelkarites who are essentially innocents, caught in the middle of all this. Si Cwan's response? "Anyone who casts their lot with Fhermus is, by definition, not innocent."

Can he really believe that? Is he so far removed from the noble, compassionate man I married that he truly thinks there's no such thing as innocents caught in the crossfire at a time of war? Has he simply gone out of his mind with anger?

Personally, I think he doesn't want to do this. I think he would give anything he could to avoid it. But because he knows he can't—because Cwan is so blinded by fury—I think he's created this . . . this persona for himself. One that's cold and distant and focused entirely on war, because that takes him out of himself and allows him to do what must be done, even though he has neither desire nor taste for it.

Then again, I suppose he opened the door for this possible "persona" the day he ordered Xyon to be tortured for no damned good reason. It's strange. The very first day I met Si Cwan, I felt as if I had known him forever. But that day when he ordered his majordomo, Ankar, to oversee Xyon's torture . . . that was the first time in my entire life that I felt I didn't know him at all.

I miss the Si Cwan who would never torture a helpless victim just out of a sense of political expediency. I miss the Si Cwan who was decent and honest and true, and those qualities shone like a beacon above all else.

I miss him so much.

Or at least . . . part of me misses him. Another part of me wonders if he ever existed at all.

i.

Topez Anat—red-skinned, round-jawed, with an open and eager face—was a young Thallonian whose father had served the House of Cwan. And his father before him had served it, and his father before him, and so on for as far back as anyone in the Anat family could possibly remember.

The Thallonian Empire had collapsed, and Si Cwan had gone into exile, shortly before Topez Anat was to turn of age and begin his service in whatever capacity the House of Cwan wished him to. Naturally Topez Anat had had nothing to do with that collapse, and could not have prevented it no matter what. Nevertheless, despite the irrationality of his belief, he felt as if he had somehow let down his father and all those before him. They had served; he had not. The reasons didn't matter. Only his failure to follow in their footsteps did.

So Topez Anat was gleeful beyond his ability to articulate when New Thallon was established, the Protectorate formed, and Si Cwan put in place as Prime

Minister. Topez Anat had been among the first to report for duty. He had knelt before Si Cwan, held Cwan's hand reverently, and sworn allegiance. He was gratified to learn that Cwan remembered his ancestors' service quite well, and had always thought fondly of the efforts they had made on behalf of the House of Cwan. Topez Anat had practically been apoplectic with joy upon learning that. The first—and only, as it turned out—meeting that he had with Si Cwan ended with him on bended knee saying reverently, "I pledge you my life and honor, my prince."

Not long after, Topez Anat had received his assignment. He was to work at Building Three of the planetary defense grid. At first he had been a bit disappointed over this notion, because he'd hoped to be serving Si Cwan directly in some sort of capacity, such as personal guard. Furthermore, with New Thallon at the heart of a vast systemwide alliance, it seemed pointless. Who would attack them? But he had offered not the slightest word of protest, since that would have been unworthy of his family's proud tradition of service, and instead taken up his monitor responsibilities with due diligence.

It would have been overstating it to say that Topez Anat was happy that civil war was brewing. Obviously peace and tranquillity were far preferable to the long-term good of the Thallonian Protectorate. But almost overnight he had gone from having a boring, dead-end job to being one of those charged with the responsibility of protecting the entire planet.

The truth was that most of the monitoring process was automated. Topez Anat didn't have to make any decisions as to identifying incoming targets, putting up the defensive grid, or opening fire. That was all done via computer. Topez Anat provided the living eyes and mind to monitor the computer and made sure that everything was functioning as it was supposed to. He was the flesh-and-blood fail-safe, as was the case with the other monitors at the other stations.

Still, his was an important job. A vital job. And the reason he knew that beyond any question was because Lady Kalinda herself had said so.

As he went through his routine duties on his last day of monitor duty, he was still shaking his head in wonderment over the encounter. There he had been, going about his business, and all of a sudden, the lady had shown up. He was astounded to be that close to her, as if she were just a normal person.

Her smile had been as dazzling as he had heard, and when she spoke, it was like bells chiming. "My brother," she had told him, "has sent me on a secret inspection tour. He wants me to make certain that everyone is particularly vigilant. Not that I think that's a problem with you, Topez Anat." She had reached out and gently run a finger along the line of his chin. He had trembled at her touch. "You are clearly taking your responsibility most seriously."

He had assured her that that was the truth. He had shown her the entire facility. He had watched in silent, trembling excitement as she had sat down in his chair to inspect the systems herself, and contemplated what it would be like knowing that henceforth he was going to be sitting in a chair upon which royalty had sat.

Topez Anat reined himself in. It was inappropriate to think such things, and he would do everything he could to eliminate them from his mind.

Even so, he still fancied he could feel the warmth of her as he sat in his customary station. He, along with everyone on New Thallon, was aware of the abuse that her new husband had tried to inflict upon her. Tiraud must have been mad. That was the only explanation. How could anyone try to bring harm to someone so perfect? Topez Anat's only regret was that Kalinda had already dispatched the bastard. He would have given anything to be the one who attended to it.

Indeed, he was in the midst of concocting an entire scenario in his head wherein he, as part of Kalinda's personal guard, had heard a ruckus within the wedding night chamber and burst in to discover Tiraud abusing Kalinda. He saw himself charging forward, dispensing with the brutish Nelkarite, and the grateful Kalinda looking up with wide, limpid eyes and saying, "What is your name, brave soldier, to whom I am so grateful, and are you doing anything tomorrow night?"

That was when he heard the explosions outside.

Alarmed, he flipped on an exterior monitor and his jaw dropped in horror as blazing red spheres—pulse bombs—fell from the skies by the dozens. Outside the monitoring stations were the vast, hundred-feet-high ground cannons that were aimed toward the sky, ever vigilant. If some enemy came remotely close enough to New Thallon to drop any sort of bombs from orbits, as now seemed to be happening, the computers would have signaled the alarms, activated the defense grid so that none of the bombs would have gotten through, and then proceeded to blast the originating intruders out of space.

But the guns remained silent, the defense grid inactive, and Topez Anat's computer was informing him that it was a bright, sunny day and there was no imminent threat at all.

For half a heartbeat, Topez Anat was almost ready to believe that his eyes and ears were deceiving him. The computer was right and his own senses were wrong.

That was when the first of the pulse bombs struck home, blasting apart the farthest gun. Several more bombs hit as well, and the gun began to tilt and twist with a rending of metal, which let out an agonized scream like a thing alive.

The pulse bombs continued to fall, blasting apart cannon after cannon.

Topez Anat tried to alert the other defensive stations on the grid. Nothing. The computer didn't send out any sort of warnings to the other stations. It simply sat there and tried to convince him that he wasn't in danger.

That was when Topez Anat realized the steady, scythelike exploding track of the bombs was drawing closer and closer with each passing second. In no time at all the guns would be gone, and the horrific pounding would fall upon the bunker within which Topez was huddled. Either the ship above was moving along with a sense of inevitability, or it was just maintaining its position and the planet's own rotation was bringing Topez Anat's bunker directly toward its doom.

He knew at that moment, without the slightest uncertainty, what his duty required him to do. He was to stay at his post, to continue trying to contact the other stations and alert them, to find out what was going on and solve it if possible. That was what his father would have done, and his father before him, and so on back down the line.

But his panicked gaze flickered from the computer screen—which was still telling him that everything was fine, thanks—to the sight of yet another massive gun exploding. Before he even knew what he was doing, he was on his feet and out the door, running as hard and fast as he could. He left behind his post, his responsibilities . . . everything that he had supposed was more important to him than anything else. As it turned out, though, the most important thing of all to him was his life. His stinking, craven life which he had supposedly turned over to the service of Lord Si Cwan.

Topez Anat stood there, looking up at the darkening sky, his heart thudding against his chest and his soul shriveling in his heart, and he had only seconds to wonder what he should do. Then he heard a creaking of metal and looked up just in time to see the last of the massive arrays collapsing without having fired a single shot in its own defense . . . collapsing right toward him.

If he'd made the slightest effort, he might have gotten out of the way. He might have survived.

Instead he threw his head back and his arms wide,

his red face streaked with tears, as he cried out, "I have no honor and no purpose. I am sorry. I have failed you, my Lord Cwan and Lady Kalin—"

That's when he realized. The image of the Lady Kalinda, seated at his monitor, apparently fascinated by the system. So wide-eyed. So impressed. So flattering. So—

"She did something to the computers!" shouted Topez Anat. "That has to be it! I must inform Lord Cw—"

In his shock over his realization, Topez Anat completely forgot about the massive collapsing metal array. When it fell upon him, crushing him to a bloody pulp, he was actually surprised, and had about a millisecond to consider that he had just failed Si Cwan not once, but twice, before blackness took him.

ii.

Si Cwan had chosen not to meet with the warlords in the vast chamber that had served as the council chamber for the Thallonian Protectorate. It was too depressing, and only served to remind everyone of what had been lost.

On occasion he would stand there alone, looking at the empty seats, thinking about how they had a united Thallonian system right there in their hands . . . and some sort of insane misunderstanding had brought it all crashing down. He would keep running the events of the past days through his head, trying to figure out how it had all gone wrong. How could Kalinda have so completely misjudged Tiraud? How could Tiraud have been such a brute?

He supposed that it shouldn't have been completely surprising. After all, Tiraud's father, Fhermus, was little better than a slightly refined brute. Swaggering, posturing, full of himself, perpetually bellicose. Perhaps it was nothing but folly to think that the two of them, working in tandem, could possibly have kept the Thallonian Protectorate together. Perhaps it was doomed from the start.

Still . . . the manner in which it had all disintegrated . . .

"My Lord Cwan . . ."

Ankar, Si Cwan's main aide and family retainer of long standing, had entered without Si Cwan's even hearing him. Since Cwan was typically hyperaware of everything that was transpiring around him, it was an indicator of just how distracted Cwan had been. "Yes, Ankar?"

"The warlords have assembled."

Si Cwan nodded in acknowledgment and started to head out. Ankar fell into step behind him and inquired, "Will you require my further services this evening, milord?"

"Not at this time, Ankar . . . although if you wouldn't mind looking in on my wife, I would appreciate it."

"Yes, Lord Cwan."

The towering Thallonian kept on going as Ankar headed off down another corridor. Several minutes later, Si Cwan strode into his secondary conference room, where the warlords were assembled. They were seated around a large, oblong table, and were looking up at him expectantly.

Another war. Why does it have to be another war? The thought went through his head unbidden, and it disheartened him that that was his basic reaction. His father had lived for war, as had his grandfather. It was almost as if they welcomed challenges to their authority, because it gave them a sense of exhilaration to beat all such challenges down. It provided them . . . fulfillment of a sort.

They would doubtless have little patience for Si Cwan's attitude. *This is your war, Cwan! Until now, the defining moment of your stewardship over our empire was to be there when it crumbled. You now have the opportunity to make up for that. You have the chance to get all the gnats, all the ants that crawl through Thallonian space as if they are your equals . . . you can crush them all beneath your boot.*

He knew he could. It wouldn't take all that much effort; Fhermus didn't present much of a threat to him, despite the fact that he had gathered some aggressive allies to his cause. There was no doubt in Si Cwan's mind that, in the end, he would triumph.

But what was the point? What was to be served by standing there with his foot upon the throat of his enemy?

There is no point. It is an end unto itself.

His heart wasn't in it, though. That was the dark and terrible truth of it. He thanked all the gods there were that his father and grandfather were no longer around, because he was certain they would see through whatever words he might offer and perceive the sorrow that hung over him like a shroud. They would have seen his chance to annihilate an arrogant enemy as a chance to reestablish himself, but all he could see were the lost opportunities.

Fortunately the warlords weren't as perceptive. Instead they merely saw their leader, the regal and confident Lord Si Cwan, gathering his thoughts before addressing them.

Most of them weren't there, of course. To be exact, only four were there at that moment. The rest were attending via video-conferencing technology. They were the ones who were back on their worlds, still working on assuring skittish populaces that they had— to use an old Earth term—backed the right horse. From what Si Cwan understood, it was a difficult sell in some instances. A number of worlds wanted to stay out of the situation altogether. It was the job of the warlords to convince them that neutrality was far less preferable to forging firm alliances with the eventual winner.

There was certainly a good deal to discuss with the warlords. Si Cwan had been putting together an attack strategy, determining how best to deploy the forces at his command. To go from a state of peace to a state of war was not an overnight endeavor. It required time, planning, careful consideration. He needed to anticipate what Fhermus would be expecting and do, instead, the unexpected.

He was satisfied that he had managed to accomplish this.

"My friends," Si Cwan began, "thank you for coming. I—"

The explosion that struck the imperial residence was so violent that it knocked everyone either off their feet or out of their chairs. Several of the warlords immediately ducked under the table, seeking refuge, as large pieces of the ceiling plummeted from overhead, smashing against the heavy stone table and shattering.

A chunk fell straight for Si Cwan, and he threw himself back to get out of the way. It shattered right where he'd been standing. He had fallen on his back, but instantly he whipped his legs around and brought himself back upright. *"Run!"* he shouted, somewhat unnecessarily; the warlords were already in the process of doing so, falling over one another or pushing each other to get out of the way.

The video screens flickered and went out. Si Cwan couldn't even begin to imagine what they must have thought was going on, although if they assumed that New Thallon was under attack, it was probably a pretty safe guess.

How?! How?! Where was the planetary defense system . . . ? thought Cwan.

There were screams in the distance, screams coming from all over the vast residence. Retainers, servants . . .

Kalinda? Robin? Were they all right? What the hell was happening?

The assault didn't stop. Explosion upon explosion rocked the area, blowing out walls, crumbling ceilings. Statues that had been carved centuries ago were knocked to the ground and shattered, and priceless paintings were buried beneath collapsing walls.

Si Cwan didn't even remember getting out of the room. The next thing he was aware of was pounding down the corridor, shouting instructions to whatever servants he could find. Everyone was bewildered, staggering around, looking to him for answers. But his words were drowned out by more explosions. Suddenly Si Cwan felt himself being lifted through the air, propelled by the concussive force of yet another bomb. He tried to catch himself, to hit the ground properly and roll, and then there was another detonation, even closer this time. Si Cwan slammed up against a wall with almost bone-crushing force, and he slid to the ground. Instinctively he threw his arms up and around his head to protect himself as an entire section of the wall fell upon him.

He lay there, breathing hard, trying to shove debris off himself. The side of his face was wet with blood. He hoped that it was merely the result of a huge gash rather than that, say, the entire top of his head had come off and he just didn't realize it yet.

There was, however, something he did realize.

This was a massive display of firepower, and not only that: Somehow a plan had been executed that had rendered the planetary defenses powerless. This sort of thing was not assembled and executed overnight.

This had been planned. By Fhermus.

It had been planned for a while. Planned long before the falling-out between Fhermus and Si Cwan that had led to this civil war.

There, buried beneath debris, with the sounds of screams still ringing in his ears, Si Cwan came to the conclusion that the death of his son had not driven Fhermus to attack New Thallon and try to obliterate Si Cwan. Instead, his son's death was merely the excuse. The plan for the attack had always been there. Sooner or later . . . Si Cwan's great ally, Fhermus, was going to try and destroy him.

It had simply turned out to be sooner.

iii.

Ankar was dodging right and left, trying to avoid the pieces of debris that were hitting the ground all around him. He was wide-eyed with terror, his blood pounding in his ears, and he kept telling himself that everything was going to be all right, that everything was going according to plan. Except that made absolutely no sense, because he could well be killed in the midst of all this, and his getting killed was most definitely *not* part of the plan.

He made it to Kalinda's room, almost being crushed once more in the process, and shoved open her door. He had no idea what he expected to find; there was every chance, he realized, that she might well be dead.

Instead she was sitting there on the edge of her bed, her hands folded comfortably and resting in her lap. There were chunks of debris around her which had obviously fallen from overhead, but apparently they had avoided hitting her as if they had eyes.

"Ankar?" she said with a slightly arched brow. "Is there a problem?"

"A problem!" he shouted as he approached her, and then fought to lower his voice when she scoldingly put a finger to her lips. "A problem? We're under attack, in case you didn't notice!"

"Of course I noticed," she replied easily, apparently unperturbed. There were still explosions, but the sounds seemed to be coming from a greater distance . . . moving away from them like a passing thunderstorm, albeit leaving havoc in its wake. "I helped make it possible," she added with a touch of pride.

He stepped closer toward her, his eyes wide. "You . . . ?"

"Just a tidy little computer virus that I was able to introduce into your system. Don't worry. With the computers smashed by this point, it's not as if it's going to spread to anything else."

"But this wasn't the plan!"

"It wasn't?" She looked at him with a remarkably innocent expression, as if unable to fathom what he could possibly be upset about.

"You—!" Ankar fought to control himself. It shouldn't have been that difficult. He was, after all, Si Cwan's chief interrogator/torturer. So he was long accustomed to being able to detach his mind, especially while engaging in some of his more repulsive activities. Then again, such sadistic pursuits were usually pursued in relative peace, the only disturbing aspect being the screams of his subjects. Ankar didn't normally have to contend with the damned ceiling crashing down around him. "You," he continued with effort, "swore to me that your people would provide protection for New Thallon in the event of war. That you and other operatives would work from within to have Si Cwan ousted or, even better, executed. That I would then be put in charge to guide New Thallon to a future more befitting a conquering race!"

"Hmm. Yes, that *does* sound like an excellent plan," Kalinda said agreeably, seemingly oblivious of the pandemonium around her. She extended her legs like a stretching cat and then stood. "A few problems with it, though . . . and they're problems I suppose you couldn't possibly have foreseen."

"What problems?!" He staggered slightly as another explosion rocked the palace.

"Well, first, as it turns out . . . there aren't actually any other 'operatives.' There's just me. Granted, yes, others of my people are around, but not here on New Thallon. They're back at Priatia. And there's a second prob—" Her eyes went wide and she looked over Ankar's shoulder. "Si Cwan! My brother, what are you doing here?"

Ankar immediately turned to see what she was looking at. He barely had time to register that there was no one standing in the doorway, and suddenly a chunk of debris bounced off the side of his head and sent him to his knees. His mind swimming, he barely had time to process the realization that the debris had not come from overhead, but from the side and from the general direction of Kalinda. A moment more, then, to comprehend that Kalinda had, in fact, thrown it at him.

By that point he was on his knees, leaning forward with one hand on the floor, trying to stop the dizziness and wave of nausea. He looked up just in time to see Kalinda standing over him with an even larger piece of debris, holding it high over her head, a look of utter dispassion on her face.

"The second problem," she said, sounding almost bored, "is that having you as an ally smoothed the process . . . but now presents a potential threat. We can't have that."

Ankar's last sight was the huge piece of rubble swinging down toward his head, and his last thought before his skull was crushed was a common profanity that was—as it so happened—the last thought that crossed many people's minds in the end.

iv.

Robin Lefler had been working in her office when the bombardment began.

She had been composing a detailed report to Starfleet of the current situation, and hated the fact that it was filled with nothing but negativity and depressing assessments.

The most difficult moment came when she had a real-time video conference with a newly minted Starfleet admiral, one Henri L'Ecole, with a mild French accent, close-cropped silver hair, and a steely gaze that—in her younger years—she would have found attractive, but now found merely slightly unnerving. L'Ecole had just been designated Lefler's contact person in the Office of Planetary Affairs, and he was still bringing himself up to speed. She could see him checking through files even as she laid out for him the disintegration of the Thallonian Protectorate. He had cut her short several times, seemingly impatient with the point-by-point manner in which she was reporting things. L'Ecole seemed to have little patience for details.

Finally he said, in apparent exasperation, "So let me summarize this, Lefler. The Protectorate is coming apart, you were unable to do anything to keep it together, and your involvement and advice has been marginalized to the point where you don't really need to be there at all. True or false?"

"Admiral, I would hardly characterize that as a—"

"True," he said again, "or false?"

She blew air impatiently between her lips. "On some level . . . true."

"Then may I ask what you're still doing there?" he demanded. "Certainly the time and resources Starfleet invested in training you would be better served if you were in some location where your presence could actually make a difference."

"Thank you for your clinical assessment of the situation, Admiral," Lefler said coldly, "but if it's all the same to you, I'm not anxious to run out on my husband just yet."

"Husband?" L'Ecole said in bewilderment. "Who's

your—?" He looked down and off to the side, obviously checking over her personnel file. He blinked owlishly upon seeing information, the specifics of which Lefler could readily guess. "Ah. You are married to Prime Minister Cwan."

"Yes, sir."

He frowned. "Doesn't that pose something of a conflict of interest?"

"Your predecessor did not seem to feel it did."

"Yes, and the fact that he's gone and I'm here might give you some hint of where Starfleet's thinking on this matter might be."

"Since you were unaware of it until just now, Admiral, I would be inclined to believe that Starfleet wasn't thinking much about it one way or the other."

He inclined his head slightly in acknowledgment. "A valid point," he conceded. "May I ask you how your relations with your husband currently stand?"

"Of course. May I ask you how things are with your wife?"

"That's out of line, Lieutenant Commander," he said stiffly.

"You see what I mean, then, Admiral."

"My marital relations have nothing to do with my job."

"Nor do mine," Lefler shot back.

"Lieutenant Commander," L'Ecole said, "I'm going to go on the assumption that you're saying that out of a determination to respect your marriage's privacy . . . which I can at least understand if not wholly condone. Because if you're saying that and truly believe it to be the case, then I would have to conclude that you're delusional."

"Believe what you wish, Admiral."

"Thank you for allowing me t—"

The image abruptly crackled, broke down, and vanished from view. Lefler leaned forward in confusion, wondering for a moment if the admiral had broken the connection, and then deciding it unlikely. So what had done so? What could possibly be interfering with—

That was when the bombing started.

From the nature of the impact and the accompanying sounds, Lefler immediately identified the source as pulse bombs. She considered running, but she had no idea where to run to, so she did the only thing she could think of: She dove under her desk. There she huddled, curled up into a ball, head tucked forward as far as it would go while she brought her arms up and over to provide her what little protection they could. The ground continued to rock under her, and she heard debris falling from overhead and around her. The desk shuddered under the impact, but did not shatter. She knew it was a remarkably sturdy piece of furniture, but she was extremely impressed to see the pounding it was capable of withstanding.

She knew without a second thought that the source of the bombing had to be Fhermus and his allies. Her mind racing, she came to the same conclusions that Si Cwan was arriving at elsewhere in the building: that Fhermus was executing a plan long in preparation. It gave the civil war a certain inevitability, which she found very disheartening. Had they all been wasting their time in the circle dance of the Protectorate? She hated to think it was the case, but was hard-pressed to come to any other conclusion.

She felt the impacts beginning to lessen, the volleys easing up. From all around, up and down the hallways, she was able to hear the cries for help from various people in the place. Unwilling to simply leave people to their fates, Robin left the safety of her desk and ran out of her office into the corridors.

She was immediately relieved that she did. There were people—servants, retainers, a couple of dazed warlords with bleeding heads—all of whom needed attention. Robin couldn't help but wonder if some higher power was watching out for her, because as she attended to the frightened and wounded all around her, debris continued to fall intermittently to her right and left, in front and behind her, but she remained miraculously unscathed.

And every person she encountered, she asked the same thing: "Where's Si Cwan? Have you seen Si Cwan?" She received a variety of mixed responses. People would shake their heads or mumble something about having seen him when the attack began but they had since lost track of him. A couple stared at her blankly and said, "Who?," and she had a feeling those individuals had been concussed and were going to need the most immediate attention.

It was some minutes before she realized that the bombardment had ceased altogether. There were any number of reasons that might be the case. Perhaps the planetary defense systems had finally come to life, although she couldn't begin to imagine what could have caused them to fail. Plus there were vessels in orbit that had transported the warlords to New Thallon in the first place. Upon realizing that New Thallon was under attack, they would have in turn attacked the planet's assailants and driven them away.

Or maybe the attackers had just run out of bombs.

Whatever the reason, the bombing had stopped, and Robin was just happy to be alive. Unfortunately, as she made her way through the palace—her heart sinking as she surveyed the damage—her fear over Si Cwan's status continued to spiral upwards.

She cut down the main hallway, stepping over debris, and headed for Kalinda's room, reasoning that Si Cwan would assume that Robin could take care of herself but that his sister might be in dire straits. She didn't let herself feel depressed over her assessment of Si Cwan's priorities. A wife was a wife, but Si Cwan had sacrificed far too much in his life to assure Kalinda's safety, and there was no reason to think that his concerns would change now.

She got to Kalinda's chambers. The doors were closed tight. Banging on them as loudly as she could, Robin shouted, "Kally! Are you in there? Can you hear me? Are you all right? Kalinda! It's Robin!"

The door suddenly opened and Robin was stunned to see Si Cwan standing there, grim-faced. A breath of relief practically exploded from her as she said, "Cwan!"

In response, Si Cwan enfolded her in his powerful arms and whispered, "Thank the gods you're all right.

I was about to come looking for you. I had to check on Kally . . ."

She hated to admit how good it felt to have her head nestling against his powerful chest. "I know, I know. I understand. I would have done the same thing. It's all right . . ."

"No. It's not all right." He turned slightly so that she could see past him, and she half-expected to see Kalinda lying there in a puddle of her own blood.

But Kalinda looked just fine. She was seated on the edge of her bed, and she looked to be in a daze. Robin didn't blame her. After everything the girl had been through recently, this latest shock might well have sent her into mental overload. Then Robin realized that Kalinda was looking down at something, and an instant later realized what it was.

Ankar's body was lying there, half his head crushed in, a massive pool of his blood coalescing under it.

Robin gasped. God knew that Ankar wasn't her favorite individual. As Si Cwan's aide-de-camp, he was frequently patronizing to her. She had been even more horrified to discover that Ankar was an experienced practitioner of barbaric torture procedures. It had been he who had brutalized Xyon, the son of Mackenzie Calhoun, and would have continued to do so had Robin not risked everything to intervene.

But as much as Ankar repulsed her, she took no joy in seeing him brought low by the cowardly assault that the palace had been subjected to.

"He saved Kalinda," said Si Cwan. "He died saving her life."

"Yes," Kalinda said with a distant, hollow tone. "He heard me screaming, and . . . and came in here . . . he pushed me out of the way when he saw debris falling . . . it was . . ."

"Heroic." Si Cwan nodded, his chin stiff. "He died a hero to the House of Cwan. His light will never be forgotten."

"No," Robin echoed him. "Never be forgotten."

Her focus, however, was on Kalinda rather than Ankar's corpse, and Kalinda seemed to know it. She met Robin's gaze levelly. Robin couldn't be sure, but she thought there was a touch of defiance there . . . as if daring her to make the observation that this was another dead body discovered in Kalinda's presence during a remarkably short period of time.

She could have sworn that Kalinda knew exactly what was going through her mind. And she could also have sworn that Kalinda's response was a very slight upturn of the edges of her mouth, as if the entire business was fraught with amusement.

That was the moment that Robin knew.

The problem was . . . she didn't know what she knew. She knew *something*. But she wasn't sure what. What she did know was that it was tremendously important, it involved Kalinda in ways that Si Cwan would not believe, and none of it was going to end well.

U.S.S. Excalibur

Tania Tobias is in a world of her own.

It is a pleasant world, warm and happy. It is not a world of starships, of weapons and shields, not one of violence and scrabbling to stay alive in a hostile and unforgiving environment.

No, it is a place where she floats and smiles as her lover looks down at her and smiles and assures her that everything is going to be all right. He invites her to see the galaxy as he does. She opens herself to him in every way imaginable, and he enters every part of her. She does indeed begin to see the galaxy as he does. For half a heartbeat that seems to take a lifetime, she knows where every star is, and where she is in relation to every star. It is as if a door in her mind that she didn't even know was there has been unlocked and thrown wide.

And then . . . things happen.

She is unable to understand all of them, and she feels as if there are now even more doors, and as each one swings open it does so with a deafening slamming noise, until she feels completely overwhelmed. She sees the stars beginning to spiral around her, descending down a vast funnel, and she reaches out, trying to catch as many of them in her hand as she can in order to put them back where they were.

Then they're gone, all of them gone, along with her lover, and she is floating there all by herself, all alone.

She has no idea how long she remains that way. But then, after an infinity of time that passes in far less than that, she sees something new.

Something large.

Something heading her way.

It is tentative at first, uncertain of what to expect. It draws closer and closer still, and it begins to have form and substance.

All is quiet.

So quiet.

It is like a mouse hoping to avoid the attention of the cat; there is nothing but silence.

Ultimately, it makes no difference.

"It sees us."

Mackenzie Calhoun was never a big fan of hiding. The problem with hiding is that it was almost inevitably a plan "A" with no plan "B." Plan A was "Don't get found." If that failed, there pretty much wasn't anything else aside from "Damn. They found us. We're in trouble now."

Unfortunately, in this case, he didn't feel as if he had a lot of options.

So instead Mackenzie Calhoun, leader of men and women, was leading them in silent vigil as they watched their situation go from somewhat bad to staggeringly worse.

The approaching ship was the incarnation of "worst-case scenario," in that it was identical to the one within which they were currently hiding. As near as they could determine, it was smaller, although that just might be a trick of perspective. But it was unquestionably made by the same individuals who had fired upon them and then consigned them to this—this wherever-they-were. Based on that, it didn't seem terribly likely that they were going to be especially happy to see the *Excalibur*.

Nor was Calhoun sanguine over their chances in a head-to-head battle. For all he knew, their weapons would prove completely impotent against it.

The ship continued on its path, and now they could see that it was no trick of perspective. Not only was it smaller, but it was considerably smaller. Even so, it was still much larger than the *Excalibur*. Bigger even than a Borg cube, as near as Calhoun could tell.

Fortunately the space in their hiding place was vast, and it was entirely possible for the newcomer to probe around within and never encounter them. That was certainly what everyone there was hoping for.

"Morgan," he said softly, "sensors may be useless, but can you project that ship's likely heading?"

Morgan gave a very slight nod. Her eyebrows flickered for a moment, and then she said, "If it doesn't change direction, it will continue on a course of 216 mark 7, and not come within five hundred thousand klicks of us."

"Good."

"Of course," she continued, "if they are proceeding in some sort of search pattern, then they could change course without the slightest warning and be practically down our throats in no time."

"Good. Thanks for expanding on that, Morgan."

"Just trying to be thorough."

Still, for the time being, it looked as if the ship was indeed continuing on its nonthreatening course. Calhoun didn't allow himself to become tense, but relief was still flooding through him as the larger ship moved farther away from them . . .

Then he sat forward, snapping to alert. "Uh-oh."

"Yes, confirmed," Morgan told him. "It's changed course."

"Toward us?"

"So it appears."

Before Calhoun could determine what to do, Dr. Selar's voice suddenly came over the com. *"Sickbay to captain."*

"Calhoun here, and this isn't the best time, Doctor," he told her.

"I have an update on Lieutenant Tobias."

"Captain," warned Morgan, "it's definitely turning toward us."

"Lieutenant Tobias," Selar continued, *"is still nonresponsive, but—"*

"Doctor," said Calhoun with mounting impatience, trying to keep his attention on the screen and the impending danger. "I really have to ask you to wait for a later time, presuming there is one."

"I simply thought you should know that she said three words very abruptly, even in her current condition."

Anxious to say anything to get the implacable Selar off the line, Calhoun said, "What three words?"

" 'It sees us.' "

A chill ran through Calhoun, and he suspected he

wasn't the only one, based upon the mute responses of the other members of the bridge crew.

"*I thought*," continued Selar, "*that it might have some significance to you.*"

"You thought correctly. Thank you."

"*Selar out.*"

The echo of Selar's voice had barely faded when Morgan announced, "Ship is coming closer on a direct intercept course."

"We're not moving," Kebron pointed out. "How can they be planning to intercept us?"

"They're not," Calhoun said grimly. "I think they're planning to ram us. They're not even going to waste the energy of shots on us. They're just going to plow right through us as if we weren't even here."

"Do we try to outrun them, Captain?" asked Morgan.

"At sublight speed? We couldn't outrun a crippled Horta at sublight speed. But if we go to warp speed," and he glanced at Xy for confirmation, "we risk possibly tearing apart the entire space-time continuum. Does that more or less summarize the situation?"

"I would have stopped short of the hyperbole," said Xy, "but otherwise yes, that's fairly accurate."

"Then we stay and fight," said Calhoun. "Sound battle stations."

"Sounding battle stations, aye," confirmed Zak Kebron.

Immediately the red-alert klaxon sounded through the ship, prompting Calhoun to think that the crew was going to be able to figure out, all by themselves, that the *Excalibur* was no longer attempting to stay hidden.

"Phasers online," Kebron said. "Charging photon torpedoes."

"Targeting capability?"

"Limited," admitted Kebron. "Nor do we know how the actual substance of our surroundings is going to affect the trajectory of our weaponry."

"We'll have to do our best. Still, first things first. Obviously they know we're here. Try to open a hailing frequency."

"Aye, sir," said Morgan. She moved her hands across the control panel . . . yet another gesture that was done in deference to making herself appear more human and normal. Linked into the ship's systems as she was, she merely had to decide that she wanted a hailing frequency opened for it to happen. She paused, waiting. "No response. Perhaps they're not capable of receiving our transmission."

"Or perhaps they simply don't give a damn," suggested Burgoyne.

"Either way, it's a waste of time," said Calhoun. "Prepare to—"

"*Captain!*" Morgan suddenly said, sounding extremely surprised.

"I see it!"

Indeed he did, as did everyone else on the bridge. The larger ship had been descending upon the *Excalibur,* moving at high speed, and suddenly it lurched as something struck it from the side. Explosions erupted along the ship's surface in response to whatever it was that had fired upon them.

"Give me a visual!" shouted Calhoun. "A visual! Now!"

The screen shifted and there it was, the new vessel that had arrived and was firing upon the ship that had been stalking them. It was not a single sustained blast, as with phasers. Instead it looked almost like a string of beads, as if an array of photon torpedoes was being fired one after the next after the next, so fast that it looked like one unending barrage.

The newcomer was smaller than the ship it was assailing, and appeared hexagonal in shape. The sides of it were flat, black and inscrutable, with no markings to give the slightest hint of the race that was in control of it (not that markings would have been of tremendous use to Calhoun, thanks to the sheer "alienness" of their surroundings).

The "molecule ship" rocked back under the attack. The barrage was definitely having an effect, but the ship's maneuverability indicated to Calhoun that it wasn't having enough effect. Dropping its interest in the *Excalibur*, it instead angled around and made toward the new vessel.

"Shall we make a run for it, sir?" asked Kebron. "While the two of them are fighting it out . . . ?"

"Tactically, it does make sense, sir," said Burgoyne.

The possibilities raced through Calhoun's head, and he responded before he had truly thought it all out . . . although if he had given it lengthy consideration, the chances were he would have made the exact same decision. "Bring us around," he ordered. "Prepare to open fire on the larger ship."

"Captain, are you sure?" said Kebron.

Calhoun, who was not sure at all, didn't let it show.

"Old Japanese saying, Kebron: The enemy of my enemy is my friend."

"Arabic saying, actually, Captain," Morgan informed him.

"I don't really care. Now prepare to—"

"Phasers locked and ready, sir," Kebron announced.

"Targeting?"

"Still nonfunctional."

"Best guess, then," said Calhoun. "All ahead full and . . . fire!"

The twin phasers below the *Excalibur*'s hull roared to life and began firing on the far larger vessel. The gelatinous mass outside trembled in vibratory response.

Kebron's best guess was completely accurate. The ship's phasers cut into the larger vessel amidships at the same moment that it shook beneath the assault from the other vessel. It returned fire at the *Excalibur*, but this was an instance where the starship's far smaller status served it well as Morgan effortlessly moved them out of harm's way, even as Kebron continued to return fire.

"Stay on them!" Calhoun called out.

Battles in space tended to be brief, violent affairs, and despite the fact that they were not in anything that remotely resembled "space" as they knew it, this was no exception. It took a minute, maybe two, and suddenly entire sections of the larger vessel were blasted free of their moorings. They didn't simply float away; instead they just hung there, unmoving in the gelatinous environment, displaying only the slightest sign of drift in the viscous surroundings.

In the final moments, the smaller vessel needed no help from the *Excalibur*. It moved in for the kill, pounding away aggressively with its own weaponry, the nature of which Calhoun could only guess at. Then the larger vessel blew apart unceremoniously, the vibrations of its violent death spreading through the glutinous ether and violently shaking the *Excalibur*, albeit without any harm to the starship itself.

Calhoun sagged back in relief, although he avoided any loud exhalation of air that might have indicated he was anything less than fully confident that his ship and crew would have been more than up to the task.

"Two against one. My kind of odds," muttered Kebron, sounding remarkably like his old self there for a moment.

"I reluctantly have to agree," said Calhoun.

"Sir," said Morgan cautiously. "The other ship is heading this way."

She was correct. Having dispatched the larger vessel, the newcomer was slowly moving on an indisputable course toward the *Excalibur*.

"Not unexpected," Calhoun said.

"Yes, but if they start shooting at us, that will be unexpected," said Burgoyne.

That was true enough. Calhoun had rolled the dice and chosen his ally. Now the only question was whether the ally was going to choose him back.

Calhoun stared at the approaching vessel and dwelled on the fact that sometimes there was no such thing as a good choice.

The Spectre

i.

Soleta stared at the approaching vessel and dwelled on the fact that sometimes there was no such thing as a good choice.

There it was, cruising in their general direction without the slightest awareness that the *Spectre* was anywhere near them. If the Romulan ship wanted to fire upon them, then aside from the ship's decloaking in order to use their weapons, the advancing starship would have no warning whatsoever before they were under attack.

But that was not an option for Soleta at that moment, even if she'd been so inclined for some insane reason. Because the *Spectre* was in deep trouble, and she was already being forced to the conclusion that the ship coming toward them might well be their only hope.

Unfortunately, the rest of her command crew hadn't followed her to that same conclusion.

"Commander, with all respect, you cannot be serious," Lucius said, stepping forward and fixing her with an intense gaze. He pointed at the screen. "Despite your long history with them, and despite whatever alliances the Empire may have forged with them in times of duress, we must not lose sight of the fact that they are, and will always be, the enemy."

"I admire your conviction, Tribune," Soleta said cautiously, "even if I do not necessarily share it."

"But, Commander—"

"They have a saying, Tribune," she continued as if he had not spoken, "and even though it's their saying, it still has measurable validity. And that saying is 'Any port in a storm.' Unless there is a significant upside to our current situation that you're not telling me, then we have to face the fact that we're in a significant storm at the moment."

"I admit the situation is dire, but—"

"Dire?" She glanced around at the bridge crew and then began ticking off the specifics on her fingers. "Life-support is on battery, which is running low. Warp engines are offline. Ion glide functioned just enough to get us out of Romulan space. Repairs may take days, presuming we survive long enough to make them. Shall I go on?"

"I know the situation is dire," Lucius said stiffly, "but if my life is at stake, then I do not hesitate to sacrifice it in the name of the Romulan Empire."

"That may be, Tribune, but it's not your life to sacrifice. It's mine. Your life is in my hands. For that matter, so are the lives of everyone else on this ship. That's my responsibility as commander, and I'm not about to shirk it simply because you believe it's time for you to lay down your life. And," she added, "need I point out that as admirable as your dedication is to the Romulan Empire, the Romulan Empire at this point in time doesn't seem interested in reciprocating."

"Isn't it possible," Aquila said, sounding hopeful, "that it was just some sort of . . . of misunderstanding?"

"An interesting notion," replied Soleta. "My understanding is that they were trying to take over this ship and, when we were disinclined to allow it, attempted to blow us the hell out of space. Did anyone else have a different understanding of what transpired in our most recent encounter with the Romulan Empire? Anyone else perceive any bright spots . . . aside from the fact that we managed to escape with our lives, barely?"

No one was able to come up with any reasonable response. Even Lucius dropped his gaze and looked away. She almost felt sorry for him. The tribune was a respected warrior and a proud Romulan. He deserved far better than to be treated as the enemy by the very Empire he'd spent so many years serving.

"Commander." Maurus reluctantly spoke up. "The starship will be out of range very shortly. If it is to be done . . . then best to be done quickly."

She nodded, and said with the resignation of one who knew she was making the right decision, even though it was at great cost, "Maurus . . . hail them. And drop cloak."

"With energy reserves as depleted as they are," Vitus observed, "we wouldn't have been able to maintain cloak much longer in any event."

"They're responding, Commander," said Maurus.

She took a deep breath. "On screen, Centurion."

The image of the starship on the screen wavered for a moment, and then was replaced by the icy, scarred visage of a severe-looking blond woman. Her lips pursed in grim amusement. "Well, well. In all the vastness of space, imagine running into you."

"You need not imagine at all, since it has, in fact, happened." Soleta studied her a moment. "Command appears to have agreed with you, Captain Mueller."

"I'd like to say the same for you, Soleta," replied Kat Mueller, "except something seems to be niggling in the back of my brain as to why I shouldn't . . . oh! Yes! I remember now. You betrayed the Federation."

"I like to think it was a two-way betrayal."

"Yes, I'm sure you do," Mueller said coolly, "as would anyone who was ungrateful for the many opportunities and freedoms Starfleet presented her. So . . . I assume this is not a social call, especially considering you're skulking around in Federation space."

"Technically, this sector is unaligned with any one interest. My ship has as much right to be here as does the *Trident*."

"You speak the truth . . . a novel experience for you, I'd say."

Soleta winced inwardly, and suppressed the anger she was feeling over Kat Mueller's snide and humiliating comments, especially in the presence of her crew.

"So," asked Mueller, "what can I do for you?"

"I suspect you already have some idea of the answer," replied Soleta.

"Yes indeed. It appears someone kicked the crap out of you."

"I would have summarized it in a different way, but yes, that's a fair assessment."

"And you . . . what? Want our help?"

She took a deep breath. "It had occurred to me, yes."

Mueller looked as if she were suppressing an urge to laugh. "Soleta . . . you're tooling around the galaxy in a ship designed specifically for espionage. Don't think we're unaware of your vessel's capabilities. Furthermore, we may have allied ourselves with the Romulans during the Dominion War, but you're still not members of the Federation. In fact, officially you're still classified as a hostile race. Under such circumstances, I'm under no obligation to offer you any sort of assistance."

"This is outrageous," Lucius said under his breath to Soleta. "Tell her to go die in burning agony and let's be done with this. It's unseemly."

"You're right, Captain Mueller," Soleta said stiffly. "You are indeed under no obligation. And the fact that you have far greater claim to humanity than I, who have none, is obviously no guarantee that you would feel compelled to act in a humane manner."

"Very generous of you to see it that way, Commander Soleta," replied Mueller. "So are we done here?"

"It would appear so. Just . . . out of curiosity. How is Admiral Shelby?"

"Why do you ask?" Mueller said, her eyes narrowing. "Is that some attempt to threaten her . . . ?"

"Threaten? Captain, we're holding our ship together with wire and willpower. We're hardly in a position to threaten anyone. No, I was simply asking because I feel I have a vested interest in her well-being. I did, after all, save her life."

"I'm well aware of that," said Mueller. Soleta could almost see frost starting to form on the viewscreen.

"Are you?" asked Soleta with raised eyebrow. "I wasn't sure. I mean, you obviously place such a premium on matters of loyalty and gratitude. I simply find it interesting that those priorities don't extend to someone who saved the life of Elizabeth Shelby, your good friend and former commander. Or perhaps you felt that Starfleet's dismissal of me was an appropriate and valid punishment."

"You weren't thrown out of Starfleet for saving Shelby," Mueller snapped. "You were thrown out for lying about your true nature."

"That wasn't my mistake, Mueller. Everyone lies about their true nature. My mistake was getting caught at it, and the reason I was caught was because I was nearly killed saving Elizabeth Shelby. Then again," she added silkily, "perhaps you resent me for doing so. After all, were she dead, you'd have a clear field at her grieving husband, wouldn't you."

The cold of space was as nothing compared to the iciness that was coming from Mueller's eyes. Nothing was said for a long moment.

"We'll take you in tow and render what aid we can," Mueller said finally. "We're on our way to Space Station Bravo; I assume you'll understand if we cut you loose before we arrive, no matter what the current status of your ship is by then."

"Understood."

"And I'll want you over here for the duration."

"As hostage?"

"As a guarantee that whoever I send over there to assist in repairs will return unmolested."

"And here I thought my giving you my guarantee of their safe passage would be sufficient."

"I'll say one thing for you, Soleta," replied Mueller. "Your time with the Romulans has finally provided you with a sense of humor. *Trident* out."

Her image disappeared from the screen. Soleta forced herself to look around at her command crew, her chin slightly upthrust, as if daring them to say something insulting or demeaning after the heated exchanges with Mueller.

All eyes turned to Lucius, whose face was inscrutable.

"That was . . . entertaining," he said finally.

Soleta relaxed slightly. "Yes, I suppose it was. I'm pleased that you approve. It's comforting to know that, while I'm fighting for our lives, I can also provide some amusement value for my crew."

"You are a female of many talents, Commander," Lucius said.

ii.

Soleta strode down the corridors of the *Trident*, looking neither right nor left, refusing even to acknowledge the stares she garnered from crewmen as she passed them. Kat Mueller walked stiffly at her side, and trailing just behind them, moving on his three legs, was Security Chief Arex. He had said nothing beyond "Welcome aboard" when he had met her in the main transporter room. He had then informed Mueller that Soleta was aboard, and escorted the Romulan commander to deck five, where Mueller had met up with them. Mueller hadn't said a word either, but merely inclined her head slightly in acknowledgment of Soleta's presence. Then the three of them headed for Mueller's quarters, with Soleta doing her best not to feel like a leper.

She knew just about every person she walked past in the corridors. None of them were anyone whom she would have considered friends, but many of them were at the very least acquaintances or people she'd worked with at one time. Seeing the way they looked at her, with suspicion or confusion or betrayal, was extremely difficult for her. Then again, why not? Nothing about any of this had been remotely easy.

"I appreciate how everyone is keeping a wary eye on me," said Soleta. "I assume I'm going to be escorted everywhere I go."

"You're not going to be going 'everywhere,' and yes," Arex told her. "We do have security issues, you know. We can't simply allow a Romulan operative to wander the ship freely."

She glanced at him in distant amusement. "You're not serious, Lieutenant. It's a starship, and I was a starship science officer. I know every square foot of this vessel. Are you remotely under the impression that there's any aspect of this ship—defensive and offensive capabilities, engines, anything at all—that I don't already know about?" When Arex made no reply, she looked toward Mueller. "You, however, have little to no information about my ship, and my people have instructions to keep it that way. If we see even the slightest hint of a tricorder taking down specifics on our systems, it will be confiscated."

"We know all we need to know about your vessel," said Mueller.

"Do you."

"Yes. We know how to blow it up. Beyond that, there's nothing of interest."

Mueller stopped outside her quarters and then gestured for Soleta to proceed her. "That will be all, Lieutenant," she said to Arex. Arex hesitated, but only for a second, and then he nodded and turned away. As always, Soleta marveled at the sure-footedness his third leg offered him. Not only that, but when he moved, it was so quietly that even with her sharp hearing, she could barely detect his footfall.

She entered Mueller's quarters, followed by Mueller, and the doors slid shut behind them. "You are aware I could have you put in the brig," Mueller said.

"On what charge? Consorting with allies?"

"For espionage. Who knows what private material you've stolen or have aboard that vessel."

Curiously, even as she spoke, Mueller was busy uncorking a bottle of something labeled SCHNAPPS and proceeded to pour herself a glass. She looked questioningly at Soleta, holding the bottle up, and Soleta nodded. Mueller poured a glass for her as well and held it out to her. Then, to Soleta's surprise, she raised it as in a toast. "To Elizabeth Shelby," she said.

"To Shelby," agreed Soleta, and they clinked glasses and drank. The liquor tasted a little too sweet to Soleta, but she said nothing.

"I was talking to her about you, you know," Mueller said.

"Really. When?"

"The other day. I believe she referred to you as 'an accident waiting to happen.' "

"I believe you'll find that all living beings can be divided into two types: those who are accidents waiting to happen, and those who have happened already."

Mueller looked about to respond immediately, but then she pursed her lips and gave it some thought. "There's a good deal to be said for that," she admitted. She studied Soleta as if they were meeting for the first time. "What happened to you, Soleta?"

"I was almost killed and then the organization to which I devoted my life deserted me. You'd be amazed how that would reorient your thinking."

"You deserted it, Soleta, not the other way around. If only you'd been honest when you first discovered your heritage . . ."

"Then I'd have been consigned to limited desk duty for the rest of my career," said Soleta. "What kind of way is that to spend my life?"

"You would have spent it in service of the Federation," replied Mueller. "If you were truly dedicated to the greater good, then serving in any capacity would have been sufficient for you."

"So you're saying . . . what? That my leaving to join the Romulan Empire was an act of selfishness?"

"That's certainly one way of looking at it."

"And do you look at it that way?"

"Yes."

Soleta stared into the top of the glass. "And does Shelby also look at it that way?" she asked quietly.

Mueller shrugged. "I wouldn't presume to speak for her."

"Of course you would."

For a moment, Mueller considered the question. "I think she misses you," she said finally. "In fact . . . I'm sure she does. Also, I think she feels responsible for what happened."

"She's not. It's not remotely her fault."

"You, of all people, should know that humans are not always logical."

"I suppose that's true. And I suppose"—she let out a long breath—"that it could be seen that my decision was based on selfishness. Then again . . . if wanting to find someplace where one can belong is an act of self-ishness, then I'd have to think that every sentient being in the galaxy is selfish. Wouldn't you say?"

"To a degree. But sometimes you have to balance that desire against your commitment to others."

Soleta rose, turning her back to Mueller as she walked slowly around the room, taking care not to jostle her drink. "I had a commitment to myself as well. Ultimately—and here's the 'selfish' aspect again—I had to do what I felt would be best for me. Yes, I could have served Starfleet, relegated to an obscure and harmless post. But I couldn't have served myself. My needs, my desires, my wish to explore the galaxy and the very nature of its composition. Starfleet has its priorities; I had mine. When they overlapped, everything was fine. When they ceased to overlap, Starfleet went its way," and she took a sip of the drink, "and I went mine. And I frankly don't see how anyone can reasonably resent me for that."

"Because the way that you went took you into the arms of an aggressive and warlike race that has tried to bring down the Federation for centuries, so who's kidding whom, Soleta?"

Soleta didn't reply. Instead she emptied her glass and put it down on the table next to Mueller's. "I certainly hope that wasn't poisoned."

"If it was, we'll both be getting burials in space," said Mueller as she downed her own glass. She put it down next to Soleta's and said, "It's ironic, I suppose. Here you went to the Romulan Empire . . . allied with the Praetor, found yourself a new 'home.' Something to be a part of. And now all *that's* ended, so you've been thwarted yet again . . . although this time not as a result of some great self-sacrifice of your own. So what's going to be your next move . . . presuming you can tell me without betraying any confidences among your new best friends."

Soleta stared at her blankly. "What?"

"What do you mean, 'What?' " asked Mueller. "Don't play games with me, Soleta. It's insulting and, frankly, I have better things to do with my time."

There was no way for Soleta to try and cover up her utter bewilderment and gain an upper hand. She'd been caught far too flat-footed to backtrack now. Besides, the bottom line was that she was too clueless to dissemble in any convincing manner. "Kat . . . what the *hell* are you talking about?"

"I'm talking about . . . You're not serious."

"Don't I look serious?"

"Yes, but you *always* look serious."

"Kat, will you please tell me what you're going on about?"

"I'm just asking," Mueller said, trying to sound reasonable, "what you're planning to do now that the Praetor is dead. Certainly you must have given it *some* thought."

Soleta stared at her and was suddenly aware that there was a tremendous pounding in her temples. The room seemed to swim slightly, and she took several deep breaths to compose herself before forming the next words. "The Praetor . . . is dead?"

Mueller looked incredulous. "Oh, come *on!* You must know . . ."

"No! I didn't know!"

"You're an espionage and fact-gathering vessel! How could you not know . . . ?"

"*Because we spy on other races, not our own!*" Soleta wondered why she suddenly felt shorter, and realized belatedly that she had sat in a chair. "We maintain radio silence for weeks at a time so as not to risk detection! I can't believe . . . no wonder when we were trying to communicate, we received no . . ." She stopped, forced herself to calm, took a deep breath. "When did this happen?"

"Fairly recently, actually. We weren't involved in any of it; the *Enterprise* was in the middle of it all."

"He's dead?!" Soleta's voice was a shout, and when the echo finally ceased, she asked in a far smaller voice, "Are you sure?"

Slowly Mueller nodded. "Information is still being pieced together and disseminated about the potential sea change in Federation-Romulan relations. From what I've read in Captain Picard's report, a Reman named Shinzon was responsible . . ."

"A Reman?" Soleta had heard of them, of the shadowy "parallel" race of Romulans that resided on the darkened mining planet that was the twin of Romulus. But the thought that one of them had been able to rise up . . . it seemed incredible . . .

"Actually," amended Mueller, "technically, he wasn't a Reman. He was a clone of Jean-Luc Picard. The Romulans intended to use him to replace Picard as part of a vast infiltration scheme." When Soleta stared at her incredulously, Mueller nodded. "A half-baked idea, I know. Apparently when a new senate came into power, word of the plan reached them, and they realized its folly. So they sent Shinzon to reside on Remus, to work in the mines. But he eventually returned and, long story short, vengeance ensued."

"Hiren . . . dead," Soleta said tonelessly. "I . . . wish you could have met him. He was a decent man. Honorable. A hard man, but made that way by circumstances. He deserved better, he . . . Was it quick? What did Shinzon do?"

"Thalaron radiation," said Mueller. "In the Romulan senate chamber, he exposed Praetor Hiren and the entire senior leadership to thalaron radiation. By my understanding of such radiation, the end was . . . He did not suffer. Then again, you would know far better the effects of thalaron radiation than I."

"Yes," was all Soleta said. She closed her eyes, trying to remove from her mind the concocted image of poor Hiren, writhing on the floor of the Senate, the deadly thalaron radiation practically obliterating his molecular structure. Her jaw outthrust, her eyes hard as flint, Soleta said, "Tell me Shinzon still lives. Tell me he's still out there so that I can kill him myself."

"No," Mueller said, shaking her head. "And a good thing, too. He created a warbird, called the *Scimitar,* and he tried to use it to destroy Earth. But Picard was able to destroy it and him. If it's of any consolation, the Federation is in talks with the new government. Alliances between us and the new Romulan Empire may be stronger than ever before. There's even talk of dismantling the Neutral Zone . . ."

"They tried to kill us, Kat. The new government. They tried to take our ship or, failing that, blow us to hell."

Mueller was completely taken aback. "Your ship was damaged from a fight with *other Romulans?* I just . . . I assumed it was as a result of an altercation with a hostile race . . ."

"Well, apparently the two concepts aren't mutually exclusive," Soleta said bitterly. She leaned forward, rubbing her hands together briskly as if they were suddenly very cold. "Whatever the Federation may think is developing in terms of their relations with the Romulan Star Empire, it's apparent that there's more going on behind the scenes than anyone wants to admit."

"A power struggle," said Mueller. "With the main leaders dead, various factions are making grabs for domination. And you're seen as a staunch ally of the dead Praetor."

"With no ties to anyone currently lobbying for power," said Soleta. "I'm a wild card. Me, and my ship. And since I'm not fully Romulan, no one feels they can trust me, so they probably figure the best thing to do is simply eliminate me."

There was a long silence in the room then as Soleta fought to take in all that she had just learned. *I'm a woman without a race. No port in a storm. The Federation is closed to me, and the Praetor is dead to me. What the hell am I going to do?*

Then Mueller said very neutrally, "Soleta . . . what of your crew?"

Soleta forced her gaze to focus on Mueller. "My crew? What about my crew?"

"How many are there?"

That was classified information, but Soleta was in no mood to worry about niceties. "Not counting myself, twenty. Command crew of four, plus an assortment of engineers, centurions, and such . . ."

"And how many of them can you trust?"

"Trust?" she echoed.

Mueller nodded. "Unlike you . . . they are full Romulans, with ties to the Empire that likely extend beyond the deceased Praetor. Wealthy families, or politicians who are now ascendant with the power vacuum. Can you count on your crew to cover your back? Or are they just as likely to stick a knife in it?"

"I don't know," Soleta admitted. She felt like she was chiming a bell of her own doom. "I . . . truly don't know. I would . . . I would like to believe they are loyal. But right now, I don't know what to believe."

"Soleta." Mueller leaned forward. "I . . . know I've said some harsh things to you. And I meant them. I still do mean them. But Elizabeth Shelby would never forgive me if she knew that you were in trouble and I did nothing to help you."

"And what would you propose to help me?"

"Turn your ship over to me . . ."

"No."

"Request asylum. I can guarantee that—"

"*No.*"

"Why not?"

"Because," Soleta said tightly, "it's my first command, and I'll be damned if I let my first command end in surrender."

And to Soleta's mild surprise, Mueller actually smiled at that. "I'll be damned," said Mueller.

"What?"

"That," she said, "may be the first thing you've said today that I can absolutely respect you for."

iii.

Mueller looked around at the stunned faces of her officers in the briefing room . . . an old world term that she far preferred to the bloodless (in her opinion) "conference lounge." As far as she was concerned, a lounge invited relaxation and supine posture. When she was receiving and disseminating information, she wanted everyone at attention, dammit.

"Is there a problem?" she asked.

"You're . . ." Desma, her Andorian executive officer, blinked furiously in that way she had when she was especially bewildered. "You're going to let them go?" Seated near her were science officer M'Ress, security head Arex, and Romeo Takahashi of ops.

"Yes."

"Just . . . let the Romulans go?"

"On what grounds would you suggest I hold them, XO?" Mueller inquired. "We didn't catch them performing an act of espionage. They summoned us when their ship was in trouble."

"But they were outside of Romulan space," Arex pointed out.

"And in the time of Captain Kirk," Mueller said, "that would have been considered an act of war. But our 'uneasy alliance' with the Romulans ever since the Dominion War means that I would need more than that to hold them."

"No disrespect, Captain, but . . . ya really don't," drawled Hash in that bizarre faux-Southern tone he liked to adopt. Mueller could have been wrong, but she thought it sounded a little more forced than usual. "Yer a starship captain. Ya have gobs of discretion. Certainly you can use some of that there discretion to keep Soleta, a known deserter, under wraps, and her ship in our hands."

"Lieutenant, for all the sins that one can readily lay at Soleta's feet, desertion is not one of them. Starfleet sent her packing. What she did with her life after that is her business."

"She was given command of a stealth vessel," Arex said. "I tend to think that makes it our business."

"A stealth vessel," said Mueller, "that her people would no doubt set to self-destruct if they thought, even for a moment, that we were not planning to let them go."

"Personally, I'm not seeing a downside on that," Desma said. "One less Romulan ship to worry about spying on us."

"She's right," said Hash. "I say we turn Soleta and her people over to Starfleet. If they decide to let them go, then fine. That's Starfleet's call to make. Meantime . . ."

"There's no 'meantime' here, Hash," Mueller replied sharply. The scar on her face became slightly pink against her pale cheek. "Granted, Starfleet might well squawk when they read my log. They might even agree with you. If there's heat to take, I'll take it. Meanwhile, we're helping Soleta put her ship back in working order and then we're letting them go . . . the sort of consideration," she continued more loudly, as several of her officers started to talk at once, "I would hope that she or others like her would extend to us were we in distress. Which, need I remind you, we were not all that long ago. The fact that we were able to put in at Space Station Bravo was a lucky happenstance. We could just as easily have run into problems a significant distance away, and then it might have been us counting on the kindness of strangers."

"And you're expecting . . . what, Captain?" asked M'Ress. "That by helping Soleta's ship, we'll be earning ourselves karmic points of some sort?"

Mueller stared at her icily, and it was as if the temperature in the room had dropped ten degrees. "I am expecting . . . Lieutenant . . . that I will be giving orders and they will be obeyed."

"No one's questioning that, Captain," said Desma.

"I am."

All eyes turned toward Hash. There was none of the typical joviality in the ops officer's face. Instead there was a coldness that Mueller had never seen before in all the years she'd known him. There was no trace of his drawl now. "Make no mistake," he continued. "I will obey your orders, Captain. Nor do I dispute your right to make them. But I am questioning them, and their wisdom, and yours." He stood, his shoulders square. "And I am officially requesting a transfer from this ship at your earliest convenience. Thank you." Without waiting for Mueller to respond, he turned and walked out of the briefing room.

There were stunned looks from everyone there. Mueller stared at the door long after it had closed behind Hash, and then—in a flat, even tone—"Executive Officer . . . oversee our people helping the *Spectre* to go on its way. Arex, as soon as their ship's ready to depart, I want a security team to escort Soleta back there. Anyone here have a problem with any of that?"

They all shook their heads.

"Good. It is so ordered."

As one they rose and filed out one by one from the briefing room, leaving Mueller to conjure up mental pictures of firing Romeo Takahashi out a photon torpedo tube.

U.S.S. Excalibur

She sees him. She knows no one else does, but she can, so easily.

He managed to reach an escape pod before his ship detonated. It is small and thus capable of eluding detection, essentially indistinguishable from debris and possessing interior devices that mask his life signs.

And now he is floating. Floating . . . and more afraid than anyone on the Excalibur *or on the other vessel. His world is now a dreadfully frightening one, and he feels very, very alone.*

She wants to reach out to him, to touch him . . . to assure him that everything is going to be all right. Except she doesn't really know for sure that's going to be the case. In fact, the odds are huge that everything will be about as far from all right as it can get.

She wants to tell him that he is not alone. She would like to do that because she knows from her own experience just what the depths of loneliness can feel like, and she would not wish that on anyone.

But she stays her hand, because she has no desire to do anything that will change the events that are about to unfold . . . if for no other reason than that she's intensely curious to see what's going to happen. She is content for the time being to be a mere observer rather than a participant.

She looks beyond herself for just a moment. She has the vaguest sense of the father and the son . . . the man and boy, normal yet abnormal, small yet vast . . . and she knows that they will be instrumental in the final fate of all concerned. But she is not quite clear yet on how, and more, she's not sure she wants to know, for it will be a great and terrible thing when the father and the son end it all.

So instead she turns her attention back to the being in the pod. The pod that is drifting right toward the Excalibur, *toward the shuttlebay, and no one knows it yet. But they will, they will . . .*

i.

Calhoun didn't know what to expect when the image of their new "friends" shimmered into existence on the bridge. Indeed, he'd been surprised that they had responded to their hail at all . . . or at least responded without making the slightest attempt to destroy them.

He'd been briefly concerned over their ability to understand their saviors. "Universal translator" didn't necessarily apply if one happened to be somewhere other than one's own universe. Nor was he certain that ship-to-ship communication was going to be possible at all, if something as fundamental as the laws of physics worked differently. But both worries turned out to be groundless when a purplish image appeared—not on the viewscreen, but right there on the bridge, a mere two feet away from Calhoun.

Calhoun involuntarily flinched back, more from surprise than from concern for his well-being. Just as reflexively, Kebron started to move from his tactical station to serve as bodyguard to Calhoun. But then he likewise realized that they were faced not with a flesh-and-blood individual but instead a light projection of some sort.

Then again, even if their new acquaintance had actually been there, "flesh-and-blood" might not have been the most appropriate term to use.

The newcomer looked like nothing to Calhoun so much as it did a giant amphibian of some sort. Its skin was thick and green and seemed to hang loosely off its frame. It had no legs, or at least none that were readily visible, since any legs it did have were hidden by the massive folds of its teardrop-shaped body. It seemed to have four arms, two on either side, jointed in the middle but still rail-thin. Each arm had a large swelling at the end that could generously be considered a hand, and a half-dozen small dangling stringlike appendages on each "hand" that served as fingers. Its head was squat, with four bulging eyes atop, and Calhoun immediately noticed that they had the disconcerting habit of blinking—not simultaneously but in sequence, from left to right. Open, shut, open, shut, four times in quick succession and then over and over again. He couldn't even begin to discern where its mouth was until it began talking, and even then he was startled because the mouth was in the general area of what Calhoun had taken to be the bottom of its throat.

"Greetings," it didn't so much say as it did warble. "I seek the mate of the vessel which aided us in our battle against the Teuthis."

"If by 'mate' you mean the captain, that would be me," said Calhoun. He stood, feeling it to be the more appropriate way to address the . . . individual. "I'm Captain Mackenzie Calhoun. You're aboard . . . or at least you're projecting yourself aboard . . . the *Starship Excalibur.*"

"A starship?" It appeared to roll the word over its lips.

"Yes."

"And what . . . would a 'star' be?"

That brought Calhoun up short. It was Xy who stepped forward and said, "They are bright islands that dot the environment from which we come. They're very far apart from one another, and we travel from one to the next to the next."

"To what purpose?"

"To explore. To learn."

"To what purpose?"

This prompted Xy to look blankly back at Calhoun. "We more or less consider it an end in itself."

"I see," said the creature, although it was impossible to determine if he did or not.

"The Teuthis," Calhoun said, wanting to keep matters moving along. "That is the name of the beings we fought?"

"What? Oh . . . yes. That is how they call themselves, and have always called themselves." Despite the holographic nature of the communication, his face still darkened slightly at the very mention of the other beings. "The Teuthis have long engaged in a systematic destruction of all who are not the same as they. They decided that all this," and he extended two of his arms to either side, "must be for the Teuthis and only for the Teuthis. And so they long ago set about to eliminate all other life until there would be just Teuthis in this realm."

"If they are the Teuthis, who are you?"

"We are the Bolgar," it said. "I am called Termic." He touched his chest lightly as if in pride, and it puffed out a bit. "Termic of the Bolgar."

"What is this realm's name?" Xy interjected.

"Name?" The being sounded puzzled.

"The name of it, yes. What do you call it?"

Termic of the Bolgar made the oddest noise that sounded as if it were supposed to be a laugh. Calhoun couldn't be sure. It might have been a strangled cough. Then Termic composed himself and said, "That is ridiculous."

"What is?" Calhoun had no idea what he was finding so amusing.

"Naming the realm." It appeared to be making the equivalent of a smile, but it was hard to be certain. "It is a symbol of supreme arrogance to think that we would have the right. It would make it seem as if we were greater than the realm itself. It would be . . . presumptuous."

This time it was Calhoun's turn to find something

being said amusing. "Like the remora trying to name the shark," he said.

"The what trying to name the—"

Calhoun put up a hand, silencing Termic. "I understand what you're saying," he told him. "That's all I meant."

"Ah. Good." Termic looked at them curiously. "You are not from this sphere, I take it."

"That's absolutely correct."

"Have you presumed . . . to name *your* sphere?"

Calhoun exchanged looks with the other denizens of the Milky Way galaxy. "No," he said quickly, and there were echoes of "No" and "Of course not" from the others on the bridge.

"Very wise. I assume you came here through the Teuthis corridor."

That brought them to a halt. "The . . . Teuthis corridor?" Calhoun asked.

"Yes. The means by which they seek to escape their inevitable fate."

Burgoyne stepped in close to Calhoun. "The conduit," s/he said in a low voice. "The transwarp conduit. These Teuthis . . . their way out was our way in. And, most likely, vice versa."

"Are you saying," said Calhoun, wanting to make certain that there was no confusion on the matter, "that these . . . Teuthis . . . are responsible for the interspatial rift that brought us here . . . wherever here is?"

"Absolutely," confirmed Termic. "For a very, very long time, they have dominated the sphere. They thought to eliminate all life except their own. They thought to dominate, to conquer. And we have fought back, battling against genocide. Once there were many races in the sphere. Now there is just us and the Teuthis. But we have not gone quietly. We have fought back and fought back, and now we have the Teuthis on the run. They seek to use their corridor to escape us. To create a beachhead elsewhere and use it as a staging ground for new conquests. If they are within your sphere . . . then I fear for the life-forms that reside there."

"So do we," said Calhoun. "But why did they send us here? If we were a threat to them, why not simply destroy us?"

"Oh, well, that seems rather obvious to me," said Termic. "They couldn't. Their weaponry was insufficient."

"You're joking," said Burgoyne. "They seemed far more powerful than we are."

"Perhaps the operative word is 'seemed,'" said Calhoun. "So their preferred means of disposing of us was simply to send us down here via their . . . corridor . . . on the assumption that we wouldn't be able to escape back to our universe?"

"Yes," replied Termic. Calhoun noticed that there appeared to be some sort of slime dripping from him and gathering at his feet, or at least where his feet would have been. Yet another reason to be relieved that he'd shown up in holographic form. The prospect of having to clean up after him was not a pleasant one.

"So you know how they sent us here."

"Yes," he said again.

"And you can send us back."

"No," Termic said. "Their technology is a closely guarded secret and we have not been able to acquire it for our own. I can assure you, however," he added, "that when you aid us in achieving the final extermination of the barbaric Teuthis race—and thus ending forever their corruption and their destructive ways—you will be welcome here as beloved and appreciated new inhabitants of the sphere."

"How . . . marvelous," said Calhoun.

ii.

Moke loved the shuttlebay.

As far as the adopted son of Mackenzie Calhoun was concerned, it was the most interesting place on the vessel. Certainly it was the most cavernous. Granted, the holodeck could provide venues that seemed far bigger, even endless. But deep in his heart he knew they were fake. He had grown up on a world with vast, unlimited vistas; fakery was a poor substitute, and so he opted for the area on the ship that had the most space in which to move about.

In addition to being huge, the shuttlebay was often unmanned. The only time people were overseeing it was when the shuttles were going in and out, or if some cargo was being brought aboard and the loading needed to be administered. So it was a good place for him to be when he was seeking solitude.

He had been seeking it a lot lately.

It had not been all that long since Xyon had returned to the *Excalibur* and reentered Mackenzie Calhoun's life. Nevertheless it seemed an infinity to Moke, who felt as if Calhoun had little enough time to accord him as it was. Now that Xyon had shown up, it was not only a further distraction for Mac, but yet another reminder that Moke wasn't in fact his actual son.

Moke had brought a rocketball down with him and was casually bouncing it off one of the shuttlebay doors. Propelled by special gloves, a rocketball was capable of moving up to two hundred miles per hour, and players had to wear light armor to protect them from possibly winding up with holes in their torsos. But without the gloves to interact with them, it was just a normal black sphere.

He knew that the *Excalibur* was in trouble. That it had wound up in some bizarre and different universe, or something like that. He'd picked that much up between Calhoun's public announcements and the conversations he'd overheard from various officers. He knew there was nothing he could possibly do about it, and he hated that. He hated that he had nothing to contribute to the situation.

He hated that his playmate, Xy, whom he had attended to when Xy was an infant, had now grown up and passed him and was an adult. He knew it was because of an ultimately tragic condition—that Xy's peculiar Hermat/Vulcan biology was causing him to age at an insanely accelerated rate. The one he should really feel sorry for was Xy. Yet he couldn't help but focus on his own problems and frustrations. And Moke knew that was selfish, but that was how he felt and he couldn't do anything to change it.

He hated that he felt like an ingrate. After all, Calhoun had taken him in when he really didn't have to. He was trying his best. So why this burgeoning resentment?

Lost in thought, Moke hit the black ball harder than he intended to, and it bounced past him and off into the far end of the shuttlebay. He heard it ricocheting around, and suddenly it ceased. His eyes narrowed as he peered into the dimly lit far corners of the bay. "Is somebody there?" he called.

For a moment there was no reply, and then a figure stepped into view.

Moke let out an exasperated sigh. "Oh. It's you. Can I have my ball back?"

Xyon palmed the ball for a moment, then flipped it in a casual overhand manner. Moke snagged it on the fly. "Nice catch," said Xyon.

Moke turned his back to him. "What do you want?" he asked.

"The captain asked me to check on you," replied Xyon. "Looked all over the place before I thought to ask Morgan. She told me you were down here."

"Well, she shouldn't have."

Xyon made as if to leave, and then paused. Uncertainty played across his features for a moment and then, as if making up his mind about something, he approached Moke. "Look, kid . . ."

"I'm not a kid."

"Fine. Look, old man, you can't keep resenting the hell out of me just because I'm alive."

"It's not just because you're alive."

"Then what—?"

"It's because you made Mac think you were dead. You hurt him. And I'm worried you might hurt him again."

Xyon gave him a look of total disgust. "Oh, please. You know as well as I that Mackenzie Calhoun can take anything life can serve up. The man's a rock. He doesn't need you keeping a careful eye on his feelings or trying to protect him. This is entirely about you not—"

Then he stopped talking and his eyes widened. "*Grozit*," he whispered.

Moke was unimpressed. "What? You're trying to scare me now or something? Takes more than that." He tossed the ball toward the doors without bothering to look where he'd thrown it. "If you think you can fool me into . . ."

Then he realized that there had been no sound of the ball striking the door.

He turned to see what had happened to it, and his throat closed up. He tried to say something, to respond to what he was seeing in some oral manner, but no sound was managing to escape.

Something was oozing into the shuttlebay between the doors. It didn't seem at all possible, because the doors should have been completely sealed. There couldn't be any sort of leak. But something had managed to . . . to pry the doors open ever so slightly.

At first Moke thought that the gelatinous mass of whatever-it-was outside was seeping in through the rift in the doors, but he quickly realized that wasn't the case. Because whatever the nature of the environment was outside, it was clearly formless. And this thing, this—whatever it was—definitely had form and substance.

It was thick and gray, and at first it was insinuating itself slowly in between the doors. But with every passing second it started to move faster and faster, and in no time at all was practically pouring in. As it did so, it continued to take shape. Moke had never seen such long, thick appendages before, and was unfamiliar with the word "tentacle." Xyon, however, knew perfectly well what tentacles were. He did not, however, know what he was seeing coming into existence about twenty feet in front of him. He had never seen anything like it, and would have been perfectly happy to have gone the rest of his life with that always being the case.

Moke backed up and backed up, and thumped against Xyon's chest, since Xyon hadn't budged from where he'd been standing. He wasn't paralyzed with fear so much as with complete shock. The jolt of Moke backing into him, however, was enough to jostle him from his paralysis. "Let's go!" he shouted, yanking Moke back as they started to make for the door.

They didn't even come close. Two of the huge tentacles whipped out and around, moving past them and blocking their means of exit. The rest of the creature was continuing to grow. The more that seeped into the shuttlebay, the larger it grew.

Another of the tentacles was fully formed and moving toward them.

"Lyla!" shouted Xyon. "Emergency beam-in, now! *Now!*"

His ship was clear on the other side of the bay, but it didn't matter. The artificial intelligence that inhabited the ship responded instantly to Xyon's call, and a split second later—with Xyon holding tightly to Moke—the two of them vanished into the shelter of the *Lyla* while the tentacle whipped around the space they'd just been occupying.

iii.

Morgan Primus and Zak Kebron reacted at almost the exact same moment—Kebron owing to the response on his board, and Morgan simply because she just knew.

"*Security breach!*" Kebron informed Calhoun, who was still digesting the information that they had no means of getting home. "Something's entering the shuttlebay!"

Meanwhile Morgan jumped as if someone had hit her with an electric prod. "Something's attached itself to the hull . . . no! Onto the shuttlebay doors! Some sort of containment pods. And whatever's inside, it's insinuating itself into the shuttlebay through some sort of molecular-displacement device."

"A Teuthis," said Termic in obvious surprise. "One of them survived. My apologies, Captain. That was sloppy of us. Pity . . . it could easily kill you all."

"Kebron—! Security detail to the shuttlebay. Full armament."

"Captain," Morgan said, clear worry in her face. "Moke is down there. And so is Xyon."

Calhoun didn't question her pronouncement. The fact that she was essentially residing within the computer core enabled her to determine where anyone on the ship was at any given moment. Instantly he was heading for the turbolift. "Kebron, with me. Burgy, you have the conn . . ."

"Captain!" Burgoyne immediately said. Calhoun turned, and the look of fire in his eyes prompted Burgoyne to back off whatever s/he had been about to say. With both his adopted son and natural-born son at risk, it simply wasn't in Calhoun's nature to sit up on the bridge while a security detail was dispatched to try and rescue them. So instead Burgoyne merely concluded with "I have the conn, aye. Good luck, Captain."

The doors closed behind Kebron and Calhoun, as Termic turned to Burgoyne and said, "Your captain is a dead man."

"Fortunately, he has practice at that," replied Burgoyne.

iv.

The security detail, ten strong, was waiting outside the shuttlebay doors. As Calhoun ran up to them, with Kebron taking up the rear, he demanded, "What are you waiting for?"

"Something's holding the doors closed, sir," said one of the security guards. "We're getting a phaser torch to cut it open . . ."

"You do that," said Kebron as he stepped forward, Calhoun barely getting out of the way in time. As large as Kebron's fingers were, they could be remarkably dexterous when the situation called for it. While Calhoun looked on, Kebron carefully worked his fingers into the slot where the sliding doors met. It seemed to Calhoun that it was taking forever, even though it was only seconds.

"Got it," muttered Kebron, and he started to pull the doors apart. Kebron's face was routinely deadpan, and this moment was no exception, but even Calhoun could perceive mild surprise in Kebron's visage when the doors did not immediately open for him. "Something's holding it shut," he said with obvious annoyance.

A security guard came running up with the phaser torch. "Kebron," ordered Calhoun, "step out of the way."

"Sorry, sir. Matter of pride now," Kebron grunted, making no move to get out of the way.

"*Kebron!* We don't have *time* for your injured pride!"

Suddenly, with a roar of effort, Kebron's arms shoved wide and the doors ripped right out of the frame, tearing apart with an earsplitting sound of shredded metal. Glancing sidelong at Calhoun, Kebron said, "I just made the time," as he tossed the doors aside.

That was when what appeared to be huge tentacles whipped past them, moving quickly, and one of them struck Kebron in the chest. He grabbed it without hesitation and yanked as hard as he could. Calhoun had no doubt that he could have ripped the thing off whatever it was attached to, but it was slick and slimy and so was able to yank itself out from Kebron's grip before he could get a firm hold on it. Quickly it withdrew into the shuttlebay.

One of the security guards handed a spare phaser to Calhoun, and he called out, "Behind me!"

"Captain," began Kebron.

"*Behind me!*" Calhoun repeated even more forcefully and—not remotely interested in discussing protocol insofar as the safety of a captain was concerned—charged into the shuttlebay even as he thumbed the phaser to maximum level. He had no intention of taking chances with whatever it was he was going to encounter in there.

His head whipped right and left, trying to see where the tentacles might be coming from next. He heard a loud *splutch* sound from the far end of the shuttlebay, as if something huge and glutinous had spilled out onto the deck. Kebron was directly behind him, and the rest of the security squad was bringing up the rear. Tossing aside caution, he shouted, "Xyon! Moke! Where are you? Where—"

Then he looked straight ahead and came to a halt. Kebron bumped into him and, save for Calhoun's reflexes, would have knocked the captain to the floor. Calhoun looked up, and up, and had never felt that a phaser in his hand was as inadequate to a task as this one was. He needed a phaser cannon. Or perhaps photon torpedoes.

The thing was gargantuan. It did not take up the entirety of the shuttlebay in terms of its width, but its height brought it all the way up to the ceiling, a good thirty feet high. It was impossible to determine how many tentacles it had; they were in constant motion, snapping around so quickly that he couldn't begin to get a fix on them. The center of its body was practically amorphous. It had an almost columnar look to it, but there were no eyes that Calhoun could discern, nor a mouth. Instead, its center seemed to serve mostly as something for the tentacles to be attached to. The entire creature was a sort of deathly gray, and it made no noise other than the thick smacking sound that was coming from its tentacles as they slapped against the wall or floor.

Calhoun looked around frantically, seeing no sign of either of his sons. A horrific dread rose within him as he feared that . . . thing . . . had devoured both of them. Fury burning behind his eyes, he raised his phaser and shouted, "Prepare to fire on my—!"

"Greetings."

The pleasant, almost mellifluous sound of its voice— honeyed, soothing tones—resounded throughout the shuttlebay. The tentacles continued to move, and the damned thing still looked like a creature spat out by the imagination of a horror novelist. But it made no move to attack. Instead it remained exactly where it was, although Calhoun couldn't be entirely sure that the thing was simply unable to move at all.

"Take me to the mate of this ship, please," it continued, not sounding especially nonplussed by the circumstances within which it found itself.

Calhoun took a cautious step forward. "I am the ma . . . the captain. The leader of this vessel." He kept the phaser aimed squarely at what seemed to be the middle of the thing's centralized "stalk," for want of a better word. "There were two of my people in here! What did you do with them!"

"Nothing," it replied mildly. One of its many tentacles stretched over and stroked the top of Xyon's small vessel, safely ensconced within the shuttlebay. "They retreated to this box. Not that it was necessary. I would not have hurt them."

"Xyon! Moke!" Calhoun raised his voice. "Are you in there? Are you in the *Lyla*?"

There was a pause, and then Moke's voice sounded over the small ship's loudspeaker. "Mac! Are you out there? It's hard to make anything out on the viewscreen in here!"

"I'm here, Moke! And Xyon's in there, too?"

"Yeah! But I can send him out to die if you need him to."

"You see?" said the creature. "I would not have hurt them, as I said."

"It's easy to say that now," Calhoun reminded him,

trying not to let the relief he was feeling distract him from the job that needed to be done. "Considering they've gotten to safety and you've got an entire array of our weapons aimed at you."

"It is easy to say because it is true. Just as what I say to you now is true. Do you know who I am?"

"I'm guessing," Calhoun said slowly, "one of the Teuthis."

"Not one of. *The.* The leader. I escaped from my escort vessel when we were savagely assaulted by our enemies. And you . . . you are visitors from outside Teuthian, are you not?"

"More like prisoners than visitors. And . . . outside what? What did you call it?"

"Teuthian. We named the sphere after ourselves. We felt it only fitting."

"Yes, of course you did," Calhoun said dryly.

He couldn't tell if the thing was looking at him or not. The center stalk was twitching a bit, and the tentacles were in perpetual motion, but it was impossible to determine where its focus was.

"You participated in the destruction of my vessel."

"At the time it seemed the wisest course of action."

"Yes. I imagine it would . . . to you. And you have been speaking to the Bolgar, no doubt. They have spoken to you of what a rapacious, destructive race we are. How it is our desire to destroy all life in Teuthian that is not our own race."

"Do you deny it?"

"Not at all. We're proud of it. For far too long there were far too many races endeavoring to destroy each other. Warfare was constant. By destroying all our enemies, we will finally be able to achieve peace."

"Peace!" Calhoun started to advance. He was immediately halted by Kebron, who placed a large and immobile hand on Calhoun's shoulder. It was unusual for the Brikar to treat the captain in such a manner, and at first Calhoun was annoyed. But then he realized that Kebron was simply doing his job and preventing his commanding officer from getting nearer to this unknown creature than was wise for him. "Your people showed up in our . . . sphere . . . and may well have started a war!"

"We started nothing. We merely defended ourselves against the inevitable threats from the warlike races that already resided there. It was nothing more than a preemptive strike to serve our interests."

"You're telling me," Calhoun said, "that you were so sure of potential danger to yourselves, that you instigated a war in order to prevent war further down the line."

"That is correct."

"That is completely ridiculous!"

The Teuthis leader made what sounded like a distant coughing noise. "You would be amazed how many there are who would disagree with you."

"You could have exercised other options. You could have used diplomacy. You could have made certain that those in Sector 221-G knew you were interested in living in peace . . ."

"Such actions would have made us look weak. Overtures of peace are not the means by which peace is achieved. War is the means through which peace is the final result. Overtures of peace simply assure your enemies that you have no resolve. Only those willing to obliterate any who stand in their way can know true serenity." He paused and then added, "You are an intellectually stimulating individual. Are all your race similar in their thinking?"

"Now look, you—"

"Do you wish to return to your own sphere?"

That brought Calhoun up short. He regarded the creature suspiciously and then said, "Yes. Of course we do."

"Then aid me in destroying the Bolgar. The technology for creating our entryway to your sphere resides in the remains of the vessel that envelops us. You cannot access it. Neither can the Bolgar. But I can. Termic is the leader of the Bolgar. Help me annihilate him and his followers and I will send you home. Throw your lot in with the Bolgar, and you can resign yourself to having many more of these intellectually stimulating discussions . . . for you will not have much else to keep you occupied."

There was dead silence for a moment, and then Xyon's voice rang out over his ship's speaker.

"If anyone's asking me, I vote for the giant tentacled guy."

"Me too," Moke's voice piped up.

Calhoun rolled his eyes. "*Grozit,*" he said softly. Then louder, he said, "How do I know you'll keep your word?"

"I swear it," the Teuthis leader replied, "on this,

the most holy of our ancient relics. The symbol of my leadership."

From somewhere within his own vast body, he pulled out what appeared to be some sort of weapon. Calhoun braced himself, ready to move fast . . . but then he realized what he was looking at.

It was the prosthetic gun-arm of a Borg.

"I've *got* to get me one of those," said Kebron.

New Thallon

Excerpted from Lefler's logs:

One of Si Cwan's greatest strengths is his intrinsic belief that, sooner or later, he will triumph over adversity and his opponents. Even at his lowest point, even when he was reduced to stowing away on the Excalibur *so he could return to Thallonian space, he was never less than one hundred percent certain that he would find his missing sister, Kalinda, and be restored to his proper place in the Thallonian hierarchy.*

And that confidence radiates to all those around him. To his associates, to his allies, to every servant at every level. Ultimately, people like to believe they're on the winning side, and when you're in Si Cwan's company, that confidence always seems to be well placed.

But the assault on New Thallon . . . it was cata-strophic. It wasn't just limited to here at the palace. Cities all over the world were devastated. Si Cwan has people off surveying the damage, trying to determine what the hell happened. In the meantime, all the survivors here look like the walking wounded. Any loud noise causes people to jump, and they look to the skies with fear and trepidation.

And when they look at Si Cwan now, there's no reverence in their eyes. Instead there's concern, unease . . . and mute accusation. They blame him for this. It's only natural, since he blames himself. I've tried to tell him it wasn't his fault, but he looks at me angrily and says, "If not mine, whose? Fhermus didn't make this happen. I allowed this to happen." He burns with a cold fury that I can't even begin to quench.

I feel as if I'm watching the slow collapse of a star. And I am just as powerless now as I would be in witnessing such an astronomical event. I don't like this feeling. I like being able to problem-solve. I like having resources.

I have none such here. This situation cannot be allowed to continue. I have to do something.

And more and more, I'm starting to believe that that something is going to involve Kalinda . . .

Si Cwan stared at the reports in front of him and shook his head in annoyance.

"You summoned me, my lord?" came a familiar voice.

Seated cross-legged on the floor in his inner sanctum, he held the reports as he gestured for Robin to enter. "I know you were going for humor in your salutation, my dear . . . but I have to tell you, I liked the way it sounded when you said that."

"Well, don't get used to it." She gestured toward the reports. "Problem?"

"I am . . . quite simply disgusted," he said, shaking

his head as Robin sat on the floor opposite him. "As near as has been determined, the entire assault against us was thanks to the actions of a single traitor: one Topez Anat."

"Topez Anat." She rolled the name around in her mouth. "Why does that sound familiar?"

"He was the latest in a long family line of service to our House," Si Cwan told her. "You were there when I accepted his pledge of fealty. His ancestors performed their service good and true for generations. And then this bastard comes along . . ."

"What did he do?"

"He *sabotaged* us, that's what he did!" Si Cwan threw down the reports in disgust. "Used his position at one of our planetary defense stations to sabotage our entire defensive grid."

"I wouldn't think such a thing was possible."

"It shouldn't have been. The sophistication of what he did . . ." Si Cwan shook his head. "Fhermus must have bought him off. Provided him with the technology, the ability . . ."

"Are you sure he was responsible?"

"He had to have been. There was no one else." He growled in disgust. "I shall issue a proclamation having his name stricken from any and all Thallonian records that have ever existed and ever will exist. He will not even be immortalized as a traitor. Instead every trace of his life will be erased. His family will not be allowed to mention him, in public or private, ever again, lest they be subject to the same disgrace that will forever accompany Topez Anat in his final voyage to the afterlife and beyond."

"That sounds . . . very thorough."

Si Cwan, still towering over her even though they were both on the floor, looked down at her. "Are you mocking me?" he demanded. "Mocking the seriousness of—"

"Mocking it? Cwan, I could have been killed by it, same as everyone else!"

"And you shall be avenged, as will those who actually died at Fhermus's hands," Si Cwan said angrily. "In short order we will launch a counterattack that will—"

"I just . . ."

"I love when you interrupt me," he said.

Ignoring the mild rebuke, she continued, "I just . . . I want to make sure that you're sure. About Topez Anat."

"Of course I'm sure! Why wouldn't I be sure?"

"Because things aren't always what they seem, and this may be one of those instances."

"Are you saying these reports are wrong?"

"I'm saying you may be looking in the wrong place if what you're seeking is a traitor."

"Robin," he said with obviously dwindling patience, "you're dancing around something, and I find it very unbecoming if for no other reason than that I don't have time for it. It—"

"Kalinda."

He stared at her. "What about her?"

"I don't know if you noticed, but she's been leaving a trail of bodies behind her lately . . ."

"Are you saying," and his voice rose dangerously, "that my sister is a traitor?"

"I'm saying your sister may not be what she seems."

"This is absurd! You're starting to sound like Xyon in his rants when Kalinda returned to us—"

"And maybe he was right!"

He sprang to his feet. Literally sprang. It was as if a string were attached to him and he'd been drawn straight up. It was just the latest reminder for Robin of just how strong and quick he was. She didn't flinch, since never for a moment did she believe her own safety was threatened. He scowled so darkly at her that she thought his skin was on the verge of going from red to purple. "I cannot believe you would be so gullible as to accept the desperate ranting of a love-starved kidnapper."

Robin got to her feet a lot less elegantly than Si Cwan did, and tried not to be annoyed by that. Why should she be? There was so much else to be annoyed by. "And I cannot believe that you would dismiss a real concern out of hand simply because it was first voiced by someone whom you dislike intensely! If Xyon has anything approaching his father's knack for gut instinct . . ."

"Are you saying I don't recognize my own sister?"

"I'm saying you're allowing yourself to be blinded by your hatred for Fhermus and for Xyon, and the people of New Thallon are being made to suffer for it!"

A deathly silence hung over the room for what seemed a long, long while.

Finally Si Cwan said, very quietly, "I think it's time."

She shook her head in confusion. "Time for what?"

"New Thallon remains a target, and this place is ground zero. Hostilities are only going to escalate. It's no longer safe for you here."

"It's no longer safe for anyone," Robin pointed out. "But I don't go willingly running from danger."

"Then you'll go dragged from it against your will." He looked past her shoulder and nodded once.

Robin turned to see what he was looking at and her jaw dropped. There were two large guards standing in the doorway, both expressionless.

She turned back to Si Cwan. "You can't be serious."

"I have servants packing up your things. They'll be meeting you out at the departure pad. That's what I brought you here to tell you. I regret that we became so distracted discussing irrelevancies. It would have been preferable to use this time to say proper good-byes. But there's no help for it, I fear."

"Are you *insane?*" She stepped closer to him. Since he was drawing himself up to his full height, it wasn't as if they could go nose-to-nose. Even so, she got as near as she could. "If that isn't really Kalinda, that's not exactly what you could call an irrelevancy! Furthermore, I'm both your wife and a Starfleet representative here! You don't seriously think you can just pack me up and ship me away!"

"As a Starfleet representative," Cwan replied coolly, "you are here at my sufferance. As your husband, my conscience is clear when it comes to acting in your interests."

"In *your* interests, you mean!" She stabbed a finger at him. "All you're concerned with doing is surrounding yourself with people who will tell you exactly what you want to hear!"

"What's your point?"

"My point is that an intelligent man surrounds himself with smart people who disagree with him!"

He took a step toward her so that he truly towered over her. "We're in a war, Robin. Whether you want to acknowledge it or not, we are in a war. I don't have time for people who disagree with me. Anyone by my side needs to be in accord with my thinking. We need to move forward with one mind, one purpose, or we will not be able to move at all. And furthermore," he continued over her attempt to interrupt him, "I don't need a representative of Starfleet reporting back with all manner of intimate detail as to what our plans might be."

"You don't seriously think I'd do anything to endanger you or New Thallon, do you?"

"I think," replied Si Cwan, "that you have your own concerns and priorities, and will do whatever you think to be right . . . even if I believe it to be wrong. In the new world order of the Thallonian Empire, my beliefs must override all other concerns."

"Don't you mean the Thallonian Protectorate?"

"Robin . . ." He sighed heavily. "If we continue to live in the past . . . we will have no future." He reached out to touch her hair, but she automatically pulled back from his touch. He shrugged as if it meant nothing. "Farewell. I hope matters change so that we may be together once more."

"Do you seriously think," she demanded, "that if you have me hauled out of here against my will, I'm going to want to have anything to do with you ever again?"

"That," he told her, "is your decision. Not mine." He gestured for the guards to remove her.

The guards started to push Robin back, and she batted their hands away from her. "You push me around, I'll break your fingers," she snarled. The threat might or might not have been a hollow one, but the guards chose not to press the matter. They kept their hands to their sides as Robin shot a final, poisonous glance at Si Cwan.

She had never hated anyone in her life as much as she did her husband at that moment.

Then, as the doors were sliding shut behind her, she turned to toss off a final, angry insult at him.

And what she saw was the mighty Si Cwan in the midst of sinking to his knees, his hands over his face, and she could see his back shaking violently as if racked with sobs.

"Cwan!" she shouted, but then the doors sealed off her last sight of him. She tried to head back to him but this time the guards were less gentle. They grabbed her by either arm—taking care to make sure she couldn't grab their fingers—and hauled her toward her destination, while no betraying sound emerged from Si Cwan's private sanctum.

U.S.S. Excalibur

i.

Burgoyne sat across from Calhoun in the captain's ready room, and slowly shook hir head. "I can see why you're suggesting it, Captain . . . but I have to say, I think you're taking a tremendous risk."

"And since we've never taken one of *those* before . . ."

"I'm just saying, Captain . . ."

Calhoun put up a hand and Burgoyne lapsed into silence. "I appreciate what you're saying, Burgy. But we're faced with risk no matter which way we go. Being forced to choose up sides in a genocidal free-for-all which—even if we don't take the Prime Directive into consideration—"

"As is our wont."

"—still thrusts us into a moral area so gray that even I'm not sure I want any part of it. But if we can access the technology that the Teuthis utilize . . ." Calhoun thought about it a moment. "The fact that he's hauling around a Borg arm makes it fairly clear from where they got the technology for the transwarp conduit."

"True," said Burgoyne. "Obviously the Borg came to this . . . universe either by accident or by design . . ."

"That," said Calhoun, "would certainly cover all the possibilities."

". . . but were not remotely prepared for what they encountered."

"So you're saying they were assimilated." When Burgoyne nodded, a grin split Calhoun's face. "You know . . . there's something to be said for irony. But when did all this happen?"

"It's difficult to say for sure. What Xy has theorized, based on his conversations with Pontalimus . . ."

"Who?"

"Pontalimus. The Teuthis leader sitting down in the shuttlebay . . ."

"He talked to Xy?" Calhoun was incredulous. "After he delivered his ultimatum to me, he informed me that he had nothing more to say! Why did he talk to Xy?"

"Xy can be very persuasive."

Calhoun leaned back in his chair. "This isn't a starship, it's an insane asylum. So what does Xy's encounter with . . ." He hesitated.

"Pontalimus," Burgoyne prompted helpfully.

"Yes, him. What does Xy think happened?"

"Xy believes that the Teuthis acquired the technology from the Borg centuries ago. That they used it to come to our universe and arrived on the planet now known as Priatia. There was either no one there, or—more likely—a race already in existence. But the environment, even the mere act of existing in our universe, may have been problematic for them. So they bioformed a new race that was intended to be the equivalent of the Teuthis in our universe. Their eyes and ears and extended tentacles, if you will."

"Bioformed. The equivalent of terraforming, but changing the biological makeup of the individuals to survive on the world, rather than changing the world to suit the colonizing life-form."

"Yes, sir," said Burgoyne.

"But . . . then what happened? Why did they disappear for so long? Why did they come back now?"

"As near as we can tell, a combination of things," said Burgoyne. "First . . . the return trip through the 'Teuthis corridor' wasn't what one would call a smashing success."

"What would one call it?"

"A total fiasco. They didn't have any more full control of the technology than the Borg did initially. So when the initial exploratory ship, after instigating the newly created race on Priatia, tried to return home to report, they wound up arriving in several hundred pieces."

"Somewhat discouraging in terms of making return trips."

"Yes. So they made no further trips until they reworked the tech and could assure that a two-way trip was feasible."

Calhoun considered that a moment. "And what else?" he asked.

"What else, sir?"

"You said it was a combination of things. What else factored in?"

"Ah. Yes." Burgoyne leaned forward, placing hir

elbows on the edge of the desk. "As you're aware, the laws of physics that we're familiar with don't always seem to apply here. Among those laws could well be the passage of time."

"Are you saying that time passes at a different rate here than back home?"

"There is that distinct possibility, sir, yes."

"By how much? How much of a differential is there?"

"Impossible to say."

"Can you do better than that?"

"I wish I had more to tell you, but this entire situation is so outside my . . ." S/he shook hir head, frustrated. "I mean, it could be anything. It could be that one minute here is five minutes there. Or five days or five years. It could be that there's an exponential decay. That is to say, our continued presence could have an impact on the very nature of this place, and the longer we're here, the faster the time displacement increases."

"So even if we make it back, a century or more might have passed."

"There is that possibility, yes. Of course, if that should happen, we could always slingshot around a sun and go backward in time."

"Oh, great," Calhoun said sarcastically, "because nothing's ever gone wrong when we attempted *that* before." Now he leaned forward, looking poised as a panther. "So what it comes down to is this: The sooner we get out of here, the better."

"Yes, sir."

"Which brings us back to my original notion. Do you still have a problem with that?"

"Yes, sir."

"All right, well . . . too damned bad. Morgan!"

She appeared in a heartbeat in response to his summons. What was slightly disconcerting, of course, was that even as her holographic image was standing in the ready room, Calhoun knew that she was out on the bridge as well. In some ways it was almost godlike. The *Excalibur* was her own little heaven and earth, where she dwelt in a mysterious place that the average person never saw. She was omniscient as far as all the mortals wandering about the place were concerned. "Yes, Captain," she said briskly.

"I have a plan," he said, and fired a glance at Burgoyne, "which my first officer doesn't exactly agree with. I'm doing this over hir objections."

"Well, I'm reasonably certain you're empowered to do that, what with you being captain and all," said Morgan. "What do you need?"

The *Excalibur* was still residing within the blasted shell of a Teuthis ship. Termic's holographic image had disappeared because of the arrival of Pontalimus; he'd felt it vital to return to his people, apprise them of the situation, and "act accordingly," whatever that meant. Calhoun suspected it meant nothing good. Now he made a wide, sweeping gesture as if to encompass the entirety of the vessel outside. "Somewhere in there," he said, "in their computer banks or whatever passes for artificial intelligence around here . . . somewhere in there is the secret to the technology that created the transwarp conduit. Or, as they call it here, the Teuthis corridor."

"And you want me to go in after it."

He nodded. "Can you do it?"

"You want me to take my electronic essence, attempt to interface with a completely alien computer system, and extract information from it that is no doubt top-secret and likely encoded."

"That's about right, yes."

"Not a problem," she said. "Do you want me to work on solving some incurable disease while I'm at it?"

"Seriously, Morgan . . ."

"Seriously, Captain . . . it shouldn't be all that much of a chore."

"Good," he said, nodding approvingly.

"Captain, once more, I must express my concern," said Burgoyne. "We have no idea what manner of fail-safes might be present in the Teuthis vessel. If something should happen to Morgan . . ."

"Commander, I assure you, nothing's going to happen to me," said Morgan. "I'll set up a simple electron pulse directed at the vessel as an exploratory mechanism, see where I can find a connect juncture—presuming there is one—and worm my way in. And it won't even be me worming my way in. It'll be an avatar, a representation of myself that I'll duplicate from my core personality. There's no danger involved."

"We have no real idea where we are or what we're

surrounded by," Burgoyne reminded her. "We're in danger just by sitting here."

"Then it seems to me we shouldn't be just sitting," Morgan said reasonably.

Calhoun said, "I agree."

"All right, then," said Morgan. "I'll let you know what happens."

"How long will you need to prepare?"

"No time at all, Captain. As a matter of fact, I'm sending the electron pulse right now. With any luck . . . ah!" She smiled. "That was easier than I could have hoped."

"You're in the other ship's operating system?" Burgoyne looked at her in amazement. "Right now?"

"Yes," Morgan said. She was all business. "Right now."

In spite of hirself, Burgoyne was clearly fascinated by the situation. "What's it like? Is it completely different from our own operating systems? What are you perceiving? What sort of data processing—?"

Morgan wasn't responding. She was staring straight ahead, and Calhoun saw that her body was suddenly stiff and unyielding. Burgoyne realized it at the same time. He was the first one to her, touching her hardlight body at the shoulder. Morgan tilted back slightly, then rocked forward, then back again, beginning to topple. Calhoun was on his feet by that point and he caught her just before she hit the floor. "*What the hell—?*"

That was the moment the *Excalibur* went dead.

There were startled exclamations from out on the bridge and shouts of "Not again!" as the lights went almost completely out. There were also a few startled profanities and the sounds of people banging into railings or chairs or each other.

"Captain!" came a shout from Kebron. "Morgan's vanished from the ops station, and we can't see a damned thing out here! Systems are out all over the ship!"

Calhoun propped Morgan up against his desk, walked quickly to the door of the ready room, and nearly slammed into it full-tilt before pulling himself up short. The doors didn't open for him. "Go to manual overrides!" he called through the door. "Bring up emergency lights! Check weapons and defensive status! Have crewmen walk everything through if they have to!"

He made his way back to his desk and yanked his sword off the wall. Then he moved back to the door and thrust the sword forward, jamming it between the two halves of the door and using it to pry the doors open. "Well?" demanded Calhoun as he did so. "Aren't you going to say 'I told you so'?"

From the darkness, Burgoyne's voice came. "What possible good would that do?"

"None whatsoever."

"Then I see no point in saying it."

"Very wise."

Calhoun got the doors open, and just as he did, Burgoyne added quietly, "But I *did* tell you."

"Thank you, Burgoyne," replied Calhoun. "Deep down, I knew I could count on you."

ii.

In the darkness of the shuttlebay, Xyon looked around in confusion and said, *"Now what?"*

He had been spending much of his time lately down in the shuttlebay, speaking at length with the resident guest/prisoner. Xyon had a mercenary's heart but an explorer's soul, and this behemoth creature, this "Pontalimus," was like nothing and no one he'd ever encountered before. He had sat back and watched as his namesake, Xy, had spoken with the strange being at length, and when Xy's duties called for him to be up on the bridge, Xyon had taken over the conversation.

The most recent topic of discussion, curiously enough, had been Moke. Although neither he nor Xyon had been in any true danger, Moke had been impressed by Xyon's quick thinking in beaming the both of them to safety. "I'm surprised you didn't leave me to die," Moke had told him.

If I did, my father would kill me was what immediately occurred to Xyon, but he didn't say that aloud. Instead he simply shrugged and said, "You needed help and I helped you. Simple as that."

That had left Moke with a good deal to ponder, and Xyon back with Lyla within his ship . . . the only company that he was truly able to tolerate. But Pontalimus was certainly an interesting enough individual on his own, and spoke to Xyon at length about whatever was on Xyon's mind (although Xyon, trying to be cautious, made sure not to make any slipups about what little he knew regarding strategic aspects of the ship).

"You were correct in attempting to retrieve the mate you desired," Pontalimus was telling him in regard to his ill-fated kidnapping of Kalinda. "Allowing lesser creatures to issue dictates is of no advantage to you."

"Does your species have . . . you know . . . females?" Xyon asked cautiously.

"It requires three of our type to mate. When we do, the most dominant simply absorbs the other two. The process can be protracted, especially if they cannot come to a decision ahead of time of who is the most dominant. Then it can become ugly."

"I would think so," Xyon had said. He was about to make further inquiries when the lights went out. He heard alarmed cries from out in the corridor as well, where a security force had been stationed for the duration of Pontalimus's stay.

Even though it was dark, Xyon could still make out the towering creature's outline. The leader of the Teuthis wasn't budging an inch.

"*Now what?*" Xyon moaned. He'd been issued a com link upon becoming a resident—however short his stay was intended—because Calhoun wanted to be able to keep in touch with him at all times. He tapped the link and called out, "Xyon to bridge. What's going on up there?"

It was a good long while—and several follow-up demands that were escalating in anger—before Xyon got his answer. It was Xy, the science officer, who provided it: "Morgan crashed! Something happened to her; we're not certain what. As soon as we have full power and some semblance of computer aid online, we'll be sure to let you know. Xy out."

"Who is 'Morgan'?" Pontalimus asked.

Xyon told him.

"Ah. That's how they attempted to do it, then."

"Do what?" Xyon frowned, having no idea what Pontalimus was referring to.

Pontalimus made a strange sound that might vaguely have been along the lines of a laugh. "I cannot be certain, mind you . . . but I would suspect that they attempted to utilize this computer entity you describe to penetrate the remaining operating systems of the derelict."

"Why?"

"To find a means of accessing the Teuthis corridor, of course. They want to be able to create one so they can return to their own sphere. An action of foolish hubris. As sophisticated as they believe their technology to be, they cannot begin to comprehend what we have achieved. Ours is the oldest, greatest race in the sphere. None can match us. None."

"And yet, from what I hear, these Bolgar have got you on the run."

One of his tentacles twitched in a dismissive manner. "It means nothing. A setback at most. Our triumph is inevitable."

"You keep talking about 'our.' I'm curious: How many of you are there left, anyway?"

Pontalimus said nothing. His tentacles twitched a bit more, and then he said abruptly, "I am fatigued.

Your computer entity will recover. The protections she encountered were not designed to be lethal. Consider yourselves fortunate in that regard. I am done speaking now."

Xyon watched as Pontalimus wrapped his tentacles around himself, one at a time, very meticulously, until he looked like one huge cocoon of tentacles.

"Great," muttered Xyon, as he headed off to the bridge to tell his father that sending Morgan in on an espionage mission—which he fully expected Pontalimus was correct about—might not have been the brightest plan he'd ever conceived. And Xyon's problem was that he didn't know if he was regretting being the bearer of his news . . . or looking forward to it.

iii.

Xy, the *Excalibur*'s science officer, was halfway up a Jefferies tube, working on some systems rerouting. Normally such endeavors were purely the province of the engineering department. But Xy was no slouch when it came to engineering know-how, and indeed it was generally acknowledged that Xy was second to none when it came to understanding how the computers operated in general and Morgan in particular. So he was pitching in where he could, in this case helping to reboot the entire computer system so that Morgan would ideally wind up unfrozen. It was, however, a vastly difficult job as systems had to be brought online first one at a time before the general restart could commence.

So when someone tapped him on his booted foot and a voice said, "Xy," he was nothing but curt in response. "Not now," he called down from the top of the tube. "I'm busy. And if you don't like it, go complain to Calhoun."

"That's something I'd pay good credits to see."

The sudden depressing familiarity of that voice was sufficient to prompt Xy to drop right out of the tube and land in the corridor at attention. "Sorry, Captain," he said.

"Don't concern yourself about it," said Calhoun. "I just had an interesting discussion with Xyon about what happened and why it happened."

"Oh?"

"Yes. Which means I'm going to have to explore some other options for getting us home . . . one of which could wind up getting somewhat nasty."

"How nasty, sir?" Xy asked cautiously.

Calhoun draped an arm around him as he led him down the corridor. And he smiled an almost wolfish smile that Xy found extremely disconcerting.

"Very nasty, Xy," he said. "And I think you may be the only one on the ship who can help make it happen."

"Captain," Xy said, choosing his words carefully. "Not to be indelicate, but . . . Xyon. Your son. Is it at all possible that he allowed you to think he was dead so he'd never have to find himself in these sorts of situations, where you're about to embark on some insanely daring plan that could wind up causing your death and possibly the deaths of anyone in proximity to you?"

"I hardly think that's fair, Xy."

"Is it an accurate description of what you're about to discuss with me?"

"Yes."

"Ah. Well then . . ."

"In answer to your question: No. Xyon didn't allow me to think he was dead in order to avoid these sorts of situations. He did it out of love for Kalinda—"

"Whom he later tried to kidnap."

"Yes. And out of pure hatred for me."

"He hated you."

"Sad to say, but true," sighed Calhoun.

"Hard to understand how."

"It is indeed one of life's great mysteries," Calhoun said. "Now . . . let's discuss this plan I have that could kill me and possibly anyone near me . . ."

"By all means," said Xy. "Wouldn't miss it."

Space Station Bravo

As the *Trident* fell into orbit around Space Station Bravo, there was a deep and uncomfortable silence upon her bridge. Words, when spoken, were brisk and efficient and lacked any sense of camaraderie or byplay.

It had been that way ever since the *Spectre* had departed. Perhaps even longer than that: ever since Hash had his barely controlled blowup at Kat Mueller. Mueller herself had spoken to no one of it, but a starship was still a confined community, and word had a habit of getting around no matter what.

Hash wasn't disrespectful to Mueller in any way. Out there, on the bridge, there were lines he simply wasn't going to cross. But there was still a tension on the bridge that was palpable. Mueller wasn't sure how to address it or even whether it should be addressed. Technically, it wasn't her problem. If Hash had problems with her command decisions, he was welcome to depart and she certainly wasn't going to stand in his way. It really wasn't something she needed to care about. Indeed, Mueller prided herself on not caring about anything except getting her job done in the most efficient manner possible.

Still . . . it gnawed at her, deep down, that she had no one on the ship she felt she could speak to as a confidant. No one she could unburden her frustrations upon . . . and her frustrations were considerable.

"Captain," spoke up Arex, "we're receiving contact from the ambassadors at the space station. They want to know when they'll be beaming aboard."

Mueller didn't reply. She simply continued to stare at the station.

"Captain . . . ?" Arex said again, perhaps thinking she hadn't heard him.

"Billions of credits go into building a starship," Mueller said, as if speaking to herself, "and they use us as a taxi service. Sometimes I don't know what the hell is going on anymore."

This prompted many exchanged looks of confusion. Before anyone could say anything else, however, Mueller stood and said, "Tell the ambassadors they can beam aboard anytime. Confirm to them that we've received Starfleet's orders and that we will be bringing them to Ares IV to greet the newly elected chancellor on or close to schedule. Then make sure that they're put in guest quarters in as remote a section of the ship as possible so that I don't have to deal with them. Also tell Admiral Shelby I'm coming down."

"You're beaming over to Bravo Station, Captain?" asked Desma.

"No, I thought I'd just open a door for an orbital skydive. You have the con."

She headed for the door as Desma called after her, "Shall I tell the ambassadors when they can expect you back, Captain?"

"When I feel like it, XO. I hear tell," she added, tossing the comment over her shoulder, "that we starship captains have gobs of discretion." Without waiting to see if Takahashi reacted to her remark, she left the bridge.

All during her fast trip down to the transporter room, she was fuming. Crewmen would greet her and she would nod briskly without even making eye contact. As aggravating as it sounded, she felt as if she were a stranger in her own vessel, totally disconnected from the men and women aboard it who depended upon her to keep them safe. It was almost as if she resented them because they needed her.

Why? Why did she feel that way?

Because you feel like you're needed elsewhere.

With absolutely no warning, she turned and slammed her fist angrily into the nearest wall. The sudden gesture prompted passing crewmen to jump back, startled, and perhaps concerned that they were going to be the next target of her wrath. Mueller shook out her hand, then kept going on her way without offering comment to the puzzled crewmen around her.

Moments later she arrived in the transporter room, and in short order she had beamed over to Bravo Station. She walked through the station, ignoring everyone she encountered. There was such rage pounding through her that she had no idea what to do with it. There was one thing she did know for sure, however:

This was beyond the recent unpleasantness with Hash. It was beyond her anger with Soleta for going over to the Romulans, and beyond her annoyance with herself for allowing the *Spectre* to depart after the *Trident* had extended succor to them.

She knew all too well what was truly getting under her skin, and there was perhaps one person in the sector—possibly the galaxy—who would understand and share her frustration.

She strode into Shelby's outer office. Shelby's aide began to rise from behind his desk and said all in a rush, "Captain, we weren't expecting to see you here. Admiral Shelby is in a meeting at the moment, but if you'd like to come ba—"

As if he hadn't even spoken, Mueller ignored him and instead slammed her fist against the closed door to Shelby's inner office. Unfortunately she used the same hand that she'd previously used to strike the wall in the *Trident* corridor. Consequently a shudder of pain rippled through her arm. She grimaced slightly but otherwise ignored it as she bellowed, "*Shelby! Let me in, dammit!*"

The doors abruptly hissed open. The aide bolted around his desk, calling, "I'm sorry, Admiral, I wasn't able to stop her—"

"That's all right, Lieutenant," came Shelby's laconic tone. "Truth be known, this isn't actually all that much of a surprise. So, Kat . . ."

Mueller stood there, looking in, and her eyes widened in astonishment. Seated across the desk from Shelby was Robin Lefler, whose eyes looked red and puffy. As for Shelby, she had a large bottle of what appeared to be Orion whiskey on her desk. There were two glasses out, but without hesitation she reached under her desk and produced a third one with a flourish, as if she were a magician.

". . . care to join us?" asked Shelby.

"More than you can possibly believe," replied Kat Mueller as she pulled up a chair.

The Spectre

In her private quarters, Soleta stared at the bottle of schnapps that Kat Mueller had given her as a parting gift. It had caught Soleta completely off guard, because she had been quite certain that Mueller had despised her and the decisions that she had made.

"I did and do," Mueller had informed her. "However, having given a lot of thought to your predicament, I've decided that you can use this," and she had held up the bottle, "far more than I can."

Now Soleta placed it carefully upon the top of her desk and then sat down, resting her chin upon her fingers and staring fixedly at the bottle. She admired the contours of the bottle, the general curves of its shape. It was strange. For all the time that she served aboard the *Excalibur* during the same period as Mueller, she'd never really had all that much involvement with her. She'd spent some time with her during the entire incident with the godlike beings who had seduced Soleta into their way of life. But ultimately, she had no sense of attachment to Mueller, and furthermore, Mueller had grilled her pretty thoroughly during her recent time as a "guest" on the *Trident*.

Yet, curiously, the bottle symbolized a bizarre attachment to Mueller that Soleta felt would be surrendered if she cracked it open.

She had no idea why she would feel any need for an attachment to Mueller, or anyone else for that matter . . .

Yes, you do. You know perfectly well. It's because you haven't the faintest idea what the hell to do or whom to trust.

There was a chime at the door. Soleta looked at the closed portal for a moment, and her fingers strayed toward the disruptor she wore on her hip. Basic logic told her that if her people were about to stage a coup of some kind, they wouldn't ring the bell. They'd charge in, try to catch her by surprise.

Then again, what better way to catch her by surprise than to pretend that business was proceeding as usual?

You're going to make yourself insane if you keep this up. Just proceed as normal, and remain cautious.

She gripped the butt of her disruptor, the careful gesture obscured by her desk, and said cautiously, "Come."

The doors slid open and Lucius entered, his shoulders square and his bearing formal. But there was far more concern in his eyes than Soleta had ever seen before. He actually looked . . . dare she say it . . . nervous. The question, of course, was: What precisely was he nervous about?

Perhaps he was still trying to process everything

that she had told them. Upon returning to the *Spectre* and setting out from the *Trident*, she had informed the crew of all that Mueller had told her. At first there were gasps of disbelief, and several of her crew insisted that Mueller was deliberately misleading them. There was no way, they told her, that the Remans could possibly mount such a coup. Soleta quickly realized that their opinions were shaped by decades, if not centuries, of prejudice. She, on the other hand, had no reason to underestimate what the Remans were capable of. Slowly common sense swayed her crew around to the realization that not only did Mueller have no reason to lie, but it went a long way toward explaining the bizarre encounter they'd had with the Romulan war vessels.

Her crew had lapsed into silence, each trying to deal with the news in their own way. Soleta had ordered Aquila to simply take the *Spectre* in a leisurely circular pattern, which seemed mildly more productive than just hanging in space. Then she had retired to her quarters to try and consider their next move.

Now Lucius had come to her, and she was alert to all the possibilities that this entailed . . . particularly the dangerous ones. He cleared his throat as the doors closed behind him, and then inclined his head. "Commander," he said.

Soleta didn't ease her grip on her disruptor, but she did cock an eyebrow. "Commander?" she asked with a slightly mocking tone. "Not 'Legate'?"

"No." He paused. "May I sit?"

That too was unusual for him, since he typically

embraced formality and stood at attention. With her free hand, she gestured toward the seat facing her. He sat, looking uncomfortable, and his hands rested on his thighs.

"Commander," he said, not acknowledging her "legate" comment. "You know as well as I that I have been . . . reluctant . . . to embrace your command of this vessel."

"Yes. The whole 'being able to kill you' thing. I'd like to think it would never come to that."

"As do I. The point is, now we have a . . . situation."

"We do indeed," said Soleta, "considering that at the moment we're traveling in a slow circle around the sector with no particular destination."

"Yes. I have studied our predicament from every angle, and I am forced to conclude that I must . . . revisit . . . my priorities. More than ever before, a unified front is necessary if we are to survive in a hostile galaxy."

"We must hang together or we will assuredly hang separately."

"Yes." He blinked. "What?"

"A quote from a human during a turbulent time in Earth history. In ancient times, they would execute criminals through hanging. Tying rope around the throat, knotting it, and then suspending them in the air so that their neck would break."

Lucius considered that and then shook his head in disgust. "And they call us barbaric."

"It has been my experience, Tribune, that barbarism is not limited to any one race. All display equal facility at some time or other." Her voice sounded relaxed, and her posture likewise seemed at ease. But she continued not to ease up on her disruptor. Although it was blocked by the desk, she was certain that the blast would easily go through the desk and strike its target.

"A fair enough point, Commander," he allowed. "Obviously, we indeed have to hang together, as you put it. But there's . . . more to it than that."

"Really."

He shifted uncomfortably in the chair, looking as if he would rather be anywhere other than where he was and saying what he was about to say. "The gods work in mysterious ways . . . Soleta." She blinked in surprise at the intimacy implied at his using her name, which he had never done before. She hated to think it, but she liked the way it rolled off his tongue. "I had never comprehended their motivation in assigning you the command of this prestigious vessel."

"In defense of the gods, I don't think any of them actually signed the orders," she said dryly.

He seemed genuinely to appreciate the wryness of her remark, and actually smiled in a manner that caused the edges of his eyes to crinkle. "I'd say that's a fair guess." Then he looked at her with sober assessment. "The point is . . . I think I now begin to understand their grand plan."

"Do you. Then I hope you wouldn't be opposed to running it past me, for I am admittedly a bit in the dark about it."

"Isn't it obvious?"

"Not immediately, no."

"When we were confronted by those ships . . . I, along with every full-blooded Romulan on the bridge, was far too trusting. You—being a half-breed—did not appraise or approach the situation in the same manner. And because you did not . . . because you did not simply trust those who meant to destroy us . . . we were able to escape. Had it been up to me, I would have taken them at their word and we would have been boarded and imprisoned by now. Imprisoned . . . or perhaps blown to bits. We have ties to the Romulan Star Empire that blind us to what is best for all concerned. The fact that you do not have those same ties makes you our first, best hope of coming out of this in one piece."

Soleta was suspicious . . . but she was also relieved. Lucius was saying exactly what she had hoped he'd say. So much so, in fact, that she practically had to pinch herself to assure herself that she wasn't dreaming it. It was just that word-for-word perfect.

Before she could respond, he continued, "Do you have any thought as to what our next move is going to be?"

By this point her hand had moved away from her weapon and was resting easily on the desktop. "I have several thoughts . . . none of them ideal," she admitted. "When one comes down to it, the proper strategy is to approach this in a logical manner."

"And what does logic dictate?"

"Two options. Either we return to the Romulan Empire and take our chances . . . or we do not."

"That sounds simplistic on its face, but truly . . . there really aren't any other options," he admitted. "And since the former would appear to be closed to us, what opportunities does the latter present? If we do not return to the Romulan Empire, whom then do we serve?"

"We serve ourselves," she said. "We go where the mood takes us. Take on the jobs that interest us."

"For which side?"

"For whatever side suits our fancy," Soleta told him.

"I do not know," he said slowly, "if the crew would be enthused over dealing with certain races that we have traditional enmity toward . . . such as the Vulcans, for instance."

"Tribune, we are in an unusual situation. And that unusual situation requires unusual approaches. If the crew of the *Spectre* is to follow me and be essentially on its own, the least I can do is attend more closely to its wishes than a command officer would normally be required." She leaned forward on her elbows, steepling her fingers. "My suggestion would be for all of you to submit to me a list of those races and individuals with whom you would not want to see us doing business. Barring something truly unusual, I doubt I'll have much of a problem with any preemptive requests."

"What if we are asked to spy on the Romulan Empire itself. Would we do so?"

Although his tone of voice hadn't wavered, Soleta knew that this was a danger-laden question. She was beginning to suspect that Lucius wasn't just speaking for himself, but instead voicing the concerns of many other crew members. They wanted to know whether the *Spectre* was going to act in a manner running contrary to the interests of the Star Empire.

"I would tend to think," she said, "that that would be one of the preemptive requests. Simply because the planet we call 'home' has turned away from us doesn't mean that we are justified in turning against it." Then she added, "Make no mistake, Lucius. It is my firm belief that the present situation is temporary only. Matters in the Romulan Empire are far too volatile to remain this way for long. Sooner or later, leadership in the Empire will change hands, and an amnesty will be extended to us. All will be forgiven . . . 'all' including our loyalty to a Romulan who no longer rules, or is even alive."

"What about . . ." His voice trailed off.

"What about what?" she prompted him.

"What about the possibility of not waiting for matters to sort themselves out? What about the possibility of going in and trying to take charge of matters ourselves?"

"You're talking about a coup."

"I'm talking about taking actions that would very likely be in accordance with the desires of the Praetor," Lucius replied. "I will admit a hard truth to you, Soleta. The Praetor thought very highly of me . . . but he thought even more highly of you. He was childless, you know. I believe he saw in you the daughter he would have liked to have. He had great plans for you, Soleta. Great plans." He leaned toward her, speaking in a confidential tone. "Your command of the *Spectre* was merely the starting point. He was watching you carefully, I'm sure of it, and grooming you for . . . well, I couldn't know for sure. But . . ."

"Are you saying he was thinking of me to succeed him when the time came?"

He nodded.

The thought had never occurred to Soleta. "The council never would have—"

"The council would have acceded to his wishes, is my opinion. Sadly, we'll never know for certain. The point is . . . if we return to Romulus, perhaps we can put you into the place that the Praetor thought you deserved."

Soleta shook her head. "No. It's far too soon for that. The struggle for power represents a potential bloodbath, and I'll not thrust my crew into the midst of that in an attempt to grab power for myself."

"It will not be seen in that way . . ."

"So say you, Lucius. But these are dangerous times, and I think it best to proceed cautiously rather than precipitously."

"But Soleta . . ."

"Lucius," she said patiently, "how could I remotely believe that the Romulan Empire would accept me as Praetor if I can't get my own tribune to honor my opinion?"

He nodded and half-smiled. "With all respect, I believe you are selling yourself short. I reserve the right to disagree with your opinion, but I honor it all the same."

Soleta felt as if she were seeing Lucius for the first time. There were still faint suspicions floating around in the back of her mind. But Lucius, for all the disagreements that she'd had with him in the past, had always been one of the more honorable Romulans. It was difficult for her to think that everything he'd said to her just now was some sort of elaborate ruse. She wasn't ruling it out . . . but it didn't seem likely. Still, she didn't want to throw aside all caution and—

And he's damned attractive besides . . .

"Quiet," she snapped and then added quickly, "Not you," when she saw his puzzled expression.

Her com unit sounded. It had taken her a little while to adjust to the wristband units the Romulans used, as opposed to com links on their shirts. She touched the band and said, "Yes?"

"Commander," came Maurus's voice, "we're coming up on what appears to be a derelict in space."

"And . . . ?" Derelicts were not uncommon, and she wasn't especially interested in risking people on a pointless salvage mission.

"It appears to be the *Excalibur.*"

Her eyes widened. All else forgotten, she said, "On my way."

Lucius stepped aside graciously and gestured for her to precede him. She came around her desk, her mind whirling with questions and possibilities. She stepped through the door, and it was only by the most miraculous of chances that her peripheral vision caught a sudden movement just behind her.

She turned and started to bring her arms up defensively, but she was too slow and too late. A bottle of top-quality schnapps crashed against the side of her skull, landing with such fierce impact that the bottle shattered. Soleta's head nearly went with it. As it was, she dropped to her knees, the world spinning, and fought off a terrible urge to vomit. The floor was wet beneath her palms, and for a heartbeat she thought it was blood before she realized that, no, it was the alcohol. She couldn't smell it. She couldn't focus on anything. Bits of glass scattered on the floor dug into her palms. Ludicrously, she was dwelling on the lack of wisdom involved in keeping genuine glass bottles on a space vessel, because look how easily they could shatter.

Soleta tried to look up and the motion alone caused her to fall over completely, her shoulder thudding against the floor. She tried to stand, her feet thrashing out helplessly like an overturned tortoise's. Desperately trying to focus her eyes, she looked up and saw what appeared to be Lucius with the neck of the bottle in his right hand. She couldn't make out his face; it was far too blurry.

"*Ex . . . cali . . . bur?*" she managed to say.

"Not there," replied Lucius. "A subterfuge to distract you for the moment I was going to need."

She fought once more to rise to her feet, but then she felt a massive weight thud against her head which, as it turned out, was Lucius's fist. The blow sent her head thudding to the floor. She tried to command her body to move, but it refused to obey her.

Lucius, continuing calmly, said, "Don't worry. No one's going to kill you. You're too useful a bargaining chip for when we return to Romulus. So really . . . this is your lucky day."

Soleta wasn't feeling lucky. What she was feeling was ready to pass out. And seconds later, that was exactly what she did.

U.S.S. Excalibur

i.

Xyon was discovering that he was starting to enjoy the concept of making himself useful. He had spent so much of his life on his own, serving his own needs and no one else's, that working for the greater good of a community was a novel experience. Not that it was anything he planned to make a habit of, of course. There was only so much "good feeling" that any sane person could be expected to withstand.

As it was, he was working cheerfully in the engineering room, working in tandem with chief engineer Craig Mitchell's staff as they sought to run systems checks throughout the ship. They had to be especially meticulous since, according to Burgoyne, there was an outside chance that miscalculations at this point—in this bizarre and anomalous realm in which they were trapped—could cause the entire vessel to blow up. That would naturally be A Very Bad Thing.

He had just extracted some damaged data chips from their slots and placed them neatly in a container. He turned to bring them over to the repair unit and almost tripped over Moke, who was standing six inches away from him. As it was, he jumped back and nearly spilled the chips.

"What are you doing here?" he demanded.

Moke looked up at him. Xyon thought for a moment that he was seeing something like dark clouds passing through the boy's eyes, but chalked it up to an overactive imagination.

"Why did you haul me into your ship?" he asked finally.

"Because I was trying to protect you," Xyon replied, putting the box of chips down carefully.

"I know that."

"Then why did you ask?"

"Because I wanted to know why you were trying to protect me."

Xyon stared at him, then glanced around suspiciously. "Did someone send you here to ask me this just to annoy me or something?"

"No."

"Then why are you asking me something this stupid?"

"It's not stupid," Moke said a bit heatedly, and this time Xyon was almost positive there were clouds in his eyes. But once again, they abated.

"Okay, fine, it's not stupid." Xyon, shaking his head, picked up the chips and headed over to the repair station. Moke followed after him like a puppy.

"You didn't answer my question."

"That's probably because it wasn't much of a question." He dumped the chips into the main slot of the repair station. They tumbled down, making a satisfyingly loud clattering.

"It's not—"

"I protected you because I wasn't about to just let you die," Xyon said in exasperation.

"Why not?"

Xyon turned and stared at him. "What do you mean, why not?"

"I mean, why not?" Moke shrugged. "You've got no reason to like me, or care about anything that happens to me. If I were dead, I wouldn't be a problem for you anymore."

"You," Xyon said, pointing a finger at him, "have an overinflated sense of importance."

"What does that mean?"

"It means you're not a problem for me."

"But . . ." Moke looked utterly bewildered. "Don't you see me as a threat? 'Cause you're really Mac's son, but he adopted me, and we're . . ."

"Kid," Xyon said with a heavy sigh. He rested a hand on Moke's shoulder. "You want my opinion, for what it's worth? You've got some serious problems to work out in your head. Problems involving where you were, and where you're going to be, and what you think your place in the world is. For as long as I'm hanging around here . . . or, for that matter, for as long as we're stuck here . . . I'm willing to help you as much as I can in sorting it all out. There's just one thing you have to keep in mind."

"What?"

He leaned forward until he and Moke were almost nose-to-nose, and then he said with an intensely grave face, "I'm sort of an asshole."

That prompted Moke to burst out laughing, Xyon to smile, and Chief Mitchell to snap out a comment about how engineering was no place to just stand about laughing over nothing.

ii.

"What are you working on?"

The question mightily startled Xy, who had been intensely involved in his work in sickbay. He had been walking past the table where the insensate Tania Tobias had been lying, studying the test results of the project he'd been working on on the captain's behalf. He wasn't expecting Tania to snap out of her comatose state with no warning at all and address him in so casual a manner . . . or any manner.

He turned in place so fast that he almost tripped, although his reflexes were far too good to allow that to happen. Sure enough, there was Tania staring at him, her gentle brown eyes looking slightly amused at his discomfiture. Naturally she was still locked into place on the diagnostic table. However, he could see even from where he was standing that all her vitals looked completely normal.

Taking a step toward her, he said cautiously, "Tobias? Are you . . . quite all right?"

She tilted her head back to get her own view of the diagnostics. "Well, those would seem to indicate I am, yes. Can I get up now, please?"

"*Dr. Selar!*" Xy called. In sickbay, under circumstances such as these, he would never think of calling out to her with "Mother!" Professional surroundings called for professional deportment and professional address.

The summons was still sufficient to draw Selar over. Her face was an obvious question of "What did you need me for?" but she didn't have to voice it. She saw Tania Tobias staring at her with a cocked eyebrow reminiscent of Selar's own lifted brow at times of uncertainty.

"Hello, Doctor," she said. "Request permission to return to duty?"

"Denied," Selar replied.

Xy looked astounded. "What? But Mo . . . but Doctor," he quickly corrected himself. "On what grounds do we keep her here? Her vitals are all back to normal."

"So it appears."

Without a word, Selar went over to Tobias and began studying the indicators on the wall. Not only that, but she pulled out a medical tricorder as if she wasn't willing to depend entirely on the scanners. Her face, as always, remained impassive. But Xy knew her too well. There was that hint of frustration in her eyes that always surfaced whenever something medically unusual was occurring and she didn't have a clue as to how to deal with it. Tania said nothing, choosing to keep a respectful silence as Selar went about her work.

Finally the Vulcan doctor stepped back and studied

Tania with an air that suggested she believed Tania had engaged in some sort of practical joke. "You appear perfectly normal," said Selar.

The comment sounded almost accusatory, so much so that Tania contritely said, "Sorry."

"Apologies are not necessary."

With brisk efficiency, Selar undid the restraints and Tania sat up, shaking out her arms. She swung her legs around and over the table and flexed her feet to get the blood circulating. Xy continued to stare at her. She returned his gaze and flashed a smile. "It's all right," she said. "I'm feeling much better now."

"But we still don't know what was wrong with you," replied Xy.

"I'm sure it was nothing serious."

Selar eyed her suspiciously. "You made pronouncements while you were in your 'coma' that were eerily prescient."

"Oh, I'm sure I didn't."

"We heard them," said Xy.

"Did I shout out random phrases that could have had any number of meanings?"

Xy and Selar exchanged a look. "I suppose that's one way of describing it," Xy admitted.

"Well, then! It was nothing. Are we on main shift?"

"Yes."

"Then I'd better get up to my post . . ."

"You are going no such place," Selar told her firmly. "You are remaining here for observation."

"Dr. Selar, I assure you, that's not necessary," Tania said.

"And you base that assessment on your many years of medical research?"

Tania scowled. "Obviously not. But . . ."

"No. There is no 'but' at the end of that sentence," Selar told her firmly. "Need I remind you—and apparently, I do indeed have to—that a crewman returning to duty is not a given. Any crewman who has been disabled requires my certification that they are fit to return to their normal post. Your collapse is entirely without known cause, and I cannot possibly predict when, or if, there will be a recurrence. Under those circumstances, I would be derelict in my duty as CMO to send you back to your post at ops. The captain requires someone he can rely on, not someone who is a threat to fly apart for no discernible reason. Have I made myself clear, Lieutenant?" When Tania didn't respond immediately, Selar prompted, "Lieutenant?"

"Very clear, Doctor."

"Good." She pointed to the isolation ward, a sectioned-off part of sickbay used for extended observation. Without a word, Tania headed off toward it, walking in the gingerly manner of someone who hasn't used their leg muscles for a while.

Selar watched her go, then turned her attention back to Xy. Her eyebrows knitted as she glanced at the work he was carrying. "And what are you up to?" she demanded.

"Trying to develop something that may kill the captain."

"Let me know how that goes," replied Selar, as she turned and headed back to the observation ward.

Xy watched her go, and then his gaze settled on Tania. She was staring out at him from behind the enclosed partition. There was a sadness in her expression, but also a quiet sense of resolve. She knew this was only temporary. *They can't hold me here forever.*

She blinked at the same time that Xy did, and he backpedaled, confused and concerned. He had no idea whether that last thought had been his own . . . or if he'd picked it up from Tania. Except, despite his Vulcan heritage, he'd never shown any proclivity for telepathy.

Which meant either he was imagining it . . . or there was a new wrinkle in his mind . . . or Tania's mind had somehow connected with his and she had been the one to initiate the contact.

Xy stared at her, but Tania quickly turned away from him, leaving him staring at her back and resolving to do some serious research into the background of one Tania Tobias.

Space Station Bravo

i.

"I hate men."

It was Robin Lefler who had spoken at that particular moment, but at that point all she was doing was echoing the earlier-stated sentiments of the other two women in the room. The room, in this instance, was Elizabeth Shelby's quarters. The get-together had moved from the more formal environs of her office to the more leisurely, laid-back surroundings of her quarters.

They had kicked off their boots and let down their hair . . . in Mueller's case, literally. Her long blond hair, usually tied back, hung down to her shoulders and occasionally obscured her face. In the earlier part of the evening as the drinking had commenced, she had endeavored to brush it out of her line of sight. By this point, she wasn't even bothering, allowing it to hang in her face while she endeavored to look between the strands.

Shelby was draped over her bed, while Mueller was slumped back in a chair. Robin Lefler had thrown herself across the couch, and was staring with intense fascination into the glass of Orion whiskey she was nursing. "I *hate* men," she repeated.

"Any particular men?" asked Shelby.

"The ones I know."

"Oh, okay. Well . . . at least it's not all men, then."

Shelby was feeling a pleasant buzzing in her head. She suspected the other two were feeling it as well. She knew better than to drink so much that she would be unable to function should an emergency come up. The joy of synthehol, of course, was that one could shake off the effects at a moment's notice. Genuine alcohol, such as what they were drinking now—a gift from Shelby's loving husband the last time he'd come by—required far more moderation. It was a fine line and she had no intention of crossing it.

As for Mueller, the woman absorbed alcohol the way black holes absorbed light. Shelby had no idea how much liquor Kat had consumed, but she didn't appear to be in the least bit diminished.

Lefler, on the other hand, was completely hammered. Propping herself up on her elbow, she looked up blearily at Kat and asked, her speech slightly slurred, "What was I just talking about?"

"Men," Kat reminded her.

"Oh. Right. Men." She flopped back down, resting her head on her biceps. "I hate Henri L'Ecole, who talks to me like I'm an idiot. I hate Xyon for causing all the problems with Kalinda. And more than any of them, I have a deep, abiding, unforgettable, immortal hatred for . . ." She blinked like an owl in daylight. "What's his name?"

"Si Cwan? Your husband?"

"Right." She pointed at Shelby, who had just spoken. "That guy. Any woman has to be totally insane to become involved with Si Cwan in any way, shape, or form."

Mueller pointedly cleared her throat. Shelby, in spite of her foul mood, smiled, knowing that Mueller had been briefly involved with Si Cwan.

It seemed that Lefler had forgotten, though, for she misunderstood Mueller's throat-clearing noise, pointed at the *Trident* captain, and said, "See? She agrees with me."

"Whatever you say, Robin," Mueller said politely.

The women had been talking almost nonstop since congregating in Shelby's quarters. Now, though, silence fell, and with it a general black mood that matched Shelby's own. She rolled back on the bed, her legs crossed at the ankles, her arms flung to either side.

Shelby said, "So this is what command comes down to. This is what having power means. Lying around, doing nothing, because someone in a higher position of command than you tells you to stay put."

"I know what you mean," said Lefler. "What's the point of having authority and power if you can't command someone to blow up someone else whenever you feel like."

"No point at all," Shelby said. She closed her eyes and stared with fascination at the insides of her eyelids. "God, I miss him. I miss Mac so much, and I want to go help him, but I can't. I can't because I have to sit here with my high rank and not accomplish a damned thing."

"At least you have a rank," Lefler reminded her.

"So do you."

"Yeah, but I mean at least you have responsibilities to go *with* the rank. I had responsibilities, but now I've got nothing, thanks to my husband, whom I hate. And now I have to sit around and wait until new responsibilities are assigned to me. By a man."

"Who you'll hate," Mueller reminded her.

"Well, not at the moment, but once I meet him, sure."

"You could," Shelby pointed out, "get your new assignment from a woman. Would that help?"

"No, it wouldn't help!" Lefler said in exasperation. She tried to sit up, but her eyes spun in their sockets and she flopped back down again. Her battered sense of dignity prompted her to pretend that she'd intended for that to happen. "It wouldn't help because I should be helping Si Cwan . . ."

"Just like I should be helping Mac," said Shelby.

Lefler managed a nod, which was not an easy thing since the room was determined to spin around when she did it. "Instead he ships me off like I'm . . . I'm . . ."

"A woman?" suggested Mueller.

"Excess baggage."

"And isn't that typical of men?" Mueller said. Disdaining a glass, she simply took a slug of the whiskey straight out of the bottle. "To regard women as excess baggage? A convenience but little more."

Shelby lay there for a time and then, still staring up at the ceiling, she said, "No."

"No?" Mueller seemed intrigued by the disagreement.

"No." She forced herself to sit up. "What are we talking about here? Making sweeping generalizations about men, as if all of any group—men, women, humans, whatever—are all the same. And we're only doing it as some sort of a . . . a group exercise in delusion. Pretending *en masse* that we don't care about the men in our lives when the fact is that we're as miserable as we are because we care so much. So who do we think we're fooling?"

"You certainly had me going," said Mueller.

Shelby made a dismissive gesture. "Knock it off, Kat. It's nonsense, and you know it's nonsense. And you're just egging us on because you don't have a man or a serious relationship in your life, and it's bothering the hell out of you."

"The lack of relationships in my life is not bothering the hell out of me," Kat replied. "It's a matter of choice. Of necessity."

"Oh, bull. It's only 'necessary' because you choose to make it so." She suddenly became hyperaware of the fact that the space station was turning in a slow orbit. This was routine, of course, and the rotation was so gradual that one couldn't feel it any more than they could sense the turn of a planet. Now, though, she was feeling positively dizzy. She forced herself to continue speaking, even though the words sounded heavy in her mouth. "You're the one who decided that captaincy requires isolation and loneliness. Mac and I were both captains, and neither of us felt the need to be isolated."

"Yes. And look how that turned out."

Shelby's gaze hardened. She pointed a finger and said, "Get out."

To her surprise, Mueller actually looked contrite. "Admiral, I . . . apologize for that remark, it was . . ."

"Go!" snapped Shelby, refusing to be mollified. She continued to point in a commanding fashion. "Go! Right now!"

"But—"

"Go! That's an order!"

Without another word, Mueller rose, bowed slightly, and then headed in the direction that Shelby was indicating. The door slid open and Mueller stepped through, letting the door close behind her.

The door opened once more and Kat reentered. Before Shelby could say anything, Mueller spoke with quiet intensity. "You know what we should do? We should just say to hell with it. We should just go after them. The three of us commiserating and being depressed and feeling helpless . . . you know what it is?"

"A waste of material?"

Mueller pointed at Shelby and then touched the tip of her own nose. "Exactly. Exactly right, Elizabeth. A damned waste of fine material. And of resources."

"She's right, y'know," said Lefler, who was working extremely hard to put coherent syllables together. "How're we s'posed to be serving Starfleet to the best of our considerable abilities when we're perfectly content to sit around on our assets."

"Who says we're 'content'?" demanded Shelby.

"I know I didn't."

"Nor did I," said Mueller. "How can it remotely be considered a reasonable use of resources, dispatching the *Trident* to transport passengers hither and yon, when we can be so much more. When we *should* be so much more."

"It's a disservice. It's wrong," Lefler said.

Shelby nodded thoughtfully. "My father always taught me that, when I see a wrong occurring, I had a moral imperative to try and make things right."

"Yes!" Mueller declared. "A moral imperative! That's what this is! Your father was absolutely right."

"He always was. Or at least he always said he always was." She considered the matter further. "Here's what we should do." The other women leaned forward, Lefler almost toppling over, to hear her next words. "I should take command of the *Trident* . . . which I'm within my rights to do, as a ranking officer. You might, of course, take offense at that . . ."

"And yet, somehow, I don't," Mueller deadpanned.

"I inform the ambassadors to Ares IV that we're going to arrange alternate transportation for them."

"Let 'em walk!" slurred Lefler.

"Then I take the *Trident* back into Sector 221-G, we find Mac, we sort out this business with the Priatians, and we get this stupid civil war under control before matters go from bad to worse."

"Hear, hear!" Lefler cried out, raising her glass and causing liquid to slosh out the sides. She didn't appear to notice.

"That, Admiral, is one hell of a damned fine plan," said Mueller before yawning loudly.

"Yeah? I'll tell you what kind of plan it is," Shelby said. "It's the kind of plan where, when you wake up in the morning, you say to yourself, 'What the hell was I thinking?' "

"I disagree."

"All right then," said Shelby, who felt ready to pass out. "Here's the plan. We sleep on it, and when the dawn comes, we're going to see things in an entirely different light."

"Sounds like a plan to me," Robin declared. Then she paused and frowned. "Wait . . . is this a different plan now? Or is it the same plan except kind of revised?"

"It's a plan to make a plan," Shelby told her.

"Hear, hear!" Robin tried to take another slug of the whiskey, but was less than successful as the glass bumped against the side of her face and the liquor spilled down her cheek. Instead of moaning or trying to wipe the liquor away, she simply laughed and pointed at it before yawning deeply and then slumping over to one side.

"Wow," said Shelby, staring at Robin's unmoving form. "She really can't hold her liquor, can she." At which point she rolled over, closed her eyes, and fell sound asleep.

Mueller studied the two of them. "All right, this is just disappointing," she said to no one. She emptied out the remainder of the bottle of whiskey, then leaned back in her chair and stared into space. Her mind went into a sort of Zen state as she contemplated the options presented her, weighed the possibilities, and realized that if they truly did undertake the endeavor being considered, it might well cost Shelby her rank. And perhaps Mueller, and even Lefler as well.

At that moment, she didn't especially care about that. All she cared about was not feeling the way she was feeling these days. She was tired of feeling lonely. She was tired of feeling helpless and out of control, the recent ugliness with Romeo Takahashi being only the latest example of that.

She felt as if this harebrained scheme might be her best shot at taking back control of her life. That she would be sending a message not only to Starfleet, but to herself, that Kat Mueller could be as wild, as unpredictable, as . . . as . . .

. . . as Mackenzie Calhoun. Well, that was it, wasn't it. Even when he was gone—possibly forever—the long reach of the way he conducted himself remained the standard for sheer ludicrous bravado that any commanding officer worth his or her salt could not help but emulate.

Kat Mueller believed in efficiency. In organization. In order. Now, though, she was contemplating tossing all that aside . . . so that she could believe in herself.

It seemed a worthwhile trade to her, and that was the last thing that filtered through her mind before she drifted off to sleep.

Hours later, when Elizabeth Shelby woke up, her mouth felt as if it had been stuffed with cotton wads.

She tried to sit up, moaned softly, and flopped back on the bed.

As soft as the moan was, it was sufficient to awaken Lefler, who sat up violently and then clutched at her head and slumped back onto the couch. Mueller, for her part, was sitting perfectly upright in a lotus position. As she became aware that there was movement in the room, her eyelids fluttered for a moment and then opened. Her eyes had rolled up into their sockets but now returned to their normal position and focused on Shelby.

There was dead silence that was finally broken by the admiral.

"I'm not ready to mourn my husband."

"Nor I," said Mueller. "Nor am I ready to do nothing in a situation where my doing something could have positive consequences."

"And I'm . . ." Lefler started to speak, then winced at the volume of her own voice and continued in a whisper, "And I'm not ready to just let my husband shunt me aside."

"So essentially," Shelby observed, "the dawn has come, which should be the time that we see things in a new and more sensible light . . . and yet we're still talking about ignoring Starfleet orders up one side and down the other, and potentially throwing away our careers. Where's our common sense? Where's our belief in the righteousness of the chain of command? Has Mackenzie Calhoun's cowboy mentality infected all of us? What, ladies, is the answer here?"

They pondered it for a time, and then Mueller

noted, "It occurs to me that there's no such thing as 'dawn' on a space station."

Shelby considered that and then a slow smile spread across her face. "That's good enough for me," she said.

ii.

Ambassador Julian Fox and his entourage were standing on the bridge of the *Trident*, waiting for the return of her captain. Fox came from a long and proud line of ambassadors. He was broad-shouldered, square-jawed, and had drilled into him by his grandfather never to allow starship captains to give him any guff. His grandfather had had a run-in with no less a legend than James Kirk, and to hear Julian's grandfather tell it, the whole damned crew of the *Enterprise* would have been dead thanks to Kirk's recklessness if he, Grandfather, had not stepped in and taken control of the situation. Julian Fox was determined to follow that fine example set by his forebears.

Fox folded his arms and said brusquely to Commander Desma, "This is intolerable. We need to be on our way to Ares IV. Where is Captain Mueller?"

"My understanding," Desma said carefully, "is that she's in conference with Admiral Shelby."

"Still? She's been there for . . . what? Twelve hours? Thirteen?"

"Apparently they have a good deal to discuss," said Desma.

Suddenly the turbolift door slid open and Mueller strode out. Then Desma saw who was behind her and immediately she was on her feet, calling out, "Admiral on the bridge!"

Instantly everyone stood as Shelby walked onto the bridge of the *Trident*. She smiled as if she found the entire thing quite amusing. "Well, this is a new experience. If you'd jumped to your feet like this while I was captain here, I might never have taken the promotion. At ease." Everyone began to sit, and then she immediately added, "Except you, Hash."

Takahashi remained standing, his brow furrowed, as everyone else sat. She walked toward him and stopped a foot away. "You're putting in for a transfer?"

He looked uncomfortable. "Yes, Admiral, but I don't see how—"

"—it's my business? Well, since I oversee the sector you're currently in, it crosses my desk first. And I stuck it in a drawer." His jaw dropped as she continued, "You have problems with your CO? You damn well work them out. I appointed you to this position because I think you're an asset to this vessel, and you have been, and you will continue to be. You leave when I say so, and no sooner. Got that?"

"Admiral, with all respect—" Hash began.

"We can discuss this in more detail later."

"Later?" said Ambassador Fox with curiosity. "Are you going with the *Trident* to Ares IV, Admiral?"

"No, Ambassador Fox, I'm not. But, as it so happens, neither are you."

"What? I . . ." He glanced at the two aides who had

accompanied him, but they simply stared blankly back at him. They had no more clue than he did what she was talking about. "I don't understand."

"You're getting off here," Shelby said patiently. "The *Stingray* is going to be along within the next twenty-four hours. I've arranged for her to bring you to Ares IV."

"The *Stingray*? I'm not familiar with that starship . . ."

"That's because she's a cargo vessel."

"*What?*"

"Crew of twelve, room for two passengers, so it might be a little tight. But the crew's friendly. Just don't play cards with them or you won't have a credit left to your name."

"This . . . this is an outrage!" sputtered Fox. "You can't do this!"

"And yet it's done."

"Captain!" Fox turned to Mueller. "This is your ship! Certainly you're not going to stand by and—"

Mueller spoke in a tone so conversational she might have been relating a tale about a date that had gone horribly wrong in her teen years. "As it turns out, Admiral Shelby has assumed command of the *Trident*. I'm afraid I don't have anything to say in the matter."

"Oh really," said Fox. His hand rested on the command chair. "Well, as it turns out, I do. And I would venture to say that Starfleet will have something to say about it as well."

"I venture to say you're right," replied Mueller. "And you can tell them all about it en route to Ares IV.

Lieutenant Arex, escort the ambassador and his party to the transporter. I have a yeoman bringing your belongings to the transporter room even as we speak, Ambassador, so you needn't worry you'll be leaving anything behind."

"We are not going anywhere!" said Fox, remembering the lessons of his grandfather. "I demand that you contact Starfleet Command this instant so that they can set you straight on what your priorities are supposed to be!"

"Ambassador," Shelby said with clearly waning patience, "you have a choice here. You can either head down to the transporter room willingly, be beamed over to Bravo Station, and continue on your way to Ares IV without embarrassing yourself any further. Or I can order Captain Mueller to have the transporter room beam you directly out of here to Bravo Station. Now what's it going to be?"

Fox said nothing, being too busy trembling with silent indignation.

Shelby shrugged, turned, and nodded to Mueller. Mueller tapped her combadge and said, "Captain to transporter room. Lock on to—"

"All right!"

Doing everything he could to maintain his dignity, Fox headed for the turbolift, Arex leading the way. He stepped in, turned to Shelby, and snapped, "There's just one thing I want you to know, Admiral. You—"

At which point the lift doors slid shut, cutting off the rest of what he was about to say.

The bridge crew looked at Shelby, and then Mick

Gold said from conn, "Setting course for Sector 221-G, I take it, Admiral?"

"You take it correctly, Mr. Gold."

"Aye, Capt . . . sorry," Gold quickly amended, looking chagrined. "I meant Admiral . . ."

"Oh, don't be too hard on yourself, Mr. Gold," said Shelby with a heavy sigh. "By the time Starfleet is through with me, you may well wind up outranking me."

New Thallon

i.

Kalinda felt growing discomfort as she moved through the wreckage of buildings and bodies that constituted the town of Gravis, a smaller suburb outside the capital city of New Thallon. It had been pounded particularly hard by the shelling that Fhermus had unleashed upon the planet, and it was a picture of misery and sadness.

The discomfort she was feeling had little to do with the misery she was encountering in the form of homeless or wounded (or both) Thallonians. They looked up at her with begging, pleading eyes, and they asked for whatever succor she could provide. The requests were for everything from food and water to the simple touching of the hem of her garment as a means of drawing strength. She granted the latter because it cost her nothing, although the proximity to the dying or wounded creatures put her on edge.

But the main aspect of her discomfort lay with Si Cwan.

They had separately surveyed damaged parts of the region, but Si Cwan had insisted on going out once more, and further insisted that she accompany him. She had tried to talk her way out of it, but Si Cwan had been quietly insistent. He was resolute in his belief that her people wanted and needed to see her. That her presence would go a long way toward buoying the battered Thallonian spirit.

"Shouldn't you be busy planning retaliation?" she had demanded.

"I am," he had assured her. "But it's important not to lose sight of the damage that's already been done. We need to buoy the people's spirits, Kally, and a mutual visit to the citizenry is the best way to accomplish that." Unable to find any way to talk him out of it, she graciously acceded to his request . . . which was really more of an order than a request, but she chose not to make an issue out of it.

The sun beat down upon them and the weather was parched. Kalinda didn't do especially well in heat, but she did everything she could to cope with it. Trying not to stumble, she stepped gingerly over fallen chunks of debris, occasionally having to balance in ludicrously ridiculous postures. She spoke to each and every individual who approached her, no matter how wretched and pathetic they were. She listened to their unhappy tales of how they were simply minding their own business, and all of a sudden their long-standing homes were no longer standing. She did her best to console them and assure them that they would be avenged, no matter how long it took or how costly the campaign that was to come.

The entire time, though, she was convinced that

Si Cwan was watching her every move. Even when he appeared to be looking elsewhere, she felt as if his eyes were upon her. But whenever they made eye contact, Si Cwan smiled at her warmly and nodded in approval of how she was handling things.

At one point he walked over to her as she was comforting a small boy, still weeping for his lost parents. "You're doing well, Kalinda," he said.

"Am I?" She stroked the child's bald pate. "You seem to be . . . I don't know . . . watching me with great concern."

"Only in the sense that I hope this isn't all too stressful for you."

A worker came over and extended her arms to the boy. Kalinda gently urged the child toward her, then turned back to Si Cwan. "It's a bit late to worry about the stress it may have on me, isn't it? I mean, if that happened to be a serious consideration, you wouldn't have brought me here in the first place."

He looked at her askance. "Are you saying you're not up for it? Kalinda, I've never known you to flinch from a challenge."

"No, of course not. I never have," she said quickly. She rubbed the bridge of her nose and forced a smile. "I'm sorry. I just . . . I haven't been sleeping well lately."

"Since the attack?"

"Yes. Exactly."

He stepped toward her, looking very concerned, and draped an arm around her shoulder. "Are you seeing them?"

"Them?" she asked.

"The dead, I mean." He waited for her to respond, but when she gave him merely a slightly befuddled look, he prompted her. "It certainly wouldn't be unusual for you, what with your sensitivity toward such things."

"No, it wouldn't be unusual," she conceded quickly.

"Can you see them now?"

She looked across the terrain before them, with its shelled-out structures and citizens with haunted looks. "Yes. Of course I can see them. Can't you?"

"I mean the dead."

"The dea—"

Kalinda immediately stopped talking. Instead she closed her eyes, reaching down, down into the recesses of the cerebral cortex that she had emulated. *The wretched creature buried it. How did she manage to bury it? She can actually commune with the deceased. Hear them, see them. See the energy auras that they've left behind them. Something that important . . . how was she able to keep it from me?*

"Of course I can," she said, hoping that so little time had passed between Si Cwan's question and her response that he wouldn't have noticed it. She looked out at the vista in front of them. Nothing. No spirits, no shambling corpses on the run from some sort of sphere from the beyond. She knew intellectually what she was supposed to be seeing, but she could perceive nothing.

But Si Cwan was looking at her expectantly.

"So sad," she whispered. "Such . . . sadness. Look at them. Many of them . . . cut down in their prime.

Doing no one any harm, and . . . and this is what happened to them."

"What do they want?"

"Revenge," Kalinda assured him. "They want revenge upon those who did this to them. Revenge on Fhermus. Revenge on all of them."

"And they shall have it," Si Cwan said firmly. "Let them know. Let them all know . . . they shall be avenged."

She smiled at him graciously. "They can hear you . . . or perhaps sense your dedication. They are grateful to you, Si Cwan. Ever so grateful for your steadfastness. And they're counting on you to do right by them."

"They needn't be concerned. The scales to be balanced are in good hands." He patted her on the shoulder. "Let's go home."

Letting out a sigh of relief, she followed Si Cwan. As she did so, she cast a final glance behind her at the little boy whom she had been comforting. Although he was being led away in the other direction, his gaze was still fixed upon her. And she noticed for the first time that there was fear in his eyes as he watched her.

Children are so difficult to fool, she thought. *I must remind myself to track that boy down and kill him before he says anything.*

ii.

Into the late evening hours, Si Cwan sat in his chambers, staring at the far wall. Thoughts swirled in his mind like a cyclone. He had already determined what to do about the current situation and had moved beyond that into determining what the likely repercussions were going to be due to his actions.

He closed his eyes for a moment, summoning his inner strength and force of will. Then he sent word through his aides that he would like his sister to join him.

Some minutes later, Kalinda entered, rubbing her eyes, her gossamer robe draped carelessly around herself. "You summoned me, my brother . . . ?"

She looked around toward his accustomed place, the mat upon which he often sat cross-legged and in deep contemplation. He wasn't there. She entered, the door shutting behind her, and just as she was about to speak again, she suddenly felt the touch of a sharp blade against her throat. She gasped, intaking her breath, and the blade pushed against it more firmly.

From almost at her ear, Si Cwan's voice whispered, "I believe you need to be disabused of a notion you may be holding."

"My . . . my brother, what—?"

"Stop calling me that, or I swear I'll cut your head off even if it means you can tell me nothing."

Obediently she shut her mouth.

He stepped forward a foot or two so that he was now within her peripheral vision. He was holding a long, fierce blade by the ornate handle. "This has been in my family for generations," he said conversationally. "A bit antiquated by today's standards of weaponry, I know. But it has spilt the blood of many an enemy of the House of Cwan. And since you may be among the greatest of enemies we've ever encountered, I thought it appropriate that you should face it as well."

She managed to force a nervous chuckle. Making sure not to address him as "brother," she said, "Are you . . . are you still asleep, and caught in the throes of some sort of nightmare . . . ?"

"A nightmare, yes, assuredly that," said Cwan, "but very much a waking one. Not that your disguise isn't brilliant. It is. Nevertheless, the only reason it fooled me for as long as it did was because others saw through it first. I refused to believe that others could possibly know my sister better than I. That others . . . particularly Xyon . . . could penetrate your imposture with facility, while I was fooled. I was determined to prove that I was right and he was wrong, even at the cost of lives. The lives of Fhermus's son, of Ankar, of my people helpless before an onslaught that you aided and abetted."

"I . . . I don't know what you're . . . ackkkk." The sword had now pressed firmly enough against her neck that she was aware of a faint trickle of blood dribbling down her throat. Wisely, she made no effort to reach up and brush it away.

"And I continued to deny that I could possibly be taken in, even though my own wife tried to point it out to me," he continued as if she hadn't tried to interrupt. "Such was the height of my towering ego. But she is gone now, and Ankar is gone . . . whether he was a dupe or a willing accomplice, I cannot be certain. Xyon

is gone. It is very quiet here, like a mausoleum, everyone walking softly lest they tempt the wrath of our
enemies. And with all the quiet, I've had time and distance to give the matter much thought, and to realize
the string of incidents which make no sense. Then
when I watched you closely today, I could tell you were
attempting desperate fabrications. The way my sister
acts when the dead are about . . . it's like nothing else.
As if she's in a waking trance. You brought nothing to
your disguise with that little attempt. You couldn't even
begin to approximate the way she acts at such times, as
if she's slipped a little into the land of the dead herself."

"Si Cwan, this . . . this is madness . . ."

"Yes. Madness that I didn't see it for what it was
sooner. You disabled our planetary defense system
somehow. It wasn't poor, pathetic Topez Anat. You did
something, Kalinda, or whatever your true name is.
And I want to know who and what you are, and what
you've done with Kalinda."

Kalinda made no response . . . at least, not orally.
But she dropped all pretense, looking at Si Cwan with
a glare of unbridled hatred.

"Was it the Priatians?" demanded Si Cwan. "That's
it, isn't it. This is some plot of the Priatians to . . ."

Si Cwan was so focused on her face and upper
body that he didn't even notice the slight movement
below her waist until it was too late. But suddenly
there was something long and slender and fast-moving
emerging from beneath her shimmering robe. It batted the sword away from her throat, sending it clattering across the room. For a heartbeat, Si Cwan was

caught off guard, and that was when Kalinda's arms morphed into tentacles, gray and slimy and dripping.

He had known he was dealing with something that wasn't Kalinda. That didn't stop him from being caught flat-footed. One tentacle lashed around his arm, the other around his leg, and Kalinda threw him across the room. He landed with a shuddering crash at the far end.

"You," she informed him, "have proven far more trouble than you're worth."

There were other tentacles emerging from beneath her gown as well. She glided forward, the lower tentacles making soft, sucking noises as they propelled her across the floor. Kalinda reached out and snagged the fallen sword. She lifted it up and examined it thoughtfully, whipping it back and forth. "A fine blade," she commented.

Si Cwan scrambled to his feet, balancing himself, ready to move in any direction. Even as she swung the sword, Kalinda grabbed a nearby heavy chair and hurled it at Si Cwan. He vaulted to the right, landing with a shoulder roll, and came up to one knee just as Kalinda swung the sword straight at his face.

Si Cwan, in a move so fast that Kalinda didn't even see it, slammed his palms together. It was perfectly timed. Kalinda's eyes widened when she saw that Si Cwan had caught the blade in his hands, momentarily immobilizing it.

"That's mine," snarled Si Cwan. He made no effort to twist the blade out of her grasp; she was, after all, holding it in a tentacle, and he correctly realized that the sword would simply turn in her grasp while she continued to hold it. Instead, taking a huge risk, he lunged and grabbed at the sword hilt. The tentacles grabbed at him, trying to pull him off, and their strength was formidable. It was all Si Cwan could do to hang on, struggling mightily.

"What did you do to her?" Si Cwan howled in fury. "Tell me!"

"Why would I do that?" Kalinda said contemptuously.

Still Si Cwan refused to let go. There were tentacles wrapping around both his legs, around his arm, around his throat. The ones below him were prepared to tear him apart, break him like a wishbone; the ones above were starting to choke off his air. He gasped, gagged, and still his hand held tightly to the sword hilt as if it were his last salvation.

"Why?" Kalinda asked again. "When it is far preferable to have you die in ignor—"

The world was graying out around Si Cwan, and strength surged through him that may well have been his body's last-ditch effort to keep him alive. Just as Kalinda was about to rip him in half, Si Cwan twisted the sword around, overriding Kalinda's strength through sheer, furious desperation and determination. The sword sliced around and neatly bisected the tentacle that had been wrapped around Si Cwan's throat.

Kalinda let out a scream that did not remotely sound like it was coming from a Thallonian throat. The truncated tentacle thrashed about on the floor, while a comically waving stump jetted a thin stream of green liquid.

The shock caused her to ease her grip on the sword ever so slightly, and it was all that Si Cwan required. He yanked it completely clear of the tentacle wrapped around it, and swung the blade in a blindingly fast arc. It cut through the tentacles wrapped around his legs, freeing them. Kalinda screeched again as Si Cwan dropped to the floor. The viscous green fluid was everywhere now, covering the floor, making it slippery and hazardous for Si Cwan to navigate. On his back, he rolled out of the way as two of the still-attached tentacles came crashing down on where he'd just been. The floor shattered beneath the impact as Si Cwan regained his feet and backed up against the wall.

Kalinda was bent over, moaning, clutching at her bleeding stumps with the still-functioning tentacles. She twisted her head around and snarled in inarticulate rage at Si Cwan, her face twisted in hatred.

He pulled a disruptor from his belt and, sword still in one hand, he kept the gun leveled with the other. "I didn't want to use this on you," he snarled. "You're an alien species and I have no idea what it'll do to you. It might kill you, and I want you alive. For proof and for questioning."

"Go to hell, Cwan," Kalinda snapped. "I'll be neither for you!"

She moved quickly, and Si Cwan braced himself for another assault. But she headed in the other direction, slamming into the large, ornate window inset into the far wall. It shattered under the impact and Kalinda vaulted toward the newly created opening.

Cursing himself for his slowness, Si Cwan fired off

a shot with the disruptor. It struck Kalinda in the back, pitching her forward out the window. Si Cwan charged forward, leaping effortlessly over the large puddle of green fluid, and stopped at the opening. He held his weapon at the ready, glancing right, left, up, and down.

All that was out there was a vast spread of grass, shadows stretching out into the night.

Si Cwan leaped through and landed catlike ten feet below. From the ground, he spun and looked up at the roof to make sure that Kalinda—or whatever the hell she was—hadn't taken refuge up there.

No sign of her.

Then he saw spots of green fluid on the ground in front of him, and immediately he started to run. There was no better hunter, no better tracker, on all of New Thallon. If it was at all possible to trail Kalinda, Si Cwan would be able to accomplish it.

That was when the first drops of water from above hit Si Cwan in the face. "Oh no," he muttered, but he kept running. The ground was a blur beneath his feet, yet he kept managing to pick out the green drops of liquid that marked his prey's trail. And as the rain started to come down harder, the words *Faster, faster* hammered through his mind.

His arms like pistons, his legs scissoring, Si Cwan was moving faster than he ever had in his life. But it wasn't fast enough. The sky above him ripped open with an ear-shattering blast of thunder, and the rain began to come down in torrents. Si Cwan kept running. When seconds passed by without the slightest hint of green blood on the ground, he still didn't slow, but he began to feel a sense of growing despair. Finally, long minutes having gone by without the slightest trace of her, Si Cwan came to a halt. He sucked in deep breaths of air, and then threw his arms to either side and screamed his frustrations to the gods. If they were there and they heard him, they didn't especially care. Instead they sent a solid wall of rain down upon him, soaking him to the skin, making it impossible for him to see much of anything, much less a trail of blood that had been washed away.

Furious beyond belief, Si Cwan trudged back to the palace. There he discovered stunned servants, summoned by the screams of the false Kalinda. They were looking at the tossed- around furniture, the shattered window, and the large pool of whatever-it-was that had soaked the floor. They were even more startled when Si Cwan climbed back in through the window. "Everyone out," he snapped. "Send in some medical investigators. I want this . . . material," and he indicated the green liquid, "analyzed. I want to know what it is." When they stood there and stared at him, Si Cwan shouted, *"Now!"* That spurred them into movement.

Si Cwan eased himself off the sill back into the room. He stepped carefully over the thrown furniture, righting it, and making sure not to step into any of the green liquid. Then he tapped a panel of the wall and it slid aside, revealing a computer screen.

"Playback last ten minutes," he said.

He watched the video log of the previous ten minutes unspool on the computer screen. He had wanted to have the false Kalinda in hand when contacting Fhermus, but this was going to have to do: an indisputable record of his confrontation with the creature, including his battle with her and her escape into the night.

This was going to stop the war before it went any further. The notion cheered Si Cwan . . . but also filled him with a deep sense of lack of justice. Fhermus had assaulted the people of New Thallon. The blood of hundreds was upon him. And Si Cwan's response was going to be . . . what? To contact him and inform him that there would be no retaliation because Fhermus had been right all along?

How the hell was he going to face his own people? For that matter, how was he going to be able to face himself?

First things first. He had to face Fhermus. At least that would be via long distance.

iii.

Fhermus watched the confrontation that Si Cwan had recorded in his quarters with widening eyes. Si Cwan, via the slightly patchy but still viewable connection he had to the planet Nelkar upon which Fhermus was located, studied Fhermus in turn, trying to discern what sort of genuine reaction Fhermus was having to the shocking images.

It had not been easy getting a communication through to Fhermus. The man who now regarded himself as Si Cwan's archenemy had not initially wanted to speak to him at all. "The time for conversation is long past" was all his representatives would say at first. But Si Cwan had been insistent, even openly calling Fhermus a coward because he refused to receive Cwan's communiqué. That, as Si Cwan had suspected would be the case, was sufficient to bring Fhermus online, demanding to know what nonsense Si Cwan was wasting his time with now.

"We have both been duped," Si Cwan had told him without preamble, and sent through the images of his confrontation with his fake sister. Fhermus had watched the transmission, at first uncertain of what he was seeing, and then gaping in astonishment when Kalinda had begun to morph into something else. Without a word to Si Cwan, he had watched the entire thing through a second time, and then a third. Si Cwan said nothing to interrupt him.

Finally Fhermus looked directly into the screen, back out at Si Cwan. "Who else has seen this?" he asked.

"You are the first to whom I have sent it," Si Cwan replied.

"This is . . ." He shook his head. "This is shocking. This . . . creature . . . murdered my son? Is that what you're saying?"

"Obviously so," Si Cwan said. "It posed as Kalinda . . ."

"Do you have it in custody?"

"As you saw in the recording, it escaped out a

window. I was unable to retrieve it. But I am already putting hunting parties out to try and track it down."

"But why? I don't understand . . ."

"To bring us to war, Fhermus," Si Cwan said. "To pit us against one another in a civil war that would ideally cause us to annihilate each other's forces . . . thus allowing the Priatians to come sweeping in and regain all the territory they have longed for."

"Gods," whispered Fhermus.

"And I played right into it," said Si Cwan, unable to hide his bitterness and self-recrimination. "I didn't recognize it for what it was. If I had been more perceptive . . . hell, if I'd believed Xyon . . . none of this would have happened. The death of your son, the attack you launched upon New Thallon . . ."

"You are being too hard on yourself, Cwan."

"And you are being too generous, Fhermus."

Fhermus's voice hardened. "It is not the time now for recriminations, but for actions. The council has shattered; it is time that the fifty-seven races came together once more."

"Imagine the irony," Si Cwan said dryly. "Your bombs just so happened to miss the council chamber. What luck."

At first Fhermus didn't respond. Then he said, "My heart is as heavy on this matter as yours is, Cwan. I do not appreciate being duped any more than you do."

"Then we are in accord as to what must be done."

"Absolutely," said Fhermus. "I will contact my allies, as I am certain you will yours. We will set up a time to convene in the chamber, and we will plan our revenge upon the Priatians."

"We cannot simply go in and start bombing their homeworld, Fhermus," Si Cwan reminded him. "Kalinda is no doubt still there, and their prisoner."

"I am aware of that, Cwan. Kalinda is but a helpless pawn in this matter . . . as was my poor son. On behalf of his memory, the woman he loved must be retrieved alive and unharmed. I will not lose sight of that priority."

"It is good to know that, Fhermus."

"As annoying as it may be to admit, Lord Cwan," said Fhermus, "we are more effective working in unison than being at odds."

"I concur, Lord Fhermus," Si Cwan replied. "I most definitely concur."

The Spectre

i.

Soleta's first awareness was a dull thudding at the base of her skull. It was, to understate it, a most unpleasant sensation. She had the feeling that things weren't going to be improving tremendously for her as her return to consciousness progressed.

Slowly she opened her eyes. There was nothing but blackness. She squeezed her eyes shut, then opened and closed them again a few times before finally managing to make out some light. It wasn't because the room was dark, but rather because the impact from when she'd been struck in the head had rattled her brain and her optic nerves something fierce. It was taking a few minutes for her cranium to rewire itself so that normal sight would be available once more.

Even so, she was able to make out enough to realize that she had been stashed down in the brig. The forcefield was humming gently on either side of the door. She didn't bother to test its durability by throwing herself against it; she already had a good idea of what the result would be.

She discovered she was sitting on the floor. "The least they could have done was put me on the bed," she muttered as she gripped the edge of the bunk and pulled herself slowly up onto it.

Soleta leaned back, resting the back of her aching head against the wall. She entered a light meditative state, taking stock of her bodily processes and making sure that everything else was operating properly.

"Lucius," she moaned softly, "why the hell have you done this to yourself?"

She looked up at the com panel inset into the brig . . . there for convenience since, in a pinch, the brig doubled as guest quarters. The *Spectre* was built for stealth and espionage, not luxury.

"This . . . is going to be unpleasant," said Soleta as she reached up for the com panel.

ii.

In the command center of the *Spectre*, the mood was tense. Lucius sat in the command chair, watching the stars hurtle past them as they headed toward Romulan space.

The entire crew had been as one in their decision to take over the vessel from Soleta. Still, now that the deed was done, Lucius found that a couple of the crewmen were having trouble meeting his eyes whenever he happened to look at them. *Damn her,* he thought. *If only she'd been capable of stopping me. Why did I have to be right? If only . . .*

"Is there a problem, Aquila?" Lucius finally asked.

"Problem? No, Tribune, no problem . . ."

"That's good to hear. Anyone else having difficulties with the current situation?"

"Not . . . difficulties exactly, Tribune," Maurus spoke up.

"Well then what, exactly, Centurion?"

"I just . . ." Maurus looked down, his control panel suddenly very interesting to him. "I've never served on a vessel where we mutinied before. I . . . would not have thought it possible on a Romulan vessel."

"And had we a Romulan commander," Vitus spoke up, "it would not have happened here either. That's because a proper commander would have known where his loyalties lay, and acted in a proper manner. She was never one of us. Not really."

"But does that excuse . . . ?"

"Yes. It does," Lucius told him firmly, rising from the command chair, fighting off his sense of guilt, trying to purge her image from his mind. "Have you a desire to see your pregnant mate again, Maurus? Or did you really desire to float about in space indefinitely, an exile from our homeworld, serving the nomadic life that Soleta would have prescribed for you?"

"No, Tribune. I would not," said Maurus, still looking down.

Lucius was standing behind Maurus. Now he reached over and patted the young Romulan on the shoulder. "When we finally get home, and you see your mate and her belly swollen with your child, you will want to thank me. And my only response to that will be to remind you that 'Lucius' is a superb name for a youngster."

Maurus smiled at that in spite of himself.

But then Aquila said, "How will we know?"

"Know what?" asked Lucius.

"How will we know that we'll still be welcome on Romulus? They tried to destroy us, remember."

Vitus spoke up. "Because they didn't want this vessel in the hands of a half-breed with no loyalties to the Empire, now that the Praetor who commissioned her is no more. Our loyalties, however, stem from shared blood and shared heritage. Our loyalty will not be questioned. In fact, we'll be heroes." He nodded as if convincing himself. "Yes. Heroes to all. Kill us? They'll want to hold us up as examples of—"

"Tribune," Maurus suddenly said. "I'm receiving a communication."

"From one of our people?" asked Lucius, looking at the unwavering sea of stars before them.

"No, Tribune. From the captain. She's using the com link that's installed in the brig."

"I always meant to have that removed," he sighed. "All right. Put her on the overhead."

"You're on with her, Tribune."

Lucius leaned back in the command chair. "Soleta. Joining us back in the land of the living, are you?"

"So it appears. Although I must say that we all won't be residing in it for the same length of time, should you not rethink your rash actions immediately."

"Rethink?"

"Yes, Tribune, as in release me. We ascribe all this to a panicked move, put it behind us, and go on with our lives."

"Panicked?" Lucius cocked an eyebrow. The others looked amused. The notion of Lucius panicking was simply too silly to contemplate. "I assure you, Legate, that this move was well considered."

"So we're back to 'Legate' now, are we? And here I thought we had an understanding."

"Well, Legate, as is the case with many things, you appear to have thought wrong."

"Let me guess: You still intend to return with me to Romulus and utilize me as some sort of bargaining chip."

He nodded, even though naturally she could not see it. "Your deductive faculties remain undiminished."

"Considering your cowardly blow from behind, I'm fortunate my ability to speak remains undiminished."

Lucius shrugged. "Your 'cowardice' is my convenience."

"Indeed." She paused, and then something in her voice changed. When her voice filtered through again, there was something akin to pleading in it. *"Lucius . . . do not do this thing. Do not force me to retaliate."*

Everyone on the bridge laughed. Everyone, that is, except Maurus, who looked concerned. "Legate," said Lucius. "You're down in the brig. We're up in the bridge, and crewmen are throughout the ship. You're hardly in a position for retaliation. Although if you'd like, I can post a guard or two outside the brig in order to make you feel more of a threat. I hadn't bothered since the force screen is quite secure and we don't have a lot of men to spare."

"*Lucius . . . I'm serious here. You don't know what you've done. You don't know what you're about to unleash. I'm giving you a chance now to do the right thing.*"

"Legate," he sighed, "that's what you don't seem to comprehend. I have done the right thing. The fact that you disagree with it . . . and are, indeed, the victim of it . . . is neither here nor there."

"*It is both here and there, Lucius. I am here, and safe. You are there, and in mortal danger.*"

"Tribune," said Maurus with a touch of concern. "Perhaps we should . . ."

"Should what? Concern ourselves over a desperate bluff?" He called out, "Legate . . . unless you have something useful to say, I will be ending this conversation."

"*I have three things to say, Lucius, if you do not mind. And then I will have said all that I need to say.*"

"Say them."

"*First, I was going to make one more, last-ditch attempt to appeal to reason. But I see now that it will be perceived by you as craven begging.*"

"True enough. Two more things, you mentioned?"

"*Yes. The second thing is that while you're busy thinking of me as a bargaining chip, you have neglected to think of me as that which is actually the most pertinent in this situation . . . namely, a former science officer, for whom it is second nature to analyze her environment and learn how things work.*"

"Tribune," Maurus said, now genuinely worried.

Lucius waved him off. "The tattered bravado of a beaten woman," he said in a low voice. Then, louder, he called, "And the third thing you want to say, so we can end this conversation?"

"Simply this: Execute Alpha Omega."

"Now what," demanded Lucius, "is that supposed to mea—"

There was a sudden shuddering, a massive vibration, throughout the ship. Instantly Lucius was on his feet, looking around. "Did something just hit us?"

"No, sir," Vitus assured him. "There's nothing—"

At that moment, the battle doors that separated the bridge from the rest of the ship slid smoothly open. Lucius turned and looked but saw no one coming through. "What's going on . . . ?"

"Free her!" Maurus cried out. "Free her before it's too late!"

"Are you out of your mind? Why should—"

"Tribune!" shouted Vitus, and simultaneous with his cry of alarm came the howls of emergency klaxons. *"Emergency protocols are being overridden! Exit hatches are being blown open all over the—!"*

That was when the winds came.

iii.

Soleta knew she had no reasons for regrets. She had not brought this upon herself. She had instead depended upon her crew to serve under her as they had promised they would do. They were the ones who had forsaken their oaths, and they deserved whatever happened to them. They were no longer her crew; they were threats. Threats to her control of her ship, threats to her liberty and very life.

One didn't feel sorry for threats. One dealt with them, quickly and efficiently.

The most depressing thing for Soleta was that she'd anticipated the possibility and planned for it, even while praying she was wrong. Instead her crew had lived down to her lowest expectations. What did that say about them as a group? About her worthiness as a commander? Indeed, about the noble Romulan race in general?

The rushing air howled past the force screen. Ironically, that which had been serving to keep her in was now serving to keep out the destructive forces that Soleta had unleashed upon the ship, simply by speaking the code words she had attached to the activation sequence. It had been remarkably simple to do, and she had put it into place the moment she'd learned of the death of the Praetor.

The simplest way to dispatch threats from a ship: Open the hatches and let the vacuum of space do the rest. Meanwhile she sat secure in the brig, the force screen keeping her and her air supply safely contained.

She stood there at perfect attention, her back ramrod-straight, as she watched anything that wasn't bolted down go hurtling past her. The ship's atmosphere was blasting through all the corridors, exploding out the half-dozen exit and maintenance hatches that her emergency program had forced open. She was already thinking beyond the current events as to what she would have to do next. The vessel's emergency air supply would kick in once she cycled the doors shut again. Since she would be the only person left breathing on the ship, that would certainly suffice until she was able to find a Class-M planet, bring the vessel down into the atmosphere, and do a complete cleansing of the system.

The forcefield sparked slightly every time something bounced off, but she wasn't concerned. She knew it would hold up.

Then the first of the bodies flew past her. It was one of the men down in engineering, his arms flailing about. He sought purchase, found none, and kept on going, his scream being lost to the rushing of air.

She set her jaw. She had just killed one of her own men. No. Why stop short of stating that which she knew so well: She had just killed all her men. She had made a plan, she had executed it, and, in doing so, she had executed her crew. And why not? They were all complicit in the mutiny. The penalty for mutiny was death. It was as simple as that. And in the harsh environs of space, Soleta was the judge and jury, and space itself the executioner.

"Commander!"

It was Maurus. He had managed to snag an overhead pipe right in front of the brig. He was horizontal, his legs thrashing about, and he was crying out to her in fear and desperation.

"Commander!" he screamed. It was hard to hear him, for the air was rushing away from him and wasn't

conducive to carrying his voice. Soleta was lip-reading as much as hearing his actual voice, but the terror on his face made clear the tenor of his words. *"Commander, I didn't want to do it! They made me! Save me, Commander! I want to live to see my child! Commander, I'm begging you! Please!"*

She could have shut it down, of course. But she knew she had to wait. She had to wait until the entire crew was gone, because even if Maurus could be trusted—which she wasn't sure was the case—the others certainly could not. And she would never have this opportunity again.

So she remained there, rock steady. She didn't avert her eyes. Instead she simply stared at him, as impassively as her Vulcan training allowed her. Maurus continued to scream, to plead, and he cried out his mate's name, and the name of his unborn child, even as his fingers started to slip.

And Soleta's will began to splinter, and then to crack, and she was about to shout out the shutdown code even though she knew full well it could ultimately cost her her life. But it was too late. Maurus lost his grip on the pipe. His scream went with him, carried off by the air, and then he was gone, sucked out the aft maintenance hatch.

Soleta continued to stand at attention. A couple more of her men flew past, while the rest were no doubt sucked out through other exits. The *Spectre* was a maze of corridors. Anyone could have wound up going in any direction through sheer random chance as they were sent hurtling through the ship. She fancied she could still hear scattered screams from throughout the vessel, being carried to her by the forceful winds.

Finally she heard nothing except the continued screech of the klaxon, alerting the occupants of the *Spectre* to an emergency that they certainly already knew about.

She tapped the com unit on the wall. "Override Alpha Omega, code zero two zero three," she said calmly.

Her words immediately triggered the ship's computer fail-safe. She heard the distant shutting of the hatches that had been opened now irising closed. That series of noises was then followed by the soft hissing of air that indicated the emergency air supply was being pumped in.

That was when Soleta suddenly discovered herself sitting on the floor. She wasn't aware that her legs had given out. All she knew was that one moment she was standing, and the next she was seated. Then her mental discipline escaped her in the same way that the air had escaped the *Spectre*. She began to sob, misery and frustration and guilt racking her body. She mentally flagellated herself all in a rush, grief-stricken over what she had done to her own people. Even though she knew it wasn't logical, or even rational, she blamed herself for the treason committed against her. Perhaps if she had been a better commander, or a better person, they would have trusted her, they would have—

They never would have trusted you. You are a half-breed. Your authority with them was dead at the point of your conception.

She kept trying to tell herself that. She tried to convince herself that, no matter what she had done, they would have turned against her once the protection of the Praetor's support was gone. That they had brought their fate upon themselves, and she had merely acted in self-defense and in the spirit of her command.

Her command of a ghost ship. A literal ghost ship. The name *Spectre* had a whole new frame of reference, because she knew that however long she remained aboard the vessel, the eyes of the crewmen's ghosts would be upon her, passing mute judgment upon her and waiting for a misstep that would bring her over to their side of the vale of tears and enable them to exact vengeance upon her.

"This is ridiculous," she muttered, as she wiped the unseemly tears off her face with the back of her hand. "Just ridic . . . it's stupid. Stupid and unworthy." She stood and said, "Override brig forcefield. Code one zed alpha zed two."

For a moment she wondered what in the world she would do if the forcefield didn't shut off as per her prearranged entry code. That would put her in a hell of a fix. No crew, and her stuck inside the brig until basically she starved to death. It all sounded very promising. *A glorious end to a glorious career. Mother and Father would be so proud.*

That made her think, ever so briefly, of the subject she most wanted to avoid: what her parents thought of the direction her life had taken. She hadn't spoken to them in two years. She didn't want to begin dwelling upon them now.

Then the forcefield powered off. She looked from one side of the field to the other, then tentatively reached out to make certain it was down. She winced reflexively in anticipation of a jolt that never came. Letting out her breath, she then tilted her chin defiantly, as if worried she was going to run into someone who would be critical of the actions she had taken.

An image came to her mind, unbidden. Maurus had proudly shown her a holo of his mate, standing there with her hand resting gently upon her swollen belly, and a look of complete bliss upon her face.

She envisioned that young female standing outside their home, looking to the skies, waiting for the return of her mate. Waiting and waiting, and not knowing that Maurus was nothing but a frozen, floating corpse in the depths of the void, never to return. And he had achieved that status because she, Soleta, had killed him despite his pleas for mercy.

"It was him or me. It was all of them or me," she said, and her voice echoed in the empty halls of the *Spectre* as she headed for the bridge to determine her next move. From the lack of resolve in her voice, she was only relieved that she didn't have to convince anyone of the truth of her words. She was having a difficult enough time convincing herself.

U.S.S. Excalibur

i.

Termic of the Bolgar was understandably cautious, which was why he brought with him two of his own to serve as guards. One did not rise to the leadership of the beleaguered Bolgar if one did not display caution.

Still, he did not truly see the harm in boarding this vessel . . . "Excalibur," it was called, which its "captain" had informed him was the name of some sort of legendary weapon back in their own universe. The organisms residing in it were of no threat. He could see it in their eyes as he and his followers moved through the corridors. They were frightened and disoriented, confused by where they were and uncertain of when, or how, they were going to be able to escape.

The Bolgar's size was also a bit of a problem. They were not as huge as the Teuthis, certainly, but they were still considerably larger than these organisms. Fortunately enough, the Bolgar's bodies were fairly malleable. All Termic and his followers had to do was extend their lower halves. It caused them to take up more room side-to-side in the corridors, but that was manageable. And their heads were consequently low enough that they were able to maneuver top-to-bottom.

Termic had been a bit uncertain when first informed by the captain that a face-to-face was required. That holographic projections simply wouldn't do. But then he reasoned that there was no harm to it. The small organisms would have to be insane to try and do harm to the Bolgar, who were more than willing to act as allies against the Teuthis . . . at least, for as long as the organisms were useful. In the future, well . . . who knew what the future would hold? Everything served a purpose, and there was no point in continuing to make use of something once its purpose had been served. Besides, Termic was admittedly curious what these creatures were like in the "flesh," as it were.

Termic was fascinated to learn that the *Excalibur* had its own matter-transport system. So, too, did Termic's vessel. Apparently it was preferable for Termic to use his means of transportation. The local concept of "physical laws" was proving to be a bit of a hardship for the *Excalibur* to adjust to, and their own transmat beams were not especially reliable.

The ship's captain, the one called "Calhoun," was walking in front of the newly arrived group of Bolgar. Close in behind them was a larger organism than any of the others. This one was called "Kebron" and he did not appear to serve any particular purpose. But Termic wasn't bothered by his presence. What difference could it make, really?

"Your hospitality is much appreciated, Captain,"

Termic said in as politic a tone as he could muster. "Although your insistence that we come to your vessel remains a bit puzzling to me."

"I told you, Termic. On this vessel, we deal with potential allies face-to-face. It's just how we do things where we come from."

"Yes. But you're not where you come from, are you," Termic pointed out with a touch of smugness. "If you were, you wouldn't be requiring our aid."

"That's a fair point," admitted Calhoun. "Since we are strangers in a strange land, think of your coming to us as a means of calming our uncertainties."

"An advanced race such as mine could do no less."

"Yes, I thought you'd see it that way."

"May I ask where we're going?"

"To a conference facility," Calhoun said. "On this vessel, we have specific areas where we discuss and work out specific things. A discussion of this magnitude certainly wouldn't be conducted in the open corridors."

"How very different your vessel is from ours," said Termic. "The interior of ours is just one vast area, acting in complete unison. No one place is functionally different than any other."

"A very unified concept. If and when we get back, we might want to take a look at developing something along those lines."

"A superb notion," said Termic. "It is always advisable to learn what you can from your betters."

"I could not agree more," said Calhoun.

The one called Kebron made some sort of odd

noise at that point which Termic couldn't quite interpret so he dismissed it as unimportant.

"Is it fair to say," Termic asked, "that you have seen that allying with the Bolgar is your best chance at survival?"

"Oh, beyond question," said Calhoun. He stopped and gestured toward a large set of doors. "It's just a matter of settling some of the fine points. This way, please."

"Good luck, Captain," Kebron said.

The doors opened wide as Termic eased through, following close behind Calhoun. The guards followed behind, but Kebron did not come through the doors. Instead they slid shut, cutting him off from view.

Termic immediately felt more at ease in this new room, which was much, much larger than the corridors through which they'd been moving. He saw several smaller ships scattered about, and correctly intuited that this chamber was used for the storage of exploratory space vessels that could go where the much larger ship could not go.

Then Termic sensed trouble before he felt it. He stopped in his slime-filled tracks and said, "Wait . . . what is . . ."

"That voice," came an all-too-familiar tone, rumbling from the shadows. "And that stench. Could it be . . . ?"

Termic spun as quickly as he was able to and faced Calhoun. It was difficult for Termic to get a sense of what was going through Calhoun's mind, since he was still new to interpreting the facial expressions of the organisms. But his own fury was mounting. "What sort of trick is this! What sort of—"

Pontalimus emerged from the shadows, towering and terrible and what passed for a visage twisted in a contemptuous sneer. He stood at the far end of the room, but nevertheless towered to the very top of it. "Termic. What an astounding coincidence."

"*Kill him!*" howled Termic.

ii.

Calhoun was never entirely sure from where Termic's people pulled their weapons. Finally he decided he didn't really want to know.

He saw that they were large tubes, about three feet long. They swung them up and aimed them at Pontalimus. Even as they opened fire, Calhoun calmly tapped his combadge and spoke into it softly.

The Bolgar were clearly surprised at the result of their assault on their despised enemy. The blasts of energy, or whatever they were, slammed into a force-field that erupted and flared before them, absorbing the impact. It was a large field, taking up the space directly in front of Pontalimus. For his part, the Teuthis leader appeared no less surprised than Termic's security guards were.

The barrage lasted for several long seconds, and then the frustrated Termic shouted, "Enough!" The guards lowered their weapons, checking whatever energy gauges the things must have had, to make certain that they were in proper working order. Termic pivoted in place and snarled at Calhoun, "Is this some sort of game to you?"

"I suppose it is," Calhoun replied easily. "A high-stakes game. Best of all, we all get to play."

"Lower that field," Termic warned him, "or you will be the next target of our wrath."

Backing up his warning, the guards aimed their weapons straight at Calhoun.

"You may find this devastating to your self-esteem," said Calhoun with a nonchalant shrug, "but I've had weapons aimed at me many times in the past, and doubtless will in the future."

"Your future may be a good deal shorter than you anticipated."

"I have nothing to say to that," said Calhoun, "other than this: Energize."

"Wha—?"

There was the familiar humming of the transporter beams. The guards let out frustrated yells as they suddenly found themselves holding empty air. Their weapons had dissolved into nothingness.

"I forgot to tell you: We managed to make some adjustments to our transporters. Ship-to-ship remains problematic, but short-range intraship beaming . . . that we can do."

"How dare you!"

"Did you like the forcefield?" he asked conversationally. "Had it rigged up special. Just in case the transporter gambit didn't work."

"That would only have prevented us from dealing Pontalimus the death he so truly deserves," snapped Termic. "We could still have dispatched you, you . . . you traitor!"

"You could have tried," Calhoun said. "But people who know me would tell you that I don't die as easily as all that. Certainly the people who have tried to kill me would tell you that . . . presuming any of them were left alive."

"You waste too much time bantering with him, Calhoun," rumbled Pontalimus. "Inform him that the *Excalibur* is going to devote its energies to reviving the control that the Teuthis have over this sphere."

"You have no control of it! You have nothing," Termic snapped at him.

"I have more than enough strength to destroy you where you stand," said Pontalimus.

"You would not dare!"

"Dare? Why would I not? I don't really see myself as asking permission or being concerned over punishment," said Pontalimus. He made a loud noise that sounded like a derisive snort. "My race was old when yours was still aborning, Termic, you upstart fool. And now you seek to drive us out? Tout your superiority as if you know anything about anything? You know nothing of the true way of things. My race is superior, and we will triumph."

"And yet you seek the help of these organisms! These—"

"May I interject something here?" asked Calhoun.

"And you!" Termic snapped at Calhoun. "We

offered you an alliance that you have now thrown back at us by providing aid and comfort to this monster!"

"I am no monster, compared to . . ."

"Let me rephrase it," said Calhoun. "I'm *going* to interject something here. Something that I think may be of tremendous interest to you both."

"And what would that be?" Termic did not sound particularly interested, but clearly he was prepared to indulge Calhoun for the moment.

"This."

From within his belt, Calhoun held up a small tube.

"There was a story written by someone in my . . . sphere . . . a very long time ago," said Calhoun. "It was a cautionary tale about the dangers of hubris. It was about a certain race—the race of men—who were convinced that they were the most dominant, most powerful species in their world. It turned out that, no, they weren't dominant at all. Because another race came along and they were far more powerful. They were alien invaders. And they mowed through the race of men and they were convinced that *they* were the dominant species and that absolutely nothing could be thrown at them that they couldn't destroy."

"Is there some point to this?" inquired Termic.

"And then the invading alien race was brought down," continued Calhoun as if Termic hadn't spoken, "by something so small . . . so insignificant . . . that they hadn't allowed for it at all. Microscopic organisms that made them ill. That killed them. The mightiest and most destructive race ever to stalk man's world was undone by creatures they couldn't even see. In their overarching confidence, they were brought low. As I said, the dangers of hubris."

"But what does this have to do with—"

In one quick gesture, Calhoun threw the test tube. It shattered.

Nothing happened. There were just a few clear shards scattered on the floor. Other than that, there was no visible reaction.

Termic stared at Calhoun. "Was there some significance to that action?"

"Here's what's significant," said Calhoun. "On the one side, we have the Teuthis . . . of whom, for all we know, Pontalimus may be among the last in this sphere. They have technology we need to return home, but the cost of that is our aiding them in destroying you."

"As if you could," said Termic.

"You, on the other hand, don't have the technology we need, but want us to help you destroy the Teuthis just the same . . . because you have, I don't know, the moral high ground or some such. Neither option is especially attractive, and I wind up trying to commit genocide, either for personal gain or just out of a sense of moral indignation. Neither sits well with me, and I find myself in the position of having to come up with a third choice. And the third choice is this: The two of you are going to come out of this chamber with some sort of accord . . ."

"Never!" Termic snapped.

"He and his ilk have done too much to warrant our just walking away from them," said Pontalimus.

". . . or you will not emerge from it alive."

There was a fearsome silence for long moments. Then Pontalimus said contemptuously, "I have no idea what you're talking about . . . and neither do you."

"Actually I do." Calhoun draped his hands behind his back and began to work in a small, slow circle. "You see, gentlemen . . . or whatever you are . . . I have very little patience for leaders who are disinclined to lead. Beings who wage war from deep in hiding in their own bunkers or secret headquarters or suchlike. Now me, I think a leader should be willing to get his hands dirty."

"Your hands are unclean?" asked Termic, looking bewildered.

"That vial," Calhoun said, toeing some of the fragmented remains with his foot, "contains—or contained, I should say—some fearsome microbes. They were hatched up by a rather talented young doctor in our sickbay. One who has more than a little familiarity himself with having a condition that one finds personally debilitating. These microbes, these . . . germs . . . are quite virulent."

"I don't understand," said Termic.

But Pontalimus stiffened (although it wasn't easy to discern that, given the way he was built) and his voice dropped to a thunderous growl. "You madman."

"I prefer 'resourceful man,' but I'll accept the other," Calhoun replied.

"What are you saying? That you've just killed yourself?" asked Termic. "That you've poisoned yourself rather than make a decision?"

"Not exactly. I simply felt that—as was the case with the old story and its hubris-destroying theme—two races battling for universal domination were really due for a reminder that it doesn't matter how big or majestic or powerful you become, or think you've become. It's the little things you have to watch out for. Let your pride go out of control, and the universe has a funny way of balancing the scales to remind you just how insignificant you truly are."

"You'll die for this, Calhoun," said Pontalimus.

"Yes, but I thought we'd already been over that." Calhoun looked back at Termic, who still clearly didn't comprehend. Either he was remarkably stupid or, more likely, he was having trouble processing the discovery that someone could do something as stunningly stupid as Calhoun had just done. Apparently he was going to have to walk Termic through it. "Here's where we stand: I have just released into the air—sealed air, I should make clear; we made sure to shut down the vents leading in and out of here—a devastating, airborne disease. It's based upon a toxin developed by a rather nasty race who call themselves the Redeemers. I assure you, the Redeemers may have been bastards, but they knew what they were about when it came to killing. Even now it is worming its way not only into my system, but yours, Pontalimus, and yours, Termic, and your guards, as well. This disease is debilitating and quite, quite fatal given time. And I assure you, we have time in abundance."

Termic uttered a strange sound that was much like a flash of nervous laughter. "But . . . you can't truly be serious. Let us say that you actually had done such a thing. You cannot possibly think that a disease fatal to you would likewise be fatal to us."

"That is, in fact, exactly what I think," Calhoun replied. "Don't forget, we've had the king of the Teuthis here for a while," and he chucked a thumb at Pontalimus. "Don't think for a moment that we haven't had the time to do scans on him, analyses. It's all very technical and, frankly," he smiled lopsidedly, "I'm merely a captain. Medical specifics are a bit out of my line. But as I said, we have someone who is very expert on ways that the body can . . . oh, what's the best way to put it?" He tapped his chin thoughtfully, and then brightened. "Ah yes. Expert on ways that the body can eat itself. Just devour itself from the inside out, and convince itself the entire time that it's doing the right thing. A fascinating science, really. I wish I knew more about science so I could more readily comprehend it."

"But this is nonsense!"

"It's really not, Termic, and I wish you'd stop saying that. It would be terrible if you hurt my feelings." Then his voice went flat and level, and there was no trace of amusement in it. "We really did develop a germ strain that could affect you, me, and Pontalimus. I really did release it into the air just now. All of us in this chamber now have a very limited period of time to live . . ."

"You would have us believe you'd murder us for no reason?"

"Not exactly, no," Calhoun told him. "You see . . . my clever officer also synthesized a cure for it. Left unattended, it will ravage your body and you will die. With the cure introduced into your systems, the breakdown at a molecular level will be reversed." They both began to talk, but Calhoun raised his voice and spoke over them. "The two of you," he said, "are going to work out your differences. You are going to come to an accord. You are going to agree to cease this course of mutually assured genocide upon which you've both embarked, and then you, Pontalimus, are going to give us the technology we need in order to get out of here. It's as simple as that. All you need to do in order to live is decide that living includes living with each other. Live together . . . or die separately."

Pontalimus and Termic stared at each other for a long moment.

"An absurd notion," said Pontalimus.

"Unthinkable," said Termic.

Calhoun let out a heavy sigh, tapped his combadge, and said, "Calhoun to Burgoyne."

"Burgoyne here."

"Burgy . . . just to let you know . . . you may want to start measuring my quarters to see whether your furniture will fit."

Priatia

"Well, that was a fiasco."

The creature who was Kalinda stands before her leader. She hears the cold assessment of her leader and feels boiling anger. "I have accomplished my mission," she informs him, barely containing her ire. "I killed Tiraud. I set the war into motion."

"You were supposed to remain for as long as possible. Your early departure is not what I would term 'as long as possible.' "

He glides from one side of the vast deck to the other. Below him the planet Priatia turns upon its axis. "We are but one ship," he says. "Mightier than any they have here . . . but still only one ship. We need the residents of these planets to destroy each other so that we may then attend to the remaining opposition with minimal difficulty."

"I know that."

"Having yourself found out so quickly makes our job harder. You were fortunate we were able to remove you from New Thallon as quickly as we did . . ."

"I know that as well."

"Were you not who you are . . ."

"You mean," she says coolly, "the mate of our glorious leader, Pontalimus?"

"Yes. If you did not hold that status . . ." He allows the rest of the sentence to drop, simply because she does hold that status and so there's really no point in completing it. Instead he changes gears. "We must prepare this sphere for the arrival of our fellow Teuthis."

"Yes. Leave the sphere of Teuthis to the damnable Bolgar," says "Kalinda" with vast contempt. "We will move on to bigger, greater things."

"Shall we reinfuse you with more DNA culled from the Thallonian?" he asks her. "Enable you to fully recover your disguised form?"

"I see no point," she says. "I believe that gambit has run its course."

"So I should instruct the Priatians to dispose of the original Thallonian, Kalinda, then?"

"Yes. No," she corrects herself quickly. "There is no purpose in waste. Besides, at the moment she seems of no use. But we do not know what the future will bring."

"And the Priatians? What of them, once we have used them to claim worlds for us upon which we can thrive?"

She shrugs. "They serve their purpose. They worship us as 'the Wanderers' who founded their race. They can continue to be useful in the future . . . as foodstuffs, if nothing else."

U.S.S. Trident

i.

Technically, Shelby could have taken up residence in the captain's ready room, since she had assumed command of the *Trident*. Instead, as the starship hurtled toward Priatia, she contented herself with simple guest quarters . . . although she had every intention of being on the bridge once they were approaching the planet that was responsible for her husband's disappearance.

Still, despite the fact that she wasn't taking the full advantages of command that her station allowed her to, she decided there wasn't any reason she couldn't avail herself of at least a few command prerogatives.

There was a chime at her door and she called out, "Come." She was seated at a desk, and now took the opportunity to lean back and interlace her fingers, as if she were in silent prayer for strength. Moments later, Romeo Takahashi entered. His perpetual sideways grin was on his face, and he looked genuinely happy to see her.

"Admiral," he said. "Those pips look good on you."

"Thank you, Hash. Have a seat," and she gestured to the one opposite her. He sat, and then she said without preamble, "You want to tell me what the hell is going on?"

The smile faded, as she had suspected it would. "Going on?" he echoed faintly, but she knew that he knew what she was referring to.

"You've requested a transfer from the *Trident*. You're alleged to be having some problems with Captain Mueller. All true?"

"Yes, all true, Admiral. But there's an explanation . . ."

"There always is," replied Shelby. "Every stupid decision ever made is anchored in the logic that it seemed like a good idea at the time. But you'd be amazed how often good ideas are actually rotten ideas, and this is one of them. You've always worked well with Mueller as your CO, and I have no idea why that situation should have radically changed."

"I had . . ."

"You had what?"

He coughed slightly and then looked at her with a level gaze. "I had no idea of the type of person she was."

"Type of person? What, you didn't know she was a woman?"

"She gave aid and comfort to a traitor."

"Ahhhh," said Shelby, "now we get to it."

His eyes narrowing, Hash demanded, "Did Captain Mueller ask you to intervene?"

"No, she didn't. And by 'traitor,' I can safely assume you're referring to Soleta?"

"Admiral," said Hash uneasily, "I'm perfectly aware that your views on Soleta may well be colored by the . . . the personal debt that you owe her."

"You mean the fact that she saved my life."

"Yes, that debt. But in my opinion," he continued, "her transferring of loyalties to the Romulans was unconscionable. We had her in our hands, and instead of arresting her or even simply leaving her to her fate, we actually helped repair her ship and sent her on her way. Now how am I supposed to have any respect for a commanding officer who does such a thing?"

Shelby tapped her fingers slowly on the desktop. "How many family members," she asked after a few moments, "did you lose to Romulan sneak attacks over the years?"

"Since you obviously are familiar with my family history, I assume you know the answer to that yourself," replied Hash.

She smiled slightly at that. "Actually, I'm entirely unfamiliar with that aspect of your past, Romeo. I simply took an educated guess. A blind man could have seen it, though."

"I'd rather not go into it in detail, if it's all the same to you, Admiral. I mean, if you insist . . ."

Shelby waved it off. "The specifics aren't necessary, Hash. Still, matters aren't always as black-and-white as you make them out to be."

"With respect, Admiral, in this instance, I believe they are."

"I see. You believe that Soleta is a traitor, and by aiding her, Mueller is . . . what? Likewise a traitor?"

"In a very real sense, yes."

"And what about me? You must know that I opposed Soleta being ousted from Starfleet."

"Understandable," he said readily. "You felt indebted to Soleta for her actions that saved your life."

"I see. So I'm in the clear with you, then."

"That's right. I have nothing but the highest regard for you, Admiral. Yuh must know that, don't'cha?" He was beginning to slip into the casual faux-Southern accent he often affected.

"And what if I told you that I knew Soleta was half-Romulan . . . and had kept that information from Starfleet, long before they discovered it? That she told me herself, freely and of her own will?"

Hash's face went slightly gray. "I . . . that is . . . wait, you . . . ?"

"I knew," said Shelby. "She told me, trusting me to keep her secret. In doing so, I aided and abetted her in a fraud. Some might even call it treason, might they not?"

Hash sagged back in his chair. "They might. Yes."

"Why," she continued in mock thoughtfulness, as if all this was just now occurring to her, "some might say that I'm not deserving of respect or the rank that Starfleet has bestowed upon me. After all, I had an obligation to report Soleta's secret to the proper authorities. I failed to do so. That makes me culpable, doesn't it. My whole career could go right down the chute, couldn't it."

Takahashi nodded, looking numb.

"Are you going to tell anyone that I knew?"

He looked up at her, his eyes taking a moment to focus upon her. "What?"

"Are you going to tell anyone that I knew?" she repeated. "Are you going to rat me out? Let Starfleet know that I concealed information? Get me court-martialed, tossed out in disgrace?"

"N-no," Hash stammered. "I mean . . . Starfleet knows now, right? So I . . . can't quite see the purpose in bringing it all up now."

"But if you don't," she pressed, "then aren't you aiding and abetting a traitor?"

"No!"

"Yes. Starfleet regs are quite clear. Despite whatever admiration you may feel for me, despite however much respect you may have for me as an officer . . . technically, you're bound to turn me in. If you don't, you're an accomplice after the fact. You, Romeo Takahashi, pride of the Takahashi family, are technically committing an act of treason."

"Only a small act," Hash protested.

Shelby let that hang in the air a moment, and then leaned back in her chair and laughed. "You crack me up, Hash. You really do."

She continued to laugh, and as she did so, Hash began to feel a surge of confidence. He started laughing as well, even as he asked, "So this . . . this was just a kind of test, right?"

"That's right," she said, nodding.

Relief clearly swept through him. "A test to see if I was trustworthy."

"Something like that."

"And you didn't really know that Soleta was a Romulan."

"Oh, no, I really knew," Shelby assured him. "That was all true."

Hash moaned and sagged in his chair once more.

"Hash," she said patiently, "I understand that you have personally strong feelings about the Romulans. I don't intend to dismiss your feelings. And you likewise have strong feelings regarding adherence to duty and regulations. That's fine. But sometimes, things just aren't as cut-and-dried as we would like them to be. I'm taking a huge chance in trusting you to keep my secret about Soleta. Was that trust misplaced?"

"No, ma'am," he sighed, shaking his head.

"All right. That's good to know. But you must realize that, in upholding that trust, you are yourself acting in a traitorous fashion. Do you think that you're wrong in doing so?"

"Yes," he said immediately, but then added with an air of reluctance, "but I don't hesitate to do it."

"Should I think the less of you for it?"

"I'd think you wouldn't."

"You'd think correctly," Shelby assured him. "And I don't think the less of you. So why should—"

"Why should I think the less of Captain Mueller for performing in a manner that is not thematically different from what you and I are doing, or have done?"

She pointed a finger at him triumphantly. "That's exactly right, yes."

"Well, I . . ."

She could practically see the wheels spinning in his

skull. Unfortunately for Hash, the wheels were running on empty. "I don't know, Admiral," he finally admitted. "But I . . . I still feel differently . . ."

"Even though there's no reason for you to?" She shook her head. "I thought better of you than that, Hash. You're a smart guy. I was reasonably sure that you were in command of higher brain functions than pure id."

"Now you make me feel as if I've let you down."

"And isn't that how you've made Captain Mueller feel? Hash, the—"

The shrill sound of the ship's hail sounded in the room. *"Bridge to Admiral Shelby,"* came Mueller's voice. *"Your presence is required."*

Shelby frowned. She knew they weren't due yet at Priatia. She'd heard no call to red alert, so she knew that the ship wasn't under attack. "Is it anything that can wait, Captain . . . ?"

Something in Mueller's tone changed. It sounded harsher, more brittle. *"Elizabeth, with all respect, get the hell up here."*

Shock rolled over Shelby even as she sprang to her feet. "On my way," she said, and gestured for Hash to follow her. Together they exited the room, and within moments were sprinting, not walking, down the corridor.

ii.

Robin Lefler was staring at the monitor screen, and she was completely unaware that she was sitting on the floor. All she knew was that everyone else on the bridge suddenly seemed much taller. When Kat Mueller reached down to her and helped her up, that was the point she realized that she had tried to sit without caring that there was no chair behind her.

"I've called the admiral," Mueller said to Robin, easing her into the command chair. It wasn't the appropriate chair for her, but it was the most comfortable. Not that she was aware of it. "We'll decide what to do once she gets here," Mueller continued. "I swear to you, Robin, everything is going to be fine."

The turbolift hissed open and Shelby stepped out onto the bridge. Hash was right behind her, but that barely registered on Mueller. "What's going on, Captain?" asked Shelby, but then her gaze rested upon the image on the viewscreen. "Oh my God."

There, frozen upon the screen, was Si Cwan. He was leaning forward, as if shouting into a camera taking his picture. Assorted Thallonians were surrounding him, holding him firmly by the arms and shoulders, although it was easy to tell from the picture that they were not having an easy time of it. There were cuts and bruises on his face and upper arms, and his clothes were torn. Clearly he'd been in some sort of vicious struggle. She realized that she was seeing something that was being broadcast from within the council chamber that had once been the heart of the New Thallonian Protectorate.

"What the hell is happening there?" she demanded.

"It's the final image of a broadcast that's been going

out all over the ethernet in Thallonian space," Arex spoke up. "We just picked it up."

"I want to see it from the beginning. Run it again."

Arex was nodding, already ahead of her. The image disappeared, briefly replaced by the customary image of space, and then the broadcast started over. They were once again in the council chamber, but the only one visible there was Fhermus. He was smiling with utter complacency, and there was a sneer in his voice when he spoke.

"This transmission," he began, "is intended for the few allies who are still foolish enough to support the usurping fool calling himself Lord Si Cwan of New Thallon. A man whose murderous sister coldly and calculatedly manipulated my son into marriage for the express purpose of killing him in cold blood. Whose actions resulted in death and destruction when I, as any aggrieved father would do, retaliated for his brutal actions.

"And what was his response to that? Did he attack in kind? Did he engage in a retaliatory strike, as our traditions and way of life would expect him to do?" His mouth twisted in a sneer. "No. Instead he fed me a ludicrous tale that you will now see him repeating here."

The screen wavered slightly and suddenly the council chamber had representatives in it. Not a full complement; it was only about three-quarters occupied. But there was Si Cwan, addressing those who had assembled, with his arms spread wide in a flourish of oratorical style. "A monster, my friends," he was declaring. "A creature of unfathomed origins, having taken the form of my sister for the purpose of killing Fhermus's son and causing war between our peoples. You have seen the video record I produced of our confrontation. Now you realize that we must set aside our grievances and join as one against our mutual enemies . . ."

Once again the picture shifted, and Fhermus was there alone. "Can you believe the audacity?" he demanded, as if sharing mutual outrage. "The sheer gall of the man! To present an obviously falsified recording in which, naturally, the heroic Si Cwan battles a monster that threatens his beloved New Thallon. He expected that we would become swept up in his fantasy to such a degree that we would believe the absurdities depicted herein. The fact is that Si Cwan has no stomach to retaliate and seeks an easy way out to avoid sustained battle. Ever since his bedroom ties with the Federaton—a union by which every right-thinking New Thallonian was appalled— he has been weak! Far less than he was! The people of New Thallon deserve more. Thallonian space deserves more.

"Consider the irony, if you will. His own people cried for vengeance against their attackers. But when it became clear to them that Si Cwan would go to any lengths to avoid such an undertaking, they turned against him themselves!"

The picture changed yet again and, sure enough, Si Cwan was under assault. There, in his throne room, Thallonians were converging upon him from all directions. Si Cwan was clearly startled by the assault, caught completely off guard. He tried to battle back, and he fought with the fury of a cornered lion. Whoever was recording it was clearly having a splendid time as he kept pushing in close, then retreating, giving a constant sense of movement to the camera. The entire battle was there, long minutes ticking away as Si Cwan took on all comers, roaring defiance.

At first viewing, Lefler had thought it was some sort of staged event. But no. Si Cwan was mowing through his opposition, snapping their necks, gouging out eyes, ripping open jugular veins with his teeth and sending blood spurting. Somehow in the melee he got his hands on a sword, and heads were flying moments later.

"Magnificent," whispered Kat Mueller in admiration. It was natural that someone like her would appreciate a battle as fearsome as this one. Mueller was, in her own way, a warrior born, and Robin Lefler was perfectly aware that Mueller and Cwan had their own history together. But she was too numb to feel even the slightest flare of jealousy over the comment. Instead she was watching as the inevitable finally occurred: A lion he might have been, but even a lion can be dragged down if too many jackals descend upon it.

So it was with Si Cwan. He fought valiantly, he fought desperately, and it seemed he fought endlessly. But the true end did finally come, and Si Cwan was dragged down to the floor, disappearing beneath a pile of bodies. When he was finally hauled to his feet, his hands were bound in unbreakable manacles and they were busy applying similar restraints to his feet.

"The people have judged," came Fhermus's voice, and then Fhermus reappeared on the screen. "They have judged Si Cwan and found him wanting. But there are still fools out there, absurd allies, who have pledged fealty to Si Cwan even in the face of all odds and reason. Don't think that I don't know you're out there. Even though Cwan's own race believes that he has betrayed their interests, and would rather throw in their lot with me, there are still Thallonians out there who stubbornly cling to the notion that they must stay loyal to him. There are other allies as well, members of other races who would rather pursue a pointless conflict against my followers and me rather than cede to the inevitable. Now is not the time for pointless, incessant conflict. Now is the time for us to come together as a true, new protectorate, before enemies both foreign and domestic endeavor to rise up against us.

"It has taken some persuasion, but Si Cwan himself will now come forward and beg for a cessation of hostilities. So that there is no misunderstanding," and his voice became low and threatening, "the continued existence of Si Cwan depends upon the total cooperation of all those who currently support him. Act in opposition to us, and he will die. He does not desire this, nor do we. Hear him explain it to you himself."

Fhermus stepped back and gestured off camera. Seconds later, Si Cwan was hauled onto the picture.

He looked as if he could barely stand, and his head was hanging down. His hands and, presumably, his feet remained manacled, and he was being supported by Thallonians on either side. "Tell them, Cwan," Fhermus said flatly. "Tell them what is at stake."

For a long moment, Si Cwan said nothing. Then, slowly, he lifted his head and leveled his gaze upon whoever was recording the event.

He spit directly into the lens.

There were angry snarls from offscreen even as Si Cwan shouted, "Don't cooperate! Don't believe him! Fhermus deserves to die! They all deserve to die! My people! Fhermus's people! The lot of them should all be rotting corpses left for carrion eaters to feast upon!" He was struggling mightily in the hands of his captors as he continued to shout, "Don't surrender! Keep fighting! My life is unimportant! They don't deserve order! They don't deserve a protectorate! Burn them all! Burn them to the ground! Let nothing be left of them! Let them die in final, glorious flames of destruction! Let them—!"

That was where the image froze, with Si Cwan's face twisted in hate and fury, shouting imprecations and calling for the death of all who had betrayed him.

There was a long silence upon the bridge at that point. Then, without a word, Shelby headed for the ready room. Lefler followed right behind her, and Mueller brought up the rear. As she did so, she stopped, turned, and looked straight at Romeo Takahashi. "Hash, you have the conn," she said.

"Aye, Captain," Hash said without hesitation as the doors closed behind her.

iii.

No one was seated behind the desk in the ready room. Robin Lefler was sitting in a chair, still with a dazed look upon her face. Mueller was pacing, while Shelby leaned against the desk, her legs crossed at the ankles.

"If we continue on our course to Priatia," Shelby said, "and it turns out that Kalinda is actually being held there—as we suspect is the case—then that will help prove what Si Cwan said was true. Plus we need to investigate the area as soon as possible if we have the slightest hope of discovering what happened to Mac."

"This isn't about proving Cwan's story to be true," Mueller shot back, a bit more heatedly than she herself would have liked, but unable to help herself. "They could have chosen to believe him. They didn't. They chose to rebel against him. If that's the case, my guess is that it was something that was coming for some time. This business wasn't the cause. It was merely the excuse they were looking for."

"But why turn against him when he was fighting for mutual peace?"

"They don't care about mutual peace," Lefler spoke up, sounding very distant, as if she weren't really in the room or was speaking while having an out-of-body experience. "They're a warrior race at heart, and they have scores they want to settle. You don't settle scores with people by sitting down in a large room and speaking nicely to each other. You settle scores by killing as many of them as is required to make them do what you want. Si Cwan understood that. So did Fhermus. The only thing is, Si Cwan tried to act against his own nature and the nature of his people because of me. It's my fault."

"Oh, Robin," sighed Shelby, "it's not—"

"It is," she said more insistently. "He tried to make himself over into something he's not because of me."

"Si Cwan is a grown man and makes his own decisions, and you can't go blaming yourself for them," said Mueller. "Frankly, I think he'd be offended if he heard you saying that he basically couldn't make up his own mind as to what was the best way to proceed and needed you to decide it for him."

"I didn't decide it for him. I never said that," and now Lefler was on her feet, anger rolling off her. "And I resent the hell out of you right now, and I think it'd be best if you shut your damned mouth!"

Mueller didn't come close to backing down. "Do you make it a habit to tell the captain of a starship what to do, Lieutenant Commander?" she demanded icily.

Before she could respond, Shelby came between them. "She doesn't, but I do, and I'm telling both of you to back off," she snapped. "Robin, we can't lose sight of our mission . . ."

"And I can't lose sight of the fact that my husband is in terrible danger!"

"What if it's some sort of hoax? Is that possible?" asked Shelby, looking to Mueller for her opinion.

Mueller shrugged. "I wouldn't understand the thinking behind it. What would it accomplish? All it would do is serve to inflame an already inflammatory situation."

"Perhaps to throw the Priatians off guard? If their goal is to create war, then making them think they're accomplishing their aim can . . . I don't know. Draw them out, perhaps?"

"Perhaps." But Mueller didn't sound convinced.

Lefler, for her part, wasn't convinced by a long shot. "It's a stretch at best, Admiral. And it's not a chance we can afford to take!"

"We can afford to take it," Mueller reminded her, "if the admiral says we can afford it."

Robin ignored her, instead focusing her attention on Shelby. "Admiral," she said, pleading in her voice, "we're standing here discussing 'what if' scenarios when it may well be my husband's life on the line."

"I know that. But in case you've forgotten . . ."

"Your own husband's life may well be on the line as well, yes, I know," said Lefler, feeling a surge of frustration and helplessness. "I . . . don't know what to say here. I don't know that my own judgment can be trusted because it's going to be colored by my concerns for Cwan."

"That would be the husband who rejected you."

"Didn't yours reject you once?" retorted Lefler.

A terrible silence descended upon the ready room

at that point. Robin lowered her eyes in shame. "I'm sorry," she whispered. "That . . . was out of line."

"You're damned right it was," Shelby snapped back.

"I . . . can't do more than say I'm sorry. I'll say it again. I'll do anything. But please, don't let resentment against me—"

"Quiet. Just . . . be quiet a moment." Shelby rubbed her temples, feeling as if her brain were on fire. "All right . . . all right, just . . ." She inhaled deeply and then let her breath out slowly. She tilted her head back, stared at the ceiling for a moment, then brought her head forward and fixed her gaze upon both women facing her. "Here's the bottom line: Kat. It's your ship. I didn't mind taking charge so I could order you to throw the ambassadors off and undertake this career-ending adventure. But we've got a crisis point now. Some tough decisions have to be made, and I think you're in the best position to make them. I'm too close to the Mac side of the equation, and Robin, naturally, has her concerns tilted entirely toward Si Cwan. I think you might have a more evenhanded view on the matter. So, as ranking officer, I'm willing to defer to you."

"As am I," said Robin.

"How nice for you," Mueller said to Robin. "However, since I outrank you, your deference one way or the other doesn't really mean a thing, does it."

"I suppose not."

"Good."

Mueller, for the first time in the entire meeting, ceased her pacing. Instead she stared for a time out the viewport, watching the stars flash past. She looked as if she were seeking guidance from them.

Finally, without saying a further word to either of the women, she turned stiffly on her heel as if she were on military dress parade and walked out onto the bridge. "Mr. Gold," she said without preamble. "Lay in a new course."

"New Thallon?" he said immediately.

She didn't even make a pretense of being surprised. "Correct."

As was his custom, Gold didn't even wait to confirm that the order was to be given. Instead he simply said, "On our way." The *Trident* turned gracefully and angled in the direction of far-off New Thallon.

Robin Lefler looked toward Mueller as she took her seat. Mueller glanced her way and Robin mouthed the words *Thank you*. Mueller's glacial expression didn't thaw in the slightest. Instead she simply stared at her for a moment, and then looked back at the viewscreen as the *Trident* headed for her new destination.

Shelby, for her part, walked off the bridge without saying a word. She knew from personal experience that one could never count out Mackenzie Calhoun. After all, he'd been believed dead and had returned from the grave. So a mysterious disappearance was as nothing to him. Why, he probably didn't even need Shelby's help to escape whatever fate had overtaken him.

Which was fortunate, because she realized bleakly that the chances of her extending that help had just dwindled significantly indeed.

U.S.S. Excalibur

Hours had passed, and Termic of Bolgar and Pontalimus of Teuthis were still storming about in outrage. Calhoun, seated comfortably on the floor, watched them with an amazing degree of passivity, considering his usual action-oriented state of mind.

"I demand the return of my guards immediately!" Termic was busy shouting at Calhoun. He had good reason to be shouting. His guards had vanished in a haze of transporter beams, sucked away by intraship beaming some time earlier. He had been expressing his displeasure about it the entire time.

"Your guards are perfectly safe," Calhoun assured him. "They're in isolation in sickbay."

"I don't care about the safety of my guards! *They're* supposed to be concerned about providing safety for *me!*"

"That's very touching," said Calhoun. "Look at the bright side. At least you won't have to watch them deteriorate and die. You and your greatest enemy," and he gestured in a languid manner toward Pontalimus, "can provide that degree of entertainment for each other."

"He's bluffing," Pontalimus said, not for the first time. "He would not dare to destroy us, and he certainly wouldn't destroy himself."

"You haven't known me for a very long time, Pontalimus. You're not really in a position to predict what I would or would not do about anything. The only thing you're in a position to do right now is save your own lives, and quite possibly the lives of the rest of your race."

"I will not be blackmailed," said Pontalimus.

"And I will not be bullied," added Termic.

"Then you will both be dead," replied Calhoun. "Oh . . . and here's an interesting thing, just so you know: There's every likelihood that, of the three of us, I will die first. Should that happen, my crew is under orders to let the two of you remain here until the disease finishes with the both of you. The window of opportunity for your safe passage, and your cure, slams shut the moment I draw my last breath. Then it's just a matter of time, and you'll get to spend it dying in each other's company."

"Do your worst, Calhoun," Termic said confidently.

"I already have. The worst is yet to come."

New Thallon

He is chained to the wall, hand and foot. He has tested his bonds repeatedly and has not yet managed to pull himself loose. Given sufficient time, however, he believes that he can manage it. And then, and then, oh, what a reckoning there will be . . .

In an abstract way, he finds it fascinating how these things seem to come full circle. His first encounter with any of those who would play such a huge part in his life was with Soleta during her own stay in the dungeons of Thallon . . . the original Thallon, long gone to space dust. And now Soleta is long gone, an outcast, and he himself is in the dungeons. He does not, however, think it terribly likely that someone will show up unexpectedly to be his savior, as he was Soleta's during her escape.

That is all right. He has always preferred relying on himself.

He continues to pull, ignoring the aches and pains that resulted from the pounding he took. It is as nothing to him. Those who put him into this situation are as nothing to him.

He is Si Cwan—Lord Si Cwan of New Thallon—and he will triumph over this.

Once again he starts pulling on his bonds, testing them, applying all his strength against them.

He has lost track of how long he's been down in this hole. Slowly he enters an almost trancelike state where he is pulling, constantly and unrelentingly, upon his bonds. In some deep, dark corner of his awareness, he starts to realize that he is succeeding. The bonds are beginning to give way. Just a little while longer. That is all he needs. All he needs.

The door to his cell abruptly bursts open. Fhermus is standing there, grim-faced and determined. He pulls his ceremonial sword from its sheath, part of a matched set that accompanies the jeweled dagger which resides in its own sheath on his other hip.

"It was always meant to end this way, Cwan," Fhermus informs him.

There are no words back and forth, no bandying about of repartee. The reason for this is obvious: At heart, Fhermus remains a coward to the end. Even though he has Si Cwan imprisoned, manacled, in bonds . . . still he fears him. Fhermus knows all too well his own limitations, but is unable to guess—or perhaps even comprehend—that which Si Cwan is capable of. So he dares take no chances. What is that line from the Earth play about the slaying of monarchs? "If it were done when 'tis done, then 'twere well it were done quickly."

But not quickly enough. Oh no . . . not quickly enough.

Fhermus approaches with rapid steps, bringing his sword back, and it is at that moment that Si Cwan lunges forward with a roar. The manacles holding his hands snap. The chain holding his left foot likewise breaks free of the wall, and Fhermus lets out a shriek of alarm.

The chain on his right foot holds.

For the only time in his life that he can properly recall, Si Cwan loses his balance and goes down, betrayed by his own forward motion. It is a split second of distraction as he glances back, then looks up just in time to see the glittering blade swinging down toward him.

Robin, *he thinks, and then all goes black . . .*

The Spectre

i.

Why is nothing ever simple?

The question pounded through Soleta's head as she eased her way cautiously down the narrow maintenance corridor of the ship. For the thousandth time she wondered if there was any way he was going to be able to gain access to the bridge, and for the thousandth and first time she convinced herself that such was not the case. The seals she had left behind were simply too thorough, too efficient.

Still, she'd thought she had everything covered when she blew her entire crew complement out the hatches, and that hadn't exactly worked out as planned, had it?

She was carrying her disruptor tightly, gripping it with both hands for extra accuracy. Despite the tension she was feeling, despite the severity of the situation, one would never have known it to look at her. Her focus was total, and her hands were not trembling in the least. Her breathing was slow and steady, and she was hyperaware of any slight movement from around her that could possibly indicate an attack.

"*Soleta,*" came the familiar voice. It sounded through the ship's intercom, reverberating. She didn't have the faintest idea from where it was originating, nor could he—naturally—determine where she was. Such was the nature of the horrifically hazardous game they were playing. "*Soleta . . . have you considered the wisdom of surrender?*"

"I could ask you the same question," she countered.

"*Yes, I imagine you could. Indeed, there are many questions you could ask me.*"

"Not the least of which," said Soleta, "is how you survived."

"*Not an unreasonable curiosity,*" said the voice. "*However, I'm unclear as to why, precisely, I should be willing to share this information with you.*"

"Because you want to, Lucius," she said, not entirely able to keep the bitterness out of her tone. "You want to boast. You want to brag. You're simply dying to explain how you, in your cleverness, outwitted the half-breed."

She paused at a corner, took a deep breath, let it out, and then swung around while crouching, bringing her disruptor up fast and smooth.

Nothing. The corridor was empty.

The process was excruciatingly slow, and the only solace she took was that somewhere on this damned ship, Lucius was doing the exact same thing, following precisely the same procedure. Hunting section by section, trying to pin her down and eliminate her.

It had almost been a very simple thing for him to

accomplish. Soleta had been on her way up to the bridge. The murder of her crew was the single most horrific act she'd ever accomplished, and yet with effort she was pushing it as far into the recesses of her mind as it could go. There were simply too many things to worry about, not the least of which was the simple concept of . . . now what? With the ship in her possession, and not owing allegiance to any one race, what was she supposed to do with herself and the vessel?

She had more or less made up her mind that she had only one choice, and then—as she had turned down a corridor that would lead her directly up to the bridge—she had seen a sight that had shocked her to her core. There, pushing his way up through a catwalk hatchway, coming up right out of the floor, was Lucius.

He had seen her at the exact same moment that she had seen him. Fortunately for Lucius, and unfortunately for Soleta, he had already climbed halfway out, so he had easy access to the disruptor that was hanging from his hip. He produced it in a heartbeat and fired it right at Soleta. Soleta, moving with speed she wouldn't have thought herself capable of, fell back even as her own disruptor seemed to leap into her hand of its own accord. She fired off several fast blasts, completely missing Lucius, who ducked down and away from her assault.

"Computer!" she called out. "Lock down bridge, code six six six! Employ unique voice-recognition subroutine, code-named 'FUBAR.' Comply!"

"*Complying*," the computer voice replied with its customary calm.

Even though Soleta wasn't seeing it, she knew what was happening at that moment. The main entrance door had sealed itself off, and the backup entrance was now alive with enough crackling energy charge to stun a team of oxen. Furthermore, if by some miracle someone other than Soleta gained entrance to the ship's control center, an array of death traps would be launched that would certainly dispose of anyone foolish enough to intrude on the locked-down bridge.

The subroutine code-named "FUBAR" was yet another little fail-safe that the computer-savvy Soleta had built into the ship's operating system. "FUBAR," or so she had been taught by her mates back in Starfleet Academy, was an acronym standing for "Fouled Up Beyond All Recognition." It was used to describe any situation that had gone so completely south, it bordered on hopeless. The slang term had seemed a convenient one to use when she had rigged up the subroutine that would lock out any vocal commands from any other officers—either above or below her—who might choose to try and take the *Spectre* away from her. The ship was hers, and anyone who tried to usurp it from her did so at their own peril.

Because of her built-in safeguards, the computer would now not respond to any voice save hers. She would bet her life on that. *Actually, I already have*, she thought bleakly.

"*You know*," came Lucius's voice after a short time

for consideration, *"I believe you're right. I do want you to know."*

"Know what?" She wasn't being coy; her mind was racing so far and so fast, she was having trouble keeping track of the conversation in which she was engaged. For that matter, she was busy trying to second-guess where he was going to be next.

Engineering. That's where I would go if I were him. Even without code clearances and computer lockouts, there was nothing to stop him from going to the machine heart of the ship and trying something potentially disastrous. Of course, whatever happened to her would also happen to him. There was every chance, though, that someone as traditional as Lucius simply wouldn't care.

"How I survived, of course." He sounded a trifle impatient (not that she cared). *"I thought you were interested."*

"Of course I am, Lucius. I want you to give me your full due before I blow your head off at close range."

It was only her heightened hearing that warned her at the last second. Soleta ducked back as a disruptor blast exploded from the ceiling. *Damn him, he's still overhead!* Soleta snarled to herself even as she threw herself backward, strafing the overhead grating as fast as she could. She waited for the sound of a body thudding somewhere, but there was nothing.

"Tell me again," his voice echoed mockingly, no longer over the com, but instead all-too-close, "how are you going to be killing me?"

She did not immediately reply, feeling that to continue to do so was to play to his own interests. Instead she crept over to an entrance to an emergency maintenance conduit, one that she was reasonably sure would be far too narrow for Lucius to fit into. But she, on the other hand, was just barely able to insinuate her smaller frame into it.

As she wormed her way through, making her way down to engineering foot by agonizing foot, Lucius's voice continued. "I only had a few seconds to realize what it was you were up to. Fortunately enough, there's a backup transporter control linked directly into the bridge."

"You had the transporter beam you from the bridge to the transporter room, programming in a time delay so that you would reintegrate after the doors had cycled shut once more," Soleta realized, chiding herself inwardly for overlooking the possibility.

"Exactly, yes."

She paused, not wanting to make mention of the next logical move. Lucius, however, did it for her. "Naturally you're wondering why I didn't simply lock on to your life signs and beam you off the ship into the depths of space."

"The thought did occur to me," she admitted.

"Because such an action would have been unworthy of me. Furthermore, it might make it seem as if I were afraid of you."

"Since it's just the two of us here, no one else would have known," she pointed out, even as she wondered why she was doing so.

"I would know," came his voice firmly. "That one is more than enough, Legate. No, I resolved immediately that the only proper way to destroy you is face-to-face."

"And yet you snipe at me from hiding."

"Well, all of us are walking contradictions, don't you think?"

She wasn't interested in waxing philosophical. She was interested in finding him wherever it was he was hiding and disposing of him once and for all. Unfortunately, the emergency shaft she was edging through wasn't making that especially easy. She felt her arms starting to go numb from the elbows down, because she'd been leaning on them for so long.

"*Tell me, Legate,*" his voice came to her once more over the comm link. "*What was your plan? Now that you'd betrayed the trust of your crew by killing them . . .*"

"You? You, of all people, are going to lecture me on the cruelties of betrayal?"

"*A fair point,*" he conceded. "*Still, I am curious as to whether you had thought beyond your actions.*"

"My main concern was survival. However, I admit I have been considering options."

"*Reached any conclusions?*"

Rather than conclusions, she had reached the end of the emergency shaft. The passage was open in front of her. Deciding that speed was of absolute necessity, she squeezed her arms in tightly on either side and allowed herself to slide swiftly downward.

Soleta sped down and out, landing in the engineering section and bringing her arms up barely in time to absorb the impact. Just as she emerged, she was certain she heard a swift movement from somewhere around her. She braced herself for a shot; at this distance, it would potentially be a lethal one. None came. She went with the impact of her body upon the floor, rolling gracefully, tucking her knees in, and coming up in a fighting crouch before ducking behind a bank of equipment.

She cast a quick glance at the readings and saw that the engines appeared to be operating normally. Nothing had been set to overload or self-destruct, so that was all positive. It meant one of four things: Lucius hadn't gotten there yet; Lucius was already there, but hadn't had time to sabotage the engines; Lucius was already there, but didn't have the faintest idea how to go about destroying the ship from the engine room; Lucius was there and had something else in mind.

Soleta didn't think the third option was terribly likely. Which meant that, logically, the next thing she had to establish was the possibility of option one. To that end, she remained exactly where she was, unmoving. She was fully prepared to remain in the same place, with the same lack of movement, for however long it took to lure out Lucius if he was hiding there . . . or to lie in wait and trap him if he wasn't.

There was no sign of him being there. His voice, however, was still coming at her loud and clear. The frustrating aspect of it was that, because of the volume, she didn't have the slightest idea whether he was five decks away or five feet away. It was simply impossible to be certain.

"*Well, Legate?*" came the mocking tone. "*I'm still waiting for an answer. Now that you've murdered your crew . . .*"

"Defended myself," she responded. It was her long years of training in the mind-set of Vulcans that prevented the heat she felt from entering her tone of voice. "I defended myself from traitors."

"*I'm quite certain that's going to make a vast difference to the loved ones of those who died.*"

"What do you think, Lucius?" she demanded, even as her instinct warned her, *Don't let him do this to you. Don't let him get into your head. You'll do nothing but regret it.* "Do you think what I did was easy for me? It was the most difficult thing I've ever done. It was the last thing I ever wanted to do."

"*And yet you did. You did it quickly and efficiently and—*"

Soleta suddenly fired off several fast disruptor shots. It was a risky endeavor, she knew. If she wound up hitting the wrong thing, and it in turn reacted in the wrong way, the entire question of who should be in charge of the ship was going to become academic.

Lucius promptly stopped talking, and that told Soleta everything she needed to know. He was down here, down in engineering, as she had foreseen. The fact that he stopped talking didn't mean she'd hit him; the chances were far greater that she hadn't. But he'd had to duck out of the way. If he'd been elsewhere in the vessel, his comments would have continued uninterrupted.

He obviously figured out that he had tipped off, at the very least, his general whereabouts. "Well played, Legate," his voice echoed in grudging admiration.

"In answer to your question," Soleta said, as if her little stunt was so obvious that it required no more comment on her part, "once I'm done murdering you—as I did with the rest of my crew—I had more or less made up my mind to turn this vessel over to the Federation and try to repair my relations with them."

He didn't respond at first, and she wasn't entirely sure why. When he spoke again, however, she immediately understood: He was so seized with rage at the very notion that he had needed a moment to compose himself.

"Outrage," he snarled. "Scandalous! Is this how you honor the memory of the Praetor whom you claim to have so admired! By turning over one of his most advanced ships to the Federation?"

"As opposed to the way you honor him? By treachery and mutiny? Besides, in case you've forgotten, the Federation is supposed to be allied with us."

"A happenstance of mutual convenience! It will never last, never. True Romulans must be prepared for that time."

Soleta crept through the system couplings, making her way around the warp core. She knew that engaging in this bizarre back-and-forth with Lucius bordered on madness. She should simply be silent, lie in wait for him, pray for him to make a mistake. Instead, against all reason and logic, she continued to engage him. "Well, thank you for the lessons you've taught me about how 'true Romulans' do things.

From my observation, true Romulans such as your old mentor exploit friendships for the purpose of personal gain. True Romulans betray their commanders. If that's a true Romulan, then I'm more than content to be what I am."

"And what would that be?"

She ducked under the cloaking device, throbbing with a gentle crimson tint that cast an eerie glow on her surroundings. "I would think you'd be ready to tell me that. After all, you seem to have all the answers. What do you think I am?"

With greater speed than she would have thought possible, Lucius emerged from the shadows as if he were one of them, and his blaster was pointed right at her skull. "Dead," he said.

She froze where she was, her disruptor extended out in front of her. Her voice flat and even, she said, "Drop your disruptor, Lucius. I have you right where I want you."

"An interesting if bizarre jest, Legate," he told her, "considering that I am standing behind and to the side of you, and your disruptor is pointed away from me."

"Nevertheless, what I say is true. Don't make me fire."

"You're bluffing."

"Vulcans never bluff."

She knew if she made the slightest turn toward him, he would fire. The only thing that had stopped him from blowing her brains out at close range was undoubtedly his curiosity over her apparent confidence.

"Very well, then," said Lucius. "Shoot me."

Soleta could practically hear his heartbeat speed up with excitement, and then she was thinking of nothing but the pounding of blood in her own ears as she squeezed off a shot with her disruptor.

The disruptor blast went exactly where she intended it to: at a highly reflective control panel that she was targeting at an angle. It ricocheted off the control panel, bounded off the security field in place around the cloaking device, and hit Lucius squarely in the chest. The only thing that saved his life was that the disruptor blast was less than fully potent because the two targets it had already struck dissipated some of its power. That, combined with the fact that he was wearing a chest plate, stopped the disruptor blast from tearing a hole in him the size of Soleta's fist. It did, however, serve to knock him clean off his feet. Lucius thudded to the ground, but he still managed to hold on to his disruptor. He fired off a blast and Soleta ducked back to avoid it. It bought Lucius just enough time to get out of the way and take refuge behind a bank of power cells. It was a good hiding place; there was no way that Soleta could open fire on him back there without crippling the ship's power.

"Lucky shot!" he called to her.

The truth was that he was right. It was a lucky shot. She'd given herself a one-in-ten-thousand chance of pulling it off even as she'd taken it. But there was no reason she had to let him know that.

"Tell me, Lucius," she called defiantly. "What

bothers you more? That I'm a murderer? Or that maybe I'm not only your equal . . . but your superior."

"I still don't think you can kill me."

"Funny, I was just thinking the same thing about you."

"Let's say you *were* my superior. Am I to respect one who would turn this vessel over to the Federation?!"

She was working on coming around him. She peeked around a corner and didn't spot him. He'd repositioned himself yet again. She muttered a curse under her breath even as she asked, "And what's your brilliant plan? To return this ship to Romulus? You'll never make it that far!"

"Your concern for me is touching."

"I have no concern for you. I don't give a damn if you live or die. I'm simply pointing out the logic that you fail to see." She flattened her back against a wall and remained in a crouch. "There is a power vacuum in the Empire right now. Individual groups have had the opportunity to form alliances. You don't represent an ally to them. You represent a prize, a bonus left over from the previous regime. That's why they tried to take this vessel over your dead body before, and that's why they will succeed in accomplishing it should you hand them another opportunity. If you think you're going to arrive in triumph, you've badly underestimated the situation. The only way you're going to wind up back on the Romulan homeworld is in free fall, indistinguishable from any other bit of space debris plummeting from orbit."

No response.

She said nothing either. Time seemed to stretch and keep on stretching. She knew he was near, and more than that . . . she knew that this was it.

Soleta pivoted around the corner, ready to fire, and found Lucius's disruptor pointed right into her face. Lucius had the same view, except naturally it was Soleta's disruptor staring at him.

They stood there for what seemed a very long time, neither lowering their weapon . . . but neither firing.

His face, which was partly obscured by the weapon that was pointing at her, was impossible for her to read. His finger was on the trigger, as her own was, and there was no reason at all not to pull her own trigger before he did. Yet she didn't. Nor did he.

"Do you have an alternative?" he asked finally, his weapon unwavering.

"I might be willing to work on one, provided I had sufficient incentive."

"A disruptor pointed at your face is insufficient incentive?"

"There's one pointed at *your* face," she reminded him, "and you don't seem to be working too hard on an alternative."

He considered that. "True enough," he said finally. "A suggestion, then. I'll lower my weapon, you lower yours, and we'll work on discussing possible alternatives."

"Why should I? Won't I be proving that I'm 'inferior' to you because I'm not killing you?"

"And wouldn't the reverse be true?"

"Yes." Her voice tightened. "Look at the body count our mutual respect requires. What do you call that?"

"The Romulan way."

"Really. Well, then . . . say hello to the Vulcan way. The only way we'll ever trust each other."

Her hand stabbed out and gripped his face. He gasped, his eyes widening.

"Our minds are merging," she said forcefully as the weapon slipped from his hand. "Our minds are . . . are . . ."

The images of her pervaded his thoughts . . . the intensity . . . the passion . . . felt to Soleta as if they were igniting her soul.

At which point the negotiations took a most unexpected turn. . . .

U.S.S. Excalibur

"It's not true, is it?" Moke demanded.

He had been running all over the ship for what seemed like hours, and he had finally managed to track down Calhoun's son Xyon. Xyon was seated at a far table in the team room, a drink in front of him and a lifetime of enmity toward his father behind him. He looked up at Moke, who was standing there with a hopeful expression on his face.

"You'd know. He'd have told you. I can't get Kebron to tell me anything. Or Xy. I thought maybe you would."

Xyon took a deep breath and then let it out slowly. "I know what you know," he said. "Calhoun has locked himself in with a couple of aliens and they're all supposed to die very slowly unless the aliens come to terms and agree to play nice."

"But he can't let that happen!"

"He's the captain of the ship, Moke. He can do whatever he wants."

Moke's face was set. "I want to talk to him," he said.

"I don't think that's possible . . ."

"Yes it is! There's an observation deck above the shuttlebay! I can look down from there, and there's a speaker and everything! It's sealed in, so I bet the disease can't get at anyone in there! If you could get me in . . ."

"Why not go yourself?"

"Because," Moke said, making a sour face, "there's guards there. They're stopping me from getting in there. But I'm figuring you can."

Xyon leaned back in his chair. "And how," he asked with mild amusement, "do you figure that? What brilliant plan have you come up with that would thwart all the resources of the *Excalibur* and its crew. What 'in' do I have that they've overlooked?"

"Your ship. Your ship's got a transporter, and you can talk to your ship and activate it from outside. Don't tell me you can't. You did it when we were in there, to get us to safety. You can tell your ship to beam us in there and then up to the observation deck."

Xyon stared at him for what seemed, to Moke, a very long time. "*Grozit*, that's a brilliant plan," he finally admitted.

"Is it?"

"Yeah, pretty brilliant. I wish I'd thought of it. Would you mind if I told other people I thought of it, if they ask?"

"Sure. It means I won't get in trouble." He looked at Xyon askew. "You . . . do want to save Mac, don't you?"

"You mean would I prefer it if he didn't die?"

"Yeah."

"I've been thinking about that a lot. Much to my surprise, I'm coming around to the realization that the answer is yes." He stared at the glass in front of him. "Go figure."

Moke waited with growing impatience for Xyon to say something else, and then Xyon reached over and tapped his wrist com unit. "Lyla," he said softly, as if concerned someone was listening in. "This is Xyon."

"Hello, Xyon," the voice of his ship's onboard intelligence wafted through the air. "I've missed you."

"Same here. Look, I need you to do something for me." He reached out, draped an arm around Moke, and drew him close beside him. Then he told his ship exactly what he needed her to do.

Seconds later, there were turned heads and startled exclamations from the other off-duty denizens of the team room as Moke and Xyon sparkled out of existence. It was still a bizarre sensation for Moke, and he always felt as if it were the rest of the world dissolving into molecules around him, rather than he himself. He barely had time to register the surroundings of Xyon's vessel around him before he disappeared yet again, and ended his atom-scrambling odyssey in the observation deck above the shuttlebay. Xyon was standing right next to him, and he rested a hand on Moke's shoulder to steady him.

Moke could scarcely believe what he was seeing.

Mackenzie Calhoun was slumped on the floor, and he looked absolutely terrible. His skin was gray and mottled, covered with blotches and wounds that were seeping pus. Xyon had flipped on the audio connect unit so that they could hear everything that was going on down there, and even from this distance, it was easy to discern that Calhoun's breathing was uneven and ragged.

There were two other beings in there with him, neither of whom Moke recognized. They were, however, extremely bizarre-looking. Moreover, they were developing lesions that were similar to what Mac had on him. They weren't as profuse as they were on Mackenzie Calhoun. It was perfectly obvious that, whatever was happening to them, Calhoun's condition was furthest along.

The smaller of the two creatures was touching his sores gingerly and shaking his head, murmuring, "It can't be. It can't be." The other was much larger, and the sores on his body were considerably bigger than those on Calhoun and the smaller one. He was pacing like a captive animal, and he wasn't speaking at all. Instead, every so often, he would let out a protesting, inarticulate howl and smash one or more of his tentacles against what was apparently a forcefield separating him from the other creature and Calhoun.

"Maaaac!" The cry was ripped involuntarily from Moke's throat. It was enough to prompt Calhoun to turn his head and look up at him—squinting as hard as he could, since he was unable to make out who it was who had called his name.

Finally Calhoun spotted him. He sagged back against the wall once more. When he spoke, his voice sounded nothing like the calm and confident, measured tones to which Moke was accustomed.

"You shouldn't be here," he managed to say, his voice sounding raspy. "You should have stayed away. Xyon," and looking like he was summoning all his strength, he managed to raise his hand enough to waggle a scolding finger at his son. "Xyon, this is all your fault. You brought him here . . ."

"I thought you might want the opportunity to say good-bye," said Xyon. It was impossible for Moke to determine just what was going through Xyon's mind. His voice was flat, his true mind impossible to predict. It might be that Xyon was keeping everything together for his own and for Moke's sakes. Or it could be that he really just didn't care, and perhaps was even a little glad to see Calhoun potentially on his way out.

"I . . . didn't want you here," Calhoun told him. "I didn't want you to . . . see me like this . . ."

"Like what?" Xyon demanded. "Deeply embroiled in the midst of another of your famous suicidal stunts? You two . . . you whatever-you-ares," he addressed the two beings who were down there with Calhoun. They looked up at him with a confused weariness. "Did you know the type of lunatic you were becoming involved with when you set foot, or tendril or whatever, on this ship?"

"Stop it!" Moke cried out.

"The fact is," Xyon continued relentlessly, "he's been looking for an excuse to get out from under for ages now, and you've gone and given him one. I almost feel sorry for you. I always thought he was an accident waiting to happen, and you're the poor, pathetic bystanders who just happened to be standing around when it did."

"You're wrong!" Moke said, and he pushed Xyon fiercely. Xyon staggered back, but did nothing to retaliate. Instead he just stared at Moke pityingly. Moke turned away from him and shouted down, his hands pressed flat against the clear surface surrounding them, "Mac, don't listen to him! I know that's not the way you are!"

"I . . . appreciate the support, Moke," Calhoun said, and then a violent coughing fit seized him. His body trembled and rattled as he hacked furiously for long seconds before getting himself under control. Once he had stopped hacking, he tried to get to his feet, but was unable to find the energy to do so. So he leaned back once more, his hand on his chest, trying to find enough breath to speak. "It . . . it means a lot to me . . ."

To Moke's surprise, the larger of the two beings below spoke to him. "Tell him . . . to end this foolishness, young creature. He has a cure for himself . . . for all of us. Tell him he cannot force an agreement to end war . . . upon one who is bent on total annihilation . . ."

"You speak . . . of yourself, of course," said the other of the two. He was scratching furiously at himself, as if convinced all he had to do was itch hard enough and the sore on his body would simply peel off. "The Bolgar . . . have never wanted anything but peace . . ."

"Oh, of course. Which is why you've tried to wipe out my people, the Teuthis . . ."

"As you would us . . . !"

"We have acted only in self-defense against those who would destroy us."

"Your actions against us have been many, bordering on the legendary . . ."

"*Stop it!*" Moke howled, his voice rising above theirs. Somewhat to Xyon's surprise, the two of them actually silenced themselves. "Mac is dying because he's that determined to try and bring the two of you together and make you stop fighting, and all you can do is keep on fighting! It's like what he's doing doesn't mean anything to you! You don't care about living or dying! You just care about who's right!"

"That's ridiculous," rumbled the Teuthis. "I want to live. We both do."

"The Teuthis are rarely right about anything, but this one is right about that," said the Bolgar. He was looking with clear concern at the sores, having stopped scratching them and instead regarding them with a growing sense of dread. "I am not suicidal, as your captain apparently is. I wish to live, and I wish for my race to live."

"Then do something about it!" Moke cried out. "Before it's too late! Look at him!"

Calhoun was indeed a terrifying specimen to look upon. He was trying to speak, but there was such listlessness in his eyes that it was truly an awful thing to see. It looked like every move he was making filled him with pain . . . and, worse, that he was beyond caring about it. He seemed to have resigned himself to the notion that he was going to die, and it was this resignation in one who was such a fighter that frightened Moke the most. *"Look at him!"* Moke said again. "Look at what he's doing to himself just to get you to cooperate!"

"Don't sing him songs of self-sacrifice," said the Bolgar. "He's doing it in order to find a way out of this sphere for his ship."

"That doesn't matter! Whatever the reason, he's doing it so other people's lives will be better! And the two of you shouldn't be trying to kill each other!"

"He's right." Calhoun had managed to speak, even though his voice sounded as if he were whispering to them from the other side of the grave. "You can . . . either act as if you were both put in this . . . this sphere . . . for mutual aid . . . or mutual annihilation. If it's the former . . . then that's what I'm trying . . . to push you toward. If it's the latter . . . then that's what I've guaranteed you . . . this day. So either way . . . you win . . ."

He gasped, trying to draw in air, and he tried to haul himself to his feet. "Running out of time . . . out of . . . this is . . . this is insane . . . you can . . . stop this . . . stop before it's . . ."

And then Calhoun stumbled forward and crashed heavily to the floor, like a sack of rocks. He lay there, facedown, arms and legs splayed.

"Do something!" Moke shouted, his voice echoing through the chamber. "Make him stop this! Please!"

"They won't," Xyon said harshly, his voice dripping with contempt. "The only thing that matters is their mutual hatred."

"You know nothing of us," said the Bolgar.

"I know enough. I've seen your kind all over our galaxy. It's nice to know that stupidity and destructive pride are universal constants."

There was silence then, punctuated only by the rasping of Calhoun's labored breathing.

"Let us speak," said the Bolgar.

"I am listening," replied the Teuthis. Then he glanced at Calhoun and added, "And were I you, I would talk quickly."

New Thallon

i.

Fhermus appeared happy to see them. That, as far as Robin Lefler was concerned, could not possibly be a good sign.

When the *Trident* had first approached New Thallon, there were a number of ships barring the way. This had naturally made Lefler somewhat nervous, because she disliked the notion of the *Trident* having to fight its way through an assortment of vessels. But when they had identified themselves to authorities from New Thallon hailing them, the revelation that Robin herself was aboard the vessel seemed to produce an immediate reaction. The message that returned to the *Trident*, however, was one that sent a chill up Robin's spine.

"Our lord Fhermus welcomes a landing party from the Trident, *and is especially anxious to greet Lieutenant Commander Lefler upon her return to her adopted home."*

This dispatch caused a good deal of uncertainty upon receipt. Kat Mueller's reaction was immediate: "You shouldn't go down there," she said, seated in her command chair on the bridge. "This is 'come into my parlor' language, and I have no desire to see you be the fly to their spider."

"What's the alternative?" Robin demanded. "That I stay up here and cower because Fhermus said I was welcome?"

"We don't know what we're going to find when we beam down there."

"When do we ever?" she asked reasonably.

Mueller exchanged a glance with Shelby, who shrugged. "She's got a point," said Shelby.

"I'm just saying that I'm suspicious of someone who appears that happy to see you . . . especially when he has no reason to," said Mueller. "Which means that he probably does have a reason, and it's not one that we're going to like particularly."

"Si Cwan is down there," Lefler said firmly. "He's my husband."

"A husband who forced you to leave your home under armed escort."

"Because he was concerned about me. However ineptly he expressed that concern, that was still what motivated him. I'm no less concerned about him now, and I do not choose to express that concern by waiting up here on the *Trident* to see how it all turns out."

"You do," Mueller reminded her, "if I say you do."

Robin looked appealingly toward Shelby, but the admiral shook her head. "This is her ship, Robin. I'm not going to countermand her judgment."

"But Admiral—"

"You could try respectfully requesting."

It was Romeo Takahashi who had spoken up. Everyone on the bridge looked to him as he sat there calmly at ops, his tone devoid of its usual affected drawl. "That's what I'd do," he continued calmly. "You want something of a commanding officer . . . you show respect. No disrespect intended to you, Robin. I'm just saying, is all." But he wasn't looking at Robin. Instead his gaze was fixed upon Mueller, whose own face was unreadable.

Lefler turned back to Mueller, and then squared her shoulders. In the most formal tone she could adopt, she said, "Captain, I am respectfully requesting permission to go ashore."

Mueller looked as if she was about to snap off an answer, but instead sighed heavily. "All right," she said. "But I'll be there with you."

"Captain," Commander Desma immediately spoke up. "As first officer—"

"I know what you're going to say, Commander. God knows I said it enough times to the admiral over there when I was her first officer. This time, however, I'm going to use some of that famed prerogative you may have heard about back in Starfleet Academy. Arex," she continued before Desma could protest, "you're with me. First Officer, you have the conn."

She started to rise to head for the turbolift when Desma said insistently, "Captain, with all respect, I must protest."

"The decision's made, I'm going down—"

"Yes, Captain, you've made that clear. My protest centers on the fact that I should not have the conn. We have a ranking officer on board, and one who has commanded this vessel before." She nodded toward Shelby. "By all rights, in the absence of her captain, the *Trident* should be commanded by Admiral Shelby."

Mueller paused. Her normally stoic expression cracked ever so slightly toward a smile, and then she gestured toward the command chair. "You heard the lady," she told Shelby.

Shelby looked as if she was about to protest as well, but then she merely shrugged and took her place in the command chair. Lefler couldn't help but notice that there was a serenity in Shelby's face that hadn't been there before. When Mueller, Lefler, and Arex headed out to beam down to the planet's surface, Lefler wasn't even sure if Shelby knew they had left.

"Hello, baby," Shelby whispered, rubbing the armrests affectionately. "Did you miss me?"

ii.

Lefler, Mueller, and Arex materialized, not within the main palace of New Thallon, but a distance away at a sort of central receiving point. This was at the specific request of Fhermus, who made it clear he didn't want Federation personnel popping in and out of thin air right in the midst of his people. "There are protocols involved," was all that the *Trident* was told, although what those protocols might be was never specified.

An armed escort of five men met them there. Three of them were Thallonian and two bore the gleaming gold skin of Nelkarites. Robin found that somewhat disturbing, particularly in the way they kept glancing at her. Mueller, for her part, appeared unfazed. Her tone was firm and commanding. When she told them briskly, "Bring us to Fhermus immediately," one of the guards replied in a harsh tone, "You mean *Lord* Fhermus?"

She fixed a withering glance on him and said, "No. I mean *immediately*." The guard met her gaze for a moment and then looked down. He wound up taking the lead in the escort, apparently desiring to be as far from Mueller as possible. Lefler caught Mueller's eye and Mueller gave her a fast wink. It almost made Robin laugh aloud since it was so unexpected.

As they approached the mansion, Lefler saw that repairs were under way. She also noticed that workers would glance toward her and then look away as if reluctant to maintain eye contact.

"So what exactly is our plan?" Robin asked in a low voice.

"Plan?"

"How are we going to get Si Cwan away from them?"

"Well," Mueller replied, "I was thinking something as simple as that we demand to see him, they bring him to us, and then we all beam up to the *Trident*."

"That all sounds workable," said Robin. "It's just . . ."

"Just what?"

"Well . . . if we've thought of that, certainly they'll have thought of it as well."

Mueller nodded. "I know. That has occurred to me."

"Do you think they've found a way to counter it?"

"I'm worried they may have, yes." But she would not go into any further speculation than that.

iii.

"Lieutenant Commander! How lovely to see you again!"

Fhermus's display of ebullience upon seeing her did anything but put Robin at ease. Then again, she had a feeling that it wasn't designed to.

Robin, along with Mueller and Arex, had been escorted to the central council chamber, the home of what had been—should have been—the New Thallonian Protectorate. They were standing in the outer rim, the customary spectators' position. Fhermus was standing in his usual spot dead center, making the absence of Si Cwan all the more stark in comparison since Cwan was usually on the opposite side of the table from him.

She noticed that there were open seats in the council chamber. Obviously there were those of Si Cwan's allies who were not yet on the same page as Fhermus and his associates.

What was most appalling to her was that the residents of New Thallon were not rising up in outrage against the despicable treatment that Si Cwan had received at the hands of his erstwhile "friends." It seemed incomprehensible to her: Here this damned Fhermus had bombed New Thallon, and then betrayed its leader, but the inhabitants seemed more willing to throw in their lot with their assailant than the man whose job it was to protect them.

Then again, perhaps it wasn't too bizarre to understand at that. It was just a matter of comprehending the Thallonian mind-set. As far as they were concerned, Si Cwan was a failed protector. Legends might have arisen about him, and in any number of places in Thallonian space his mere presence was enough to make jaws drop and onlookers fall to one knee. But it's said that no one is a hero in his own home, and as far as the residents of New Thallon were concerned, Si Cwan didn't have the greatest track record in the galaxy. Not only did their original homeworld of Thallon get smashed to space dust on his watch, but he was the one responsible—either through his actions or those of his sister—for the bombing that had besieged them not long ago. Granted, Fhermus had been doing the bombing, but the citizenry can view things very oddly, and there might well be the general belief that Si Cwan had provoked it. That Thallonians had died because Si Cwan's sister had had a fatal argument with her husband on their wedding night.

She could just imagine the discussion among Thallonians. "His sister has a homicidal urge on her honeymoon, and we die because of it!" That concept alone

would undoubtedly lead to lengthy discussions center-
ing on many more of Si Cwan's transgressions, real or
imagined. Plus there was the practicality aspect of it. If
Si Cwan, the alleged protector of the Thallonians, was
unable to keep them safe from attacks by their enemies, what better way to forestall attacks than by wel-
coming that same enemy into your bosom?

The very notion of it—tossing aside their prince,
their lord Si Cwan, in exchange for this launcher of
cowardly terrorist attacks—made Lefler bristle in
indignation. But she knew all her bristling wouldn't
make the slightest difference to the present situation.
Instead what she had to do was remain calm and stay
on top of her feelings in the matter.

She remembered what Si Cwan's people had done
to Xyon while he was in their possession. She had no
reason to assume they would be any more gentle in
their treatment of Si Cwan. She had steeled herself for
anything.

Fhermus was gesturing expansively for them to
approach. "Come, come," he called out. "There is
nothing to be afraid of. We are all allies here. All of
New Thallon is united in our desire for peace, pros-
perity, and a new direction for the New Thallonian
Protectorate . . . although," he added with a wink to
his associates, "I admit there is some discussion of
transforming the name into the New Nelkarite Protectorate. But that is merely in the talking stages."

"Indeed," said Mueller as she approached Fhermus, Lefler and Arex following her. "How nice to hear
from you that all of New Thallon is behind you."

"Yes, yes . . ."

"Although," continued Mueller, nodding toward Arex, "my security head here has been monitoring transmissions and such on your world, and I'm not exactly hearing tales of total unity. What I'm hearing about are stories of resistance. Of your soldiers trying to seize hold of, and control, various cities on New Thallon, and not exactly having the easiest time of it."

Fhermus waved dismissively. "Insurrectionists. Last gasps of rebellion. They should be snuffed out within days, once they've been made to realize that we've relieved them of a weak and uncertain ruler."

"Si Cwan was not their ruler, as I understand it," said Mueller. "He was a co-counsel with you. With all of you," and she took in the lot of them with a cold gaze. "He willingly shared his power."

"That merely underscored his weakness of resolve," replied Fhermus. "His people have now realized that."

"His people don't know which way is up or down," Robin said, stepping forward. She felt buoyed by what Mueller had just said, for she had been unaware that the entirety of New Thallon had not simply fallen in line behind Fhermus and his thugs. "The fact that you've taken the capital here means nothing. You're nothing but an occupying force on this world, outnumbered and out-gunned. Occupations always fail. Always."

"Really." Fhermus chuckled at that. "I seem to recall the Klingons have created rather successful occupying forces in the past."

"*That's* who you wish to model yourself upon?"

demanded Arex, his face distorted in a grimace. "The Klingons?"

Lefler didn't entirely blame Arex for his attitude. He had, after all, fallen through time from a distant past in which Klingons were still bitter enemies of the Federation. Even though he had been in the present for several years, he was still working on adjusting to the notion that Klingons were Federation allies.

"I'm modeling myself on no one," Fhermus replied. "I'm simply saying that the Thallonian people will adjust."

"Where's Si Cwan?" said Mueller.

"Ah. I was wondering when we would get to that."

"Then wonder no more."

"If you'd like a record of his last great adventure as ruler of New Thallon," said Fhermus casually, "then treat yourself to this." He tossed a data crystal toward them, which Arex promptly reached out and snagged. "It's very entertaining. Si Cwan battling some sort of monster. It's a very good fake; our researchers have been unable to figure out how he did it. I suspect something as simple as a hologram. After all, he did install a holosuite for you, his loving wife. Not difficult to put together a monster-hunting scenario in that venue, is it."

"We saw how you treated him in your broadcast," Robin said. "It was appalling. Revolting."

"And yet revolt was what we desired to quell. Our hope was that Lord Cwan would be more cooperative. Such did not turn out to be the case." Fhermus shrugged as if it were a minor matter.

"Where is he?" said Lefler. She stepped around Mueller, bringing herself to within a few steps of Fhermus. She was repulsed by his arrogance and smug satisfaction.

Fhermus smiled at her. "He's dead."

A silence fell upon the room, and Robin felt a distant buzzing in the back of her skull. For just a heartbeat—for reasons she didn't yet comprehend—she suddenly wasn't in the council chamber. She was back at Starfleet Academy, she was in a course, and an instructor was intoning, *Officially, we don't teach you this . . . officially, this is not in the curriculum . . .*

Then she was back, jolted to reality by Mueller's harsh response: "You're lying."

"Am I?" asked Fhermus, his face the picture of innocence, as if he were stunned that anyone would accuse him of such a thing.

. . . ultimately, our job is not only to prepare you for going into space . . . but coming back in one piece . . .

She felt as if her mind were splitting. She was hearing what Fhermus was saying, but as if through a distance of years, her thoughts ricocheting back to the Academy . . .

"Yes," Mueller said firmly. "You wouldn't be that stupid. You must have some idea of the danger involved in turning Si Cwan into a martyr."

"Yes, I do have an idea of that danger. By the same token, I also have a fairly clear idea of the danger involved in keeping someone like Si Cwan alive. He is very resourceful, and sooner or later, he would have managed to overcome whatever restraints or predicaments we put him in and come looking for my head . . ."

. . . these techniques are for defense only, and are to be used only in matters of last resort . . . when it's your opponent or you, and you are unarmed or in such close quarters that you can't draw your weapon . . .

Fhermus reached down under the round table at which he was standing and brought up something covered with a cloth, positioned upon a platter.

. . . there are, of course, wide varieties of alien biology, so not every move is going to work on every opponent. This, however, is a fairly effective technique on seventy percent of known humanoids, effectively crushing the breathing apparatus and bringing death within thirty seconds . . .

He gripped the top of the cloth, like a magician about to perform a trick . . .

. . . now . . . face your holosimulation opponent . . .

. . . and whipped it off with a flourish, and the world spun sideways around Robin as she looked into the dead eyes set in Si Cwan's head, which sat square in the middle of a gleaming bronze tray, and it was a joke or a hoax, it had to be, it wasn't real, it couldn't be real, and she reached out to touch it, to shove her finger deep into its fake flesh, and she knew the moment she touched its cold red surface that it was him, it was her husband, and every second of the time that she had known him from the moment she'd first set eyes upon him on the *Excalibur* slammed through her mind, and Mueller was shouting something in outrage at Fhermus, but Robin couldn't hear her because the pounding between her ears was too loud, and Fhermus's laugh was cutting through the noise, and Robin fought the urge to scream because she knew she wouldn't stop, not ever, and she didn't even remember picking up Cwan's head, and cradling it in the crook of one elbow as she turned toward Fhermus, who was still laughing, and there was applause from all around them by the allies who apparently thought the expression on Robin's face was simply priceless, and Fhermus was saying something about Si Cwan begging for mercy at the end . . .

. . . *and now, with your fingers extended thusly, thrust like a spear toward the throat* . . .

. . . and Robin's free hand moved of its own accord and suddenly Fhermus was no longer laughing, instead his eyes were wide in astonishment as if they were going to bug out of his head, and then Robin wasn't holding Cwan's head anymore, she had lost track of it, she didn't care, she had both her hands upon Fhermus, and she was screaming and right up against him, and Mueller was atop her, trying to pull her off . . .

. . . *of course, if a weapon should present itself, use it* . . .

. . . and there was Fhermus's dagger, in his belt, and she was reaching for it, and time seemed to collapse completely around her, folding in and down upon itself, for everything had become flashes of images now, no longer coherent events unspooling one after the other, and she had disconnected from her own body, she was watching as if seeing everything from outside herself, and there were her hands upon Fhermus, and the dagger was in the sheath, and then out, and she no longer felt her hands or any part of her body but saw the dagger drive home into Fhermus's chest, splitting his heart, and blood was absolutely everywhere . . .

Kalinda wakes up screaming.

She has fallen asleep on the floor of the cell that the Priatians have continued to keep her in all during her stay there. She has not given up hope of rescue. She has never doubted that, sooner or later, her brother will show up with the might of the New Thallonian Protectorate backing him up. She knows there is no reason to think that her fiancé, Tiraud, will not do the honors. And even Xyon, her former lover, is enough of a wild card that he might be the one who steps in to help. Still, every time she runs it through her mind, it is Si Cwan who is coming for her. It may take him time, but eventually there will be shooting outside the door, and a ruckus, and much screaming. And then the doors will slide open and Si Cwan will stride in, looking slightly put off with her in that way he has. Then he will scoop her up and carry her out, and she will sink with relief against his chest.

That knowledge has sustained her through her imprisonment.

Now it is gone, replaced with a new knowledge: Her brother is dead.

It is impossible that she could, or would, know this. Her sensitivity to the departed is usually limited to the planet upon which they perished. New Thallon is many light-years away . . . unless Si Cwan has actually come to Priatia, but she does not believe that has happened yet.

Besides . . . she senses the distance. As impossible as it seems to her, she knows that Si Cwan is gone. That he died with no loved ones on hand. It is all becoming clear to her now, and Kalinda realizes she senses it not simply because of his passing, but because loved ones have learned of it, and their agony is like a psychic reverberating howl audible to Kalinda even across all this distance. Their grief is hers, signaling to her like a light in the darkness.

She sits up violently fast, and for half a heartbeat, she sees him. She doesn't know if he's truly standing there, or if it's a dreamlike impression left against the backs of her eyelids just before they snap open. Either way, he is there, and he is in pain, and he is possessed of fury beyond imagining, and then he is gone, just like that. She lunges for the space that he no longer occupies and she shrieks his name and keeps shrieking it until one of her captors, Keesala of Priatia, oozes into her prison chamber and asks in that infuriatingly mild voice of his whatever could be distressing her.

At first she doesn't want to tell him, but then she looks up at him with cold, burning fury and says, "My brother is dead."

"Si Cwan?" says Keesala, looking surprised. Then he considers the announcement and finally says, "You have my condolences on your loss."

"I neither want nor need your condolences," Kalinda says with a snarl, getting to her feet and facing her squidlike jailer. Her hands are curled into tight fists and barely contained fury contorts her face. "I want your life. And I will have it. Yours and every other damned soul's on Priatia. You and your people, who started this all for the purpose of causing a civil war that would enable you to then sweep in and

*take back all the worlds in Thallonian space. You will not
succeed, and I will make sure to kill you myself."*

*"Then perhaps," Keesala says mildly, "we should kill you
first. Just to be safe."*

*"Do it," snaps Kalinda, advancing on him. "Do it if
you've the nerve. Do it and be damned with you. Unless you
think I'll kill you first."*

*Keesala does not attack. Instead he backs up. Without
even turning around he glides away from her, his tentacle-
like feet moving with their customary silence. Seconds later
he is out the door. It slides shut in his wake, and Kalinda is
left slamming her fists in impotent fury against it.*

U.S.S. Trident

i.

No time at all seemed to have passed for Robin Lefler, and suddenly she realized that Elizabeth Shelby was looking down at her.

The screaming and shouts from the representatives all around her ceased all at once, and then she realized in a detached way that the noise had, in fact, ceased for some time. It took her a few moments to register that she was no longer in the council chamber, and almost a full minute to realize that she was no longer on the planet at all, but rather in the *Trident* sickbay.

"Doc!" called Shelby. "I think she's focusing on me."

Doc Villers, the ship's rough-hewn CMO, stepped into view. She looked down at Robin, then extended her index finger and brought it back and forth past Robin's eyes. Robin watched it pass by with curiosity, and then Villers nodded in her customary brusque manner. "Yeah. She's coming out of it." She glanced up at the diagnostic panel on the wall. "About damned time, too."

"What . . . happened?" Robin managed to say, except her voice was little more than a croak. She frowned, confused. "How . . . how long was I . . . ?"

"Eleven hours," said Shelby.

"Are we still in orbit . . . around New Thallon?"

"Are you joking? The moment we had you people up here, we got the hell out of Dodge before the other ships orbiting the planet realized what had happened. Otherwise we'd have had to fight our way out, and I can't say I would have liked the odds."

At that moment, Kat Mueller stepped into view. "She's coming around, I see. Good timing on my part." She sounded even more distant and formal than usual.

"Good timing?" snorted Villers. "You've been down here every twenty minutes checking in."

"Cwan . . ." Robin managed to say. She was astounded how numb she felt. No crying. Nothing.

Shelby looked grim. "It was him. We tested the . . . his remains. Arex recovered it before he had us beam the three of you out of the middle of the melee. I'm . . . I'm sorry . . ."

"Fhermus."

The admiral paused a moment, and then said, "He's dead."

"Stabbed."

"Yes."

"Who—?"

"Robin," Mueller spoke up, "now may not be the best time to—"

She locked eyes with Mueller and then said firmly, "No. Now is the perfect time." She forced herself to sit up and almost pitched forward before Mueller steadied her. She looked straight into Shelby's eyes and said, "I remember now. The shock . . . it took me a moment to . . ."

"Lieutenant Commander," said Shelby, "the captain may be right. This isn't . . ."

"I killed the bastard."

The words hung there, and then Lefler said again, nodding in confirmation, "I killed him. I crushed his windpipe and then, just to make sure, I grabbed his dagger off his belt and I planted it in his heart. The same way his son, Tiraud, died. If he was stupid enough to carry a weapon so that it could be used against him after what happened to Tiraud, then to hell with him. In fact, to hell with him in any event."

"Robin," said Mueller softly, "I already told Admiral Shelby that it wasn't you."

"What? What are you talking about?"

"Captain Mueller," Shelby told her, casting a look at Mueller, "told me that although you did assault Fhermus, your attempt was unsuccessful . . . and that she, in a moment of rage, pulled out the dagger and killed Fhermus. I have not yet launched a full investigation into the—"

"There will be no investigation required, Admiral," Robin told her, and there was a look of fire in her eyes. "I was there. I killed him. Captain Mueller is now clearly attempting to claim responsibility in a misguided attempt to spare me . . . I don't know. Future grief. In any event, her concern is misplaced. End of story."

Shelby laughed uneasily. "I'm . . . look, Robin, I

wanted to delay this until later, when you'd had time to recover from . . . until everything was . . ."

"I said it's the end of the story, Admiral, and it is." She slid off the edge of the table, and wavered for a moment on her feet before steadying herself. "I was within my rights to do as I did."

"Within your . . ." Shelby and Mueller exchanged confused glances. "Lefler," said Shelby, "you're still a Starfleet officer . . ."

"I'm a head of state and I executed a traitor."

"What?" said Shelby, her voice rising. "What the hell are you—"

"Oh my God, she's right," Mueller said in sudden realization. When Shelby turned and stared at her, Mueller repeated, "I think . . . she's right. I'm almost sure she . . . I read up on Thallonian law ages ago, when we first started the assignment in Sector 221-G. And I . . . I seem to remember . . ."

"According to law," Robin Lefler said, "if a head of state—a lord, such as Si Cwan—dies, and there's no blood family member eligible to assume his responsibilities, but a spouse is available, then his spouse is expected to step in and take over his position. With the . . ." She took a breath and let it out. "With the death of Si Cwan . . . I am now the ruler of New Thallon. 'Protectorate' or no, I still take his place as Lord of New Thallon with the right of high, middle, and low justice. I condemned Fhermus to death for his actions, and carried out the sentence."

"But a Starfleet officer can't simply—"

"I resign my commission, effective immediately."

Shelby began to speak, but then didn't. Instead she looked slightly deflated. Instinctively, Robin knew what was going through her mind, and she put a hand on Shelby's shoulder.

"I know what you're thinking," she said. "You're thinking this is Soleta all over again. But it's not. I swear to you, it's not. You're not responsible for this."

"The hell I'm not."

"Elizabeth . . ."

"I should have kept us on course for Priatia!" said Shelby angrily. "If I hadn't given in . . ."

"We can make up for that one right now," Lefler told her. "We head for Priatia now." Her face tightened. "And we don't go alone. If Fhermus thinks . . . if Fhermus *thought*," she amended, "that he was the only one who could use the ether to get things stirred up, he's about to find out how wrong he was."

ii.

Robin received a steady stream of visitors to her quarters over the next several hours, each of them extending their condolences. The one who seemed the most upset was the Caitian, M'Ress, which made Robin wonder in the back of her mind whether something hadn't gone on with them at some point in the past. She hadn't the faintest idea when that might have been. Then again, her husband . . . her late husband . . . was nothing if not resourceful. She did not, however, have the nerve to ask M'Ress if her suspicions were correct. Instead she simply nodded and accepted her condolences, as she did with the other crewmen who came by.

She did not spend a good deal of time talking to any of them, though. She explained over and over, maintaining her politeness, that she was busy writing something regarding Si Cwan's death and it was of the utmost importance. Everyone nodded in understanding, even though none of them truly understood.

All the time that she was working, and all the time that people came up to her, she kept waiting for the grief to kick in. And still nothing happened. There was no welling up of tears, no moistening of her eyes, no dramatic collapse. The fact that there was nothing began to bother her. She knew it was customary to be in shock over something like this, but she didn't feel as if she was in shock. Her mind was clear, her priorities were focused. What the hell was going on?

She wondered if Si Cwan's exiling her had somehow, in some small way, killed her love for him. But no: she was positive that wasn't it. She couldn't possibly have gone over the deep end as she had, tried to kill Fhermus, if she hadn't still loved him with all her . . .

That was when she stopped working on her speech and came to a full realization. It stunned her for long seconds, and then she tapped her combadge and said, "Lefler to Captain Mueller."

"Mueller here."

"Captain . . . would it be too much trouble to ask

you to come down to my quarters for a moment? I . . . wanted to run a draft of the speech by you."

"On my way."

She remained in her seat, unmoving, until Mueller arrived. Then she stood when the captain entered, as protocol suggested. They both sat and Mueller said quietly, "I was wondering when you would want to chat, the two of us."

"This isn't about what I'm writing."

"I know."

"You killed Fhermus."

"I know."

Her ready admission stilled Lefler for a moment. In the ensuing silence, Mueller nodded slightly and said, "Ever since you came to, you've been far more forceful and commanding than I remember. It looks good on you."

"You killed Fhermus."

"Yes, we've been over that. And I admitted to it."

"Why?"

"Why what?" asked Mueller. "Why did I kill him, or why did I admit to it?"

"Both, I suppose."

"I killed him because Si Cwan deserved better. He deserved a majestic death, a death for the ages. A death battling a hundred attackers at once, and he would die with his teeth buried in the throat of his killer. I killed him because it offended my sense of what is right and just and the sort of death a true warrior is entitled to. I killed him because his knife was there in front of me, as was his chest, and if anyone is going to be wielding a blade, it should be the woman with the Heidelberg fencing scar. Besides, no offense, but you weren't getting the job done. That choke hold they teach us in the Academy is all well and good, but doesn't work worth a damn on Nelkarites. I killed him, and given a dozen times to make the choice, I'd make the same one again. And I confessed to it because a Starfleet officer doesn't hide from the consequences of her actions."

"Yet Shelby thought that you were confessing in order to cover for me."

"Yes."

"Why?"

Mueller shrugged. "Comfort level, I suppose. Admiral Shelby felt more comfortable in a universe where a Starfleet captain nobly takes the blame for a crime she didn't commit in order to cover for the actions of a distraught wife. A far superior construct to a universe where a captain of the line mercilessly kills a man because he executed a former lover . . ."

Lefler smiled mirthlessly. "Funny. You didn't mention that as being one of the reasons. You just spouted lots of high-flown rhetoric as to how Si Cwan deserved better. You acted like it was a matter of balancing cosmic scales."

"It was."

"And the fact that you and Si Cwan were lovers at one point?"

The high cheeks of Mueller's face flushed ever-so-slightly red. "All the reasons that I cited were why Fhermus deserved to die. That last one . . . is the reason why I decided to be the one to do it."

"Instead of his wife."

"You get to kill the next one. I promise."

The comment was supposed to sound humorous, Robin supposed, but instead it was simply cold and bitter. The fact was that, as appalling as the concept was to her, Robin had to admit that she was relieved Mueller had been the one who had actually done the deed.

"Are you going to tell Admiral Shelby?" asked Mueller with a cocked eyebrow.

Lefler shrugged. "Not exactly sure I see the point. As you said, the admiral has her view of the universe. She has her report to make to Starfleet . . . presuming, of course, that anyone in Starfleet is still talking to us after this insanity is over."

"Ah yes," sighed Mueller. "I almost forgot I conspired in the hijacking of my own ship. A ship, I should think, I'd be well advised to get back to running for as long as I'm still in command of her."

She rose from her seat and as she headed for the door, Robin said, "Kat." Mueller turned and looked back at her. "Thank you," she said.

"Don't disappoint me," replied Mueller. "And more importantly . . . don't disappoint *him*." And she turned and headed out of the room.

iii.

The broadcast went over the subether in the exact same way that Fhermus's had. Citizens, space vessels, worlds throughout Sector 221-G, aka Thallonian space, all of them saw the same thing. The impact it had was as varied as the races that witnessed it.

There was Robin Lefler, seated on the bridge of the *Trident*. Shelby was to her left, Mueller to her right. She looked calm and determined and seething with quiet anger.

"This message is going out," she said, "to all sentient beings within the sound of my voice. I am Robin Lefler . . . late of Earth . . . late of Starfleet . . . and now the ruler-in-absentia of New Thallon. My husband, Lord Si Cwan, was assassinated by the usurper, Fhermus, of the House of Fhermus. He did this in the belief that Kalinda of New Thallon was responsible for the death of his son. He was wrong. This error led him to ambush and then slaughter my husband. That was also wrong. I have rectified this error . . . by taking Fhermus's life. This will no doubt make me a target for allies of his. Fine. However, as the new power in Thallonian space, I have taken it upon myself to summon aid from Starfleet. If you wish to go up against not only myself but the combined might of the most powerful spacegoing fleet in existence, be my guest. I assure you my hospitality will be forthcoming . . . and lethal.

"You can be against me . . . or you can be with me. And the place you can be with me is Priatia. At this moment, I am heading toward that world . . . a world where I firmly believe that the true Kalinda, sister of my late husband, is being held prisoner. I intend to retrieve her from captivity, and the Priatians will be forced to admit to their culpability in the death of Si Cwan. For those of you who believe that the Priatians are a helpless, marginal race . . . a mere shadow of their former selves . . . I believe they have powerful allies. Allies not of this territory. Allies who may well show themselves if the Priatians are directly threatened.

"We have the video record of my husband's battle with the creature who impersonated his sister. Fhermus endeavored to dismiss it as a hoax. It was not. We are going to continue to play it on an endless loop on an adjacent frequency, so all of you can see the heroism that my husband possessed . . . and so you can see the face of the enemy. We will produce more with that same face, I guarantee it.

"Those of you who are loyal to Si Cwan—who reveled in his greatness—I say this to you: Fhermus and his followers tried to pretend you did not exist. That you were few in number and of no consequence. I call upon you now to show them that they were wrong. That you have consequence. That you are willing to fight in the memory of your lord, and avenge yourselves upon those who were responsible for this pointless civil war. Join me at Priatia, and we will rain down justice upon them. It will be a battle that will be spoken of for ages, and remembered by all future generations. If you are with me . . . join us there. If you are not," and her voice dropped to a deep, threatening tone, "then I suggest you stay the hell out of our way. Robin Lefler . . . out."

After a few moments, Arex called out, "All right.

We have it. It's going out now." He paused and then said, "Uh . . . Captain . . . Admiral . . . 'rain down justice'? Not exactly in our mission parameters."

"I know that, Arex," said Shelby. "But those hearing the message don't know that. Officially, we're simply escorting her. We will fire on no one first."

"And if someone fires on us?"

"Then," Mueller spoke up, "we will ask them to stop."

"And if the Priatians see through my bluff? If they believe it's a joke of some sort . . ." said Robin.

"I suspect that will not be the case here," Mueller told her. "And I further suspect that, when word gets out . . . the Priatians will not be laughing."

Priatia

The Wanderers loom over Keesala and the others of his race. It is a size disconnect that Keesala has never quite become accustomed to, always feeling daunted and uncertain in their presence. Now, however, he feels none of that. He feels nothing except escalating panic. And for the first time, others of his species, such as Pembark, who is standing next to him, are likewise looking concerned. Until now, Keesala's flutelike voice has been alone in suggesting that they are heading for certain disaster. Now, though, others are echoing his concerns, and the Wanderers who had deigned to descend from their vessel and talk to them about it do not look particularly concerned.

"You received the messages! You must have!" Keesala is saying. "A force of ships—who knows how many—are coming here! Here! We are simply unable to withstand an assault of that magnitude!"

"You doubt us?" rumbles one of the Wanderers. "You dare to doubt us? We who established your race? We who hold your future in our grasp?"

"It seems that the Thallonians and their demented new leader have something to say about it as well," Pembark says. *"We encountered this female before. She was more rea-sonable at that point. Now she is crazed. Implacable. You saw it. We all saw it. Her husband is dead thanks to our machi-nations, and now she wants all of us to pay for that!"*

"Of what consequence is that to us?" demands the Wan-derer.

"You swore that you would help us! That you would aid us in regaining our past glory!"

"And so you shall. But you will not cover yourselves in glory if you excrete panic. Let them come. You have seen our power. You have seen what we can do. Do you truly think we cannot withstand an assault by them?"

"We don't know how many ships there will be!"

"Perhaps," Keesala says, *"the wisest course would be to do as they say. Release the Thallonian. Explain to them that—"*

One of the Wanderer's tentacles lashes out and envelops Keesala before he even knows what's happening. He is lifted high, high into the air, brought to eye level with the fright-ening orbs set into the Wanderer's face. For a moment he's convinced that a maw is going to open somewhere in the creature and deposit him within.

"We . . . explain nothing. We maintain that which interests us and destroy that which does not. Do you desire to be destroyed?"

"N-no," stammers Keesala.

He is abruptly thrown toward the floor, where he lands with a fairly loud splat. He is nearly boneless, so the impact does not hurt him very much. It does, however, stun him.

"Then have a care to continue to interest us," warns the Wanderer.

The Spectre

i.

Soleta lay back on her bed and exhaled heavily. It was rather narrow and not remotely designed for two people, which made it both uncomfortable and yet pleasingly challenging as Lucius dropped his head onto her shoulder and matched her exhausted sigh. Her bare skin was starting to cool, and she drew him closer so that he was half atop her, his naked left leg draped over her loins.

"Some aspect of me," Soleta observed, "thinks this was inevitable."

He lifted his head with effort and looked at her bleary-eyed. "You're one of those females who likes to talk a good deal afterwards, aren't you."

"I'm not sure," she replied. "Past lovers usually have leaped screaming from the bed and run out into the night. So I've never had the opportunity to explore it one way or the other."

"I see," and he chuckled slightly. He pulled down the blanket, smiled at her breast, and rested one large hand upon it.

"Worried it's going to wander away?" she asked.

Nevertheless she put her own hand atop his. "Well? Are you going to answer the question?"

"You didn't ask me a question."

"Yes, I . . . all right, I suppose, technically, I didn't. I was wondering whether this . . . the two of us . . . was inevitable. All our talk of sex and what it would take . . ."

"Perhaps," said Lucius. "I mean, I knew I hated you far too passionately. There had to be something more. You simply weren't worth despising that much."

"Thanks *ever* so," she said and punched him in the shoulder. "Have a care. My previous lover was a god. By every reasonable measure of comparison, I'm slumming."

"I suppose," he observed, "for a hatred as deep as ours, there are only two ways to express it. One is in mutual destruction . . ."

"And the other is mutual gratification?"

"So it would seem."

This time when they made love, they did it far more slowly, with none of the fierceness-bordering-on-hostility that had accompanied their first coupling. There was no tenderness yet. That would come later, if it ever did at all. But there was slow exploration of what pleased the other, the meticulous and thorough inspection of the curves of each other's bodies. And when they were once again spent, Soleta fell into a dreamless sleep, wondering if she would be alive when she woke up.

A beeping alert startled her to wakefulness and for a moment she thought they were under attack . . . or perhaps Lucius himself was trying to attack her, although that thought didn't really make a tremendous amount of sense. But Lucius was startled awake as well, and it took only moments for Soleta to realize what it was that the system was reacting to.

"A recorded incoming message," she said. "One that the computer feels requires immediate attention."

"Our computer is capable of doing that? Of making that determination?"

"It was after I got through with it."

She rolled out of bed on one side while Lucius bounded off the other. They pulled on their clothes and headed for the bridge.

Once having arrived, Soleta said, "Computer. Play message."

And then she and Lucius watched in silence as Robin Lefler made her open appeal for aid in raising an assault on Priatia. All during the announcement, Soleta was not watching Lefler, but instead Captain Mueller. She wanted to see her reaction to all of this. But her face was as immobile as that of a Vulcan's, and not for the first time, Soleta couldn't help but wonder if Mueller perhaps didn't have a little Vulcan blood somewhere in her family line.

"It will be a battle that will be spoken of for ages, and remembered by all future generations," Robin Lefler concluded. "If you are with me . . . join us there. If you are not, then I suggest you stay the hell out of our way. Robin Lefler . . . out."

Her last words hung in the air for a short time, and then the message began to repeat automatically. "Computer, recording off," said Soleta. She leaned back against a railing and stroked her chin thoughtfully.

"It sounds like a rather impressive undertaking," Lucius observed.

Soleta nodded. "An undertaking being . . . undertaken . . . by the vessel that offered us aid when we were crippled, even when it was under no obligation to do so."

"That is true." Lucius considered that. "Do you think that large vessel . . . the one that manhandled us on our last encounter . . . will show up?"

"I think it eminently likely. If they have some sort of proprietary interest in the Priatians, certainly they would make an appearance in order to protect that interest."

Lucius nodded, and he smiled in that satisfied way he had when anticipating inflicting damage upon someone. "It would be most pleasing to even the score with that monster of a vessel."

"She's bluffing, of course," Soleta said. "It's a starship, not her personal battle vessel. Still, most people won't know that. Things could get interesting. Still . . . vengeance is, and always will be, a hollow pursuit. It has neither purpose nor goal."

"Can it not be an end in itself?"

Soleta considered this. "I suppose it can be, yes."

ii.

Soleta wasn't sure exactly what to expect upon approaching Priatia. She had a number of scenarios worked out in her head, trying to anticipate everything. They covered the entire range of possibilities, from mildest to worst case.

She didn't actually expect the worst case to be already in play at the point that she arrived. She estimated that one having a likelihood of one in twenty-seven. But as the *Spectre* dropped out of warp space, still maintaining its cloak, she realized she had to adjust her estimate somewhat.

"Gods," said Lucius, when he saw what was in front of them. He vaulted from the navigation station toward tactical. Soleta immediately took his position at navigation, content to let the more battle-experienced tribune handle the weapons array.

The vastness of space over Priatia was alive with weapons fire. There, sure enough, was the gargantuan vessel that had—as Lucius had put it—manhandled the *Spectre* in its previous encounter. This time, however, the ship was under assault from all around. The *Spectre* hung back, assessing the situation. "How many ships do you make, Tribune?" she asked.

"At least two dozen, Commander."

She turned and looked back at him. *"Now* it's 'Commander'?"

He shrugged and then added, "Eyes front, Commander."

"Ah. Right."

Despite their number, the ships were outmatched in terms of size. But the inhabitants of the massive vessel clearly didn't know where to look first. "Why aren't they simply immobilizing the ships, as Xyon claimed they did to his?" Soleta wondered aloud, and then answered her own question: "It must have a range. As long as the ships are staying out of that range, their energy-dampening field can't be used."

"Perhaps it's not even a field," suggested Lucius. "Perhaps it's a specific weapon that must be aimed and fired, same as any other weapon."

"Interesting notion . . . and one that suggests possibilities."

She spotted the *Trident* in the midst of the fight. Obviously the ship had been fired upon, freeing it up to defend itself. The starship had separated its saucer section from its secondary hull, effectively doubling its battle potential. It also made sense since they had two combat-savvy officers, both of command level, on the ship. Mueller was probably aboard the saucer section, while Shelby was on the battle bridge of the secondary section. That would likely be Mueller's thinking, since the engineering section had the warp engines and therefore greater capacity for escape should the need arise. And since Mueller would be concerned about the admiral's survival, she would naturally make sure that Shelby wound up on the battle bridge.

They were coming at the vessel from two directions in a deftly coordinated attack, and Soleta marveled at the way the saucer section spun out of the way of blasts fired at them by the larger vessel. Even in a battle situation, the *Trident* was displaying admirable restraint.

And then one of the smaller ships was struck by a blast from the gargantuan ship. Having a chance to observe it from a distance, Soleta was astounded by it. It was like nothing she'd seen before, a sort of spiral blast that simply seemed to drill into the ship like a corkscrew made of pure energy. It smashed the smaller vessel apart in one stroke, bisecting it and sending each half spiraling off in a different direction.

Then a second ship was picked off, and then a third. "It's starting to get their range," Lucius said grimly. "They're not going to be able to withstand it."

"Prepare to decloak and charge weapons."

But Lucius did not immediately acknowledge the order. With a faint buzz of alarm over his failure to do so, Soleta turned to check what was going on—half-expecting to see him aiming a disruptor at her and saying, "Surprise." Instead he was studying the tactical arrays, his elegant arched eyebrows knit together.

"What is it?"

He looked up and said with mild surprise, "They have no shields."

"Are you serious?"

"Yes."

"Are you *serious?*"

"Never more so," he reaffirmed.

"How can they not have shields? *Why* would they not have shields?" And then again, the science officer who resided in Soleta's skull answered the question before Lucius could. "That transwarp corridor of theirs may well be some sort of link to another dimension, rather than simply another section of our universe. And if that's the case, it's possible that differences in physical laws might preclude some of their armament from working properly."

"That is, I suppose, possible," said Lucius. "Unfortunately, it does not appear to be making much difference in the long run. The assaults from the other ships do not appear to be taking a significant toll upon the larger vessel. Perhaps they simply can't get close enough to penetrate the ship's hull."

"Maybe they can't," she said grimly. "But I don't see that that precludes us from doing so."

"I had a feeling you might say that."

"Are you game?"

"Keep us alive long enough for me to do some damage, and I'll be more than satisfied."

Soleta nodded in acknowledgment of the challenge, and then studied the nav station. She took a deep breath and then let it out slowly to steady herself. This was not remotely what she had been trained for, and was unlike anything she had ever done. At that moment she would have killed to have Mark McHenry there, taking confident control of the vessel and sending it sailing into danger, deftly maneuvering around all the hazards that awaited it.

But McHenry wasn't there. There was just Soleta, who hadn't trained on any sort of navigation equipment since her Academy days . . . and had never operated the navigation system of a Romulan vessel in her life. At least, not in anything approaching combat conditions.

"Perhaps today," she said defiantly, "is a good day to die. Hold on to your station. This is going to be . . . interesting."

Soleta cleared her mind and then, keeping the computer guidance lock under close observation, sent the *Spectre* slamming forward toward the huge ship ahead of them.

Naturally they did not face jeopardy only from the huge vessel. There were also the other ships to consider. Swooping this way and that, firing freely at their opponent, naturally they didn't see the *Spectre* because she was cloaked. So Soleta had to worry not only about possible assaults from their target, but also about friendly fire from those she was trying to aid.

The *Spectre* swooped and dove, rolled completely over, and then came up again. Soleta kept the ship moving, with her shields on maximum to handle any additional damage that might come their way.

"Steady!" Lucius called. "Steady! You're doing well."

"I appreciate that," Soleta replied, just as the *Spectre* was jolted by a passing blast. She couldn't even determine from which direction it had come, and she didn't have the time to find out.

The ship loomed large on their viewscreen, and yet she felt as if they weren't getting any closer to it. Suddenly the saucer section of the *Trident* cut right in front of them, so close that the "T" in the ship's name looked enormous. Soleta cried out even as she cut hard to aft, and the *Spectre* came within a whisker of colliding with the saucer before the two of them passed each other.

"*That* would have been ironic," Lucius said with remarkable sangfroid.

Soleta ignored him, instead recalibrating the attack course in a heartbeat and then sending the *Spectre* howling toward the larger ship.

All this time it had seemed distant, and abruptly the opposite was true: Soleta felt as if it was all around them. The bizarre molecular shape of the vessel made penetrating its inner sections that much easier. The blasts from the other ships dropped away as the *Spectre*, running silent, penetrated far more deeply into its opponent than anyone could have anticipated.

It loomed around her, majestic, like something left over from ancient times. In the heart of the ship, surrounded by its many cross-tunnels and passageways, Soleta felt as if she had stepped into the heart of creation itself. "There were giants in those days," whispered Soleta.

"Commander . . ."

"Yes. Of course." She shook off the growing sense of awe and said, "Are you getting a reading off any particular section of the vessel? Something that could indicate an energy or power center? Engines, perhaps, that we can destroy and thus cripple it?"

He shook his head, and although he was far too experienced a warrior to let frustration show, she could tell it was there all the same. "Nothing. There's a uniformity to it, such as I've never seen."

"All right, then. I suppose we have to start somewhere." She studied the ship's structure and then, taking her best guess, propelled the *Spectre* as close to an intersecting joint as she dared get. "That's your target, Tribune. Full array of disruptors and torpedoes."

"Locked in and awaiting your word, Commander."

They exchanged a look, each knowing that the moment they decloaked so that they could have energy for their weapons system they would be visible and vulnerable to the beings within the ship.

"The word is given, Tribune."

U.S.S. Trident

"I'll be damned!" Mueller cried out.

From her vantage point aboard the saucer section of the *Trident*, Mueller couldn't quite believe what she was seeing. "Arex, forward sensor sweep! Is that—?"

"It's Soleta's vessel, yes," said Arex. "They just decloaked."

Gold said, looking at his navcom, "Considering the angle they must have come in at, we're lucky we didn't collide with them."

"They're opening fire on the vessel, Captain!"

Sure enough, the *Spectre* was letting the larger vessel have it with everything in their arsenal. The interior of the vast ship was illuminated by the display of firepower as the *Spectre* let fly.

"They're targeting several junctions all at one time," M'Ress said from the science station.

"Any effect?"

"Scanning now, but it's difficult to say, Captain."

"Find a way to say it."

M'Ress studied the sensor sweeps, then looked up

at Mueller with a flash of hope. "Some structural damage, yes. They're making some headway . . ."

Suddenly the *Spectre* vanished from the screen, mere seconds before the larger ship returned fire. One of those devastating corkscrew blasts ripped through space right where the *Spectre* had been, and Mueller was on her feet. "Did they hit it?"

"Unable to determine—"

She rounded on M'Ress. "Don't you *dare* tell me that. I don't want 'unable to determine.' I want 'yes' or 'no.' "

"*Captain!*" shouted Arex.

Instantly Mueller knew what was happening. "Evasive maneuvers!" she shouted, bounding back to her chair.

The saucer angled away, just as another blast from the ship cut across, nearly creasing the starboard side. Judging from the strength of the other shots, it would have ripped a gaping hole in the saucer if it had made contact.

"*There!*" M'Ress said. "*Got* them on sensors, at 214 mark 7! They're attacking again!"

She was right. The *Spectre* had reappeared, looking entirely whole, and it was firing once more at the same juncture points.

"Arex. Target those same points and open fire. Full torpedo array."

"Aye, Captain. Torpedoes away!"

The photon torpedoes flashed out from the saucer's underbelly and streaked across space. Earlier attempts along those lines had been thwarted as the torpedoes had bounced harmlessly off the larger vessel's hull. This time, however, the photon torpedoes found their mark and crashed into the juncture points just as the *Spectre*'s own blasts did.

The larger vessel swung around, and the sector under direct assault from the blasts actually looked as if it was starting to bend under the pounding it was taking. The *Spectre* pivoted, dove, and darted under yet another blast and opened fire a third time upon the same area.

"Are we damaging it, Arex?" demanded Mueller.

"Some structural damage in evidence, yes."

"Keep firing! Contact other vessels, give them the coordinates! Tell them to concentrate whatever fire they can! It's too far in for standard phasers to be of much use," she added, knowing of their own frustrations in that regard. "Torpedoes only!"

"But why that specific section, Captain?" asked M'Ress.

"Soleta's in command of that ship, Lieutenant," Mueller reminded her. "One of the most brilliant scientific minds I've ever known. She's got her reasons, I'm sure."

The Spectre

Soleta had no idea what she was doing.

This, she thought, *has to be the most half-assed battle strategy I've ever come up with*. Then it occurred to her that she hadn't actually come up with all that many battle strategies. She'd spent most of her career as a science officer, and when she assumed command of the *Spectre*, her main job had been to stay out of pitched battles such as this one.

She wasn't giving thought to anything except staying out of the way of the return blasts from the larger ship and trying to keep her own vessel on course. Then Lucius called out, "We're getting company, Commander. Other vessels now firing on the same target we are!"

"Why? We picked it at random. It was the nearest thing to us."

"Perhaps they think we knew something they didn't!"

"Wonderful," muttered Soleta. "So we've got the bulk of this assault force firing on what they assume is a vulnerable point when, for all we know, it's the enemy's lunchroom. Meantime it's all we can do to keep out of their way as well." Even as she spoke, she sent the *Spectre* diving to one side, blasts exploding practically over their heads. "This is insane. We need to tell them to pull back, to try and find some sort of—"

And that was when a huge plume of flame erupted from the vessel. It blew out of the section that they had been assaulting, and the round section that had been anchoring the long tubes flew apart. The entire vessel lurched as the connecting tubes crashed together, and then more flames, fueled by internal energies, began to appear all along the ship's lower half.

A chain reaction. I don't believe it, thought Soleta, even as she shouted, "Cloak us! I'm getting us out of here!"

"Cloak activated! We're running silent!"

The *Spectre* banked hard, down and away from the source of the explosions, which seemed to be spreading by the second. Lucius had obviously been correct in his guess that the larger ship required a target to aim at in order to shut down an opposing vessel. The *Spectre*'s cloak had kept it from making itself an easy target, and during the times it had been visible, it had kept up too steady a stream of fire for the now-beleaguered larger vessel to fire back.

Soleta kept the ship moving as quickly and as deftly as she could, swinging the vessel around in a random pattern to avoid any chance of the larger ship getting a bead on them somehow. Seconds later the *Spectre* emerged from under the vast cover of the invading vessel, whipping back around and decloaking as they approached the *Trident*.

"The *Trident* is instructing all vessels to fall back. They anticipate an explosion is imminent!"

"It can't be that easy. It can't," muttered Soleta, even as she piloted the *Spectre* on a course away from the massive ship.

And yet it seemed that it was indeed going to be just that easy. The vessel was shuddering, explosions continuing to burst forth along the surface. Soleta held her breath even as her ship and the others drew to a safer range. She could only imagine the panic that must be ensuing on Priatia at that moment as their protector seemed on the verge of . . .

. . . of . . .

"Shit."

The flames were snuffing out. All along the surface of the vessel, the shuddering was ceasing.

"I don't believe it," said Lucius.

"Why wouldn't you?" she said grimly. "For starters, there's no air in space to feed the flames. If they cut off whatever was fueling the fires, naturally the flames are going to snuff out."

"Orders, Commander?"

Soleta's mind raced, trying to determine what to do.

That was when warning klaxons went off all over the *Spectre*, and Lucius's voice rose in alarm for the first time in the entire encounter.

"Commander!" he called out. "Off the port side! There's—"

"I see it!" she replied. Sure enough, there it was: Space itself was twisting and writhing upon itself, forming the same sort of whirlpool that had drawn in the *Excalibur*. Obviously the huge vessel had deployed its ultimate weapon.

And it was going to pull in the *Spectre* and every other damned ship in the area to wherever Calhoun and his ship had been drawn into.

Impossibly, even through the soundless vacuum of space, a roar enveloped them. The *Spectre* began to shake violently, and Soleta blasted the engines at full strength, trying to pull away, knowing it was hopeless . . .

That was when she noticed something. "It's backwards!" she shouted over the howling of the energy whirlpool.

"What?!"

"Get me the *Trident*! Now!"

Seconds later, Mueller's voice crackled over the subspace com. *"I'm not sure this is the best time, Soleta! We're trying not to be dragged into—"*

"It's not trying to pull us in!" Soleta shouted back. "It's turning in a different direction from the way it was when we last saw it! Don't you see? It's not pulling us in. Something's coming out of it—!"

And that was when energy erupted from the hole in space, so blinding that Soleta gasped in pain and threw her arms across her eyes to block it out. There was still a burst of brilliance seared into her retinas, as if she'd been foolish enough to stare directly into the sun. Then she blinked as, from the depths of another dimension entirely, a brand-new ship emerged.

It was different in design from the one they'd been battling, but it was just as gargantuan. And it looked just as formidable, if not more so.

"Oh joy," came Mueller's sarcastic voice. *"We're saved."*

U.S.S. Excalibur

"We're *through!* Captain!" Morgan called from the conn. "We're through! We're back in our own universe!"

A ragged cheer sprang up from the bridge crew, and Mackenzie Calhoun sagged into his chair like a balloon relieved of air. He rubbed his hand across his face and let out a heavy sigh before he murmured, "*Grozit* . . . I never thought it would work. Up until this very second, I was sure that Pontalimus had booby-trapped the Bolgar vessel . . . rigged it somehow so that the transwarp conduit would collapse in on them and us, smashing us to atoms."

"I believe I speak for the entirety of the bridge crew," Burgoyne spoke up, "when I say that I'm pleased you decided to keep that to yourself."

"Uh-oh," Kebron said. "Captain . . . sensors indicate we have an audience. A fairly large audience."

Kebron was correct. Below them was the planet Priatia, and all around them was a staggering assortment of vessels, big and small. The most commanding of them in terms of presence was the same vessel that had propelled the *Excalibur* into another sphere to begin with . . . the ship that he now knew was operated by the race called the Teuthis. There were other ships as well, ships he recognized as belonging to an assortment of races in Thallonian space. Plus there appeared to be the engineering section of a starship, devoid of saucer . . . no, wait. There was the saucer, all right, and it was . . .

"The *Trident*, sir," Kebron said. "It's hailing us . . ."

"Both halves are," added Morgan. After a moment, she said, "I think you'll want to take the engineering section first. It's your wife."

"My w—?"

He didn't even have to tell Morgan to put that one through. The image of Elizabeth Shelby, standing on what was clearly a battle bridge, appeared on the screen of the *Excalibur*. She gasped, at first obviously unable to believe what she was seeing. There was a choking noise as if she didn't know whether to laugh or cry. But she instantly composed herself, squaring her shoulders and saying, "Captain Calhoun. You certainly took your sweet damned time coming back."

"My apologies, Admiral," replied Calhoun, forcing himself not to smile. "We had a few bumps along the way."

"So I see. And I see you brought a friend."

"Yes. The vessel that preceded us through the corridor is commanded by the Bolgar. And the one that was already here . . . that is a vessel of another race called the Teuthis. Their respective leaders are still aboard here, to ensure their mutual cooperation . . .

although we did return his guards to their vessel as a show of good faith."

"I'm confused. Are they enemies or allies?"

"Allies now," Calhoun said with a weary smile. "Getting the two heads of their respective races to come to terms took . . . a bit of doing. But now they're—"

"Captain!" Morgan suddenly shouted. "The Bolgar ship is opening fire on the Teuthis vessel!"

Shelby's image vanished, to be replaced by a horrific vista: The Bolgar ship was indeed firing upon the Teuthis ship. Had the Teuthis been operating at full strength, they might well have been able to resist it. As it was, they had no chance whatsoever. Powerful blasts cracked apart the Teuthis ship, pounding it every which way.

"*No!*" shouted Calhoun. "Morgan, get me Termic down in the shuttlebay! Right now!"

It was too late. The Teuthis vessel tried to put up a fight, but it only got off a few random shots that bounced harmlessly off the surface of the Bolgar ship. And then, seconds later, the Teuthis ship blew apart, shattering and sending pieces flying off in every direction, spiraling away into the darkness of space.

And then, seconds later, the Bolgar vessel swept back around and into the transwarp conduit, which had never actually closed and was now turning in the other direction. Then it simply vanished. Except for the floating pieces of debris that were left to mark the spot of the vessel's destruction, there was no sign that it had ever been there at all.

Priatia

Kat Mueller hadn't known what to expect when she beamed down to the continent of Nemosia, in the capital city of Cheng. She had never been there before. It had, however, been the exact spot where the false Kalinda had been stationed when the impostor had been fobbed off upon them. The coordinates had been given them by a Priatian named Keesala, who was, obviously, one of the masterminds behind the entire nasty business.

Mueller had, however, taken the precaution of bringing a sizable security force with her, over two dozen strong, armored and armed for trouble. Furthermore, she was also accompanied by Calhoun's son Xyon. Xyon had barely had to look at the impostor to know that she was a fake. If only Si Cwan and the others had listened to him at the time, a lot of death and blood could have been avoided.

Still, even without knowing what to expect . . . she certainly hadn't anticipated what she found.

Scattered all over the streets were the bodies of

Priatians. They were simply lying there, staring life-lessly up at the night sky.

"What the hell . . . ?" said Mueller.

"What happened here?" Arex asked.

A voice that was all too familiar to Mueller spoke up from the darkness. "Isn't it obvious? They killed themselves."

Moving slowly toward her, with a much smaller figure next to him, was Keesala. He looked weary and wasted. The guards leveled their weapons at him, but Keesala made no sudden move toward them. "The Wanderers are dead. Our hope is dead. Our future is dead. And many of us . . . chose not to live in a future that has nothing to offer us."

"And you?" demanded Mueller.

"I am ambivalent." He gestured toward the smaller figure as he said to Mueller, "I thought you would come to this place. I believe you're looking for this."

He stepped back and Kalinda stumbled forward, wrapped in a cloak that was too large for her.

"Keep back," Mueller ordered her troops, and then nodded for Xyon to step forward.

Xyon did so, approaching cautiously, studying her scrupulously. She had a stunned and distant look on her face, but then she seemed to focus upon Xyon for the first time. She stopped in her tracks, staring at him, and then tears began to run down her face.

"Oh, Xyon," she said, the words escaping like an agonized whisper, and she sagged into his arms. He picked her up, cradling her, and she sobbed, "You're not Si Cwan . . ."

"I know," he said, having heard from Mueller the fate of Kalinda's brother.

"He never liked you."

"I know. But I always liked him."

"You're lying. Thank you for lying," and then she sobbed into his chest. He held her tightly against it, then turned toward Mueller and simply nodded, telling her what she needed to know: In his opinion, this was the genuine Kalinda.

"Of course she's real," said Keesala as if capable of reading his mind. "What possible purpose would there be in continuing the charade?"

Mueller wanted nothing so much as to pummel him with a blunt object, or perhaps run him through with a sword. If Keesala was able to tell that was what was going through her mind, he didn't let on. Instead he simply said wearily, "May I go now?"

"You can't be serious," Xyon snapped at him. "After everything you've done? After—"

But Kalinda reached up and put a finger to his lips, stilling him. "I want it over," she whispered. "Let it be over."

Xyon looked over to Mueller, whose decision it was. She gave Keesala a long, hard look, and then tapped her combadge and said, "*Trident*. This is Mueller. Beam us up."

Moments later the entire landing party had shimmered away, leaving Keesala standing there, with dead bodies as far as the eye could see, and a future that he neither understood nor desired.

He stayed where he was and prayed for guidance.

And he stayed there and prayed and prayed and prayed until he completely lost track of time . . .

And that was when the two huge masses of burning, lifeless flesh fell from high above and smashed him to a pulp, answering his prayers and solving his problem in one fell swoop.

U.S.S. Excalibur

i.

Calhoun practically exploded into the shuttlebay, stepping onto the observation deck above so that he could look down at his two "guests." His fury was directed entirely at Termic as Pontalimus—still separated from his longtime foe by a forcefield—looked on in a very placid manner.

"You bastard!" he shouted. "We had a deal!"

"A deal forced upon us by you," Termic said calmly, a stark contrast to Calhoun's outrage.

"But you agreed to it nevertheless! I gave you the cure for it!"

"And saved yourself in the process."

"That doesn't matter. What matters is that you gave your word, and your people went back on it!" He hesitated, and then said, "Pontalimus . . . I'm sorry to have to tell you this, but . . ."

"They destroyed the ship. My people. The remainder of my people." Pontalimus spoke in a hollow, disconnected tone. He oozed backward so that he was up against the shuttlebay doors. "I dared to dream of greater things from the Bolgar than that. It was my fault, Captain. You merely tried to bring peace. I am far older than you, and should have known better than to hope."

"And you should have known better than to think that my people would willingly overlook the history of your barbarism," replied Termic. "Now your people are dead. All dead, with any luck. And mine is the dominant species in our sphere. The so-called Teuthis sphere. And if I never have the opportunity to return there, as appears to be the case . . . well, my life and fate are insignificant things. Only the welfare of my people truly matters."

"My mate was aboard the vessel that your people destroyed, Termic. I sensed her violent passing before the captain even came down to inform us. I owe you for that, Termic. I owe you for that . . . and for a great many things."

"Don't whine to me, Pontalimus. Your people were attempting to take over this sphere. Your motivations and your plans are no better than mine."

"That, Termic," Calhoun said angrily, "is not the point . . ."

"No, Captain," Pontalimus rumbled. "Perhaps . . . it is the point, at that. Perhaps Termic and I . . . deserve each other. That is certainly my belief in the matter. I would hope . . . that it is yours as well . . ."

And with absolutely no warning, the shuttlebay doors opened.

It should have been impossible for it to happen. But Pontalimus's strength was clearly beyond anything that the *Excalibur* had been designed to prepare for.

Calhoun would never know whether it was that his tentacles had somehow seeped into the supposedly air-tight joints of the door mechanism, or whether he had simply "suctioned" his tentacles to the doors and applied brute strength. Either way, the result was the same: The bay doors were shoved apart before the exterior forcefield could be brought online. The result was that Pontalimus, the last of the Teuthis, was pulled out tumbling into the vacuum of space.

The air rushed out of the shuttlebay. Termic was hauled forward by the rush of air at the outer edges of the forcefield that had separated him from Pontalimus, but then slammed into the field before he could be dragged any farther. Termic screamed as the field crackled around him, and he howled for Calhoun to do something, to shut the far doors.

And looking down at the struggling form of the Bolgar, Calhoun's face became as animated as a corpse.

"I've decided Pontalimus is right."

He slammed the base of his palm down on a panel control, and the forcefield disappeared.

Termic had a split second to realize his jeopardy and then he was gone, writhing and twisting as he went, sailing into the depths of space behind his foe.

"You deserve each other," said Mackenzie Calhoun.

ii.

Termic flails about, certain that this is some sort of terrible, terrible joke. That Calhoun would never deliberately do such a thing, just . . . condemn him to death.

There is no air for him to breathe. There is nothing but cold, cold all around . . .

And something suddenly grabs him. For half a heartbeat (not that he has all that many heartbeats remaining) he believes it is some sort of grabbing beam that has come to his rescue.

Then he realizes that it is, in fact, the tentacles of Pontalimus. They are wrapping around him, getting a firm grip.

He fights back as best he can.

The two enemies begin to plummet, struggling furiously. By the time they reach the outer atmosphere of Priatia, they are all but dead.

By the time their massive bodies begin to burn upon reentry, they are completely dead.

As a result, they're not remotely aware of it when they come crashing down upon the praying Keesala, although they have managed to make yet another argument on behalf of a long-dead Earth philosopher named Voltaire who maintained that God was a comedian playing to an audience afraid to laugh.

iii.

Mackenzie Calhoun sat in his ready room, feeling as if he'd just run a marathon. Elizabeth Shelby was behind him, rubbing his shoulders, pressing her fingers in deep to loosen the tension.

The *Excalibur* was on its way back to Space Station Bravo. The *Trident*, meantime, was taking Kalinda and Robin Lefler back to New Thallon, to try and sort out the political mess that had enveloped that world.

"You've got so much tension in there," Shelby told him. "You feel like you're carrying the world's weight on your shoulders."

"What else is new?" He paused, then asked, "What do you think's going to happen to you? You did technically hijack a starship, you know."

"I don't know," Shelby admitted. "I'm figuring, worst-case scenario . . . they bust me down to ensign, and I get assigned to a starship to work my way back up."

"As it so happens, I have a few ensign slots available."

"I'll bet you do."

He sighed. "Damn. When I think of poor Si Cwan . . . Kebron was a wreck when he got the news, you know."

"Kebron? I thought he couldn't stand Si Cwan."

"That was the old Kebron. This is the new, more sensitive Kebron. And Robin . . . my God, how is she holding up?"

"Surprisingly well," said Shelby. "I'm not sure she entirely—"

The chime to the ready room sounded. "Come," said Calhoun.

The door slid open and Moke was standing there. Calhoun gestured for him to enter and Moke did so tentatively. "What can I do for you, Moke?" he asked.

"I want to know . . ." He paused, as if struggling for the words.

"Moke . . . ?"

"I want to know why you didn't tell me about the disease being a fake."

Calhoun looked thunderstruck. "How did you—?"

"Xy told me. Don't be mad at him; I didn't give him much choice. I was yelling at him, telling him he should never have done something that could have made you die. And he blurted out the truth. At least he told me the truth . . ."

"Mac, what is he talking about?" asked Shelby.

Calhoun rolled his eyes, acting like a young boy who had been caught out with his hand in the cookie jar. "I was trying a desperation ploy to get the Bolgar and the Teuthis leaders to play nice. I approached Xy about creating an illness that would be contracted by the Bolgar, the Teuthis, and me. The concept was that, with all our lives on the line, they'd be forced to come to terms with each other. Xy worked on it for a time, and then came to me and said that he could not, in good conscience, go through with it. That it was against his ethical code of conduct."

"First, do no harm," said Shelby.

"Exactly. So we came up with a backup plan. By this point we have holographic projectors in just about every major area of the ship, so that Morgan can get around. That includes the shuttlebay. We used them to project a deteriorating disease on me and our 'guests.'"

"You mean on your skin?"

"Yes. Then I acted as sick as I could because, naturally, the outer symptoms were the only ones that existed. But I was depending entirely on the power of suggestion in the case of the other two, and I was concerned that might not be enough." He looked sadly at Moke. "So I enlisted my son, Xyon, to help me out . . ."

"By having him get me in there so I could beg you to live," said Moke coldly. "And the only way I could sound like I meant it . . ."

"Is if you really did mean it. If it's of any consolation, Moke," he said, getting up from behind his desk, "you really sold it. I mean, yes, the so-called truce fell apart, but Teuthis would never have cooperated, we'd never have managed to get back here to—"

"Why didn't you tell me later?"

"I . . . well," he said, "I didn't really see the point. I thought—correctly, as it turns out—that you might be upset. Feel like I used you. And—"

"I am upset," Moke interrupted him. He stepped closer toward Calhoun, and it could have been Calhoun's imagination, but he felt as if the air had suddenly become colder, a stiff wind blowing through (which was impossible), and it even seemed darker suddenly. "And you did use me. And if you ever treat me in such a disrespectful manner again . . . you're really, really going to regret it."

Moke turned on his heel and walked out, and Calhoun and Shelby stared at each other.

"Am I crazy," said Calhoun, "or did it suddenly feel like there was going to be a thunderstorm in here?"

"Can't it be both?" Shelby asked.

New Thallon

Kalinda stands upon a vast plain, and there is a loving smile upon her face. The wind moves around her gently, as if caressing her.

"You would have been proud of her," she says. "She took command on my behalf . . . she was so decisive . . . in many ways, she's become like her husband. We all have, I think.

"Oh, and you'll appreciate this. Soleta and her associate have formed an alliance with New Thallon. They said that as long as Robin and I are working here . . . working for change, working to pull together the New Thallonian Protectorate . . . they will devote their services, and the services of their ship, to our behalf. They can be very useful.

"I am . . ." She hesitates. It is not easy to speak about this. She does not know completely what to say. "You are . . . bigger than life. So much bigger . . . I just . . . I never thought it could ever happen to you. I thought you would live forever. And I . . ." She took a deep breath and let it out all in a rush, as if hoping that speaking the words quickly would garner his assent. "I want to join you. To be with you. I don't want to be here anymore. My fiancé is dead, and my brother is dead, and everyone is looking to me to rule now,

*and even though Robin is going to help she would actually do
much better instead of me, and I'm not afraid, gods know
I'm not afraid, because it would just be a step into something
new rather than an ending of everything, I know that, and
so if it would be okay with you . . ."*

*He stands before her, smiling gently, understanding, and
shaking his head. He points down toward the ground, indicating that she is to stay where she is. That she still has work
to do.*

*She tries to keep her chin from trembling and doesn't
succeed. "Do I . . . do I have to stay? I swear, I'll find a way
that isn't too painful. Please . . ."*

Again he shakes his head, this time more firmly.

*"All right," she sighs in acquiescence, and she reaches
out toward Si Cwan, and through him. She feels an odd
sensation that is a combination of both warm and cold, and
then he steps toward her and envelops her, a misty shroud
that she finds comfort in . . . if not forever, then for a little
while.*

Robin Lefler sat in her quarters, her head resting upon
her hands. She stared off into space, wondering what
she was going to do next and not having the faintest
idea. She knew there was so much to be attended to,
but she couldn't decide which thing was more important than any other. She was stuck in neutral, unsure of
how to shift herself over into forward.

She glanced out her window and saw Kalinda
standing some distance away. She frowned as she
watched the young Thallonian lady—the last in her
royal line—stand there with her hands out to either

side, her head tilted back. A gentle breeze seemed to be swirling around her, rustling the folds of her cloak, and Robin could have sworn that Kalinda was talking to someone. But there was no one there . . .

"Robin . . ."

The soft female voice called to her. She looked up in confusion in the direction of the holosuite that Si Cwan had once built for her . . . the room which had miraculously survived the bombing inflicted upon the mansion. She rose and headed toward it.

"Robin," the voice called again, and even though it was muffled, she realized who it was. She touched the release and the door slid open.

Her mother was standing there, pain and sympathy in her face.

She put out her arms to her.

"Mother," said Robin, "what are you doing h—" And then, before she even realized it was happening, tears were pouring down her face as if they had a will of their own. She tried to complete the sentence, but she had no speaking voice. Instead all that emerged was a deep, agonized moan, and a sob of misery. She took one step forward, then another, and then practically fell into her mother's arms. She cried piteously, as if someone had cut out her heart, and Morgan held her tightly and kept swearing to her that she would never, ever let her go.

Somewhere . . .

The father and son sit on a dock at the edge of a vast cosmic river that exists through many realms of time and space. Once, millennia ago, this river overran its borders, carving a moment of cosmic memory so deep that it's the reason every known civilization—even those on desert worlds—has a flood story buried in its mythology.

"Worlds within worlds, my boy," the father says archly to the son. "That's what it's all about." He dangles his fishing line in the river, trying to pull something in. "Worlds within worlds."

"What do you mean, Father?" asks the boy.

"What do I mean?" The father makes a face of disgust. "Now, what sort of omniscient being are you going to grow up to become if you have to ask questions such as those."

"Then how am I going to learn?"

"By observing," he says with his trademark petulance. "If I were just going to answer questions, we could have both stayed in the Continuum."

"All right," the boy says cautiously. "Then . . . what do you want me to observe?"

"Well . . . let's see." He studies the water thoughtfully, then points. "See that jellyfish over there?"

"Yes."

"I'm going to dangle my line toward it. And you reach out and sense the thoughts inside."

"The thoughts of the jellyfish?"

"No, son. The thoughts of what's inside the jellyfish."

Without fully understanding the instruction, the boy does as he is told. He probes a few moments with no results, and he is about to admit his frustration when suddenly he perceives it.

There is a race there. An entire race . . . no, an entire universe. Or a subsection of a universe. The race calls itself the Bolgar. It lives in its sphere in triumph. It believes itself to be the ultimate power in its universe. Perhaps in the multiverse. It has recently triumphed over its greatest enemy. It is confident in its manifest destiny. In fact, when the time is right, it intends to return to another universe it has just left and endeavor to conquer it. Nothing can stop it. Nothing can deter it. They are conquerors. They are supreme. They are like unto gods.

"You sense it?" his father asks.

"Yes."

"Is not its arrogance monumental?"

"It's certainly deserving of punishment." The boy smiles.

"I couldn't agree more. It's never a good idea," says his father, "to become too full of yourself."

His hook snags the jellyfish and he reels it in. And within the universe inside the jellyfish, the world of the Bolgar is ripped apart. The entire race screams as one, its arrogance replaced by terror and supplication and complete *lack of comprehension as to what is happening. It doesn't even have words to frame what is transpiring.*

The jellyfish is yanked out of the water, or at least what passes for water in the universal miasma. The moment it hits the air it begins to shrivel and fall apart. The father allows it to land splat *on the pier. All the toxins that the jellyfish contain that render it so lethal to sea life mean absolutely nothing on dry land. There, in the heat of day, under the punishing light of the sun, the jellyfish and the universe contained within it crumble and die.*

"Look on my works, ye Mighty, and despair," intones the father, smiling down at the remains of the masters of their sphere. Then Q casts his line back out into the water and says, "Let's see who else could stand to learn a lesson or two . . ."

About the Author

PETER DAVID is the *New York Times* bestselling author of numerous *Star Trek* novels, including the incredibly popular *New Frontier* series. He has also written dozens of other books, including his acclaimed original novel, *Sir Apropos of Nothing*, and its sequels, *The Woad to Wuin* and *Tong Lashing*.

David is also well known for his comic book work, particularly his award-winning run on *The Hulk*. He recently authored the novelizations of *Spider-Man*, *Spider-Man 2*, *Fantastic Four*, and *The Hulk* motion pictures.

He lives in New York with his wife and daughters.